"Through These Doors"

The Manoir at Bout L'Abbé

By Diane Condon-Boutier

For Robyn---
Hoping you enjoy and
your trip to Albert and
that later you'll like
this story!
All the best
Boutier
12/12/12

Through These Doors: The Manoir at Bout L'Abbé

For my Dad,

who loved walking with me to Sage Library to pick up my Mom after work

Author's foreword

Most everyone has entered an old house or building for the first time and felt a sudden awareness of its place in the fabric of history. If this has happened to you, remember your thoughts at the time. You might have said: "What if these walls could talk? Can you imagine what this place must have seen and heard?"

As we live, love, laugh and cry our bodies dispense a certain amount of energy. Elementary physics teaches us that energy does not disappear, rather it's transformed from one state to another: much like liquid when boiled, changes into vapor.

If this is true, where does human energy go? Could it be absorbed by the different porous materials surrounding us in our homes and workplaces: these stages upon which our lives unfold? Are they the true witnesses to our existence?

Just for once, let's allow the images and impressions to be retrieved, and recounted by one of these silent spectators. A manor anchored in northern France, in a region named Normandy.

CHAPTER 1

Normandy countryside – 1985:

A shiny new Renault 25 pulled up in front of my facade, tires crunching the gravel of my circular drive. I was anxious to see who would climb out, wondering if they would say *oui* or *non* to the offer of sale. I hoped they possessed good taste and wouldn't consider repainting my oak ceiling beams some hideous shade of orange.

There was something unpleasant in the usual commentary regarding my qualities, something tiresome and offensive. Measurements and technicalities of plumbing and electrics were superficial details meant to sway the ignorant. I was aiming for a match with someone I could enjoy, someone with depth of character, someone who could hear me. Such a person would never be influenced by the state of my pipes.

Paying more attention than usual to the humans in my space, I dissected their thoughts and words drifting by. A decision must be made whether I should douse their interest by springing an opportune leak in the kitchen or by letting a few mice loose in the bathroom.

"Bout L'Abbé? Doesn't that roughly translate as 'Abbot's piece'?" Debra asked Philippe. "What could it possibly mean? A piece of what? It's actually kind of vulgar when you think about it!" Repressed humor twitched around a corner of her mouth.

"Well, I should think it doesn't refer to a piece of the abbot, per se, silly! Maybe this house and its surrounding land once belonged to the church."

"Hmmm, I guess that would make more sense." As they approached my front door, she squinted through the falling dusk at the wide lawn stretching toward the orchard.

Crossing the stone paved terrace, Debra couldn't refrain from peeking through my crocheted curtains. The warm, orange glow of firelight and the fragrant smell of burning apple wood won her heart on the spot. She could make him happy here.

As the estate agent extended a hand to the iron knocker on my imposing oak door, Debra grabbed Philippe's arm, and pulled him closer- this older, stoic man who she tried so hard to please,- and whispered into his shoulder blades "Let's take it".

He responded with a tiny smile and a "harummph", without turning to look at her.

Grinning, she buried her nose and chin in the wool of his overcoat, trying to keep hold of her excitement, certain the deal was already done.

I observed him as he straightened his shoulders, sure of himself, and of his capable manipulation. It was obvious, even to the casual observer, that Philippe knew what to do in order to keep a tight hold on Debra: what to agree to, what to allow, when to let her think she had made the right decision. He carefully weighed the consequences of these *arrangements* ensuring he would gain maximum results with a minimum of trouble to himself. A selfish compromise, underscored by his expensive suit. He thought highly of himself.

Debra was vaguely aware of some this, yet attributed it to their personal dynamics. He was, after all, much older than she and should be a better judge of things.

For a moment she allowed herself to believe that he desired her happiness. Pride welled up at the idea of having any measure of influence over this man, he who had taught her so much and who continued to impress her daily. She wallowed in it, on the verge of drowning.

#

These thoughts danced about in Debra's optimistic heart when I first recognized her presence. I heard their excited patter while observing her inhale with satisfaction as she followed the realtor and her husband across my threshold. At that precise instant, we both knew that she had stepped into her future.

Three months later, the others said goodbye, and Debra settled in with her rather demanding man. I could tell she'd have trouble with him, so I planned to assist her whenever I could, for I knew that she loved me, and that I would love her in return.

It was rare indeed when one of my favorites did not see their first daylight from inside my walls, or at least from somewhere on the estate. Still, ferns can be transplanted from one container to another and thrive, so why not humans? Never mind that this particular specimen had changed continents as well, for Debra was American.

Being notoriously American, for her accent instantly revealed her origins, was rather hard to live up to. People expected her be different: to dress differently, to think and eat differently, and who knows what else? On a regular basis, her husband fielded pointedly indiscreet questions regarding their love life. Sometimes it was exhausting. Yet, she was a foreigner in a land that felt like she belonged in it.

And, she had a new name to live up to. Debra loved hearing herself referred to as 'Day-bor-ahh'. Christened with a name sounding like an English curse, with a hard accent on the first syllable, she was entranced by the soft French pronunciation of her name. She melted the first time it wisped from Philippe's mouth, the last syllable more a sigh than pronounced letters. Hearing this sweetened version of her name made her turn the page on herself, starting over as a new person. However, it carried a certain price.

Debra had chosen an older man. Or rather, an older man had chosen her on a whim, and she had decided to keep him. His wit and knowledge of worldly things brought into focus the small life she'd led before meeting Philippe. I watched her evolve; transforming herself into the brilliant woman she held the potential to become. She owed it to him, and to herself.

To this end, she set about learning food, wine, literature, cinema and music. She took pains with how she dressed, yet was disappointed by the rarity of his compliments. She finally understood that his lack of criticism was a compliment in itself. When he didn't like something, he suggested a change, no matter what it was. When he said nothing, all was well. His apparent indifference forced her to strive for his elusive approbation. She worked hard at selecting the appropriate home furnishings in creating a nest to please him. Mild blues and greens decorated my rooms, a balm for potentially volatile nerves.

Debra had the good manners to ask before undertaking major changes, although she never mentioned this to any living soul. How could one explain conversing with a house?

Men knocked down walls and added windows, changing my outward appearance, yet not touching my heart and soul. They applied new paints and tasteful wallpapers, making me feel attractive and up to date.

Although she didn't know why, Debra always took care to sleep in the oldest part of me, even though her choice of bedroom changed over the years to accommodate her children born in the hospital. Sadly there would no longer be birthing for me to watch over. This was the 20th century, and I must be satisfied with a second hand account.

CHAPTER 2

But it wasn't always so. My other favorites
opened their deep blue eyes for the first time to me. They
drew their first breaths, full of my smells. Their hands
and knees scuffed my floors when they began to crawl.
They learned to run in my orchards, to climb my trees
and when no one was looking, to bravely slide down my
banister on the grand staircase. They were my children.
Their names were Marie, Angeline, Emile, Liliane,
Cécile and Paulette without forgetting Jean-François,
Michel, and Roseline. The list is as long as my history.

Beneath their tears and laughter lie the echoes of
those who came before my walls were rebuilt, whose
voices still ring out in the stone underground passages
and kitchens: Hubert, Thibaut, Reynaud, Hugues and
Simon, their stern voices tempered by the softer tones of
Agnes, Constance and Flore. Their remnants are scorched
with fire, as I was reconstructed under the watchful eye
of Henri-Louis de Rochefort, the man who took over my
lands and rebuilt me on the foundations of the ancient
Commanderie of the Knights Templar.

Like the phoenix, I rose from the ashes and ruin
of the old order of fighting monks whose master had
been the abbot from which my new name sprung. I am
the repository of each and every one's living memory. I
share those memories with those who know how to listen

to me, who have the bond imprinted in their souls, linking them to these stones, to these oak beams and to the very ground on which we all stand, tied together through eternity.

My story is inextricably linked to theirs. Voices pulled back through time can be deciphered by the willing and hushed by those too afraid to understand. For those who choose to hear me, I will whisper tales of knights and soldiers, washerwomen and priests, lovers and enemies, the blessed and the damned.

#

Paulette was the illegitimate fruit of a union of lovers. She wasn't fortunate enough to be recognized as the grand-daughter of the master. Yet his blood flowed in her veins, blood sweetened by the temperament of her mother, Liliane, a laundry maid, too attractive to be effectively hidden by her drab workday attire.

Her conception was a beautiful thing, taking place one spring evening under the flowering lilac bushes in a corner of the kitchen garden. The succulent blooms dropped purple petals, sweet with perfume on the young couple, although they took no notice.

Liliane had been swayed into thinking that the handsome eldest son was as much taken with her as she was with him. He had the good grace to believe it as well, mistaking his enthusiasm for the young maid's fresh-cheeked, natural good looks for love, as selfish young men often do.

Later, in exchange for his attentions in the garden, she presented him with the irresponsibly unavoided complication of a burgeoning midriff. His parents would have none of it, as could be expected, and Liliane was hastily married off to an earnest young man, named Marcel Fournier, who accepted her as a gift, along with a sum of cash and the use of one of the nicer cottages on a small parcel of land adjacent to the outbuildings on the estate, ironically, not too far from the kitchen garden where it had all begun.

Marcel never remarked upon her speedy acceptance of his proposal, nor did he exclaim at the early arrival of their first child. Marcel loved Liliane and employed his energy at making a life for them. Liliane did her best to forget the young man to whom she had given her first love, never quite able to forgive him for not fighting for her. Instead, he had left for university far away, to learn useful things which would allow him to run the estate when it would be his. In time, Liliane turned her attention to the efforts of Marcel, her heart warmed by his unfailing kindness toward her.

#

Paulette looked nothing like the brothers and sisters following in her stead, yet never questioned their dark hair and brown eyes, so different from the blonde hair and blue eyes reflected back at her in the spring belonging to St Catherine. She wore her stepfather's name, certain that it was her own. Marcel and Liliane, being of the hard-working-nose-to-the-grindstone sort, claimed no enemies. So it was that Paulette's parentage was never openly speculated upon.

She was a kind, lively child who did her chores quickly, gaining precious minutes to run off to play in my fields and woods surrounding the estate, or to hang about in the stable, conversing with the huge work horses while they munched their grain after a long day's work.

This part of Normandy in 1932 was steeped in the traditions of the preceding centuries. Agriculture was labor intensive, implementing techniques handed down from one generation to the next. The master employed a handful of families to produce grain, flax and sugar beets. They raised dairy cattle and sheep, keeping chickens, ducks and a sow with her piglets for their own consumption. Goats trimmed my lawns and provided milk for fresh, soft cheese. Recently, the master had developed extensive orchards of cider apples, boiling the mash to produce the stronger *calvados*, which represented a source of ready cash. All in all, everyone prospered.

The master began to equip me with indoor plumbing and electricity. *Mon Dieu*, how I protested against the holes being drilled in my baseboards, and to the hanging of ugly wires along my walls! My complaints animated the nights with much creaking and groaning, inadvertently frightening several of the house maids sleeping in the small rooms along the top floor.

For the most part, my efforts concentrated on disturbing the workmen who were the instigators of these invasive alterations to my innards. I did my best to shift, causing their tools to meander away from the spot where they had been put down. I let gusts of wind blow off their caps and any nail falling from their hands would, of course, skitter off to lodge in an inaccessible cranny. Yet it was all for nothing, as I was hammered and drilled into a more modern era, increasing the status of the master and his family.

These improvements did little for Paulette or her family. Their rural existence unfolded much in the same way as that of the generations of farm workers before them, with the notable exception that their children attended the village school. A governess taught the master's children in the early years, and then tutored them until they were old enough to be sent to the boarding schools in Rouen or Dieppe, run by monks or nuns depending on the sex of the child. The boys were later sent off to university, and husbands of suitable lineage negotiated for the daughters.

Farm workers didn't have access to education of that caliber for their children. The boys regularly missed classes because of the imperatives of nature: at harvest when extra hands were needed to bring in the grain before rainstorms could ransack the fields, attacking and flattening the swaying stalks.

Thus, the girls ended up with a more comprehensive education, although their options were fewer that those open to the less educated boys. As young women, they dreamed of breaking free of the mold imprisoning the females of past generations, by obtaining a post as a secretary or shop girl in the city. There, they could hope to meet a man with better prospects, releasing them from a life of manual labor. No eligible men appeared at the farm, proposing to sweep them away from the drudgery of their after-school chores. That sort of luck was only to be found in the city.

#

When Paulette turned sixteen in the spring of 1940, her dreams of moving to Rouen to look for work as a shop girl were squashed beneath the treads of German tanks rolling across the eastern border into France. It appeared as though the Great War of twenty years previous hadn't resolved a thing. Everyone Paulette knew spoke of war, praying that life in Normandy would go on much the same as it had the last time. The battles of the past war had been contained in the east, along much disputed borders. The locals hoped it would be the same this time. Still, Paulette wasn't allowed to go to Rouen, her parents insisting she remain on the estate where she would be safe from the excesses of invading soldiers. Unfortunately, the invading soldiers did not stay in the east; they invaded Normandy as well as the rest of the northern half of France.

Six months later, the master and his family abandoned me, fleeing south to stay with cousins. The house staff and farm workers watched their cars drive away after promising to keep the estate safe during their absence. Cowardly folk with little backbone, leaving the paid workers to cope, I decided not to miss them at all, instead waiting to see what the future might bring. Waiting with some trepidation, I must admit, and not wishing to be burnt to the ground once again. For flames leave scars which never disappear. The stench of one's own burning is not to be forgotten.

Shortly thereafter, shiny black boots stomped in my halls and the harsher intonations of German smothered the softer chatter of French. Fortunately, the acquisition of a large estate farm was a worthy asset to the Germans. They enjoyed the food we produced and the spirits as well. Many an evening was spent laughing and drinking in the drawing room, near the fire. The laughers and drinkers wore uniforms instead of evening dress, yet the festive atmosphere was familiar. We were, all of us: peasants, livestock, buildings and resources alike rather lucky to be presided over by this particular officer. He obviously came from a good family- albeit German- and he did his best to keep things running much the same as before.

His men were courteous, and while they imposed strict rules of conduct—backing them with threats which Paulette's parents and co-workers had no desire to test— there were no scenes of pillage or plunder. The difference lay in the recipients of the goods we produced. Instead of the family benefiting from their profit, it was the Third Reich. There were soldiers garrisoned in some of the outbuildings and throughout the house, and much more mud in the yard. Yet, after a while the occasional lady visitor laughed in my dining room, while foxtrots tooted coppery notes from the gramophone.

Life trudged on for the farm. The inhabitants were grateful to have food and shelter, while waiting to see what else might be in store for them.

Paulette did the soldiers' laundry, keeping her face turned down to her task.

CHAPTER 3

1941:

Liliane wrung her hands in anguish while Marcel whispered quietly with the fathers of the other renegade sons, authors of another sabotage on the German supply trucks used to load up the farm goods regularly hauled to storage warehouses on the outskirts of Dieppe.

"He's such a young lad to be getting himself involved in this," Marcel said, keeping his voice down, not wishing to be overheard by any soldier passing on his rounds. "He doesn't know how dangerous it could be."

Another father spoke up, shaking his head in disbelief. "Colonel VonEpffs is a reasonable man, I won't complain of him...or his treatment of us, but still in all, he surely won't tolerate any more trickery! Michel, Guillaume and the other boys should know better than to put us in such a dangerous position, *les idiots*!"

Michel was Paulette's little brother, two years her junior, which made him all of fourteen when the soldiers arrived last year, taking over the running of the estate. He was the self-proclaimed leader of the small group of adolescents who had grown up together and who now worked the farmyards, tending the animals and seeing to the everyday chores involved in the smooth running of a large estate. He was the youngest of the lot, yet in spite of his small stature, his enthusiasm for all things forbidden rendered his popularity amongst them uncontested. Unfortunately, his scrawny size also made him rather susceptible to teasing, and his pride tended to surpass his good judgment.

Paulette's parents were terrified of the risks undertaken by the young rebels. What had started as a silly dare, provoked by the resentment the boys felt toward the German soldiers garrisoned on the estate, ballooned into explosive proportions.

Lack of understanding made the boys feel that each burst of laughter coming from the soldiers was a direct affront to their personal pride. Sons of barely literate farm workers and crofters, they had no knowledge of the German language. Therefore they couldn't realize that the bulk of laughter was simply the result of *risqué* jokes, the sort with which men far-from-home entertain themselves. Conjecture about *les dames* whom the Colonel made welcome, and his activities when one or another of them stayed overnight, made up most of the material for their banter. The glances thrown about while gossiping in such a manner were to avoid being overheard by one of the officers, and taken to task for their disrespect. But the young lads felt they were the targets of this laughter and took offense.

The first incident was almost accidental. Michel, when bending over to pick up his shovel, found himself in a tempting position to release the air from a tire valve on the already loaded truck of chickens, just as it was set to roll off down the drive. He made himself scarce, hiding to watch with glee as the truck lurched to a halt before reaching the gate, the tire already flattened.

Later the same week, drunk with pride at his success in annoying those *'bâtards de Boschs'*, Michel enlisted the help of his friends to sabotage another of the vehicles. This time they broke one of the headlights and clogged the exhaust pipe with cow manure, resulting in a spectacular explosion of shit.

It was with some discomfort that Colonel VonEpffs made a decision. The broken headlamp and the flat tire could be passed off as incidental wear and tear on the vehicles. But there could be no mistaking an exhaust pipe clogged with manure, cows being not quite that agile, even in Normandy. There was no longer any doubt that a trickster was amongst them and must soon be caught and dealt with.

He ordered the assembling of the entire household in the yard in front of my door. Michel and Paulette were present with their parents, as well as the other lads and their families. Being a soft spoken man who had learned French as a boy from his private tutor, he addressed the uneasy group with care.

"One of you knows why I have asked you here this morning," he said with a slight accent in spite of his near perfect pronunciation. "I have no desire to identify the culprit. I wish that all of you simply be aware that these unfortunate events must stop immediately, or jeopardize the working arrangements which you are enjoying presently."

He paused, taking time to look specifically at each of the boys scattered amongst the adults. They all seemed quite interested in their shoes, and each of their fathers looked straight ahead, shoulders squared. He needed no further convincing the instigators of the pranks were the boys, and finished his speech undeterred.

"Stricter rules and sanctions will be placed on everyone, in reparation for lost time and cost. No more of this sort of thing will be tolerated without punishment. I hope you understand my position. Good day to you all." He turned on the shiny heel of his tall black boot and returned to the library.

Pulling aside the heavy drapes, he observed the dynamics of the group as they dispersed behind the second layer of filmy gauze, returning to their tasks. Long ago he had learned that much could be discovered from an uncomfortable group of people harboring a wrongdoer. He expected to see angry glances thrown in the direction of the boys, effectively identifying the precise source of trouble.

He'd guessed beforehand that it could only be the work of youngsters, considering the material used to clog the exhaust pipe. Having grown up around farm animals himself, he remembered being prey to a bizarre tendency, inbred in mischievous lads, to employ fecal matter as the stuff of pranks. He was reminiscing about a particular incident involving his cousin and a cow pie, when a discreet knock at the door pulled him back to the present and his responsibilities. Wiping a nostalgic smile from his face, he turned to the door, voicing admittance to a young lieutenant bearing provisions requests from the supply house in Dieppe.

Heinrich VonZeller was a tall, yet slightly built, blond-haired man, recently free of the skin troubles associated with youth. Colonel VonEpffs had chosen him from the ranks of junior officers of good family who, as a rule, enlisted of their own free will, believing in the tradition of the second son distinguishing himself and his family via a military commission. Hitler's rise to glory, and the desire to return the luster to the Fatherland's

somewhat tarnished allure following their undignified
loss of twenty years previous, motivated these proud
young men of high ideals to step forward. Heinrich
possessed a good education and was gifted with an
unusual propensity to correctly judge human nature. He
had proven his worth to Colonel VonEpffs, time and
again, indicating specific situations which had the
potential to sour. This was particularly useful to the
Colonel, who preferred by and large, to avoid letting
situations develop which would need to be punished. It
was more efficient to prevent rather than to cure.

"Lieutenant?" inquired VonEpffs as he dropped
the curtain, once again camouflaging the front yard, from
which the assembled workers had now disappeared.

"Sir?" replied Heinrich.

"Did you decide which of the boys was the brains
of the operation, as it were?"

"I did, Sir. I believe it to be the smallish dark-
haired one: Michel."

"The one with the lovely sister?" VonEpffs turned
to observe Heinrich.

Blushing furiously, the Lieutenant took a nervous
step backward as if he had been slapped. Stuttering, he

spat his reply with very little grace of elocution. "I, er, sister, Sir? Ummm...I've been mostly watching the boys, Sir." It was now his turn to inspect the shine on his boots.

The Colonel took pity on him, dismissing him with a short word. "Very good, Lieutenant. That will be all."

Listening to Heinrich back out of the room, and escape across the hall, he was struck by how young this man was, how young most of them were.

He settled back in the ancient, cracked leather desk chair, planning to examine the goods requests, and instead abandoning them in a limp pile on his lap, thinking of his youth.

His parents possessed an estate much like our own, in the Rhineland region of Germany. He grew up expecting to spend his adult life overseeing the growing of grapes while enjoying the wine pressed from them. This would have allowed him ample free time to read, listen to music and contemplate the meaning of life, being something of a philosopher at heart. Having some difficulty at not finding fault with his own actions, he was reluctant to advise others on their conduct. Grapes didn't seem to care much if he struggled with moral conundrums on occasion, hence it would have been the perfect occupation.

Sadly, life doesn't always wander along the path one expects. Being in charge of a number of men, situations arose with an alarming frequency requiring him to prove himself worthy of his Colonel's cap and braid. All the more important to surround oneself with men capable of alerting him, with sufficient notice, to these volatile situations, in hopes of diffusing them before an inevitable explosion.

He truly regretted the war, misunderstanding the Fuhrer's overwhelming thirst for revenge, or whatever it was which drove him so relentlessly. However, patriotism being one of the undisputed traits of the aristocracy, the Colonel and the Lieutenant stood the same ground regarding their sense of duty.

The rank soldiers represented another case altogether. After the fall of the Austro-Hungarian Empire at the turn of the century, the common man underwent several generations of relative poverty, the gap between themselves and the wealthy upper classes widening with the passage of time. They were recruited amongst the poor, with promises of a better world governed by people like themselves, free from those who threatened their jobs and ambitions. Hope was the powerful tool misused to motivate the unfortunate.

A good deal of the soldiers were hopeful, and therefore blind to the means used to achieve their much desired New World order. The Colonel's job was to harness that hope, transform it into a disciplined work ethic, keeping the soldiers' enthusiasm focused on the advancement of the domain, in order to exploit the farm to the fullest potential, while preventing its destruction. A delicate balance was necessary between the usefulness of the local population and the manpower of the occupying army. One couldn't survive the war successfully without the other. Maintaining order between the two was a difficult task for a peaceable man, such as the Colonel, naturally inclined to observe instead of imposing himself, which was why Heinrich's insight was so valuable.

Unfortunately, Heinrich was the sort of young man, who could foresee disaster where it threatened others, but was surprisingly inept at judging situations in which he himself was concerned.

Paulette's blue eyes wrought havoc with his common sense.

CHAPTER 4

1987:

"I know you're getting tired, Madame Dubois, but you really do have to make an effort to push very hard. A few more times and we'll be done." The midwife's voice zoomed in and out as if someone were diddling around with the volume button on a transistor radio.

Debra lay on the verge of giving up, wanting to die, as long as death supplied an end to the pain. The pain surrounded her—the left, right, top and bottom of her existence. She could no longer think straight and certainly couldn't control her muscles.

She remembered Philippe being in the room. Turning her head on the sodden pillow, looking for him, she only succeeded at wrapping damp strands of hair over her nose and mouth. She wanted to beg him for help.

Over the last eight hours he told her ridiculous jokes in the vain hope of reducing the drama of the situation. He looked fuzzy around the edges. Horrified at the suffering taking place before him, angry at his inability to do anything, she could tell he wished duty wasn't keeping him from an immediate escape.

Debra looked out of a hole at the delivery room, capacity for peripheral vision erased by physical distress. Tidal waves of pain screamed from her lower back, radiating to her extremities.

Philippe watched, with visible annoyance, the mounting needle on the monitor, squeezing her hand as another contraction climbed to its peak. The incessant flux of wave upon wave appeared as if it would never stop. He scowled, obviously wishing to crush the machine, as if the monitor were responsible for the contractions it tracked. He readied himself, checking his breath in sympathy for her suffering until the crest was reached, and the needle journeyed downward, aimed at relief.

Debra hadn't expected as much from him, and through a haze of sweat, appreciated his staying by her side. She thought it much to his credit, and later if she survived, she would remember to thank him for it.

He had explained to her beforehand, that she was the one who had insisted on having this child, not him. He had a teenaged son from a previous marriage, whom he rarely saw, and who always seemed to be getting into some sort of trouble. There were numerous occasions when he would hang up the phone, announce that he had to leave to sort out some problem with Stéphane and drive off into the evening, only returning in the small hours of the morning. After each of these incidents, he refused to discuss Stéphane with her, saying that he and the boy's mother were responsible, not Debra.

At only forty one, for some bizarre reason Philippe kept saying things such as "I'll most likely be dead by fifty anyway, so you must be prepared to shoulder responsibilities for yourself."

The only response possible to such a statement was to hug him and while holding him tight, she would whisper that he led a charmed life and would certainly live forever. She never understood his fear of death, instead suspecting it interfered with his enjoyment of living. She guessed that he took no comfort from her whispers, as he made light of them by saying that she would see what it was like when she got to be as old as he was. She hoped he was wrong.

And he was, because death seemed a good option just now, and certainly not a thing to be feared. She wondered what in the bloody hell she had been thinking when she accepted the doctor's suggestion of a natural childbirth, with little or no painkillers. For that matter, she was seriously rethinking her decision to have a child at all.

Although she couldn't imagine never having children- that is, up until about four hours ago- she hadn't been quite ready to become a mother. The question of having children had somehow morphed into an ultimatum between the cheese and salad courses served at an expensive restaurant in Rouen. It seemed most logical to her that they discuss having children, as most married couples do. When she broached the topic, his negative reaction jump-started the entire business leading to this moment of agony on the birthing table. Well, to be honest, her stubborn streak had something to do with it as well.

It had simply never occurred to her to doubt the natural sequence of human existence. As a woman, one starts life as a child, progressing through adulthood, taking on the successive roles of girlfriend, fiancée, wife, mother, eventually grandmother and if you were lucky, great-grandmother.

It was unthinkable to stop partway through life, teetering there as if in limbo, tragically waiting to move forward with the normal flow of the living, and instead existing immobilized. It would feel like being stuck in an elevator between floors.

Of course, it would be an entirely different story if, for whatever reason, one or the other of them couldn't conceive a child. Medical reasons were irrefutable, inescapable, and dauntingly definitive – the cause of mental anguish to the unlucky. But to choose to stagnate on her path? Certainly not.

By the time dessert arrived, she had achieved a significant level of indignation and injustice.

"How could you possibly think that I, as a healthy woman of twenty-four, wouldn't want a child? It's not my fault that you've already done that! I want a family of my own! It's not as if you want to share Stéphane! He's off limits. We don't see him. We don't talk about him. And he barely knows me!" She scowled across the table while tapping the tip of her fork on her dessert plate with such percussion, he had to reach across the table to still her hand before the china plate broke under the jack-hammering cutlery.

"Why can't we be happy, just the two of us?" The sigh accompanying this remark held an air of resignation. For once, a situation was escaping his grasp.

She didn't answer out right, because secretly she feared not having children would confirm the disgusting premise which she was driven to refute to the world. People assumed he was with her because she was young, firm flesh. Debra simply had too much self-respect to let things stand as they appeared: summer hooked up with autumn. This image was so incredibly demeaning, that she once again took up her battle weapons and launched the child crusade. Obviously, she couldn't explain this to him, so she countered differently.

"Because I want more."

The look on his face was clearly one of shock. Debra had surprised herself almost as much, and toyed with her napkin as he withdrew the hand imprisoning the drumming fork. They drank their coffee in silence and the subsequent trip home seemed terribly long. But when they pulled into the drive, and parked the car, he finally spoke.

"Alright. If it would make you happy. But I'm not getting any younger, so we must start at once."

They came inside, went upstairs, and did, after throwing the box of condoms in the bathroom rubbish bin.

She was carried on a tidal wave of grinding pain from that night nine months ago back to the immediate needs of her body, as the double edged sword of self-righteousness drove itself deep into her lower back. Following close behind the stabbing came a ripping sensation, as though her entrails had been turned inside out, spilling onto the table. Just after, an unexpected gush of pleasure lifted her from the depths of hell, leaving her tingling and exhausted, yet so very alive, as someone laid her daughter across her belly.

Covered in all manner of gunk, the dark blue eyes opened and Debra struggled with her seemingly rubberized neck muscles to get a look at Susanna's face. A frenzied check of toes and fingers ensued before she relaxed, holding tight to her precious bundle. The doctor severed the cord, and took the child for a check-up before Debra thought to look around the room for Philippe.

He stood away from the table, once again sporting a shocked countenance, this time awash with tears, and once again, she was surprised.

All she could think to say was, "Did you see her?"

"Yes...and I saw you, too." He paused, leaning close to her before continuing. *"Tu sais que je t'aime?"*

The question was intense: the kind of question that matters, and not simply a phrase repeated often enough for the meaning to diminish over time. Her answer would carry weight.

So, she didn't give one, choosing instead to look closely at his face before smiling into his eyes with a heartfelt response, stronger than words could ever be.

She felt incapable of coherent speech anyway, and especially not in French. She closed her eyes without looking away, falling into a deep sleep, chasing peaceful darkness.

He admitted to her much later, that he thought she'd died just then, bleeding unchecked from the episiotomy incision, the doctor's attention turned to the baby. He'd called across the room to the doctor and nurses, alerting them to the situation. A few minutes later, he'd been relieved when afterbirth contractions started and she was wrenched back to the birthing table from oblivion.

She would have much rather stayed in oblivion, ignoring the staff who kept poking at her, doing unpleasant things. Until finally, someone carried the baby back and taught her to nurse.

It felt a bit like having your life sucked from your breast and spread through another being. It was much more than sustenance. Debra instantly locked into the bond created by nursing. It was a promise of nurture, combined with everlasting, unequivocal protection. Debra pitied every person in the room, because they couldn't feel what she was feeling, her child at her breast. And most especially, she pitied Philippe.

Of course she would shoulder the responsibility for this baby. It could never be any other way. He would never feel a link to Susanna which could compare to the one born in her soul that instant in the hospital. He would certainly love the child, work to feed, clothe and educate her, most likely spoil her with toys and sweets. But Debra's mothering love was undisputed, and would remain so, forever.

A week later, Philippe drove them home from the hospital. My nights were punctuated with the mewling cries of a fussing infant. I kept Debra company during those long winter nights of their first few months together.

Philippe was busy elsewhere.

CHAPTER 5

They had been home for two days when the phone rang.

The unfamiliar voice sounded desperate, filled with anxious despair. It took her some time to realize it wasn't a wrong number. The names repeated over and over were ones her heart recognized.

"Yes, Monsieur Dubois is at work...I spoke with him not over an hour ago...Where did you say you saw him?...Well, he leaves the office for meetings elsewhere in the city quite often...No, I don't know the names of all the secretaries in the building...Why are you telling me this? And who are you anyway?.. No, I don't know her...I'm sure you're mistaken, you've most likely seen someone else and mistook him for Philippe...Please don't call here again...I'm sure Philippe would be quite angry about this call."

She dropped the burning handset onto the receiver.

Of course she knew Philippe had a secretary named Sophie. Still, it was a relatively common name in France.

Debra felt a bit sorry for Sophie. Somewhat chubby, she poured herself into suits a good size too small for her, made of materials which were either too bright in color or too flashy in texture to be worn by anyone who wasn't stick thin. She distinctly remembered one low cut, peacock blue outfit, worn with matching shoes and eye shadow. That day, the peacock blue suit day, when Sophie left the room, having ushered Debra into Philippe's office, Debra couldn't resist mentioning the obvious overkill and general lack of good taste displayed by the young woman.

Philippe looked at her with an expression much like one bestows on a child who makes an impolite comment about one of their school chums. Condescending pity filled his voice when he reprimanded her for being unkind.

"Really, Debra, I'm surprised at you. She's just a young girl who doesn't know any better."

Ashamed at his accusation of cattiness, Debra bit her lip, yet couldn't bring herself to revise her initial opinion. Sophie reminded her of nothing so much as an overblown flower of an audacious species. She couldn't keep from wishing someone would pluck the outlandish orchid from the vase of daisies where it didn't belong, removing it to a vase by itself. Elsewhere would be best.

She was surprised at Philippe's tolerance. He always reprimanded her when she dared wear a skirt too short or a neckline with even a bit of a provocative scoop. He should instigate a specific dress code for work and she told him as much.

"Oh good heavens, Debra, will you stop being so jealous! I won't get involved with how my employees choose to dress. Do you realize what you're saying? I'm a man. I barely notice what they wear. As long as they come to work! Now what did you come here to speak with me about?"

Subject changed. Debra had taken a deep breath before handing him the estimate from the auto repair shop, trying in vain to swallow her distaste for Sophie. In fact, she choked on it.

She was aware that Sophie was seeing an older man who spent rather a lot of money on her, taking her shopping and getting her hair done every week in new colors and styles. Her nails were always perfectly painted with a color corresponding to whatever brilliant piece of attire stood out the most.

Debra's nails were most often chipped or crooked, having the disappointing tendency to break, unfailingly, just after she found the time to file them all to the same length. Never mind the nail color! She was a woman with a baby and a large house to run, complete with a set of dogs and a cat. Enjoying swimming, bike riding and growing vegetables, nail polishing was nowhere near the top of her list.

Sophie's to-do list was clearly condensed to a single entry: primping. Debra assumed Sophie must possess something else intriguing to this older man, to keep him dishing out cash for her fashion whims, but refused to entertain distasteful thoughts about what that might be.

And now, as Debra stared at the telephone squatting on the kitchen counter like a malevolent toad, and bringer of bad news, she was certain the voice on the phone was his.

She couldn't bear listening to his distress. He said he'd seen Sophie, his fiancée, entering a hotel with a man he'd mistaken for Philippe. He was clearly very upset and calling her was wrong of him. It was too late though; his panic had screeched through the phone line and infected her ear. Peace of mind was no longer to be had.

He could only be mistaken.

Debra was torn between the urge to rip the phone from the wall socket and hurl it across the room to crash into the brick fireplace, hoping to silence the messenger, and alternatively, using it to put her suspicions to rest. The second option won.

In a gesture born of desperation, she decided to call the office directly and speak with Sophie, and with Philippe. An excuse about inviting some friends around for dinner on Saturday evening would show Philippe what a great wife she was. Not many women could be up for entertaining friends so soon after having a child. A small reception would prove that she was handling her new status as mother without breaking her stride in her other roles of wife, friend, and hostess.

The phone call would set her racing heart to rest. She dialed the number.

Patricia informed her that Sophie was off sick today, so she was filling in for her, screening Monsieur Dubois' phone calls. She was sorry not to be able to put Debra's call through to Monsieur Dubois, because he was out of the office this afternoon visiting a new client across town, but she would give him the message as soon as he returned.

"Is everything alright, Madame Dubois? You sound upset. Is the baby doing well? And you're doing fine yourself, I hope?"

"Yes, everything is perfect. Susanna is asleep and I just wanted to ask Philippe about something, but it's not urgent. I'll speak to him about it this evening. He needn't call me back. Have a nice afternoon, Patricia, and...well...I do hope the extra work load isn't too inconvenient for you. Will Sophie be off long? What does she have, a cold or the flu?"

"Errrr, I'm not quite sure what she's down with. No one told me."

"Well, let's hope it's not too serious," Debra answered briskly, anxious to hang up. "Take care. *Au revoir,* Patricia."

She was stunned.

Off sick? My eye, she thought. If she'd have been off sick that man would have known about it. She'd have been home, with him.

A vicious suspicion snaked its way into her guts, while another part of her, the place where optimism lodged, prepared for a siege which might last for a substantial amount of time. Her thoughts galloped one after the other, panting in their sprint, new troops arriving to support the opposing factions of her inner conflict.

She hoped she didn't communicate to Patricia the shock and desperation submerging her. That man had sounded so very pathetic: anguished and incoherent. Did she sound the same way to Patricia?

Philippe would be angry at her for phoning the office, causing people to worry about her state of health and well-being. He liked his wife to be self-assured and self-contained.

He greatly disliked scenes of any sort and prided himself on his capacity to stomp out arguments before the flames of fury took hold.

Usually, she flung herself out of the room and slammed the door when she was in a huff. That way, she left him alone for some time before any confrontation could get out of hand. For she had learned, at her expense, that he possessed the enviable talent for saying just the right horrible thing to her, grinding an argument to a halt and resulting in hurt feelings: her own.

Invariably, he would apologize later, claiming that he always said things he didn't mean when he lost his self-control. Debra should know better than to provoke him. Yet, hurtful words slithered out of his mouth so easily, as if he'd rehearsed them beforehand. *Au contraire*, Debra was at a loss to fight back with any sort of eloquence, let alone coherence. Bursting into a fit of tears, followed by an undignified escape through a slammed door was her most common response to his attacks. Most importantly, she never said anything in anger that she didn't mean.

All of which didn't help to reassure her regarding his proficiency at argument. Were those nasty remarks born from his true feelings about her?

Was he having an affair?

Did everyone at his work know already?

Was she the only fool left out of the joke?

Her mind jumped around like a caffeine drunk rabbit.

Susanna woke, protesting at an empty tummy.

Breast feeding was wonderful. Being a mother was wonderful. But just then, Debra wished she could escape to her own mother and seek comfort, not be the one to dry someone else's tears. Mom was five thousand miles away, and had no clue that all wasn't perfect in her daughter's seemingly charmed life. It probably wasn't worth it to call Mom and upset her when she couldn't even stop over for a cup of coffee and a hug to set things right. It would be unfair to dump this on Mom. To worry her would be just as unkind as that man calling Debra in the first case.

So, she was reduced to a whimpering mass of shaking, shell-shocked femininity, not quite knowing what to do with herself and very much alone.

She picked up Susanna and sat down in her favorite spot, the comfy old chintz covered armchair. She'd planned on dragging it out to the dump, before comfort while nursing a baby became a priority. It was a bit of an eyesore in an otherwise well decorated room, in a well decorated house, in a well decorated life.

The day she found it in the attic, removing the dirty dust sheet before sitting down with a sigh of well-being, she'd taken a liking to it. Now it seemed like a silly thing to keep. She would have it removed this weekend when Hubert, the gardener-handyman came.

He would take it away. Things would be all right. The room would look so much nicer with the chair removed.

She could ignore the phone call. She was silly to let herself get so upset over a conversation with a man crazed with jealousy.

The leather settee was just fine for nursing if she spread a comforter over it.

Susanna fussed, refusing to latch on correctly for the milk to flow. She had read that a mother's stress could keep a child from nursing enough to grow. Taking a deep breath, she attempted, somewhat unsuccessfully, to clear her mind. What were her options at any rate?

She was twenty five years old in a foreign country in possession of a residency permit, which she'd only obtained because she had married a Frenchman. In fact, the very Frenchman her parents told her not to marry.

Call them and go running home with a newborn? So much for her glamorous life in France! Could she bear to leave here and the home she so dearly loved? Give it up and flee back to the States because of a phone call from an unidentified nut?

Little by little she calmed her mind and resolved to wait and see.

A phone call wasn't proof of anything. More importantly, she wasn't ready to believe that it could be. So she didn't. The armor-clad optimistic thoughts were enthusiastically digging trenches, hunkering down, settling in for a lengthy battle, and erecting defenses against pessimism.

I set about humming my soothing hum of furnace, hot water heater and refrigerator, the noises which unconsciously punctuate my inhabitants' lives, capable of serving up a plateful of normality when it is most needed. I could feel both Susanna and Debra relax to these little noises of a peaceful, well-ordered life.

Debra had made her decision. I was relieved, and hummed for a while longer.

CHAPTER 6

Spring 1942:

More and more often, Heinrich found himself drawn to the window overlooking the west side of the house. From here, he enjoyed an unobstructed view of the walled kitchen garden with its sections for spring vegetables, herbs, winter vines, potatoes and berries. Along the inside stone walls grew trellised flowers, gooseberry bushes, raspberries and an entire section of fragrant tomato plants.

This was the domain of Emile, a fellow of rare gardening expertise. He was an older man, always dressed in a blue canvas workman's jacket and pants, sometimes coiffed with a straw hat. He refused to wear gloves and his fingers were gnarled and calloused.

Yet, looks can be deceiving. Heinrich would sometimes see him pause of an afternoon, take out a sheet of paper and a stubby pencil, his twisted fingers and knobby joints flying as he sketched a bird or one his lovingly tended plants. Intrigued, Heinrich would have liked to steal a look at Emile's drawings. Still, his position as an occupying officer, whose job it was to keep the workers on their toes wasn't conducive to personal *rapprochement*. On every occasion Heinrich conversed with Emile, the drawings were carefully stowed away, somewhere out of sight. Guessing it would make the old man uneasy if Heinrich let on he'd been observing him draw, he never requested a look at Emile's work.

I thought this was a shame. However, this was war, and friendly overtures were not always welcome between opposing parties.

The upstairs room which Heinrich and two other officers used as workplace and sleeping quarters had most recently been the bedchamber of the young lady of the house, decorated accordingly with floral chintz curtains and wall coverings. The cherry wood furniture had been removed to an attic where it sadly awaited use by a future female occupant. For now, plain oak tables covered with papers and ledgers filled the center of the room, while three camp beds lined two of the inside walls.

From the table where he worked most often, Heinrich could get a glimpse of the garden if he lifted his head and shoulders upright, stretching muscles tightened by bending too long over small print. He'd perfected this cat stretch, using it every time he caught a flicker of movement between the neat rows of vegetables. Most of the time Emile pottered about, weeding and digging up plants past their prime. But every now and again, he would be rewarded with a view of blond hair tied back under a kerchief, tumbling down a young back, bent over some plant or bush. He hadn't dared to speak with her, but he knew her name was Paulette.

Two years had passed since the day the convoy arrived, vomiting men in boots and uniforms into my front yard. Heinrich had been given the job of assembling the farm workers, house staff and their families, in view of the obligatory 'we're here to invade you' speech.

It was then he first noticed a startled pair of blue eyes, peeping from beneath the arm of a man with whom Colonel VonEpffs was speaking. Apparently the man was the employee of the absentee landholder: the one in charge of overseeing the working of the domain during the owner's southern sabbatical. Heinrich tried very hard to pay no attention to the blue eyes, mostly out of respect for the obvious youth of their owner. In addition to this resolve, maintaining an air of command was necessary when face to face with the people whose help was needed for the smooth running of the estate. Hoping to obtain another promotion this year, he must not appear to be distracted by such a young girl. In the meantime, the blue eyes scrutinized every move made by the newcomers.

"It must be a bit overwhelming for you," the Colonel was saying, "but we will try to maintain as closely as possible, the duties which had been assigned to each of you by your previous employer. We will be here to assist you...to make things easier for you. Whenever you have a decision to make about something, you must come to me or one of my officers who will help you make the right choice. If you do this and continue to work hard, you will see that things will be fine between us and you will be happy to have us here."

Well, it certainly sounded wonderful, even to me.

Many maintenance tasks had been neglected by sheer lack of man power and financial means. When the landowners fled in a flurry of agitation two years before, taking refuge in the unoccupied zone in the south of France, the running of the domain had been left to Paulette's father.

The decisions made about which crops to plant and how to negotiate crop prices were discussed amongst the workers who'd been there the longest. A sort of coalition was formed, with voting on the most important issues. Maintaining the buying and selling relations formed under the direction of the master had proved difficult, as many of these men had fled for the south as well.

In fact, quite a lot of the country's aristocracy and bourgeois businessmen had packed up, abandoning the north when it became clear the French army was vastly overpowered. Only those who had no connections south stayed on, as well as some of those who had never known any life other than farming. Those conscientious few couldn't bring themselves to leave the livestock to fend for themselves, or to let the fields lie fallow. These families stayed, much to the benefit of the flown, making sure there would be something for them to return to, if the occupation ever came to an end.

These haphazard conditions were effective for a time, but still in all, there were improvements to be made. German money and directives would be welcome. That is, if the occupying *Wehrmacht* kept their word and didn't treat them like chattel to be exploited.

#

Heinrich was nineteen when he enlisted in the army, buoyant with hopes of climbing through the echelons to a commissioned post where his sound head and heart would assure a future. He benefited from a good education, with time spent at university, and yet expressed no desire to enter into the business dealings at which his father and older brother, Rolf, excelled. No other viable opportunities presented themselves, so he enlisted.

Being in the army, and away from home afforded him the chance to avoid any sort of competition with his brother, who was a bit of a bully, enjoying trampling those who crossed his path.

Heinrich had learned, out of self-preservation, to anticipate Rolf's every move when they were youngsters. This made Rolf very angry whenever he played chess with his younger brother. Quite often the chess set would, at a strategic point in the game, waltz off across the room, scattering its knights and pawns beneath the furniture. Sometimes, it flew directly toward Heinrich, who knew when to duck and in which direction to make his escape. Rolf was a sore loser.

He managed to take credit where it wasn't his due and tried to lay blame for his misdeeds at feet belonging to someone else. Heinrich learned to abandon the scene before the crime took place, making sure to spend time with a valid witness; one who could attest to his innocence whenever he guessed Rolf's plans might go awry.

Rolf claimed most of their father's attention, be it praiseworthy or involving the inevitable punishment paid out by a heavy paternal hand. This situation suited Heinrich just fine, and because of it he was considered to be a trouble free child, if somewhat insignificant.

His decision to join the army was quite well accepted by his father who wasn't at all certain of his second son's capabilities. A military career would be just the thing for him. His mother, while reluctant to see her gentle, second son leave the family home, accepted without question her husband's relief at Heinrich's enlistment. She would have preferred to see him continue his studies at university, possibly becoming a professor. However, no one asked for her opinion.

Now, at twenty-two years, the last four of them spent in the army, Heinrich was free from Rolf and their domineering father. He did as he was told, submitting a well prepared suggestion here and there to his superiors. His efficiency and insight purchased favorable attention, and he was rewarded with frequent promotions. Enjoying the camaraderie supplied by army life and lacking in his childhood, he made friends and got on well with his peers.

#

Heinrich's duties supplied many reasons for moving about the estate, causing him to cross Paulette's path from time to time. She would be helping her mother launder the officers' shirts and underclothes, look up and follow his back with her gaze as he crossed the yard carrying a clipboard with fluttering papers, scribbling things along the way.

She noticed he liked to spend time with the horses in the evenings after dinner. He would bring them carrots and apples, sometimes brushing their coats. The horses liked this just fine, taking no notice of his uniform or political alliances. They munched the apples and enjoyed the extra attention. Even Polka, the Saint Bernard, wagged her tail, approaching him to claim a rough fur tousling.

Paulette was of the persuasion that animals, especially dogs and cats, never took to bad people. Little by little her attention was caught and held by the young man who talked to the horses and dog. She, like they, no longer noticed his uniform.

#

"Would you like some help with that?"

Startled, Paulette turned, squinting at the blond-haired lieutenant approaching her along the pathway separating the sugar peas from the *courgettes*. She was blinded by the late afternoon sunshine, yet had no trouble identifying the accent. The voice pronounced a simple, clearly stated question which would change her existence. Her instinct about this slammed her heart against her ribs.

She could supply no answer, although for months now she had hoped, in a frightened sort of anticipation, that he would approach her when she was alone. Imagined conversations took place between them, during which she would reply coquettishly, her behavior modeled on a movie star in one of the latest films. Her witty repartee would leave him swooning at her feet in admiration. Alternatively, they would have enlightened conversations about music or literature, when she would impress him with her knowledge. She could prove herself worthy of his attentions, banishing the image of ignorant, farm girl. He would be so pleasantly surprised, that his heart would be won to her instantly.

The disappointing reality of the moment was illustrated by a complete lack of inspiration for speech, resulting in an appalling silence which he had the good grace to ignore. He simply stepped across the row of sugar peas and rustled through the plants, searching for appropriately ripe pods to add to the basket slung over her elbow. Looking up at her frozen figure, he reached across the row, gently removed the basket from her stricken arm, and hung it from his own.

They plucked plump pods, advancing slowly from plant to plant for several minutes, burdened with a bushel of unspoken words and squelched questions. Silence hung between them, heavy and increasingly uncomfortable. The basket was near to overflowing as they reached the end of the row. At this point, a decision had to be made.

Paulette mustered her courage and reached to retrieve the basket from his arm.

"*Nein*," accompanied by a slight frown, was the close to inaudible response to her gesture.

Left with no choice, and unable to meet his gaze, she turned at the end of the path toward the door to the underground kitchens. He followed her at a respectable distance, descended the half flight of steps and placed the basket on the table where two of Paulette's young colleagues were chopping vegetables, helping the cook prepare the evening soup.

The trio of occupants looked up in surprise, their chatter abruptly stalled. Luckily for their fingers, they also interrupted the chopping. The cook cast a sharp look at Paulette just as Heinrich executed a small bow, clicking his heels together, followed by a rather hasty exit back up the steps, all composure lost: an embarrassed boy in uniform.

Before the others could recover their wits and get their tongues back in working order, Paulette chose to follow suit, escaping through the garden toward the back gate, where she grabbed the bicycle from the shed. She pedaled off furiously down the lane, chasing the solitude required to let her thoughts tumble free.

Watching her go, I was reminded of her mother with her own garden beau and wondered what it was about vegetable patches that seemed to so inspire young people. I did hope these two would fare better than the last generation, much preferring to absorb the overflow of happiness in lieu of tears. For now, I felt quite drunk with their anticipation.

#

She was panting heavily as she turned her bicycle into the little lane leading to the spring. The path meandered through the woods and Paulette had to dismount after about a hundred meters, littered as it was by large rocks and fallen logs. A better access to the spring came from the other direction, but this was the path Paulette had taken since she was a child, hunting for faeries in the woods.

Her thoughts were all jumbled, possibly from hyperventilation, for she hadn't succeeded at catching her breath or slowing her pounding heart since the moment she brushed his hand while attempting to re-take possession of the basket of peas.

"What in heaven's name is wrong with me?" she cried, dropping the bike and stomping about in last autumn's leaves. "Surprise him with my intelligence! Sweep his heart away with my wit and my charm! A...a mute, disfigured, idiot would have made a better impression on him! *Bon Dieu!* Why does my heart hurt so badly? Why, oh why, do I have to be so stupid?" Her angry diatribe escalated into a plaintive wail, frightening roosting birds into flight.

The noise made by their chaotic take-off brought back a smidgen of her calm. Stopping, she listened closely, thinking she could hear voices ahead of her. It was bad enough to be mortified by her behavior in the garden, but to be caught having a fit in the woods would demand an explanation she was not prepared to supply.

Picking the bicycle back up, she leaned it gently against a tree, as if in apology for having chucked it to the ground in anger. A sigh of resigned frustration escaped her lungs as she descended the trail to the spring. When she entered the little clearing she saw no one. As she made her way along the slippery path leading to the tiny stone hut covering the spring, she scrutinized the surrounding forest. There was no one to be seen. Her imagination must be playing tricks on her.

The spring was the home of a local legend. Saint Catherine's spring produced crystal clear, very cold mineral water, drawing people from miles around who came to drink it, hoping to improve their health. They carried out brimming earthenware jugs and glass bottles to take home, in order to prolong its positive effects. There was indeed something magical about this spot. The slow gurgle of water welling up from the rock strewn pool sang a soothing melody which echoed about the clearing, reverberating off the trees. The overflow trickled into a tiny, meandering stream which disappeared into the forest, carrying away secrets.

Dusk fell through the trees, as Paulette stopped, feeling faint. She knelt on a rock and scooped water into her hands, splashing it on her face and forearms. The shock of the frigid water cooled her racing heart. When she noticed her reflection in the translucent pool, she automatically made the typically feminine gesture of smoothing her hair while smiling at herself, dissecting the image seen by the young lieutenant in the garden.

As she touched her hair, two pins fell from it into the spring. She dipped her hand into the water, fumbling for the hairpins, which if not exactly a luxury, were nonetheless in limited supply on a farm. She swished around in the silt, searching for the pins and found in their stead, a metal button and three nails. This find slid a smile across her lips, making her wonder whose wishing objects she had disturbed.

The nails she dropped back into the spring but the unusual shape of the button caught her attention, and she turned it over in her hand, rubbing encrusted silt between her middle finger and thumb from an unidentifiable design. The contours of the button itself were flat, octagonal, but a raised curlicue pattern covered a domed top made of ivory. As the dirt came off, the long neck of a swan appeared curving delicately around its body, while trailing vines of some sort of plant entwined the rest, almost as if the swan struggled to swim free from a carnivorous predator. The miniature sculpture was so fine that the image jumped from its tiny resting place. She sat back on her heels, holding the small button in her hand, wondering who might use such a beautiful thing to hold a bodice closed, and how that person could bear to sacrifice it to the spring. This led to the last question, of who this woman yearned for, that she might accept giving up such a beautiful item as a wishing object.

For Saint Catherine was the patron saint of unmarried girls, and every November, on Saint Catherine's day, young girls would bring useful pieces of domestic metallica such as needles, pins and -she realized with somewhat of a shock -hairpins, to toss into the spring in hopes of meeting their true love within the year. As if scalded, she dropped the button back into the water, rising to her feet as the concentric circles from the tiny splash lapped against her shins.

What had she done? Did she want a German officer for her true love? It was unthinkable! What was she starting?

She considered herself much too sophisticated and educated to actually believe in such a legend. The dropping of all this metallic paraphernalia most likely served to keep the iron content of the mineral water on a high, but as for finding true love? Then again, ancient legends have a written-in-stone quality about them which force even the most skeptical to respect, if not adhere to their claims. And Paulette wasn't a true skeptic. She had grown up with the legend and accepted it as such.

Every year, the villagers enjoyed something of a holiday, with a small procession of unspoken-for young girls, dressed in their finery, leading the way to the stone hut. This was reputed to be the site of Saint Catherine's grave, the spring welling up unexpectedly when the young woman was buried there many, many centuries ago. As with most Catholic legends this one was rooted in a much older, pagan tradition, revamped to fit Christian ideology.

The *fête* heralded a welcome lead-in to the Christmas and New Year's celebrations, and was a good excuse to have a few hours off work in anticipation of these grander holidays. Paulette participated in the procession every year since the age of ten, as was the case with all the local girls, not taking part never entering her mind. She neither believed nor disbelieved the legend.

Like most of the girls she knew nothing more about Saint Catherine, or why she, amongst the other saints had been attributed the task of revealing future husbands to young girls.

Dipping her hand back into the water she swished it to and fro through the silt searching for her hairpins, not at all certain she wanted to abandon them to the talents of Saint Catherine and hoping to catch hold of the button once again. The design teased her with a fleeting memory of something she couldn't quite grasp.

As she fished about in the spring, moving pebbles around, she daydreamed about the young lieutenant, realizing she didn't know his first name. What was he doing in the garden anyway? Had Colonel VonEpffs sent him out there to count the peas, to make sure she wasn't pilfering any for her own use? He had strict rules about the strawberries, having punished several of the soldiers for a nocturnal raid on the berry patch last summer, but peas? Why would he care so much about peas? The more you picked them early, the more pods they grew. These peas had been steadily producing for the past three weeks.

Her vegetable musings were cut short by the distinct sound of people approaching down the other path. Paulette quickly lifted her skirt above her knees, crossed through the spring, scooping up her shoes along the way, before slipping into the cover of tall ferns growing between the trees. There she stopped, hidden from view, to put on her shoes, straighten her skirt and hair, alas, without the help of the two lost hairpins, while peeking through the brush to see who she had avoided.

She was disturbed to see Michel, her little brother, with Guillaume's sister, Manon, a plump girl with a sly smile about her which caused Paulette to dislike her. When they were younger, Paulette often had charge of the littler girls, watching over them as they did their lessons and feeding them their after-school *goûter*, the snack made of cheese and crusty bread served with *café au lait*. The mothers could thus continue working, knowing one of the older schoolgirls kept an eye on the younger group, until suppertime rolled around and the families gathered for the evening. This surveillance was all the more important now that armed soldiers were garrisoned on the farm.

While it was true that Manon had never exactly done anything wrong, her constant attempts at ingratiating herself to those in charge made Paulette distrust her. It was as if she were paving the way for future misbehavior, something really awful which none of the adults would think of pinning on her, since she was invariably so sickeningly sweet. Paulette was wary of her motives. And seeing her here, hanging on Michel, was not reassuring.

Paulette stayed put, certain she'd do well to keep an eye on these two, now that Michel was fifteen and Manon, a much too physically mature thirteen. Who knows what they were up to? Neither of them carried water jugs as an excuse to visit the spring.

As Paulette watched, camouflaged by the ferns, Manon took off her shoes and lifted her skirt a little higher than necessary, wading into the spring. Michel, eying her greedily as if she were a puff pastry filled with cream, whipped off his boots, rolled up his trouser legs and waded in after her. Manon squealed like a piglet, giggling as she made to escape. Unexpectedly, she feigned slipping to catch herself against the low stone edifice protecting the spring, while giving off a fraudulent moan of pain.

"*Aeiii*! I think I've turned my ankle!" she whined, turning large, limpid, cow eyes to Michel. "It hurts dreadfully!"

Instantly, he was at her side, bending down to look at her ankle, happy to have a reason to slide his hands around her foot and up her wet calf. Bent slightly backward against the sloping roof of the low stone hut, she inhaled deeply, puffing her breasts up into the air. Michel stood up and gawked down at the cream puff, entranced.

"Aw...poor you!" he purred, evidently enjoying her predicament. "Do you think you can walk on it?"

With no real originality, she whimpered, "No, I don't think I can...But, I suppose I must try, if you'll just help me." She punctuated this with a long, languid look up into Michel's face.

Paulette rolled her eyes and snorted in disbelief as her brother took the bait, pulling Manon close to his chest, to help her out of the pool of water. She crashed out of the undergrowth just as Michel clamped his mouth onto Manon's. The startled couple tipped sideways into the pool with a plopping splash, dousing their ardor and their pride.

"Papa is looking for you, Michel. Come home with me right away." She ignored Manon, who shot Paulette a murderous look while struggling to regain some dignity in spite of dripping drawers.

Michel, being a boy, thus used to being wet and dirty, helped Manon to her feet and to the edge of the pool, with quite a gentlemanly air.

Paulette waved her hand at Manon, shooing her off as if she were an annoying insect. "You should get back home as well, I think your parents wouldn't want you wandering around alone in the woods after dark!"

"I wasn't wandering around alone in the woods," Manon muttered under her breath, "I was with somebody!" Lifting her chin in defiance, she added, out loud this time, "I'm on an errand for *Maman*."

Paulette and Michel both looked at her with lifted eyebrows, but only Paulette remarked on this obvious falsehood. "Oh really? She sent you here specifically to wrangle a kiss from my brother?"

"I did not wrangle a kiss from anybody! I hurt my ankle!" She stomped her wounded foot, to punctuate this claim, forgetting how badly it was supposed to hurt.

Further argument was useless. Night was falling and none of them should be out of the farmyard for much longer. Intending to let the argument drop and get home, Paulette lowered her voice to a more soothing tone, "Alright, alright, but let's all get going, it's getting dark."

"I can make it home by myself, thank you!" Manon stomped off through the trees, in the direction of the short cut through the fields back to the farm.

"Suit yourself!" Paulette called to her hastily retreating, bedraggled backside. "But no dawdling or I'll tell your parents!"

Undecipherable grumbling wafted over angry shoulders as Manon disappeared round a bend in the path.

Michel looked over his shoulder with obvious regret as Paulette herded him up the slope to where she had left the bicycle. He turned back to ask, "What did Papa want with me? When I left him he was in the south plot with Flo and Maurice, turning up the new potatoes. He said I should go get the cows from the east pasture."

"Well it didn't look to me like you were anywhere near the east pasture and even if you were with a cow, I'm pretty sure that's not the one Papa wanted you to be moving!"

He smirked at this, incapable of stifling his laughter. "*Oh là!* Come now, Paulie! You're not going to tell on me, are you?" Michel bestowed his most charming smile on his sister.

"Stop it right this minute, Michel! I think you've done enough sweet talking for one evening!" She gave a playful swipe in his direction, not really aiming to cuff his ear. He ducked anyway. "Those cows need to get to the barn for the milking. You'd make better use of your honey voice on them, so they let you get the milking done fast, and maybe no one will notice how late you are!" She sat on the bicycle and placed her foot on the highest pedal. "Now hop on. We'll get home as fast as we can, and I'll help you with the cows. But I'll hear your promise to stay away from Manon. She's nothing better than trouble!"

He let her pedal him home although strictly speaking he was most likely better suited to be the one pedaling as his leg muscles were developing into stronger ones than her own. Still, old habits die slowly, and they were used to this configuration. It didn't occur to them to switch places, not yet. He was her little brother and she was still in charge of him. For now.

He leaned forward to speak to her over the creaking of the old bicycle, not used to bearing their double weight as they'd grown heavier now. "Oh! *Mademoiselle est parfaite*! You'd think you never even looked at a boy before!" he teased. "I know you've got a soft for that Henri fellow from Pierreville. I've seen you staring at him with gooey eyes in church! So don't you go

Page | 70

playing all high and mighty with me, or I'll tell him what you think of him myself. Then we'll see who catches who, kissing in the bushes!"

"You'll do no such thing!" She reached down to pinch him smartly on the leg, making the bicycle wobble precariously. "I'll have your backside tanned by Papa, the very next time I catch you at something! And I'll tell him about the other things you're planning! Those tricks are going to get everybody in a pile of trouble, Michel. You have to stop playing little games!"

"I am not playing little games!" His tone was defiant, overflowing with indignation. "I'm trying to make things as hard as I can for those nasty German bastards! They try and run us as if they owned us and the land they make us work! I just don't give in like you do, I have courage, and … and pride, and... and I want to stay French! I don't want to have to learn their ugly language or salute their hideous flag and insane *Führer*! I won't ever be a *Boche*! I'll die first! And you should feel the same!"

They rolled the rest of the way home in silence, Michel pouting and Paulette lost in her thoughts. How upset he'd be if he guessed what had brought her to the spring! She hoped he'd never discover it, and was relieved it hadn't occurred to him to ask.

They sped to the field, gathered the cows and escorted them back to the barn where two women arrived to help with the milking. Michel, ever the clown, invented a silly excuse which made the women laugh, reaping him no more than a gentle scolding, thanks to his most charming smile.

No more was mentioned about the spring as the cows were relieved of the heavy load of rich milk to be turned into tasty cheeses and creamy butter. Michel almost always was able to slip some aside to sell to the butcher or the baker in Bacqueville, who in turn sold it off on the black market, happy to keep some profit from German pockets.

#

Curfew for the French was at nine in the evening. Night falls quite late in the early summer in Normandy, and the supper hour is pushed back to get as much work done in the daylight as possible.

Paulette had finished her chores and was in the stables daydreaming in tune to the contented munching of Flo and Maurice, the huge draft horses who had just returned to their well-earned dinner of oats. They were a matched pair of Percheron horses, mild by nature but unrivaled in strength. Paulette had always enjoyed their company but now, she'd fallen in love with Flo's foal whose arrival she had witnessed this past March.

He was a loveable, cumbersome baby who nuzzled everyone who came near him. His favorite game was to approach Paulette from behind, butting her between the shoulder blades while nibbling on her kerchief. She was charmed by his sweet nature, and she named him Flynn after her favorite movie actor: Errol Flynn. This, in spite of the fact that most of her kerchiefs were now spitty and a bit frayed.

As she scratched Flynn between the ears, she hummed an unidentifiable little tune. She wasn't much of a singer and while she remembered the words to the songs she had learned in school, the melodies had escaped her. Flynn didn't seem to mind her disjointed music as long as there was no interruption in the ear scratching.

He snorted and danced, hearing quiet footsteps entering the barn before the noise reached Paulette's ears. Instinctively, she ducked between the walls of the stall occupied by Flynn and his mother, to avoid being caught outside a bit too late without valid reason.

Slipping a glimpse from behind Flo's shoulder, she recognized the lieutenant's profile as he entered the next stall over, where Maurice greeted him with a snort and a hoof stomp. She watched through a knot hole in the wooden partition as he blew gently in Maurice's nostrils, then whispered softly in his ear. Following this greeting with any sort of a treat was a surefire method of ingratiating oneself to horses. They automatically reach their noses out to snuffle a hand or listen to a soft voice in hopes of such attention.

The lieutenant pulled a withered apple from his pocket, cut it in half with a Swiss folding knife and let Maurice pluck it from his open palm. The horse munched, rolling his tongue around the tart taste of last fall's apple, and shaking his enormous head as if in thanks. Heinrich patted his withers and finger combed his mane while murmuring what could only be described as sweet nothings in German.

Paulette backed away from the partition, afraid to be caught spying. As a rule, she wasn't attracted to the harsh, chopped intonations of the German language. Yet, hearing it like this, she too easily imagined herself in his arms with his voice wafting around her ears. The tiny hairs at the back of her neck rose in anticipation, and a shiver danced through her body as she flushed with the fresh excitement the voluptuous thought inspired in her insides. She closed her eyes to better listen.

#

Heinrich caught her leaning up against Flynn, eyes closed and lips parted in a trance, her right hand covering her heart. The scene in front of him stopped him in his tracks, but he continued softly sing-songing. He stood still, contemplating Paulette for a full minute before the smell of the sliced apple in his hand made Flynn lose patience in anticipation of his treat. He sidestepped, and Paulette lost her balance. Her eyes flew open as she grabbed at Flynn to right herself. When she turned to look at Heinrich, her already flushed skin turned a brilliant red as she realized what he must have seen. She coughed to cover her embarrassment, and then choked, swallowing down her windpipe instead.

A fit of coughing and choking ensued. Heinrich rushed to her side, pounding her gently on the back. Flynn snuffled around in the straw, found the dropped apple and sidled away from them to munch with audible pleasure. After quite a long struggle to catch her breath, she let out an undignified croak resembling nothing so much as an enormous belch, as air re-entered her lungs in a rush. A few seconds passed in shocked silence before they both broke out in a fit of laughter worthy of hysterical hyenas. This exercise left them sitting on a pile of straw holding their aching sides.

Heinrich found himself thinking this was much better than the uncomfortable silence of their first *tête-à-tête,* though he kept this opinion to himself, instead speaking to her about the horses. Their conversation was relaxed, having passed the trial-by-fire period supplied by the hawking and belching.

"And are you the one who chooses the names of each of the animals here?" he asked in his softly accented French.

She was enchanted by the slur placed on some of his words, although their syntax was practically perfect. She'd completely forgotten how she had thought of German as a harsh, unpleasant language. His tainted version of French sounded divine coming from his lips. She watched his mouth as he spoke, then shook herself awake while he waited for her answer.

"Er, no. I just fell in love with this one when I watched him being born. It was wonderful!" She warmed to her subject, losing her self-consciousness. "He was so cute when he tried to stand, all wobbly, flicking his little tail around as if he was trying it out for the first time! And when he started to walk, it was so funny. He would stand up, then Flo would nudge him and he'd fall down again. But Papa said we musn't help him. He had to learn by himself where to find his supper. And when he did, he pushed so hard, that Flo grunted, and he just kept at it, flicking his tail all the time." Her eyes danced as she remembered the night she had spent in the barn, on special permission from the Colonel. "It was...beautiful, actually. I've seen lots of cows drop their calves, and of course the piglets are so sweet and silly when they race around bumping into one another and falling off their mama's side when they lose their grip on...well...um...on a teat." She blushed again, realizing too late, that it was a delicate word to use when conversing with a young man.

He looked at her with a question tilting one eyebrow. "A *teat*? What is this word?"

Her heart sank, "Euh...well...it's for babies to drink, you know, on their mother?" She lifted her eyes to search the rafters of the barn for an explanation, afraid to look directly at him while hoping he would understand enough that no gestures would be needed to perfect her sketchy definition. To keep from using them to show what she meant, she folded her hands under her arms.

"Oh! A teat! Alright, I never used this word before." It was his turn to blush. They both laughed in discomfort and simultaneously changed the subject, speaking at once as the clock turned its arms frantically toward a perilously late hour.

They spoke for a few minutes longer before Paulette looked out the barn doors at the darkness outside.

"*Ah zut*! My parents are going to be worried about me. I've stayed out longer than I had planned!"

"May I escort you home?" he asked, helping her to her feet. "I wouldn't like anyone to question you before you get inside."

She stopped brushing the straw from her skirt and touched his arm in a natural way which he found endearing. "Oh please, don't be offended! But, I think it might be better if I go back alone. I wouldn't want anyone to think...well...I'm sorry." She was genuinely worried about hurting his feelings and her concern was written on her face, plain for anyone to see.

His voice was just a bit more serious as he replied. "No, of course not, I understand, but know that I will be watching you, to make sure you get home without any problems." He kissed her hand in a salute to her loveliness, and she answered with a mocking but charming curtsy, accompanied by a brilliant smile and a laugh. She skipped off toward the door, then stopped midway turning to walk slowly backward to look at him yet still retreat.

"I don't know your Christian name!" she exclaimed shaking her head in surprise.

"Lieutenant Heinrich VonZeller, at your service, *Mademoiselle*." He bowed with gallantry in her direction.

"*Je suis Paulette!*" she whispered loudly as she reached the door and slipped into the night.

He stood frozen, speaking to the silence left behind her, "I know, *mein Schatz.*"

CHAPTER 7

Spring 1989:

Two years later, Debra introduced me to her second child, another baby girl. They named her Victoria. I observed Susanna's struggle with this turn of events, but in the long run accepted the inevitable with a natural amount of sibling jealousy. More moving of furniture and rearranging of rooms ensued, in an effort to make sure everyone had their own place to feel settled.

I do so like it when my spaces are re-utilized in this fashion, especially when my old bones are cared for, sanded down and repainted to keep my facade fresh and attractive. Being admired is more important than most people imagine. It counts to aging people and it makes a huge impact on aging edifices as well.

How devastated must my peers feel when someone deems them unworthy of expensive restoration. They might be stripped down to fragments, demolished, their memories dispersed and hauled in broken bits to the landfill. The hard work and sweat of those who labored to make us into comfortable shelters to be cherished are erased forever. As if they never existed at all.

A new building, even the fanciest, most modern design is void, and indeed remains so for a very long time. It takes many years to ripen a house into a home, with an aura of being all its own. Things need to happen there: laughter to ring out, tears to be shed, love to be made, doors to be slammed, songs to be hummed, many lives to be started and ended, before a balanced feeling can reflect back to comfort those who are lucky enough to live there.

The truth is, no one can *own* a property of my caliber. Quite the opposite is true. The value of a home hangs in the balance of the delicate relationship between owner and possession. Some homes possess the homeowner, as it were. They're the ones passed from one generation to the next. Others are shuffled around every ten years or so, until presented to the person or family who feels the potential for a long term commitment. Still others are destroyed by the perpetually dissatisfied: those who continually seek, yet never find their equilibrium. When the perfect match is made, it's a miracle for both parties. A new life is shared between the home and the inhabitants, satisfaction infiltrating every fiber of both.

Debra instinctively knew of this harmony and I felt her understand it, even though she never spoke of it other than to pronounce the standard response of, "Oh, I love living here in France." I know she loved living here because of me.

She could look through my aptly named French doors from her bedroom, contemplating a vibrant sunset across the terrace and her contentment would seep through every one of my rooms. It was balm to my soul. I absorbed, then radiated this peace back to her whenever she was unsure of the path she was on, which was becoming more and more frequent as her time with Philippe progressed.

He had decided she must work and found a place for her in his company.

The arrangement was proposed one evening, when he came home in a bluster about a traveling salesperson who had unexpectedly quit work, claiming health problems. This person covered the sector closest to home and Philippe insisted Debra should fill in as they risked losing certain clients who had appointments the following week. It was the start of the high season, with a good percentage of their annual sales to be made.

"*Chérie*, if you would just give it a try for the time it takes to recruit and train someone else, it would help me out. We can't do without these orders. I'm not sure what would become of the company if you can't lend a hand just this once. We might have to sell the house if we miss out on this season's business." His voice was wheedling and petulant, as well as blatantly manipulative.

The unfair advantage of knowing someone well enough to tickle them where it hurts factored into their conversation. His perfidy reinforced my inherent distrust of him. I groaned and squeaked, though Debra remained oblivious.

"But, *mon amour,* surely there's someone better suited to fill in who already works for you. I really don't know anything about wholesaling. Don't you think I would do more harm than good?" Debra wasn't very keen on getting hooked up to a job she felt she hadn't been trained for. She barely knew the line of products Philippe's company distributed.

"You have it in you to be very good at whatever you choose to do. None of my employees can say the same. You have a vested interest in your success, because it would be our shared success. I could never trust anyone else to do their best for me, not in the way I can trust you to do so." His smile seemed genuine, and its appearance made her feel ungrateful and mean-spirited, balking at helping out when times were rough. She was at a loss to contradict him.

My boiler belched in response to his overtly cunning compliments. But they hardly took notice. It was a rather windy evening and my warning manifestations were largely ignored.

While I could tell there must be an additional motivation buried in Philippe's not-so-pure heart, Debra couldn't see it. She reluctantly agreed to let Françoise, the cleaning lady, take care of the children come Monday and climbed the stairs to their bedroom, burdened with misgivings. It wouldn't be the last time.

#

Debra climbed in her car, armed with a map of the region, her trunk full of the sample cases she would show to the clients with whom the absentee salesperson had made appointments. Today there were only two, but tomorrow's schedule listed four. She was anxious about entering a building, introducing herself and pulling off a sale, but as luck would have it, the weather was fine and her spirits lifted in spite of her fears. As everyone knows who has ever been here, nowhere can hold a candle to Normandy, decked out in the flowering springtime of a sunny day.

She tooled off down the two lane road taking her to Caudebec and her first *rendezvous*. Forty-five minutes of pleasant driving through bucolic scenery later, the reality of the situation slapped her in the face as she pulled up in front of her destination. Apprehension developed into nausea while she parked the car. Chiding herself, she grabbed her briefcase, leaving the samples in the car, hoping to feel less like a packhorse, and pushed open the door.

Stomach churning, she waited for the receptionist to finish a telephone conversation. She hoped either the buyer would be sick or too busy to meet with her, providing an excuse to escape and give herself a serious pep-talk before the appointment this afternoon. The wait was torture.

Finally, the receptionist looked up and smiled. "You must be Madame Dubois. I'm Sarah. Pleased to meet you. Sophie from your office phoned and said you'd be here to replace Madame Leclerc who seems to have fallen ill. I'll just go see Monsieur Talbot to let him know you've arrived."

Well thank goodness for small miracles! Relieved that Sophie had paved her way, she made a mental note to thank her the next time they spoke. Maybe Sophie wasn't so bad after all. The unpleasant business with the crazed boyfriend was enthusiastically shoveled under the rug once and for all. Sophie wouldn't do her such an obvious kindness if she had set her sights on Philippe. Full of positive energy, she rose and stuck out her hand to firmly shake that of her client, following him into his office.

They emerged an hour and fifteen minutes later, with what she considered to be a good sized order. She remembered to ask when they thought they would need to see her again, before thanking everyone and saying goodbye. Penciling in the appointment for the following month using Madame Leclerc's date book, Debra drove off in search of a telephone and some lunch.

She phoned the office planning to thank Sophie. Instead, Patricia answered the phone. "Just one minute Madame Dubois, he's not in his office, I'll try to locate him for you."

She could barely contain her excitement when she finally had Philippe on the line. Expecting congratulations of some sort, she was cruelly disappointed at his bland response. Philippe cut her short and wished her good luck for the afternoon appointment, explaining he was busy with paperwork that couldn't wait.

Only slightly deflated, she took a stroll around Caudebec, planning on enjoying her success with a short stint of sightseeing before lunch. She stopped into a shop selling children's clothing, and purchased a sweater for Susanna and a sun hat for Victoria. She thought these small presents might help make up for her being away all day. She bought herself a sandwich and ate it while walking along the Seine River. A quick half-hour drive, passing the Abbeys of Saint Wandrille and Jumièges took her to her next *rendezvous* and face to face with the second trial of the day.

This time however, the client in question was a blustery little fellow sporting a drooping mustache and tiny-man-hates-the-world complex. Debra squared her shoulders and met the enemy head on, deploying as much charm and enthusiasm as she could muster. If he could like her, she might overcome his objections to the change in personnel, work habits and the multitude of other complaints he dumped at her feet. After two hours of continual bowing and scraping, they finished the order and he blessed her with a tiny smirk of a smile, peeking from beneath his unattractive facial hair. They shook hands and bid their goodbyes until next month.

"Whew!" she exclaimed once safely back in the car, "That was character forming! The little creep! But I'm done, I did it! I'm free!" She did a seated version of the happy dance as she turned the key in the ignition. Taking the scenic route home, Debra rolled the car window down, a song on her lips and in her heart.

#

August:

Philippe was late coming home from work, so she took the time to have a short wander around the garden with the girls. She wanted to enjoy the late summer sunshine, and she missed spending time with them. Work had kept her busy for the past three months. They were happily chattering away about the flowers and listening to the birds chirping as they settled in the hydrangea bushes for the night, when Philippe's car pulled in the drive.

She swallowed her greeting as he launched into a diatribe about the upcoming trade fair in Paris he was forced to attend. Debra attempted to cheer him up.

"Non, *mon coeur,* this will be an excellent opportunity for us to spend the evenings together and go to some restaurants we've not yet had the chance to try. Just think! Evening strolls in the Jardins du Luxembourg, or along the Champs Elysées. We could even go up to Montmartre and watch some of the street entertainment. We've never been up there together. It will be great fun! I'll find some shopping or museums to occupy myself with during the daytime when you're at the show and we'll have every evening to spend together in that romantic city...just as if we were newlyweds!" She was gushing excitement, eyes sparkling.

"Well, it sounds like you've got it all planned then, don't you?" he remarked, a sour taint of sarcasm in his voice. "Who will take care of the girls if we're both gone? Do you think it's wise to leave them with someone else for seven days. And what about your job? Who will visit your clients if you're away? I hope you're capable of taking your job seriously Debra, because you know we're all counting on you. Other jobs depend on you doing yours well."

He was reluctant to have her come. I could hear it. She was deaf, or at least so energized by the prospect of a trip to Paris with him, that she was incapable of hearing his squirming attempts to convince her to stay home. Nor did she weigh the clump of responsibility he shoveled onto her shoulders when mentioning jobs which depended on her own. I was appalled to hear him remove himself from the equation in such a wily fashion. After all, he was the owner of the company, not Debra. I was indignant for her, since she was forgetting to defend herself. I blew a cool draft up his pant legs, aiming to raise goose bumps along his hairy ankles.

Debra clung tightly to her wishes, doing her best to convince him to let her come along. "Françoise has told me time and again, that she would love to have the girls over for a sleepover. You know she and her husband can't have children. I'm convinced she loves our girls like they were her own. I trust her completely. And if we can trust her to care for them in the daytime when I'm at work, then why can't we trust her to care for them if I'm with you in Paris?...As for work, I'll simply put in a few longer days before and after the trade fair. I can get all the clients' orders if I just condense my days a little. You'll see it will be wonderful!

Much to my petty satisfaction, Philippe did a small two step to move away from the draft, proof that I had annoyed him. Although I knew he wouldn't heed my message of warning. His heart was too full of selfish considerations to listen to much of anything which didn't suit his desires.

I turned my attentions to Debra. 'Oh dear girl,' I breathed in her ear, 'he doesn't want you to come with him to Paris. He's up to something else, and you're not included.' She would fall. I could feel it coming. But exceptionally, she wasn't attentive to my warnings either.

#

September:

How unfortunate that Debra had to return home early from Paris! What dumb luck that Philippe hadn't thought to order in extra fuel for my heating system before they left. But, as fate would have it, France was in the grips of a freakish cold spell and Françoise didn't know how to start up my ancient boiler.

Debra was forced to leave the trade fair two days early, taking a train back through Rouen and into Dieppe, where she paid a taxi to drive her out to the house. She arrived rather too late in the evening to drive to Françoise's home and pick up the girls. She lit a fire in the bedroom hearth, heated up a bowl of soup and climbed into bed with the cat and a good book. Mulling over the events of the past few days, she sipped at the soup, enjoying the comfort of the fire.

She had convinced Philippe to let her come to the trade fair. However, her plans of shopping and visiting museums had been unceremoniously dumped when Philippe issued the snide remark that since she was dead set on coming, she might as well help out on the stand.

"Can't you see how bad it would look to everyone else who'll be working there, if you're lording it around town, shopping and having a good time? We'll be on our feet twelve hours a day, five days straight, not to mention the setting up and ripping down days. Not very good for employee relations, I would think! How irresponsible are you?"

She was stung, but recognized the logic in what he was saying. "I never thought of it that way. I guess you're right," she conceded, sheepish and looking rather crushed.

"No, you just didn't think. Sometimes I wonder if you realize how hard we all work to keep this company afloat. The money doesn't come in without effort, Debra. Really, I should think you'd have guessed that by now." He spat his words at her, a far cry from the soft conversation he had once used to seduce her.

Tears welled, but she swallowed them along with her sarcastic response, knowing it would just make things worse. Still, she was determined to come along and when they left for Paris in the van, she was excited and ready to apply her talents to making this a successful show.

She was helping to unload sample cases from the van in the back parking lot of the trade fair at Villepinte, just outside of Paris, when she heard female voices calling out to her husband.

"Oh there you are Monsieur Dubois; we've been looking for you!" Sophie's dazzling smile froze, stuck to her glossy lips, when she noticed Debra, arms piled high with sample boxes.

Patricia's cheerful voice filled the awkward silence left by Sophie, who didn't bother to come greet Debra, instead hanging behind Philippe mumbling something Debra was too far away to hear. Debra looked at Patricia who was chattering on, reminding her of one of the fat little sparrows who hopped on the kitchen windowsill every morning after Debra shook the crumbs from the tablecloth out the window. "What a pleasant surprise, Madame Dubois! We had no idea you would be here to help us," she chirped as she reached to take one of the boxes from the top of Debra's teetering pile while Debra tried, in vain, to keep an eye on Philippe and Sophie's conversation. "I'm afraid this is going to be a lot of work and you'll be a real asset to us, since you've been doing so well with your clientele. Monsieur Dubois says you're doing much better than Madame Leclerc ever did!"

This last remark caught Debra's attention. "He said that, did he?" and grumbled to herself, "well, he never told *me*."

"Pardon me, Madame Dubois, what did you say?" Patricia asked.

"Oh, I'm sorry, nothing, nothing at all." She gave up trying to eavesdrop on her husband and smiled at Patricia who was blocking her view. "I'm glad to be here,

I've never been to one of these things before. It should be interesting."

She took heart at the sincerity in Patricia's voice and warm, welcoming smile. The woman was a bit older, how much Debra didn't like to guess, but she had the beginnings of a matronly air about her, dressing in longish floaty skirts and dresses. Debra felt young enough to keep to knee-length outfits or jeans when she knew she'd be getting dirty, like today, hauling things and unpacking boxes.

The sales staff was present, logical, but she couldn't help wondering why Sophie, a secretary, and Patricia, the accountant, had been asked to come along. She also wondered what in the hell Sophie had been thinking when she got dressed that morning to help set up the stand. The young woman was dressed in a rather tight pleather skirt, which couldn't quite be described as a mini, but it certainly did not look appropriate for box carrying. In a spurt of unspoken cattiness, Debra wished Sophie would fall off her skinny boot heels and break her plump neck. She kept this to herself, knowing she would only be accused of being jealous. As if!

Her face must have given away her thoughts. When she looked up, she noticed Patricia's stare. Debra flashed a quick smile and a shrug of her eyebrows at Patricia, who smothered a grin, looking down at her own

Page | 94

sensible flats. At least Debra now knew that someone else held an opinion regarding Sophie's extravagant attire. She was strangely comforted by this discovery, liking Patricia for it. Debra's natural good humor won out and she turned to the back door of the exhibition hall with a light step in spite of her heavy load.

She worked tirelessly all day, hauling boxes and tables, helping out wherever she could and supplying cups of espresso and sandwiches for lunch. She did her best to be pleasant, in spite of the stress of getting everything perfect before the show opened the next morning.

This trade fair could mean new clients from all over France and even Europe. It was the very first time they'd participated as sellers. There had been quite a lot of preparation in Dieppe before loading the van with samples, tables, supplies, and the *décor* they were using as a backdrop for the displays. The expense of the show was enormous and it was quite a gamble on Philippe's behalf. They were under serious pressure to get things just right.

The next two days flew by in a whirl of activity. She did her best to help out the sales team and met prospective clients. Some of these came from their province and she tried to sell, if not a firm order that day, at least an appointment with her for the near future.

Philippe appeared satisfied with her work. After the first evening meal shared with the entire team, he announced that while arrangements had been made for the others to dine at the hotel, he was taking Madame Dubois out on the town. The camaraderie which had built up throughout the first two days of hard work gave rise to a little whooping and whistling from the guys and sly winks from the ladies, or maybe it was the effects of the before dinner drinks. No matter, it made Debra feel special.

She had worn a new outfit for the occasion, receiving a rare, appreciative once-over from Philippe when she emerged from the bathroom at the hotel, ready to go. He was usually so stingy with compliments that she glowed with pleasure, smiling even now in bed with the cat, remembering the look he gave her and the subsequent enthusiasm with which he divested her of the new outfit before they'd left the room. An hour later, pink with impromptu lovemaking and late for their dinner reservations, they rushed out of the hotel into the taxi that would take them downtown. His attention made her feel like a young girl in love, and the feeling was wonderful.

The following two days slipped by without a hitch, copies of the previous one, inclusive of the sex and fine dining. They dropped into the gigantic bed at night exhausted, but for Debra at least, completely satisfied with life.

Then came the phone call from Françoise. She wondered if Monsieur Dubois could give her the name of the company holding the service contract for the boiler, so she could call them herself. Francoise apologized for bothering them, but it was quite chilly in the old house and heat would be necessary, even in the daytime. She was afraid the girls would catch cold.

Of course Debra was the logical one to go back and sort it out. Philippe had to stay. He was the boss. So she wished them all *bon courage* and went back to the hotel to pack up and take a taxi to the Gare St Lazare, where she could catch a train back to Normandy.

I tried to welcome her as warmly as I could in spite of the chilled north wind which rattled my shutters a good month too early.

So why the niggling uneasiness just behind her left ear? The cat settled down to sleep and stopped purring. Debra put her empty soup bowl on the nightstand and picked up her book. As the pages turned, the fire died to a glow, heat reverberating from the stone surround. She found insomnia was best treated by delving into someone else's problems, instead of rehashing her own. This was a particularly interesting novel about a woman who accidentally travels through time and ends up in eighteenth-century Scotland. Debra plunged into the time of Bonnie Prince Charlie and tough, kilt-clad warriors.

A good hour later, she was jerked back to twentieth-century Normandy when she heard the distinct sound of tires crunching the gravel of the drive. My boiler being off, I was completely silent. The sound drifted up the stairs to the bedroom, dimly lit by the nightstand reading lamp. Debra rose and went to the window, drawing back the drapes only slightly, already frightened.

There at the end of the house where the drive curves around to approach the entrance, she saw a car with its lights off but motor running. Three figures emerged from the unlit interior. She went out to the landing, grabbed the telephone off the hook and dialed seventeen, the emergency number for the police.

The person who answered sounded sleepy and didn't seem to understand what Debra was frantically trying to whisper to him.

"Madame, don't be so excited. Calm yourself and tell me exactly what you heard." Debra rewound, trying to be as clear as possible, summoning all her concentration in an attempt at sounding coherent.

The voice at the other end of the phone line didn't seem to get it. "But surely it's just someone driving by, who stopped for a moment to stretch their legs."

"*Non, non! Vous ne comprenez pas!* They are in my yard. They're not on the street and I have no neighbors close by. They've come here to my home on purpose. None of my friends would ever drive all the way out here in the middle of the night. Not without calling first! It's someone who's trying to break in! I know it!" She was terrified and frustrated at the lack of comprehension from the other end of the emergency line.

"Alright, Madame Dubois, is it? Put the phone down, but don't hang up and go look out the window again. Then come back and tell me what you see."

Meanwhile, the team of would-be thieves had organized themselves with flashlights and what looked like a tool box. They milled about the yard, scanning the façade of the house with the lights.

She rushed back to the phone. "They've got flashlights and tools!"

"Don't panic, I've dispatched a patrol car. Do you have exterior lights? Are they on?"

"Yes, but no, they're not on...and...the light switch is downstairs!"

"You have to turn on all the lights and make a lot of noise. They need to know the house isn't empty. Don't hang up, but go right now and do as I say. A car is on the way."

She set the phone down once again, and inched her way toward the staircase, her heart pounding a staccato beat sure to be heard by the men outside. She crouched down the steps one at a time, peering around the turn of the stairs when she reached the halfway landing. She was met there by Mac and Cheese, her two Scotty dogs who didn't seem the least bit interested in the men outside, but who happily waggled their backsides at her.

My front door, being made of oak with cathedral glass panel inserts, allows light into the foyer. To Debra's extreme dismay, the electrical switch for the outside lights was located next to the doorway. This meant if she were to turn them on, she would have to cross the hall and approach the glassed-in door. She could see a shape on the outside, holding a flashlight, already fiddling with the lock.

Drawing one choking breath, she flung herself across the hall shouting, "Philippe! There's someone outside! You get the gun and I'll call the police!" as she slapped at the light switches in an attempt to deter them before they opened the door.

I flooded the front yard with light.

She sped through the other rooms flipping on lamps as she went, Mac and Cheese yapping excitedly at her heels. When she made it to the kitchen she grabbed the downstairs phone.

"I did it!" she shouted into the handset.

"Good, now stay on the line with me, until the officers arrive. They will honk several times as they pull in, so you'll know who they are. Are the men still outside, or have they left?"

"I have to go look again?" she whined like a petulant child when asked to do the dishes.

"Well, that way we'll know, won't we?"

"Ok, but I can't see the side yard or out to the road from the house. All I can see is the front yard. Hang on."

Five minutes later two patrol cars pulled into the yard honking, sending Mac and Cheese into a frenzy of barking and growling.

"A lot of help you two are! I'll remember to post a sign at the gate, 'Burglars: please honk before entering!'"

She opened the door for two police men who escorted her into the sitting room to question her about what she had seen.

"I've no idea what kind of a car it was, I couldn't see the plate from the bedroom window, and I know absolutely nothing about cars. It was a kind of darkish color, that's all I can tell you. There were three medium sized guys in dark clothing but I didn't hear them speak to one another and I couldn't distinguish their faces or hair color through the cathedral glass of the door."

Her nerves finally gave out. Teeth chattering and shoulders shaking, sobs clogged her throat.

One of the officers took pity on her. "If it's all right with you, Madame, we'll stay here with you for a little while. The other officers will patrol the vicinity and see if they run across a dark colored car with three occupants."

"Aaawl-rrright," she blubbered, ashamed of not being able to regain her calm.

"Well, Madame Dubois, we don't have much to go on, but I think it was a one off thing. This is a quiet place and there isn't a lot of crime in this area, just some routine burglaries. I'm pretty sure they won't be back. But to avoid anything like this ever happening again, lock the gate at the road, keep outside lights on every night and keep at least one light on inside the house, preferably upstairs. That way the house will always look occupied even if you're away. And get a big dog. These guys are cute, but not very good as guard dogs go."

He reached down to pat Mac and Cheese, who washed his hand: top, bottom and in between the fingers. The officer was sympathetic, making small talk and questioning her about why she was alone in such a big house at night and where her husband was.

The chit chat carried on for nearly an hour, as little by little Debra's breathing returned to normal and her heart beat slowed enough for her to speak correctly. In a fit of verbal diarrhea, she spewed information about who she was and how she got here from the States, about her daughters, the trade fair and the boiler.

He asked her to show it to him and she led him out through the kitchen door to the cellar where the ancient furnace squatted in a corner. He looked it over, then pushed a lever or two, opened a valve, switched a switch and my boiler chugged to life.

A pleased grin on his face, he brushed the dust from the stone floor of the cellar off the navy blue knees of his uniform

"My grandma's got one just like this. Well, at least you've got some heat for the rest of the night. Can I suggest you go to bed now? We'll be driving by the house about every twenty minutes for the rest of the night and we'll come back around here for the next few evenings just in case they try to come back. The dispatch center knows who you are now and where you're located, so don't hesitate to call them if you hear anything funny."

He spoke to her gently as if speaking to a frightened child. "If you don't call every time, we won't have much hope of helping out. It's our job. But try and rest easy tonight, we'll be around keeping an eye on things for you. Just keep your outside lights on and we'll close your gate when we go. Goodnight now." He tipped his hat and was out the door.

"Lock up behind me!" he shouted from outside.

"I will! And thank you!" Debra clicked the key in the lock then climbed the stairs, patting the dogs as she left them on the landing.

Her book lie on the floor, where she'd dropped it. The cat stretched sleepily, grunting in feline annoyance as Debra slipped under the duvet, disturbing her sprawled position across the middle of the bed.

About as wide awake as she ever could be, she tried to dive back into eighteenth-century Scotland. After reading the same page six times over, she finally managed to turn it and ease her mind into the story. Much later, she closed her book and switched off the reading light just as dawn teased the horizon.

Slipping into a fitful doze, she got a little rest.

I chugged out heat, and boiled up water for her shower, while feeling lucky that my windows hadn't been broken or my interior invaded by men looking to do harm. We were both glad to be safe.

CHAPTER 8

Late spring 1942:

Abbot's Wood was a self-sufficient farming enterprise. Long ago, estates on a scale as large as my own had to be, bartering being the principal means by which people obtained what they could not produce themselves.

We had a *laiterie,* or dairy, for the fat milk cows that grazed amongst extensive apple orchards. We raised sheep, pigs, goats, geese and chickens, and grew our own vegetables and herbs. Our cash crops were flax and wheat, as well as rough corn used for fodder during the winter for the livestock. In addition, we produced hard cider and calvados: the apple-based brandy, boiled from cider.

In times of peace, the domain was a source of considerable revenue for the landholders, supporting five families of workers, in addition to the owner and his family, all housed on the property in small cottages. We had a large barn, two granaries, a carriage house, what used to be a smithy's forge, a smoke house, chicken coop, dove cote, stables and sheep shed.

The cider house sheltered an ancient stone cider press to which a horse or team of donkeys was harnessed to turn the huge stone wheel in its trough. The apples left over from the previous autumn were arranged there to dry upside down on slatted shelving. These were used throughout the entire year following their harvest in the making of cakes, pies and compotes. When they dried too much the horses enjoyed them as treats. Inside was the entrance to the underground cellar where the bottled spirits were stored.

Polka plodded along behind Paulette late the following morning as she headed there to draw a fresh jug of cider to wash down her father's lunch.

Approaching the open door, she heard German voices raised in some sort of argument.

She looked through the door to see Colonel VonEpffs, Heinrich with clipboard in hand and three soldiers dressed in the more casual work uniforms indicative of their corps, the *Wehrmacht*. Last evening's conversation with Heinrich gave her the courage to do something she would never have done before. Instead of retreating to the yard until they had left the building, she went inside.

It was a rather gloomy, dusty building, and the sunshine streaming through the open doorway made dust particles from the straw swirl about in the air, mimicking miniscule creatures dancing a whirly jig. The same sunlight lit Paulette from behind, outlining her body through her thin cotton dress, and producing a halo around her blond hair, *sans* kerchief today, as they were all set out in the sun to dry after being freshly laundered free of Flynn's affections.

Heinrich sucked his breath through his teeth in a noisy reaction to her unexpected appearance. Colonel VonEpffs clucked his tongue with disapproval, before turning to address Paulette, whose sudden blush was disguised by shadows falling over her front side.

"You were looking for me, *Mademoiselle?*" the Colonel politely articulated.

A small squeak of a voice was all she could summon as she noticed the scarily admiring looks on the soldiers' faces: expressions rather like that on the tomcat's whiskers when he found a nest of baby birds within his reach. Polka sensed this as well, pushing out a low growl at this unwanted interest, sensing it as a threat to her friend.

"*Non, Monsieur*, I only came to fetch some cider for the lunch that I'm to take out to my father in the north potato field. I hope I'm not bothering you too much. If you'll just let me, it won't take but a minute to draw from the keg."

"Of course, *ma chère,* go right ahead," was the polite answer, though conversation did not resume, all five of them watching her back as she set about her task.

It was the most uncomfortable three minutes she'd ever spent, as five pair of eyes burned her shoulders, neck, and backside all the way down to her feet. She was regretting her bravado, remembering her mother's advice to do her best not to attract the soldiers' attention, to steer clear of any buildings they occupied, especially if she were alone, and to keep her hair covered at all times. But this morning, having run out of spit-free kerchiefs, she had decided to forgo these morsels of motherly wisdom. Too late, she realized her folly, with the hindsight which invariably produces useless tidbits of good sense.

She would have to turn and leave, facing their aggressive, leering faces. Understanding that if she looked timid or regretfully guilty, she would present herself as easy prey, she squared her shoulders and turned with a defiant lift to her chin and a glare in her eyes. Showing a serious face to the Colonel, without a hint of a smile, she thanked him. In turn she threw a withering, pointedly disapproving look at the three soldiers, and at Heinrich as well, before leaving with Polka trotting along behind.

The Colonel lifted his eyebrows and let out a small chuckle, before pivoting on his heel to face the soldiers who were blinking surprise at this interruption.

"So, back to our business." The Colonel's smile changed to a frown. "I had insisted that you account for each and every bottle of *calvados* stored in the cellar this winter. Now I find there is a rather large discrepancy between your numbers and the truth. I need to know where it has gone, and I must know if the same is true of the bottled cider." There was some shuffling of feet at this. "You will, once again, go through all the storerooms, count all the full bottles as well as the empty ones stored on the bottle trees. We need to find out exactly what we have and what was consumed before we prepare the delivery to Captain Bierduempfl in Dieppe. I do not wish to appear to be a fool, producing contradictory accounts. Lieutenant, when you are finished here, come immediately to me with your findings."

He left on a wave of respectful saluting, abandoning Heinrich to try and get to the bottom of the missing calvados, a task the young officer wasn't particularly looking forward to.

In the meantime, a slightly sweating Paulette hurried toward the basement kitchen to help finish packing the workmen's lunch. She was to carry it out to the field where they sifted through overturned plants, harvesting the first potatoes of the summer. Grumbling to Polka about her foolishness, she took a short detour across the yard and pulled a dampish kerchief from the clothesline to tie over her hair.

In a fit of childishness, she stuck out her tongue at the other clothing drying on the line: a large collection of white undershirts belonging to whichever group of soldiers whose turn it was to have their laundry done by Liliane. The offended, freshly bleached whites flapped at her, shooing her away to her next job of pedaling out to the field, laden with a much awaited meal for her father and his co-workers.

The basket was heavy, so she positioned it carefully on the mudguard, strapping it to the bar holding the seat of the bicycle, before setting off down the dirt track to the north.

Far away toward the horizon, she could see the line of wispy clouds indicating the moister, heavier, salt-laden sea air of the coastline. Up here on the plain, the sunshine flowed down around her, warming the dirt and setting the gnats and other tiny insects to buzzing around her nostrils and open mouth as she breathed heavily with the exertion of hauling the loaded basket on the rapidly deteriorating bicycle tires. Swatting them away with one hand set the bicycle to wobbling along the rutted path.

After picking a small black bug from her tongue, she decided she would tell Heinrich about the need for new bicycle tires, as it was an indispensable means of transportation for them all. If new tires were impossible to come by for the French, certainly Colonel VonEpffs would be able to order some through the army supply lines. Everything seemed to be available to them. Her throbbing leg muscles and her bottom would be relieved to ride once again on a properly cushioned tire.

In fact, she thought she might as well approach the Colonel herself. He did say they were to come to him if they had any sort of problem. He seemed like a polite enough man. Surely he would understand the need to replace the hard rubber tubing Emile had split open as a home-made replacement for the blown out front tire last winter. Not that she could use her sore bottom as an argument, but if she highlighted the increased speed which could be obtained from proper tires, maybe his natural Germanic affection for efficiency would motivate him to order new ones. She knew what her Papa would have to say about her intervening directly with the Colonel, but she thought maybe it was time for her to assert herself. She was a grown-up now at eighteen.

Her discomfort during the confrontation with him in the cider house not twenty minutes before was blown

away with the gnats, as a gust of wind added its
resistance to the slight incline of the path.

A small bend, and a few huffs and puffs later
brought her into view of Flo and Maurice attached to a
large wagon partially filled with dirt-encrusted potatoes.
Her father was bent over at the waist with a pitchfork full
of dirt and the fat brown globs of tuber which the
Germans seemed to be so inordinately fond of, asking
Marthe, the cook, to be sure they were present in some
shape or form in every meal she served.

Marthe did her best to respect this request, having
to bend to the wishes of the army's version of herself, a
wiry little fellow with a bad temper, who had invaded her
domain under the house when the Colonel arrived in
1940. For the past two years, she and this unpleasant
little man shared the space in the half-basement as the
grudging arrangement of task repartition slowly evolved
into a sort of competitive cook-off between the two, to
the great delight of our consumers as they reaped the best
of two culinary cultures.

Franz harassed Marthe when she didn't let the
roast beef brown all the way through to the center,
claiming that if the French chose to eat raw meat,
civilized people weren't cannibals, and they must serve
fully cooked roast beef to the Colonel.

In turn Marthe loved to irritate Franz by calling him François to his face, in an effort to Francophile him, insisting that no one hailing from the east side of the Rhone River, could have anything but an elementary idea of what food preparation was all about. As time went by in the relative peace of the occupation, the soldiers, officers and the other inhabitants of Abbot's Wood enjoyed an abundance of good food as France and Germany waged daily culinary battles in the kitchens.

They were extremely fortunate in this, as the rest of occupied France was getting by on ration tickets distributed by the government, restricting daily food intake to a minimum for inhabitants of the cities. Luckily, we were self-sufficient regarding food, and our Colonel was somewhat of a *gastronome* who believed in the power of a contented stomach. Had he chosen to be stingy with the workers' diet, quite possibly things wouldn't have run so smoothly during his occupation of our domain.

However, it was this *largesse* which was making Paulette's basket so heavy and she was happy to empty it for her father and the others. She passed slabs of *paté* and cheese around after breaking off large chunks of crusty bread for each man and for herself. They picnicked alongside the muddy, overturned potato field, on the grass bordering the track.

Flo and Maurice were unhitched and they plunged their noses into the juicy grass. There were water bags for them hung on the outside of the wagon, as their comfort was of extreme importance to the job at hand. We had no tractor or motorized farm equipment of any type. Flo and Maurice were the only source of useable power available, and as such, were invaluable.

Lunch drew to an end. Paulette packed up the leftovers, kissed her father on the cheek and pedaled back toward the house and an afternoon of pressing shirts with the heavy flat iron, still mulling over the best way to get the bicycle back in smoothly rolling condition.

CHAPTER 9

Summer, 1942:

The skies above Dieppe were frequently disturbed by air strikes over the past eighteen months. Allied forces focused on the Germans as they busily fortified the western sea front. Homes were destroyed and civilian lives lost, as the bombs aimed at shipyards, the train station, or more rightfully at German infrastructures went frightfully off target, landing instead in shopping districts and residential areas. The market square was hit several times although it was located in the center of town, away from any logistical mark. Unfortunately, stray bombs weren't the only problem the population had to contend with. New restrictions were put in place.

Earlier curfews had been placed on the local population. Silly rules were invented about which side of the street pedestrians must walk on, determined by the direction they were taking. Bicycle traffic was to flow in single file and riders could only execute right hand turns, which involved some rather ingenious route planning in order to return home from one's excursions.

The Mayor's office issued these constraints in the form of new laws created for the protection of the local population, and published them in the local press.

However, the people knew their true source was the "*Kreiskommandateur*" who stretched his imagination with inventive limitations. Strangely enough, he was particularly fond of soccer and the wide lawns bordering the seaside, while of forbidden access to the population, were still open for use by the soccer club. Matches continued on in a semblance of normality, the absence of cheering spectators the only obvious contradiction to sport.

This was the era of the Vichy government, led by the Maréchal Pétain, who at eighty four years of age, had risen through the ranks of the former elected government to find himself collaborating with the German occupation forces. The President of France, Albert Lebrun had been shoved off the political stage shortly after the decision to stop the useless fight against the invading German army. So many lives had been lost in a struggle against odds of such magnitude, that capitulation seemed the wisest way to avoid the massacre of the entire French male population. The French artillery was under-equipped. The Germans had a seemingly endless supply of tanks, and sophisticated weaponry which they'd been steadily developing since the Great War. The odds were completely off kilter as there was a quarter century of technology and preparation separating the two adversaries. It was as if Napoleon's army were trying to counter attacks from the Nazi Panzer division. Patriotism wasn't enough to win the day and an armistice was signed on June 25th, 1940.

Thus the tanks had lumbered in and everyone tried to make the best of it, survival being the issue at hand. The Germans had initially attempted an attitude of friendly teamwork, but the French, in general being a rather prideful people, didn't accept German authority in an amicable fashion.

Every village housed a contingency of soldiers and the much feared *Geheimefeldpolizei,* or rural secret police, kept a watchful eye on the comings and goings of farm laborers, frequently setting up blockades on country roads to inspect the working papers which had become mandatory. Any male over the age of seventeen must be gainfully employed and able to prove it, or risk being sent off to Germany to be employed there.

The Germans conducted a yearly census and the Mayor of each village was forced to provide the names and addresses of every young man turning seventeen that year in view of exiled recruitment to the German work camps. One such Mayor refused to do so and was himself imprisoned. His life ended in Germany.

Colonel VonEpffs was careful to accept the sons of our farm laborers at sixteen, ensuring they obtained appropriate work permits and would be safe to go about their business. However, there were no more outings to the town, no more cinema trips and no more window-shopping for trinkets. What they needed was ordered through the Colonel, but those orders didn't include much of anything for the working families.

While the limitations placed on city dwellers were of the sort designed to render their daily lives sufficiently complicated to keep them short of the necessary time and energy to cause the Germans serious problems, those placed on the rural population were of a more practical nature. In 1941, we were forced to hand over our pigeons, who had for hundreds of aviary generations been living happily uncomplicated, if useless, lives in the brick and stonework dovecote.

In the 17th century, only residences of the nobility claimed possession of a dovecote, the size and beauty of which was directly related to the social standing of the owners. A specific number of pigeons was allotted to each precise rank in society. Since the pigeons reproduced, the excedent provided fowl for the dinner table. A favorite dish was roast pigeon with sugar peas.

Regrettably, the German occupying army decided at one point that these birds might be used as carrier pigeons and therefore must be destroyed. We watched the truck drive off with our caged pigeons and wondered just exactly who would dine on carrier pigeon *aux petit pois* that evening. They were never heard from again. Obviously none had escaped the pot or they would have returned to the sadly empty dovecote which now adorned the yard in stricken silence.

Few local workers were allowed to leave the farm. A select number accompanied the soldiers for deliveries to the storage facilities on the outskirts of Dieppe. In general, they were forbidden to exit the cabin of the truck until it passed through the gates of the warehouse yard, only then unloading whatever cargo of goods was being delivered at the time. They weren't allowed to speak to anyone or to each other during the unloading and the chosen men were rotated, preventing the creation of habits or contacts with those to whom the crates were passed. Paulette's father never went to Dieppe and he did his best to keep his son, Michel from this task.

As was the case in every village in occupied France, a list of notable inhabitants was made, and these people comprised the list of *hôtages*. They were never allowed to leave their village. They lived under constant threat, for any wrongdoing taking place in the village was paid for with their blood. The Gestapo didn't waste time finding the culprit and punishing him, or her, they simply chose a hostage and punished the hostage. Paulette's father was on this list.

Marcel understood his position and could only hope his friends and neighbors would understand it as well, and respect him enough to keep their heads down and do what was asked of them. His son was a different case. Numerous quiet talks were had over the evening soup, with admonitions raining down on Michel's stubborn head, but rolling off unheeded like summer rain off a duck's tail feathers.

Michel couldn't accept that his father, whom he loved and respected, chose to continue working and taking orders from tyrants parading around in black boots and sporting swastikas on their arm-bands. Where was his father's pride? And his patriotism? How long would it be before they were made to speak German instead of French? They were no better than prisoners as it stood, so they owed it to themselves to break free!

Liliane and Marcel tried in vain to reason with their son, while never suspecting the existence of a budding friendship between their daughter and a certain German soldier.

Paulette fully measured the risk she was taking and was certainly aware of the volatile reaction Michel would have if he thought for an instant his sister fraternized with the enemy.

Still, one can only think so much when the body insists on celebrating the stirrings of attraction between the sexes every time one crosses paths with a certain young man, be he uniformed or not.

Such things are uncontrollable, as Paulette was finding out. She lost herself to her emotions and the physical reactions they provoked in her healthy, eighteen year old body.

#

As fate would have it, I was once again pondering the question of the romantic attraction of the kitchen garden. Was it the warmth of the sun retained by my ancient stone walls? Was it the luxuriousness of the plants at maturity? Although, a tomato plant in itself, in my humble opinion, doesn't exude a blatant air of sexuality. However, when young people are inspired by each other, the backdrop is of lesser importance than when age sets in and romance develops the need for a stage. My enthusiastic young people met once again, seemingly by accident, during the harvesting of some tomatoes requested by Marthe, the cook.

These grew in a small area of the garden, well protected from the wind: against a south facing wall. The plants enjoyed the extra heat reverberating from the stones, successfully ripening on the vine. This was quite a feat and it gave Emile a great source of satisfaction, because if the growing season needed for tasty tomatoes was a sure thing in the south, sunshine with sufficient intensity was a rarity in Normandy. Thoughtful planning and care allowed these plants thrive. This year's crop was abundant; meaning the task at hand for Paulette should occupy her for just a minute or so, notwithstanding interruption.

She was, however, quite interrupted, having pulled only one fat subject off its vine, when another hand reached out to cover hers, still cupping the prize. The tomato had found a nest; two hands providing better protection than just the one for such a delicate, thin-skinned treat.

Although it should have been secure, it was instead crushed after dropping to the ground the worse for wear, trampled by uncalculated footwork, as Heinrich pulled Paulette close to his chest, up against the wall. He touched her face and plunged into the blue of her eyes asking if he might kiss her. She had no words, instead pushed her body closer to his. Uncertain of each other, but sure of themselves, they each made a distinct movement forward, resulting in a brushing of noses, then lips. When he tilted his head, twisting his mouth over hers, the world spun around them, as their inexperience of each other was brushed aside by an innate knowledge of what must follow.

The trellised tomato plants were crushed, resulting in unsightly stains on their clothing, but neither noticed as the kissing progressed, coordinating with frantic manual activity. The basket was kicked away as any parcel of skin accessible in the broad daylight was caressed, and cherished. Their kisses developed a semblance of violence as the days of waiting and dreaming of each other were compensated for in just a few short minutes.

Anyone watching could see Paulette's heart swell and open like the ripe figs which couldn't grow here. It should never have happened, not here, not now. There was a sadness about the whole affair making it unbearable to watch. I had to look away as Paulette's innocent heart took flight, mimicking the swooping parade of barn swallows in a joyous but erratic quest for freedom.

Several moments later, she pushed back on his chest, terrified, as if someone had already caught them. He was suddenly awkward as he tried to grasp the fleeing intimacy engulfing them a second earlier. She shook her head, shoulders and torso, like a wet dog fluffing its fur, effectively shaking off the spell his mouth, lips and tongue had placed on her.

The frightfully crushed tomatoes drooped from their trellis, itself askew. It was a mess: the tomatoes, their spotted clothing, the trampled ground and indeed their lives. At the same time, all of it was impossible to repair or disguise.

Heinrich, unhappily surprised at her abrupt about face, found himself in the unpleasant position of feeling responsible for impending doom, especially when it had started with just a touch and a desire to speak to her once again. He hadn't planned on crushing the tomatoes, or her body to his chest, nor had he come outside with the intention of exploring her with his hands, while plundering her lips.

Still here they were, dripping tart, red juice, cheeks flaming and lost in a time when adventures such as these had little chance for success.

As before, there were no words between them as she slipped out of his arms, out of the garden and out of sight. He picked a few of the least damaged tomatoes, put them in the basket and placed it on the top step descending to the kitchen, before abandoning the garden, leaving behind him a curious scene of conflict along the south facing wall.

#

Plagued by the matter of the missing *calvados*, the Colonel could find no trace of the bottles, either full or empty, which could only mean one thing: both the product and its containers had left the farm.

A booming economy worked in parallel to the one officiated by the government. Stamps for meat, eggs, milk, butter, shoes, metal objects of all kinds and indeed just about everything, were allotted to each inhabitant and varied with the age and needs of each specific person. The quantity of each of these items was so ridiculously low, that survival was practically impossible if one played exclusively by the rules. But, if someone was in possession of money, either francs or marks, just about everything was miraculously available, provided the holder of said cash was in the confidence of a dealer. The black market, while not cheap, was abundant and supplied extra income for everyone involved. Von Epffs suspected, but as yet couldn't prove, that the calvados had disappeared via this illegal system of distribution. He suggested that Heinrich pay more attention to the habits of the farm laborers and their families.

So Heinrich took notes on his clipboard about the state of their clothing and shoes, describing the presence of jewelry on the women: who had earrings, who wore a baptismal medallion, who had wedding rings and of what general size and shape were these items. Noting these things unofficially, he hoped to remark any changes or discrepancies which might indicate the spending of money not justifiable by the salaries paid to the workers by the German administration.

Heinrich didn't find any visible increase in lifestyle and since there was sufficient food available for everyone linked to the farm, it was difficult to check for extra amounts of meat or milk. Still, he watched and kept notes, waiting for some clue to the identity of the person making a profit. He was thorough about it, but couldn't help feeling as if it were a waste of time. He highly doubted they would ever find a trace of the missing spirits. Still, he had his orders, so he took notes.

Michel didn't have much immediate use for the money he was making from the sale of his skimming. He hid it away in a small tin behind a loose brick in the fireplace conduit which traversed from floor to ceiling the bedroom he shared with his younger brother, Yves. One day soon, when the time was right, he planned to escape, maybe to England, or even to America, where he hoped to join up with the soldiers actively fighting to free Europe of the Nazi occupation. He didn't have enough to pay for passage south, nor nearly enough for a spot on a boat headed west. Yet the tin was becoming pleasantly heavy.

It was terribly frustrating to think that just a few years ago, he could have walked the eight miles into Dieppe, strode right down to the center of town, bought a ticket and taken the steamer across the channel to England. In fact, his entire family could have done so about the same time the owner had sent his wife and daughter to Menton. Unfortunately, his father didn't have the foresight to protect his family in this way.

Instead, he felt obligated to stay and continue milking the cows, tilling the earth and harvesting the grain. Michel couldn't understand his father's sense of duty to a chunk of land not his own, but belonging to a man who had chosen to run away, abandoning the responsibility for his property to a paid laborer. Michel was unfair with his criticism of his father's work ethic, not feeling the pull the land and the farm itself had on his father's heartstrings. His father, grandfather before him and who knows how many generations of the men in Michel's family had worked my land, caring for it, moistening the ground with their sweat and taking pride in doing so. However, Michel was young and he felt the need to *do* something, preferably something which would help take down the Germans.

There were rumors amongst the laborers of an invasion planned in Normandy. General DeGaulle was in England, speaking in poetic code over the wireless, warning the French to get ready. Tracts were dropped from Allied planes in several areas of Normandy informing the population of planned air raids and invasions, but since the population had no where to hide and their movements were restricted, these warnings did more harm than good. For they served to whip up suspicions amongst the German forces, who instigated even more sanctions against the people in retaliation for the hope supplied by bits of paper floating down from the sky.

One morning in August, Paulette had found such a tract stuck to a branch on a holly bush while returning from St Catherine's spring. She had been gathering acorns from the surrounding woods.

Formerly part of the pigs' diet, the acorns were roasted, ground and boiled in gauze bags to make a beverage which, while far from being confused with coffee, was still of some comfort to those who remembered the real thing. She made the mistake of bringing the paper home in her basket, hidden beneath the acorns.

Over supper, the tract was dissected and translated as well as possible, given Paulette's limited knowledge of English. This provoked a frenzy of enthusiasm in Michel, whose hope for an Allied invasion of their coastline reached a peak. Now was certainly the

Page | 129

time to prepare to attack the main house, murder the German occupants, steal their trucks and charge into Dieppe to assist the soldiers landing on the beach to overcome the garrison in town. His father had great difficulty in keeping Michel from running off toward the main house with a pitchfork straightaway that very evening.

"We must wait and see," he admonished.

Poor Michel had difficulty waiting for the sun to rise each morning, let alone to sit, doing nothing, waiting for exciting, historical, courageous feats to happen around him, without taking an active part. How could his father even suggest they wait? How sweet the victory over these oppressors would be! He entertained visions of himself covered with streamers thrown by the ecstatic population, dozens of girls running out to greet him, covering him with kisses as he paraded down the hill into Dieppe to free the city. Wait and see? Unthinkable! He must be there when it happened, to get involved and by doing so, to cover himself in glory.

Such are the vainglorious dreams of young men. Michel was not alone in dreaming this sort of dream. His was similar to the one Adolph Hitler had played out in his own head as a young man, every night on his pillow. The roles of the victorious and the vanquished had simply been inverted.

CHAPTER 10

September 1989:

I watched the next few days spin by uneventfully. The little girls were happy to have their mother home and Debra stayed there, not working, enjoying the time spent playing with them and trying to forget her close encounter with would-be criminals.

Philippe came home on the third day after the attempted break-in, a day later than initially planned. Apparently, there had been some difficulty with the dismantling of their stand at the trade fair and he had stayed to finish up. Debra hadn't been able to reach him through the hotel to share what had happened to her at home. He mumbled something about having to switch rooms because of a leaking toilet. She frowned at this. There was something strange about him: as if he didn't smell quite the same.

I thought he stunk of deceit. Leaking toilet, indeed!

Philippe was impatient when she explained how terrified she'd been when then men were in the yard that night. He dismissed her pride at being courageous enough to go down the stairs, cross the foyer and flip the lights on, rolling his eyes and accusing her of being melodramatic.

"Come, come now, it's not as if you were ever in danger. Wasn't it just the wind you heard? Maybe branches scraping the outside walls or roof?"

Debra was shocked and immediately indignant. "What about the car in the drive? Did I imagine that? Do you want me to phone the police, so they can tell you exactly what happened?" she demanded.

"And just what would they tell me?" He turned on her, his face stern with anger, as if she'd done something wrong. She stared back in disbelief as he continued, "...exactly what *you* told them, what you *think* happened, but not anything they saw for themselves. Did they catch anyone? No. All I mean to say, is that I'm not surprised you got scared: being home alone at night in this big, creaky old house. It would be easy to imagine things, that's all. We should sell up and buy something smaller in town. A nice flat, closer to other people where you wouldn't be so afraid." By the end of this speech his expression had settled to impatience and his voice dripped with condescension, efficiently throwing oil on her already lit fire.

"Excuse me, but I am *not* a silly child, scared of monsters lurking beneath the bed! I distinctly saw three men with flashlights in the yard, come up to the front door, shine their lights on the lock and try to break into the house! I did not imagine it! How can you treat me like I'm lying, when it was bad enough anyway? And now you insinuate that I've invented this? What have I ever done to make you doubt my word?"

She was beyond angry. She was hurt, and frustrated that he didn't offer sympathy or applaud the strength of character which had pushed her across the foyer floor to hit the light switch, knowing real danger was present on the other side of the door.

Philippe stood and grabbed her arm, as she leapt off the sofa and turned to make for the door. He tried to take her in his arms and soothe her like one would try to calm an out of control child, but Debra would have none of it. She pushed him away.

"Stop it! I'm not your little girl! Just leave me alone!" She stomped off, slamming the door.

"Then you must stop acting like one," he murmured, scowling at my still vibrating door.

#

October came, and the nights grew longer and cooler. Debra and Philippe never again spoke of the attempted break-in. Still ever one to harbor a grudge, she couldn't forgot how his reaction had offended her. She thought it best to take action herself, to make sure her children would never be in danger.

Debra decided to follow the policeman's advice, thinking a bigger dog was a good idea. It didn't take a lot to persuade her that a dog of any sort was a good idea, for she absolutely loved animals. She began leafing through the phone book looking for kennels. Nothing turned up in their vicinity holding any promise of satisfying her long list of criteria.

"Labradors are too friendly. Saint Bernards drool and they're not very energetic. Dobermans give me the creeps, and German Shepherds can be unpredictable. This is going to be tough."

She'd invested in a pile of dog lover's magazines and was sipping tea in the kitchen while scrolling through the advertisements in the back pages. She wanted a big dog who didn't slobber, who was loyal and lovable with their masters, intelligent, gentle with children, with a coat not needing constant attention and who had a natural tendency to guard their loved ones. Tough pick! She came across an article about the Charplaninatz, or Yugoslavian shepherd dog, the kind favored by General Tito. Amazingly enough, there was a kennel in Brionne, about a two hour drive from home. Debra knew where it was. She had a client in Brionne. She phoned.

Luckily, there was a four month old female pup available and the price, while rather high was still affordable for such a unique breed. Debra made an appointment with the kennel for the following Tuesday, late afternoon. She planned to stop on the way back from an appointment in Pont Audemer.

On Tuesday, when she pulled up to the kennel gates her heart skipped a beat as several shaggy, rather mean-looking, massive dogs barked at her. A shabby, youngish fellow came to open the gate and instructed her to drive up to the kennel building. The huge canines followed the car and when she boldly got out they approached her, sniffing her all over, even where they shouldn't. She patted several huge heads with surprisingly soft ears. They took to her right away, as did most animals.

The young man smiled broadly. "You're fine; I'll sell Elsa to you."

"Oh! Well, thank you. So which one's Elsa?" She looked around for a pup amongst the enthusiastic crowd of beasts surrounding her and pushing on her legs, all vying for attention.

"She's right over here with her mother. Come here little girl!" he hooted in the direction of a separate enclosure. Mother and baby trotted over to the fence.

"I'll let Elsa out alone, because her mother is still kind-of protective of her," He opened the gate for an enormous, white, fluffy creature carried by huge feet and wearing a completely black fur, face mask.

Unlike the males, the puppy, although she must already weigh fifty pounds, didn't seem to like Debra much, staying between the man's legs while peering out suspiciously at her.

"She's not used to women," he explained.

"And she can tell I'm different from you at her age?" Debra inquired.

"Madame, anyone, at any age can tell the difference between us." He grinned, stuffing his hands in the pockets of his rather grubby jeans. "She'll get used to your smell quick enough"

Debra supposed he was trying to reassure her and make the sale. In spite of her misgivings about Elsa herself—for goodness sakes, the dog was white!—she had found the males to be charming and more or less exactly what she was looking for. She asked which male was the father. It happened to be the biggest, friendliest, one of the bunch. Still, Debra was worried about the color of the pup's fur. A white dog in the yard in winter when it got muddy and the grass was thinning was going to be just awful.

"If these are her parents, then why has she got white fur? I really don't want a white dog."

"Oh don't worry, that's still her baby fur, she'll have the salt and pepper, wolf fur grow in over top of this white, downy fur. She'll look just like the others when she gets older."

"Well...I guess I'll take her, then."

"Did you bring a cage for her to ride in?"

"Er, ..." Well, that was some good planning! Debra hadn't thought to bring a blanket, a leash, a cage or anything at all except the money for the asking price. It was a two hour drive back home and she didn't want to make the trip all over again. Just then a fine, misty drizzle started and Debra hastened things up a bit, as she was dressed in a smart trouser suit and pumps, with no overcoat. "No, but she can sit on the floor of the passenger side," a quick estimate of her size revised this remark, "...or on the seat. I'll just move my briefcase."

The young man, money in pocket, looked dubiously at the beige leather interior of her car. "I'll go get some empty food bags to rip open, to protect your seats."

"Oh, it'll be fine. She seems calm enough, and leather is very easy to wipe hair off of. I do think I should get going now. It's a bit of a drive home yet. Come on little Elsa, hop in the car!"

Right.

The dog had absolutely no intention of hopping in the car. In fact, she had to be dragged, wriggling furiously in her too large suit of skin and fur, through the mud, lifted, shoved inside and the door quickly shut. The two humans stood in the drizzle, watching as Elsa careened around the inside of the car, looking desperately for an exit, front to back, back to front, side to side to front to back, Debra's water bottle and Kleenex box flinging in each of these directions, following the crazed animal.

"Well, I guess I'll open the gate for you," said the young man in a helpful sort of way.

He held the driver's door open just enough for Debra to slide in and helped push Elsa back inside as she tried to escape. They managed to shut the door and he turned to open the gate. He waved and watched her drive away, choosing not to stop her when he noticed her silk Hermès neck scarf sticking half way out the bottom of the car door.

About an hour into the journey, Elsa actually did calm, her dejected furry body crammed onto the floor of the passenger side. Debra was covered in white fuzz and spit, with muddy pawprints traipsing across her white blouse and navy pantsuit. Tiny claw punctures drew abstract patterns in the leather of the passenger seat, attesting to Elsa's frenzied flight around the car. They were most likely all over the other seats as well. But, nothing was to be done about that right now. Debra was simply relieved the dog had calmed down enough to allow her to drive in relative safety. She reached over and patted Elsa on the head, crooning to her, in an attempt at some bonding. She really was an unusual looking animal with her fluffy, white body and black face.

Just then, as the rain started to fall in a more determined fashion, Elsa vomited.

"Holy crap! How much did you eat before getting in the car?"

The only answer forthcoming was pathetic whining punctuated with hawking, as more vomit was deposited on the carpet. Elsa soon became uncomfortable staying put in the spot she'd thrown up in, so she hopped in the back, retching on the back seat as well. Debra pulled off the road and put on the parking brake.

She found the Kleenex box, where it had landed on the floor of the backseat. Bending over the seat, she tried to clean up some of the mess with a wad of tissues. This proved quite difficult as her behind pushed on the horn of the car, located in the middle of the steering wheel. She got into the back seat directly.

The dog spotted the open door and bolted.

Debra ran across the road after Elsa, who trotted off looking over her shoulder at her pursuant. They crossed a freshly plowed field of mud, toward a farm house about three hundred feet from the car. The driver's door of the car stood open and the engine continued running, abandoned alongside the dark road in the rain. Elsa evidently recognized a house as a refuge from the unfamiliar woman dragging her away from her home and her mother, and slipped between a pile of firewood and the building.

Debra was on her knees, calling to the dog, when the yard lights went on and a gruff looking elderly man came out of the house with a rifle in hand.

"No! Wait! I mean no harm; I'm just trying to get my dog back!"

"I don't have your dog! Go away before I call the police!" he pointed the gun in her general direction.

Realizing exactly how she must look: dirty white blouse, legs and feet caked with mud up to her calves, bedraggled wet hair and to complete her ensemble, interesting black stripes drawn by her eye make-up, drizzling down her cheeks, she chose to beg for help in getting the dog out from behind his woodpile.

"Please, *Monsieur,* I know how this must seem, but look out toward the road. That's my car out there. I stopped because my dog got sick. She escaped when I tried to clean it up and now she's come to hide here in your woodpile. Do you have a flashlight? I can show you I'm telling the truth. If you'd just help me, I'll be happy to be on my way."

Apparently her beseeching tone gave him enough confidence to come toward her, albeit still holding the gun, ready to shoot her if needs be and glance at the back of the wood pile. Elsa was cowering in the shadows. Since part of her white fur still showed through the mud splotches, the glimmer from the yard light showed her position.

"If that's your dog, why won't it come to you?" he gestured with the gun toward the woodpile.

"That's exactly the problem. I just got her and was driving her home to my house. She's just scared from riding in the car. Could you help me get her out from behind the woodpile?"

The old man bent down and whistled softly to Elsa, who unexpectedly came groveling out to lodge between his legs in their crouched position.

He grabbed the thick ruff of fur at her neck, rubbing his hand in it to reassure the dog, but still keeping a firm grip.

"You should at least have a collar on a dog, and a leash when you're traveling with it in your car," he scolded her. "It's dangerous, what you're doing here."

"I know, I just wasn't thinking," she admitted.

"Most women don't," came the comment, tossed in her direction, with a smirk thrown in for good measure.

Under different circumstances, Debra would have challenged that sort of remark, but all things considered, what with his gun and all, she bit her tongue and decided that best thing would be to get herself and the dog back to the car. She stood up. The old man finally put down his rifle and helped pick up Elsa, settling her fifty odd pounds into Debra's arms.

He pointed out to the road as soon as he'd deposited the dog, now limp and heavy. "Is that the police over there by your car? You'd better get back there before they haul it away."

"Oh God! Well...er...thank you for your help, and good evening."

He watched with some interest as Debra waddled off across the field, her shoes squelching in the ankle deep mud, her expensive investment surprisingly calm in her arms.

It was a good thing that Elsa had calmed down because her weight was so overwhelming that Debra had to stop to catch her breath every few yards. The trudge across the field seemed to take much longer going back. Debra swore she was making no progress at all. The police had a large spotlight out and were sweeping the beam around the surrounding fields when they finally landed it on Debra.

"You-hoo! I'm over here! Please help me!" she shouted to them.

The police men trained the spotlight on her, but maintained their position on the hard dry shoulder next to their car. "Stop where you are! What are you doing there in the dark? And what have you got there? A sheep?"

"This is getting better and better," she grumbled, panting with the weight of the dog pulling on her arms, she mumbled under her breath "I'm going to end up in jail for nocturnal sheep rustling!"

Drawing a deep breath, enough to shout out a response, "No, no, Monsieur, It's my dog, but she weighs a ton, can I please put her back in my car?...Then I'll explain everything to you," Debra called out, in a pleading tone of voice.

"Advance slowly toward our vehicle, please," came the warning.

"As if I could possibly run carrying this damned dog." Debra slogged across the remaining fifty yards of sludge.

Chucking the filthy, wet dog into the front seat of the car, she trod on what remained of her Christmas present from Philippe: the Hermès scarf. She turned a face worthy of Alice Cooper on one of his scariest make-up days, in the direction of the policeman.

He shined his pocket flashlight directly at her. "Is this your car?"

Again, a desire to respond with irony to this ridiculous question was stifled by good sense and a need to get the hell out of there and drive the remaining thirty miles home. So, she bit her tongue and rummaged about in her imagination for a polite answer. Trying to sound sane and look normal was a bit of a difficult task at this particular moment, still she made an effort.

"Yes sir, the registration and my driver's license are in my handbag. That's it there on the backseat of the car, but if you really don't mind, I'd rather not open the door and let the dog get loose once again."

Ten minutes of stupid questions later, including a demand to supply her mother's maiden name—go figure!—she squeezed into the front seat, careful not to open the door wide enough for the beast to escape again. She hooked her seat belt before waving jauntily at the police and drove off in the rain, leaving the cadaver of her scarf on the shoulder of the road. She cranked up the heater as both she and Elsa shivered in their wet outfits.

Arriving home much later than planned, she carried Elsa into the house and dropped her on the floor. Philippe and the girls were waiting. They fell, fawning over the puppy and ignoring Debra.

She abandoned them for a shower, a shot of whiskey and dry clothes.

Knowing that Philippe might accuse her once again of being melodramatic, she chose to keep the story to herself. She would discuss it with Elsa at a later date.

I absorbed the lively tale with a chuckle while warming Debra with a hot shower.

CHAPTER 11

Autumn 1991:

Debra worked hard over the past two years developing a clientele in the region. This meant getting up early, dropping the girls at school, then hitting the road for an appointment in the morning and frequently two in the afternoon. By now, she now knew the surrounding countryside quite well. Between her *rendezvous* she squeezed in time to visit a castle or a museum, go shopping or explore a village she'd never been to before. In addition to these perks, she had a lot of time for reflection, driving alone for many miles each day. Sometimes the solitude was welcome, other times not so much.

As time chugged along, she gained self-confidence. She learned to fake professionalism so well, it became second nature. For once, being American worked to her advantage, with customers not expecting her to exactly fit the mold of other sales people. She could dress a bit more casually, be a bit more open: less strict than her competitors. Instead of being criticized for this behavior, it intrigued her French customers.

Her new found self-assurance came from being forced to accept a job which had at first seemed overwhelming but at which she now excelled. Unwittingly, Philippe, having pushed her to take on so much, had provoked the one thing he didn't want. She had evolved right out of his grasp. She'd found a niche, a purpose, a thing she was good at: a thing in which he had no part at all. The people she dealt with through work knew and liked her. Her clientele was her own, as was her success, although she never gave it much thought.

She also learned to round the corners off things a bit more often. A natural tendency to strive for perfection and to expect it from others, made her rather difficult to please. Consciously lowering her standards, she chose to focus on lightening up a little. It was a new experience for her.

She stopped continually trying to please Philippe, eventually realizing, with quite a lot of disappointment, that she would never be able to wring a compliment out of him. He always pushed her to do more, to bring in more customers, to continually prospect for new ones. This advice she ignored. Ultimately she stopped telling him about her days, knowing if she followed his suggestions, she would be as unhappy as she suspected him to be.

Although she didn't know why he was unhappy, she was sure of it just the same. Their love-making continued at more or less the same frequency, so she couldn't attribute his dissatisfaction to the bedroom. That is, unless he was expecting something exotic from her which he wasn't getting. Since he never spoke about their sex life, she didn't know.

The girls adored him and basked in the tidbits of attention he dispensed, a kiss here, a pat there, and sometimes a walk hand in hand in the garden. However, he never played with them, and Debra thought he didn't know how. Debra took every opportunity to read stories or sing songs to the girls. Once they were asleep, she would turn her remaining energy to Philippe, but their conversations were shorter and shorter. The volume of the television tended to drown out their past complicity.

He spoke mostly about work and because she no longer regarded his opinion as absolute truth engraved in stone, she found herself less inclined to talk to him. Knowing she did her best, she was satisfied with her work. So she simply refused to listen to his stressful pushing for her to do more. Since they made a comfortable living and their savings were growing strongly, she closed her ears to his constant worrying.

Once a week she went to the office to renew her samples, always on Friday afternoon. So when she showed up late one Tuesday to grab a few extra invoice books, she caught glances of great surprise. She was in a hurry, wanting to stop at the greengrocers to pick up the fruit and veg before heading home early for once. She'd condensed her day, skipping lunch for an afternoon appointment, then making the long drive home without stopping.

Instead of lingering to chat, she simply waved as she whizzed by the receptionist who was on the phone. Patricia tried to catch her attention as she walked down the hall toward the supply cupboard just outside of Philippe's office. Debra pretended not to notice, hoping to make the stop short and sweet. Having missed the opportunity to make eye contact with her, Debra heard, with a sense of guilty relief, Patricia retreat into her office, shutting the door.

As Debra closed the door to the supply cupboard, she turned to Philippe's office, meaning to stick her head in to say hello, not that she particularly wished to see him, but it would be unspeakably rude not to do so. When she heard strange murmuring noises coming from inside, she stopped to listen, moving closer to the door. Realizing with astounding clarity what she was hearing, time froze, leaving Debra incapable of doing anything but listen in horrified silence until the rhythmic noises stopped.

She leaned her back against the wall of the hallway, concentrating on breathing, while fighting off a growing dizziness and nausea. A bit later, there were a series of toilet flushes from the adjoining bathroom. Still a few minutes later, Sophie emerged, red faced and blotchy. She froze in her tracks, a perfect imitation of a deer caught in the glare of headlights. Debra caught a glance of Philippe straightening piles of papers on his desk just as she turned and left, unable to face either of them.

The invoice books slid from her hand to the carpet, as she slowly made her way through the office, and out of the building in a daze. Philippe caught up with her just as she turned the key in the ignition. He had the abandoned invoice books in his hand.

"Did you forget to take these?" he asked, as she rolled down the window to the driver's side.

"Yes...yes, I did actually. Thank you." She turned to look over her shoulder as she put the car in reverse.

"Wait...don't leave like this...don't you want a cup of tea or something?" He was grasping at straws. She watched him squirm, not certain of how much she had seen or guessed.

He looked like a little boy caught with his hand in the cookie jar. She paused, taking a deep breath before responding. "Yes, I'm quite certain Sophie would love to make me a cup of tea, now wouldn't she?" While keeping her voice calm, rage climbed the walls of her ribcage, venting itself as sarcasm.

"Listen, Day-bor-ahh, I don't know what you think you saw but..."

She chopped off his sentence immediately before the lie could weasel out of his mouth. "Do not mispronounce my name! It's not 'Day-bor- ahh'! It's Debra for God sakes. I'm American and that's the name I was born with, now say it right or don't say it at all! I do not want to hear anything about what I just saw," she hissed. "Next time, just please have a little respect for me and don't screw people I have to work with. And most certainly not on your desk in front of the other workers! Everyone in the building knew what was happening. Patricia even tried to stop me before I got to your office. Do you realize how humiliating that is for me? Now just leave me alone."

His hands were still on the edge of the car door, as he started to puff up in self-defense. It was as visible as a cat that ruffles its fur and arches its back to scare off predators.

"You need to stop inventing things! You didn't see anything! Just because you're jealous of Sophie and the other women I work with..."

She backed up and squealed away, her anger making her drive like a demon, going nowhere, fast.

But that was exactly the problem. She was going nowhere, because she had nowhere to go. She drove around for a while to calm herself before making her way back home where she kissed the girls and explained to them that she had a headache and needed to go lie down in the dark awhile. She asked Francoise to wake her if Philippe wasn't yet home when it was time for her to leave. Then she opened the door at the top of the staircase which led to the next set of stairs up to the attic, where she took the dustcover off the old chintz armchair. Debra curled up to cry.

She stayed there for several hours, embraced by the arms covered in dusty cabbage roses. In spite of her anger, she bizarrely found herself hoping he would make the effort to look for her. She would have loved to be able to tell him to go away and leave her alone once again, in hopes of hurting his feelings just this once. Although she seriously doubted he had any. It might have done her pride some good though, knowing he cared enough to search her out; it might have been a balm to her crushed dignity.

However, he never came up. She eventually had to go down, with no plans left up her sleeve, save thinking to ignore him for a good long time, which wouldn't resolve a thing. I had no advice to give, observing a complicated play for power being implemented by a man who had years of experience in manipulation. I was afraid my girl would be no match for him.

#

The following day, knowing Philippe would be out of the office for the afternoon, Debra canceled her appointments. She'd decided to go and speak with Patricia. She needed some advice and a friendly shoulder to cry on. It was obvious Patricia was aware of what was going on since she had tried to stop Debra the evening before when she had been approaching Philippe's office door. No sense trying to save face with Patricia at any rate. The cat was out of the bag. She hoped Patricia would be sympathetic to her cause, being a bit older and probably wiser in the ways of the world.

Finding Patricia at her desk, Debra asked for a few minutes of her time as she shut the door to the outer office.

Debra started out slowly, "You know what happened yesterday." She stopped, not sure how to proceed.

"Well, actually, I'm not sure, I think you had a bit of an argument with your husband, but he didn't speak to me about it," Patricia replied cautiously.

"Oh come on, I'm sure you know what's been going on between Sophie and Philippe. I just need to talk to someone about it."

"Madame Dubois, I will be happy to listen to you, but I really don't know anything at all about any going's on between your husband and Sophie." Her tone of voice held no sympathy and was in fact, cold.

Debra was stung.

Obviously Debra had been mistaken when she believed there had been a sort of friendship between herself and Patricia, a while back at the trade fair. Just now she could see the ravine separating them was deeper than she'd guessed. To her surprise the ravine appeared to be rapidly filling with icy water.

"But, you must know! You tried to stop me yesterday as I was going down the hall!" Debra was becoming frustrated. "...and I know you don't approve of her any more than I do."

"Actually, I was trying to ask you a question. I'm missing some receipts for the gasoline for your car and wondered if you had them with you. As for approving of Sophie, it's not for me to approve or disapprove of any of the people your husband has working for him, unless they do something which affects my capacity to do my job. But I truly don't think there's anything for you to worry about in regards to Sophie. She does what she's supposed to do, in spite of her taste in clothing which, granted, is sometimes a little out of the ordinary." At this point she added a small conspiratorial grin. "But she does her job quite well."

"And just what would that job be? Keeping the boss supplied with some daytime entertainment on the desk, to break up the ho-hum of the day?" Debra was exasperated at Patricia's willingness to cover for Sophie. It made her turn catty.

Patricia let out a sigh before answering. "I can see you're very angry, and I hope I can put your mind at ease when I say, that I have seen absolutely nothing to make me believe there's anything untoward going on between Sophie and your husband. I hope you can believe me." She gave Debra a sympathetic, sad, little smile and patted her hand.

Incredulous, Debra pulled her hand away slowly and got up from her chair, feeling distinctly that she was being dismissed. Her vision blurred with anger as she followed the hall towards the exit of the building.

Halfway out, she crossed paths with Sophie, whose crimson face turned left and right searching for an escape route. Finding none, she stared at her boots, glued to the gray flecked, industrial carpeting. They didn't appear to supply her with much of a solution. She kept her eyes trained on them nonetheless, waiting.

Debra glared at her, incapable of pretending she didn't wish for Sophie to be attacked by a pack of hungry wolves right there in the hallway. Sophie did eventually look up, for someone had to move to the side for the other to pass. Debra was damned sure it wouldn't be up to her to step out of Sophie's way.

Sophie obviously felt guilty. The look on her face was proof enough for Debra in spite of Patricia's denial of anything untoward having taken place. Standing stock still in front of Sophie, Debra waited. Sophie started to speak, all the while looking around desperately for help to materialize from the ceiling, the floor or the walls. Debra was aware of extra sets of ears listening behind doors set ajar. Tomorrow's coffee break would be a lively one.

"I'm afraid you misunderstood something yesterday, Madame Dubois," Sophie hesitated.

"And what would that be?" Debra asked politely, while staring her down.

"I'm afraid you think I'm having an affair with your husband," she blurted out.

"Yes, well I guess if I were you, I would be afraid of that too," Debra answered. In spite of her interior agitation, she was still outwardly calm, if furious.

"Well...I just wanted you to know that your husband has never made any sort of inappropriate advances to me. Ever." Sophie was starting to regain some of her confidence, not having been devoured on the spot by an angry wolf. Her tone of voice was even turning a bit toward self-righteousness. "I have a *fiancé* and he would be really mad if anybody bothered me, he has a very short temper. He's really jealous."

Debra, being of the conviction that given enough rope, the Sophies of the world could easily hang themselves, let her meander on.

"He would probably even beat-up any man I talk to! You should see how possessive he is of me when we go out at night. And I certainly wouldn't want him to get a hold of Monsieur Dubois!" she rambled.

Debra wasn't expecting this and let out a surprised little "huh?" noise, as she scrambled her wits about, searching for an appropriate response to such a remarkable comment.

Sophie stood still, watching, a smug look on her face.

It wasn't terribly long before Debra shook her head, settling her thoughts to where they could get back on top of the wave of anger which had carried her this far.

"Hang on a second, Sophie. Let me get this straight. Are you warning *me,* not to inform your boyfriend that you've been jumping my husband on his desk on Tuesday evenings, let's see now, for about the past two years, if not longer, hoping I would be worried your boyfriend might come and beat up my husband?" She burst out laughing at this idea, struck by the absurdity of the situation.

"My dear, if you don't want that to happen, then there's only one solution: stop. No more jumping on my husband, irresistible though he is. Or I just might join up with your boyfriend and come and help him wring your necks myself!" She continued laughing with a twinge of hysteria, adding, "Sophie, I do hope you sleep well tonight!"

Debra slipped on down the hallway but before she was out of earshot, called down the hallway loud enough to please all the ears just pulling back from the cracked open doorways separating herself from Sophie, "I would rather you go and have the Aids test though, since we're sharing the same man's bed. It's always nice to know who I'm sleeping with, indirectly," and marched out through the main office, amazed at the turn their conversation had taken.

Of course by the time she had left the building, she was once again so angry she hesitated about turning around and stomping back into the office to chew on both Sophie and Patricia, for their seeming complicity in making sure her husband got enough of what he was used to at work.

How dare Patricia stand up for Sophie? And how dare Sophie try to threaten her with repercussions against her husband, when she was the one who was causing the situation to begin with? Was the world insane or was Debra the only person to find this situation absolutely incredible?

As bad luck would have it, Philippe's car pulled into the parking lot before Debra could reach her own.

"What are you doing here?" he asked. "Why aren't you at your afternoon appointment?"

"Well hello there, my darling husband! And how are you this afternoon?" She was determined to fight back this time and sarcasm was her armor.

The look on her face and the tone of her voice alerted Philippe to the imminent danger.

"If you came here to cause trouble, then you can forget it right now! This sort of discussion should take place in the privacy of our home. I won't have you making a scene in front of the employees and embarrassing me." The angry cat defenses were in place once again.

"Oh that's rich! I'm embarrassing you now! You know what? The three of you can have at one other! I've had just about enough of being made out to be the bad guy in this scenario. You and Patricia and Sophie, and what the hell, throw in her boyfriend for some extra excitement, you can just do whatever you want together! Just go for it! I'm done!" Once again laughing in an exasperated, incredulous manner, she made for her car and escape to wherever. Just anywhere but here.

She drove for two hours toward the west, checked into a hotel room and took a long walk along the unfamiliar beach at Cabourg. The cold, salty air helped calm her heart. It cleared her mind enough to concentrate on feeling the cold of the October sand between her toes. She let the icy water freeze her feelings of despair into a small, condensed lump: one which took up much less room in her chest than a throbbing beleaguered heart.

What was it that counted in her life as it stood? The girls and their physical well-being, first of all. In second place was their sense of balance and emotional stability. She could simulate her own, at least for a while, for she knew that how she reacted outwardly would determine how they would accept any decision she needed to make. She didn't feel capable of staying frozen forever, just long enough to organize her future. She needed time.

She was kicking the cold water with the balls of her feet when it hit her like a brick. Having run off today, she was playing directly into Philippe's hands. If she wanted the girls, and they were her girls, he had made that clear long ago; she would have to be very careful. Turning in her tracks, she left the beach, paid for the room, got back in her car and sped back toward home. She could make it before the girls' bedtime if she hurried.

#

I was relieved when she pulled into the drive an hour and a half later and caught her, out of breath when she charged into the house calling out to the children.

"Just where have you been?" Philippe stopped her on the landing as she was tearing up the stairs.

"What do you care? I'm here and I want to see my girls. Where are they?"

"You were completely out of control this afternoon and I was afraid you'd harm them, so I let them go sleep at Patricia's house."

"You did what?" She was surprised to hear her voice screeching at him. "How could you possibly think I'd harm my own daughters? They've done nothing wrong, you're the one who's been lying and acting despicably! If anyone deserves to have harm come to them, it's you!" She gulped back tears, struggling to breathe, sob and shout at the same time, and finding it impossible. "Did you know that your little sweetheart is afraid her boyfriend might come and beat you to a pulp? She specifically asked me not to tell him! You can at least be comforted by the fact that she worries you're not tough enough to fend for yourself. That must make you feel quite strong and virile to know your women are watching out for you behind your back." She specifically tried to aim below the belt, hoping he'd experience some difficulty next time he planned a *rendezvous* on his desk. As for herself, she could no sooner imagine having carnal relations with him than with a serial killer.

He moved as if to hit her. She stood her ground, face to face with him, snarling with menace and hate: "If you touch me, you'd best kill me straight away, because otherwise I will make sure you regret it for the rest of your slimy, worthless life. Now, get out of my way. I'm going to the police to report the kidnapping of my children. Would you care to accompany me?"

Grabbing her by the arm, as she turned to speed off down the stairs, he sneered in her hair, "They won't believe you; they already think you're insane for having called them in the middle of the night when you imagined being burgled. You'd better just stay here, or you'll end up being sorry for acting like a crazy woman. Someone just might believe it to be true someday, and lock you up out the way." His tone of voice was menacing, and she suddenly understood he had a plan, and which direction it was taking.

It was a horrifying slap in the face. He was intelligent, that much she knew, but she had never imagined him to be so Machiavellian. Having the tables turned on her, finding herself to be his adversary as opposed to his accomplice turned the light on his true character. She found him to be a snake, and a poisonous one at that. She wasn't prepared for it, so she backed down.

"Well, can you at least go get the children and bring them home? They must be worried, and they hardly know Patricia. Why did you take them to her house?

Françoise usually takes them when we're away. They're used to her and to her house."

"You should have thought of that before acting like a fury. It's too late to go get them now, they'll be in bed, and quite frankly, I'm not sure you're calmed down enough to look after them tonight. We'll see how things are going in the morning, now come to bed."

They climbed the rest of the stairs, his hand holding tight to her elbow. At the top, he reached out to slam the door to the stairs leading to the attic. "Damned old pile of rubbish! The doors don't shut, the windows leak air and the fireplaces smoke. I don't know why I ever let you convince me to buy this old heap. It's like throwing money into a cesspit!" he grumbled as they made their way down the hall to the bedroom.

I was deeply offended, having been referred to as many things in my time, but never as a cesspit. However, I didn't think much of him, either, and an insult is only worth the respect one bears its author.

Debra hated herself for it, but fear carried her into their bedroom, and forced her to lie down beside him. She understood how much was at stake, and that she needed to be very careful not to forget who she was dealing with.

Her only option was to concentrate on survival as he plied his unwanted attentions on her. There was desperation in his touch, as he did his best to make her respond to his lovemaking. Her heart was battered. So she pretended to climax, to get it over with, and get him off her.

She'd turned a page. This man, who had been the center of her life, had been shoved to one side, and because of it her world was completely off kilter. She felt empty and spent a long moment in the adjoining bathroom after he rolled away. I wished I had the arms necessary to hold and comfort her. Alas, I could only bless her dreams.

The toilet seat, being a most comfortable place to sit and ponder, she eventually came back to bed, slipping silently between the sheets, afraid to disturb his sleep. God forbid that he become aroused once again, and impose himself on her unwilling body. She lie awake throughout the rest of the night, planning. I listened.

I wanted the children to stay here with her. We belonged together, and I was certain I could be a comfort to the three of them during what was sure to be a test of her character.

CHAPTER 12

August 1942:

Heinrich found Paulette in the barn combing brambles from Flynn's tail. Her heart sank as she saw him penetrate her sanctuary: the only place she found peace, the only place she could think. His arrival shattered that peace.

It's not that she didn't dream of seeing him again, her dreams were full of his caresses and of his eyes delving into her soul. He had introduced her body to feelings she hadn't guessed existed. She'd been expecting the stuff of romance novels and Hollywood films: a love comprised of chaste, pecking kisses and hand-holding. Instead she found herself floundering, drowning in something much more intense.

She was frightened by it: the overwhelming need to kiss him, the violence of her reaction to his touch and most of all, the ease with which the teachings of chastity and modesty from her Catholic upbringing flew out of her head when he looked at her. Never had she imagined being so deeply involved with someone. She couldn't explain to herself, nor to Heinrich, the reason for her sudden flight from the garden some mornings past.

Paulette shouldered the destruction of the trellised tomatoes. She'd searched out Emile, explaining how she'd been overcome by a spell of dizziness while picking tomatoes in the warm sun. She was a lovely young girl and Emile, being a kindly older man, assumed she had swooned as a result of some feminine complaint and was more concerned for her well being than for the crushed tomatoes. Still wearing the stained dress when she had returned to confess, no further explanations were required. This was a good thing, as her heavy conscience could not have withstood serious questioning. After all, she had been consorting with the enemy.

The enemy as such, had invaded her thoughts from the moment she'd been struck by the danger of the situation. She couldn't hope for understanding from any member of her family or from her friends. Her only ally was the source of this grief. And here he was, standing in front of her. Heart thumping, she wasn't sure she wanted him to be there. Afraid of surrendering and throwing herself around his neck, she grabbed onto Flynn's mane for support.

Heinrich saw this, and his heart fell in disappointment as well. He'd been hoping she would smile. Instead, he saw her flinch in fear of him as he spoke. "I've been worried about you. I had to speak with you, to apologize. I didn't intend to scare you. Can you forgive my lack of self-control?" His quiet words voiced genuine concern.

"It's not only your fault. I was there and I didn't push you away. I didn't *want* to push you away! I *am* afraid, only not of you. I'm afraid of myself and of all this," her arms flung wide to encompass her universe, "and of hurting my family. This situation...our situation...it isn't what I was hoping for. Ever since I was a little girl I've dreamed that a rich, handsome man from the city would meet me on the street some day when I was dressed-up, shopping in Dieppe," she paused, as nostalgia washed over her.

"Before the war, we used to go to Dieppe, as a treat. We would take the train and go to the shops and drink chocolate in a *café*. We'd walk along the seafront and look at the rich people on holiday." She smiled at her memories. "I admired the ladies' clothes, shoes and hats and dreamed that I would dress like that some day, and that a charming man would notice me. We would talk for hours before he claimed to love me."

She blushed in shame, realizing how childish this must sound to a grown man, but struggled along, determined to make him see. "He would marry me. And I wouldn't have to work on the farm, and iron shirts and tend chickens to help my family stay alive. I know it was a silly dream, but I can't help it. I'm just so sick of this war and not knowing what's going to happen. I wish it would simply end, no matter what...as long as it's over...and I can have a future again. I deserve to have a future again, don't I?"

She began to cry, not the sobbing, uncontrollable crying of a hurt or wound, but the welling of silent tears, rising from a buried pool of frustration and disappointment. Angry at her lack of self-control, she quickly brushed the tears away, turning her face back into Flynn's side.

"I'm not a knight in shining armor, but I do have feelings for you." It was his turn to pause for an instant. "They are maybe inconvenient, but they are real...and I can't hide them...not from myself, or from you." His reply voiced heartache; she took it as regret and guilt.

I was amazed at how two people could have such a connection, yet so completely misunderstand what each was saying to the other. I wished I could tilt the ends of the barn floor and force them to approach one another, to somehow stop this silly mis-communication.

Paulette turned back to Heinrich, as the flood gate overflowed. "But you don't understand! You're not the problem! I have feelings for you too! They're real, and yes they're very inconvenient! But what hope is there for us? You're German. You're occupying my country, and you're supposed to be my family's *enemy*! And I'm in love with you? What sense does that make? None at all!"

I finally saw the 'eureka!' light in his gaze as discovery struck him full force.

"Good sense doesn't matter," he whispered, reaching to pull her close into his chest.

Flynn snorted, for they'd stopped giving him the attention he craved. Now they were just in his way, and he stomped his hoof with horsey impatience.

"You said you were in love with me," Heinrich's voice was filled with awe as he murmured in her hair.

Heinrich kissed her then, in a much different way than in the garden. He was a man who was learning to love, not just succumbing to physical desires. He was tender, intense and thorough as he held her face in his hands and loved her with his lips. Feeling her respond brought him great joy. He had her back again.

She continued crying as their kisses wrought havoc on her body. She wanted him to love her. She wanted to love him back and to be free of all restraints and obligations. She wanted everything to be good and desperately wanted to live in a land at peace, where she could love who she chose to love, without fear of repercussion. The tears were for that: knowing that this wasn't the case, and might never... ever...be so.

They were aware that the time wasn't opportune for joyous love-making. It was a time of uncertainty, but also of a driving need for some small *thing* to be right. So they latched onto each other, searching for that thing. Once again, their gestures expressed desperation, something unavoidable, something like a love which might escape them if they didn't deal with it seriously, and do so immediately. Theirs was a stolen love, one which they might regret. But even knowing this, they were powerless to walk away without tasting it. And in large gulps.

Bit by bit their clothing fell to the straw, Flynn stepping on Heinrich's coat, their lips never leaving each other. The last scraps of material gone, Heinrich lifted Paulette in his arms to lay her on the pile of clothing scattered on the straw.

When he lay beside her, propped on one elbow, his free hand smoothed her skin and combed her tangled hair, before commencing a slow exploration of her body. Her tears faltered as her breathing accelerated. His breath was hot on her face. Her skin tingled. She could no longer tell exactly where his hand was, as it left behind a scorched path. The fire spreading through her flushed skin caught his own as she copied his gestures. She used her hands, the fingers splayed wide to cover as much territory as possible with each caress.

There was no turning back.

Heinrich lowered himself over her, covering her body with his as nature took its course. She cried out with surprise and panicked when he entered her. But he stilled and kissed her tenderly, waiting for her to signal the moment when her body was ready to move ahead on the path toward each other.

It took but a moment before she felt the urge to squirm and he recognized her need for movement. He tried his best to keep a tight reign on his enthusiasm, to make certain she was accompanying him this time. He didn't want to lose her *en route*, as he had in the kitchen garden. He wanted her to be there with him, for them to make this particular journey together. So he slowed, coaxing her to keep up with his desire.

Keep up she did and her eagerness urged him on. Following her lead, he moved faster. She tightened around him, as if trying to absorb him. He could wait no longer. Her release followed his, flowing through their bodies and bringing tears, his of relief and hers of surprise.

She hadn't expected such a thing. In fact, she hadn't expected any of this. Even in her dreams she had always woken too soon. Now she understood the too-soon-for-what part.

They lay still, locked in position for some minutes before Flynn stuck his moist, furry nose somewhere unexpected, causing Heinrich to fling sideways, severing their bond. Cool air rushed over burning skin and a fit of shivering overtook Paulette.

It wasn't only the change in temperature that shook her. It was also the realization of what they had just done. Their lovemaking catapulted her from girlhood into becoming a woman. She could never go back. She would never be the same. She would be ruled by different feelings: emotional and physical, for the rest of her life. Her childhood was over. She didn't know if should be happy or regretful. These thoughts, and the straw, were becoming itchy.

Once again, she said nothing as she clutched a random item of clothing to her breast and tried in vain, to stop her chattering teeth. Heinrich bent over her, vigorously rubbing her arms and back, trying to help Paulette regain some of her lost composure. He helped her pull her full slip back over her head and to re-button her blouse. When she reached for her underpants and skirt, he stood to dress himself. They were strangely self-conscious, about an hour too late. Dressing seemed to be so much more embarrassing than undressing.

She wanted to leave, to run away and think. She mumbled an excuse and fled.

After he watched her leave, running headlong toward her cottage, he climbed the back stairs to the room he shared with two other junior officers, retreating to his bed, not able to face his friends who were downstairs drinking, playing cards and laughing amongst themselves, soldiers at their ease.

Heinrich, however, was not at ease. He was deeply troubled by what had just transpired. He didn't know what he could offer Paulette, just yet. Later, he could take her home to Germany as his wife, but right now, he was still on duty, and things didn't seem to be approaching any sort of end. The occupation of France stretched endlessly before them and he had no way to bring about any change. The events in the barn carried heavy responsibility toward a young woman he wasn't sure how to protect.

Still, being a man, and a very young one at that, these sober thoughts were crowded over to one side of his brain while the other images, the ones of her face between his kisses, and the soft feel of her skin beneath his fingertips, rising in gooseflesh as he trailed them across her belly, brought a pleased expression to his mouth. The sensuous thoughts won out, dancing across the movie screen of his dreams.

Paulette's escape was much the same, claiming an upset stomach and going to bed early. She heard her family downstairs talking and clearing the table, carrying out their usual activities. Their voices had a surreal quality, as if she were at the end of a long tunnel, separated from their reality, removed from the life she had led before tonight, before their loving. She didn't sleep.

CHAPTER 13

August 19, 1942

It was still dark when the rumble of canons and the screaming of fighter planes woke the household and the barnyard, disturbing the early morning of the countryside. The absence of the usual pre-dawn chorus of birdsong made the cows move restlessly in the fields, their rustling proof of an ignorant anxiety. Usually they were lying down, stick legs folded along their sides quietly chewing their cuds and dozing until the sun rose, forcing them to lumber to their feet and resume eating the thick grass, damp with dew. Nature's routine had been perturbed by man.

The noise came from far away, but the threat it carried set hearts pounding. There had been Allied bombing before, but scattered, more of the hit and run type, each episode of short duration. This time the aerial activity was continual, each faction's planes streaking inland to turn and attack, again and again. The quantity of aircraft was phenomenal. Seen from afar they might be mistaken for large bats performing an erratic ballet, rather like they were swooping to catch bugs in the night sky, their paths illuminated by machine-gun fire.

The pounding of the mortars and long range guns from Dieppe murmured a continual low rumble of distant thunder. The horizon burned with red and orange splashes of light, diffused through the fuzzy haze announcing a warm summer day on the coast. This glow couldn't be confused with dawn. It announced an assault of men and air power of a dimension previously unseen in this war.

At home, the German and French cohabitants assembled, hastily dressed, in front of my door. Questions asked found no answer, for neither group had been privy to the intelligence leading to this morning's events. It was obvious something on a large scale was taking place, although no one knew exactly what.

The German occupying force stationed in Dieppe totaled roughly fifteen hundred men. Each village and town along the seaside and inland had its own contingent, though much smaller. The army had spent the past two years of the occupation digging in, getting organized and building extensive defenses.

Every beach was cut off from land by a first line of defense. In Dieppe, it was comprised of a sea wall, topped with barbed wire. Guns were mounted on the tops of block houses dug into the cliffs to the left and right of the beach, which could sweep their fire across the wide lawns which should have been used for strolling and enjoying the summer sunshine after a dip in the sea.

The only building directly on the seafront was the casino, once an area dedicated exclusively to pleasant distractions, with large terraces, a restaurant with sea views and rooms for the games of chance attracting rich Parisians to this popular seaside resort. It was now a fortress of cement and barbed wire, housing soldiers who were presently attacked by air and sea.

Set farther back in, about a hundred yards from the beach was the row of houses and buildings marking the entrance to the city. In the past, tall stone walls protected the town from attacks such as this one, emanating from the sea. As was the case today, the English were usually at the origin of these attacks, having been at war with the French over and over again throughout history, as they disputed the rights to this fertile countryside. Unfortunately for the Germans the protective walls had been dismantled. Still the only access to the town center was via the rather narrow streets leading inward from the gates in those defenses. Piles of barbed wire barricaded these narrow arteries, slowing possible incursions to the heart of town.

#

Steve pulled up on the stick with both arms, straining his abdominal muscles for extra leverage, bringing the nose up hard on the Spitfire fighter plane. Mike, his right wing man, hooted with joy as he shouted news into his radio of a successful hit on the casino.

"Sonovabitch!!" yelled Warren, his left wing mate as the Focke FW190 flew at them, emerging immediately to their right from a tower of billowing brown smoke. Steve veered to the left and the plane groaned under the strain of violent maneuverings. "C'mon baby! You can do it!" he grunted to his plane. "You're a good girl! We can outrun that bastard!"

Staccato gunfire zipped around the plane, pinging on metal, the twanging "zzzzzzz" being the grimmest of all noises, the sound of a bullet finding its way through the fuselage, and lodging itself inside. The instinct to duck was useless. Each man kept to his job, shouting to each other frequently, maintaining a noisy headcount.

The three pilots zigzagged above the beach once again, Mike emptying the cartridges of the machine gun into the narrow slit in the cement as they flew over a blockhouse near the castle. The paneless windows watched the battle in shocked silence, their dark holes "o"s of surprise, while smoke curled upward along its ancient stone walls, witness once again to the folly of man.

Plunging into the smog above the cliffs, they headed southeast, the FW 190 in pursuit. Steve hoped to draw him inland away from his compatriots, better to turn and nail him when he was isolated.

A sharp turn south brought them under the other plane, the surprise on the face of the German gunner made them all laugh as Mike flipped him a Royal Canadian bird with the middle finger of his right hand. Another sharp turn west and they caught his broadside, Mike screaming with the pulsating vibrations of the machine gun, shaking the blood in his veins, the grip of his hands sending shots of pain up to his shoulders and jaws. "Here, you shits! Eat this!"

The German plane swerved up and turned in a large, graceful arc, before swooping to bear down on them, gaining extra speed through the pull of gravity in a face to face plunge. The pilots aimed at each other, in a horrific game of chicken. They did not collide, but their simultaneous gunfire hit each other's engines, and smoke plumed from both the left and right wing aircraft.

Heat spread through Steve's shoulders as he gripped the stick, keeping a steady course, while the wings fought to rock the trajectory of the plane. The windscreen spider-webbed into an intricate pattern, catching Steve's attention as he watched it spread outward from a small hole in the center. A strange thud resounded and another pattern started to the right of the first. Steve stared, mesmerized, until reality hit home and he understood the importance of the designs. He shook his head to dissipate the fuzziness brought on by the intensity of the blood pumping through his heart. He re-focused on the controls, beeping frantically and red lights blinking.

The German Focke FW190 dropped beneath them, falling from the sky. "Ycsssss!" Steve shouted when he saw the results of their encounter, looking at an angle behind him, watching out the side window as the German plane crashed into the trees, bursting into flames.

Turning back to look ahead through the haze of smoke billowing in puffs before him, Steve called out to his team. No answers.

He looked down at his shirt front and the eloquent ooze of dark liquid spreading down to his pants. To his left, Warren slumped forward as if inspecting his knees. "Fuck!" Steve whispered, not able to remove his hands from the controls, fighting to keep the damaged "Sweet Sally" aloft. "Mike!" he shouted. "Mike! Are you alright?"

Still no answer came.

#

On a foggy morning, some six thousand Canadian and English soldiers, most of them greenhorns from the 2nd division commanded by General Roberts, faced the steep incline of the beach. The coastline at Dieppe has a rock beach, with round stones the size of flattened tennis balls, piled many feet deep and smoothed by the incessant movement of the water. Walking is difficult, especially as the water's edge is close to thirty feet lower than the lawns. The rocks move underfoot like quicksand when one wishes to climb to and from the seaside. Many a turned ankle caused as many ladies to be carried off by their heroes to firmer ground.

That was the stuff of romance.

Today, with no help at hand, a speedy climb up the moving incline and across wide open lawns to the cover of the buildings, themselves infested with the enemy, was the only way out for the men who had jumped off rocking boats into the cold water of the English Channel in the pre-dawn gloom. Soaked to the neck and carrying their weapons above their heads, they threw themselves into an attack which was to last only six hours, although it would take a toll never to be forgotten.

Despite the covering fire from the Allied ships waiting offshore, as well as the continuous air attack, the soldiers on foot faced impossible odds as they did their best to reach their objectives. The tanks which were to help crush the German entrenchments had landed, unfortunately, too far to the west, subsequently lumbering along under the cliffs, avoiding huge boulders and rock formations, delaying their arrival on the main beach.

In the meantime, the people of Dieppe watched in tears as their saviors were mowed down under the rising sun. Hopes were crushed, dejection and overwhelming helplessness the only results of this enormous loss of young life.

Over five hours worth of destruction later, the master plan had included a retreat, picking up the invaders and hopefully, their prisoners at an 11AM rendezvous. The men who had succeeded in reaching the town, and there were quite a few, found themselves trapped. Most of those who followed the plan, knew the return trip across those lovely wide lawns, through the sweeping gunfire from the blockhouses still harboring the enemy, would be fatal.

Substantially less than half of the soldiers who'd thrown themselves into the water that morning reached the beach once again. A third were taken prisoner and marched off to Germany to spend the next two years starving. Even less lucky were the thousand plus whose bodies littered the beach, some of which were taken out to sea by the rising tide. Over a hundred Allied airplanes never returned to their home bases in England. "Sweet Sally" was among these.

The Germans lost a total of some six hundred men, only three hundred of whom were killed, the rest reported as missing in action; a feeble comparison. Still, they were furious.

#

While this scene of carnage played out along the beach, anxiety ran rampant amongst both factions occupying my space. Little or no news was relayed out to the countryside and Colonel VonEpffs was as anxious as the rest. All anyone could do was to watch and listen from afar, knowing the outcome could change their situation. As of course, it would.

Both Heinrich and Paulette prayed in silence that what they heard would herald the end to the stalemate of the occupation. Selfishly, neither cared much about the identity of the victors, just so long as it was finally over. However, they had no opportunity to share their thoughts, unknown to each other, identical nonetheless. Each of them had a role to play and no contact between them could be risked while so much uncertainty danced around the yard.

Still, the cows had to be milked and the other animals tended, although no other work was done as the wait for news was shared in an almost companionable silence. There was at least one exception to this relative calm and it was embodied in Michel.

His limited patience had expired and after finally satisfactorily kissing Manon, he abandoned her with the duty of holding her tongue as long as possible before breaking the news of their departure. Michel had convinced her brother, Guillaume, his long time accomplice, that their hour of duty had come. Michel emptied his tin and stuffed some bread and cheese into a haversack before slipping away while attention was focused on the horizon. They were joining up with the resistance, and it might be some time before anyone would have certain news of their fate.

When the radio finally related the morning's events to Colonel VonEpffs from the commander in Dieppe, the news of the Allied defeat was underscored with an urgent order to search for any pilots or airborne crew who might have parachuted to safety before their planes crashed. The Colonel ordered a group of soldiers to deploy immediately to search the fields for traces of any such escapees.

The Colonel also gave instructions for all women and children to stay inside their cottages until further notice, mostly because he was at a loss regarding a further plan of action. Fearing a rebellion brought on by such a crushing defeat, he thought it best to restrict the movement of his French charges.

Thus, the disappearance of two young men went largely unnoticed by the Germans, but wreaked havoc amongst the French families. Manon was shook until her teeth rattled when she refused to say where the boys had gone. She could have avoided this, had she been able to disguise the look of knowing pride painted on her smug face once their absence was detected. The anxious questions flying about the room landed in a resounding splat at her feet, effectively identifying the one who could supply the answers.

By then, there was no logical course of action. The risk of sending a search party weighed light in the scales against the danger of the German patrols looking for escaped flight crew who might have parachuted to safety. They couldn't enlist the aid of Colonel VonEpffs, for once they were found, he would have no choice but to send the boys off to a work camp in Germany. Indeed the best course of action was to take none and hope for the best. The women prayed fervently and entertained a vain hope that their sons would realize the folly they were committing and return home for supper before being caught.

When this didn't happen, Michel's father was joined by Guillaume's, stealing away after nightfall to search for the boys. They checked every cottage and barn along the road toward Rouen, thinking the boys would try to head south. They were careful to stay off the road to avoid being seen by the patrols. They went as far as possible, leaving enough time to return before dawn broke and their presence at the farm would be missed.

Marcel, being a hostage, was not allowed to leave the farm at all. He would be shot if caught. They returned empty-handed but with the news that the boys had been picked up by another group headed to Yvetôt to join up with a resistance group based there. This was of meager comfort to the two mothers.

They decided to keep their silence, to pretend all was normal in hopes of dissimulating the boy's absence. When inevitably, The Germans would notice sometime the following day, everyone would claim the boys had planned on sleeping at the other's cottage and that each family had been duped by their sons into believing they were safe with the others' family. Thus, the parents might avoid punishment for the boys' escape.

The only consolation was the knowledge that they weren't alone and unprotected. But the company they now were keeping was dangerous company indeed. Anyone associated with the Resistance was a prize for the Germans.

CHAPTER 14

Autumn 1942:

The disastrous raid on Dieppe prompted an increase in sabotage and reprisals on the population. Previously, the Germans had assumed that while the war had stalled on the other fronts, at least the western front and northern France were relatively calm. The attempted invasion of Dieppe was proof that the German situation was more precarious than the Nazis had imagined. Hitler had bitten off more than he could chew.

The occupying army increased their demands upon the citizens of Dieppe. Young local men were obliged to guard the electrical and telephone lines from sabotage. If by chance, an incident occurred during an individual's guard duty, he was held responsible as if he had committed the crime himself. The penalty was death.

Existing restrictions were enforced with vigor and movement of the population was limited. More locals joined the underground resistance, whose goal was to harass the occupying army, as well as any collaborating government employees and officials. The patriotic French made themselves known to one another, organizing themselves into groups. They produced and distributed subversive tracts filled with suggestions of how to antagonize the enemy.

The group Michel and Guillaume had joined were based in Yvetôt and involved in sabotage and burglary missions on the occupying army's depots and weapons caches. Overseas Resistance forces parachuted grenades, rifles and munitions into various locations to supplement the meager pilfered supplies. These packets contained instructions on how to assemble and use these weapons, for the recipients were for the larger share, farm laborers, some of whom had never used a gun, even for hunting. However, a willingness to torment the usurpers compensated for their ignorance in the ways of war.

Some of the commanders of these groups were retired French army officers. They organized miniature training camps in the heart of the forests for enthusiastic rebels. Michel and Guillaume participated in these exercises, feeling more useful than when plowing the fields or herding the livestock at home.

They camped in the woods, supplies coming from local farms and business, sometimes as donations, sometimes stolen from those suspected of collaboration. This wasn't always true, but scruples were a luxury they could ill afford. If it weren't for the danger factor, these young men would have been living the Robin Hood sort of adventure most young boys dream of. However, bitter reality struck when one or another of their comrades was caught and executed or shipped off to a work camp in Germany, never to be heard from again.

#

Captain Steve Winthrop did his best to slowly lower his crippled plane, coasting inland some distance before crumpling his wings and landing gear in a field several kilometers from Doudeville. His wing men were dead, but for some reason, fate had chosen to keep him alive, seriously wounded but with his instinct for survival intact. This instinct encouraged him to drag his body from the wreckage of his 'Sweet Sally' Spitfire and into the cover of the surrounding forest.

It had been several days before he reached the pig farm, finding refuge in the smelly but pleasantly warm barn containing several dozen oinking, snuffling, spotted creatures.

He'd hoped this particular farm hadn't been acquired by the Germans. So many other places he'd seen from afar bore tell tale signs of occupation. Apparently, this farm wasn't grand enough to attract their attention. The house was a mean-looking little place, barely more than a hovel. He observed the comings and goings of an old man and his equally aged wife for quite some time before moving out from the cover of the trees, and into the barn.

By then Steve was so hungry, he considered the possibility of killing and eating one of its occupants raw. The memory of how delicious ham could be was physically painful. Luckily for his roommates, he didn't have the strength to act on this impulse. The following morning, the farmer found him asleep in good company, with a filthy, crusted bandage wrapped around his shoulder and chest.

The farmer's wife dug out little bits of metal and glass embedded in his flesh alongside a bullet, a cousin to those which had killed his companions. He spoke to them in a drunken version of the French he had learned at school, tainted by his Canadian accent and blurred by the large quantities of alcohol he was given in lieu of an anesthetic. His conversation amused Pierre and Ginette Duchemin. Laughter deepened the creases in their faces and showed off their lack of viable teeth, but as he tried with some small success to understand their local *Cauchois* dialect, he found that their faces disguised two very large hearts, filled with equal parts of disgust with the Germans and gratitude to the Allies.

Goodwill was one thing, but they had learned to be very cautious. Germans patrols policed the roads, frequently taking time off to raid small farms such as this one, confiscating whatever took their fancy. Germans being notoriously fond of ham, Steve's presence must remain undetected, barring his admittance to the relative comforts of the house.

He took up residence in the wine cellar, situated under the floor of the barn, accessed through a trap door, dissimulated under piles of undeniably filthy straw littered with pig droppings. He rolled himself in blankets in the daytime, sleeping his way back to health. When evening came and twilight confused light with darkness, Pierre and Ginette came to free him from the cellar, bringing a hot meal and warm water to wash with. Ginette checked his bandages, prodding his wounds with her fingers.

When she found him in the grips of a fever, she ignored his protests and forced spoonfuls of willow bark tea through his tightly clenched teeth. This job was a difficult one, for unlike his nurse, Steve had a complete set of teeth and they were in fine condition. Still, Ginette punched insistently at the enamel until he un-clamped his jaw enough to dribble the bitter liquid inside. Her will won out, and little by little his head cleared of the foggy nightmares brought on by fever. He would have preferred alcohol, but Ginette refused to understand his request. She had a selective understanding of his demands, smiling and nodding in apparent assent, yet doing as she originally intended.

Ginette was also oblivious to the stink of the poultices she applied to his wounds before re-bandaging them every evening, he: protesting against their necessity and she: smiling and nodding and reapplying them anyway. Steve finally gave up protesting, fearing offending her more than he feared death from poultice poisoning. However, unless he ate before her ministrations, the odor would leave him retching and unable to enjoy the delicious smoked pork so vital to his recovery. After they left him for their own rest, his cleansed body was as smelly as the other occupants of the barn.

Steve's mother would have had a fit, had she witnessed the practices used on her beloved son. Mrs. Winthrop was a doctor's daughter and the proud owner of home so spotless, stray germs refused to come in through the window, certain they would find nothing to sustain them. Still, lack of hygiene notwithstanding, Ginette's methods were effective and Steve's body slowly knit itself back into condition.

Several weeks later, Ginette came tearing into the barn as fast as her crooked legs could carry her, flung open the trap door and unceremoniously chucked a half dozen piglets into the hole on top of Steve. She made a silent motion with her left hand, mimicking someone having their throat slit before quickly lowering the trap door and scuffling dirty straw over the top of it with her wooden soled clogs. Bits of debris drifted down onto Steve's head as he organized the squealing piglets off to one side, crouching in readiness for whatever might ensue.

A herd of boots tramped into the barn, causing a commotion and from the sounds of it, bothering the pigs. Their squealing and grunting was punctuated by cursing in German before things became quiet once again. Luckily the noise coming from above disguised that made by Steve's disgruntled piglets, and their hiding place was left undiscovered. Steve knew the time had come to take leave of his hosts, for their own protection.

Two days later, he huddled in a wagon bed under empty feed sacks, next to a crate of clucking chickens. He wore an unusual outfit made of clothing once belonging to Pierre, but bearing inserts, allowing the shirt and jacket to cover the wider expanse of his shoulders. Ginette was no seamstress but he would be less noticeable than if he wore his nicely fitting uniform jacket and pants, especially now that these were torn and bloodstained. The extra cuffs added to the pants were long enough to partially disguise his Air Force issue boots, to which he added a camouflage of mud and sticky pig poo.

Thus attired, he hid in the back of the wagon driven by Pierre, seated on the front bench next to Ginette, herself clutching a basket of eggs close to her chest. The lurching of the wagon as it fell into chuck holes bruised Steve's still tender ribs, yet he kept quiet, swallowing the grunt of pain caused by each jolt.

Anyone witness to this scene could easily have mistaken the year for 1842 or even 1742: the timeless rural activity of Normandy seemingly unaltered in spite of occasional airplanes rushing across the sky, periodically dropping bombs on small villages locked in a time capsule. The bombs were to blame for most ruts in the roads, which sometimes veered around a gaping hole several meters in diameter. Other craters were left in fields and in the surrounding forests, silent signposts warning of a dire future. It was almost as if Hitler had decided to bomb the peaceful countryside straight to hell, wiping any traces of charm from the earth's surface and no one knew exactly why.

Still, the locals continued their trade. Pierre and Ginette had to eat, so they braved the patrolling soldiers and the projectiles falling from the sky, driving to attend the Market at Yvetôt, still held on Wednesday mornings. They must exchange their goods for those they lacked.

In one of the lanes leading to the market square, Steve slipped from the back of the wagon, without a goodbye, as was the plan. He was on his own now and thought it might be a long time before he would see Pierre and Ginette again, if ever.

The market was a sad little affair. Steve guessed it to be a pathetic facsimile of the markets from before the war. A few farmers bartered between themselves while the bravest housewives scurried about and made their meager purchases with ration tickets and what little money they possessed.

Like the others, Pierre and Ginette left after a pair of hours, a different load in their wagon, making their way back along the rutted road to their hamlet, turning into the track leading to their farm, hoping to reach home without their goods being confiscated. They were sad to lose their tenant, yet relieved the danger he represented was gone. They dragged the bags of corn into the barn and removed any traces of Steve from the cellar.

During this time, Steve hid in a lean-to garage filled with broken bits of tractor and car parts. Rusted metal would screech if bumped, therefore making any movement at all was impossible. His muscles cramped and his shoulder ached in the cold damp of November, the feeble sunlight failing to heat the garage through the corrugated tin roof. When night fell, he stayed put, afraid to move lest an inquisitive dog hear his movements.

At one point Steve heard a racket, followed by an explosion and gunfire. Shouts sounded close to Steve's hiding place, but the inhabitants of the houses in the street where the garage was located stayed put, inside, away from the commotion, whatever it was, curiosity being a dangerous luxury in wartime.

Later, when the evening German patrols passed by the garage, shining their flashlights routinely in and around every nook and cranny, he stopped breathing, afraid his puff of warm air might signal his presence. He held it in as long as possible, feeling faint before their quiet conversation led him to believe they were far enough away for him to safely expel his frosty breath.

Cautiously he moved his arms and legs before attempting to stand. Dizzy with stress, hunger and cold, his shoulder ached, but he needed to move from the garage and make his way behind the patrol to the door of the safe house, several streets south of where he had been hiding. Lurking through the streets, staying a safe distance from the patrol, he followed until he reached a red painted door marked *"Officine"*.

It belonged to the pharmacist, a local player in the resistance organization. Pierre had obtained this information through carefully composed questions during last month's visit to the market. He had given Steve instructions to the door last night, warning him to stay hidden, knowing that if anyone spoke to Steve, his accent would betray him away immediately. His gait was conspicuous enough. Most tall, young, blond chaps with perfect teeth were either dead or working for the Germans. A stranger had no place in such a small town.

At first try, no one answered his triple rap. He waited a full minute, scanning the darkened street in both directions before knocking once again.

Someone's granny opened the door, peering up at Steve's face through vintage spectacles. She immediately kissed him on both cheeks twice, saying in a cheerful voice, *"Ah, mon petit neveu! Comme je suis contente de te voir! Rentre! On allait s'asseoir pour manger. Tu te joindras à nous. Comment va ta mère, ma nièce Claudine?"* This speech poured forth as she bundled him in through the door, then locked it, wedging a metal bar across the frame.

Her delivery was so smooth that Steve wondered if perhaps she had mistaken him for her nephew. He kept silent until she gave him the opportunity to speak in a safer place.

Once barricaded inside, the granny was strangely quiet as she led the way down a darkened hallway, knocking on a closed door. A young woman's voice called out "*Mé-mère?*" before the granny answered back. When the door opened, the occupants of a kitchen stared at him anxiously, while a man, who was obviously the *chef de famille,* spoke.

"Who are you, and what brings you here?"

Steve responded as he had been instructed, "Pierre Duchemin".

A collective sigh of relief later, the room sprang to life.

The man assisted two wounded lads as they crawled from behind a hutch, sat them down on stools in front of the fire, while two women, visibly mother and daughter, assembled knives and sewing kit on the table. Steve had arrived at a bad time. These people obviously had more important things to deal with than his presence.

Granny sat Steve down, farther along the heavy oak table and placed a bowl of steaming stew in front of him, before turning to help cleanse the young men's wounds.

They spoke rapidly in low voices. Most of the content escaped Steve's weary, limited comprehension. He watched as he ate, guessing at what was happening. The young men responded in low groans of pain. Steve noticed the serious looking burns on their faces and arms as Granny cut at the shirt front welded to the youngest one's chest. Gentle washing removed some bits of cloth while producing flinching and stifled yelps of pain. A pot of pungent goose grease appeared and the women applied bandages over a thick swab of grease.

The next few minutes saw heavy alcohol consumption by the young men, while the daughter woman scalded a sharp knife. The smallest fellow was chosen to perch on a stool at the table.

Granny stepped in front of him and grabbed his chin, forcing the boy to look into her eyes. She recited a sort of prayer or incantation while passing her hands in front of his upper body slowly, not touching him, instead weaving her hands to and fro about a half inch from the bandaged burns. After a few minutes of this, she used the tip of the scalded knife to trace the sign of the cross on his forehead, scratching the surface of the skin without drawing blood.

Steve had stopped eating during this ritual, watching with grim curiosity as Granny placed a leather strap usually used for sharpening straight razors between the young chap's teeth. The subject bit down, eyes round as saucers, the scratch of the cross shining bright pink in the lantern light.

The large man grabbed hold of the boy's arms and the young woman grabbed his ankles while Granny, wielding the knife, dug around in the poor fellow's shoulder. He puffed through enlarged nostrils like a horse straining against a heavy load. A particularly wrenching cry produced by a flick of the knife, sent a bullet plinging onto the tabletop, to roll down the length of the table stopping just in front of Steve's supper.

Spoon in midair, Steve was struck dumb when Granny turned to him, holding the bloodied knife, an expression of glee on her face. He gulped back a mouthful of stew with the macabre impression that she might like to come after him with it.

She looked disturbingly like a Granny gone mad, ready to gobble up little children in the forest. Steve felt uncomfortably like Hansel, and involuntarily pressed his six foot stature into the wooden rungs of the chair back. The scene was surreal and Steve contemplated running into the town square to suurender to the Germans.

Granny relinquished the knife before approaching his end of the table. She drew out a chair and sat next to him, fingering the bullet. Since he'd stopped eating, she nodded and pushed the bowl back in front of him in a gesture meant to encourage him to continue with his meal. Thinking it best to humor her, considering her prowess with the knife, he turned back to the stew, feeling quite like a child who'd best do as he was told. She smiled as he ate, her hand on Steve's knee, patting it absently while watching the younger women at their task of sewing up the holes she'd made with her knife.

Steve couldn't keep from glancing down at her hand between mouthfuls of stew; feeling is if a large unwelcome spider was hopping up and down on his knee. Her touch was repulsive. He repressed a shudder of revulsion, but didn't move away from her, as incapable of action as if she had placed a spell on him at the same time as the young man.

By the time Steve had swallowed the rest of the stew, which proved to be a difficult task considering the lump of horror lodged in the back of his throat, the sewing had ended. By now, the young man slumped in his chair, thoroughly drunk. The mother tied bandages about the patient's shoulder and chest, before the older man who'd asked for Steve's name, hauled him from the stool to deposit him on a cot before the fireplace.

The other fellow, who'd been busy throwing back cups of liquor while his friend was under the knife, hobbled to the recently vacated stool by the table. Granny got back up, pushing on Steve's knee for leverage. Her fingertips dug into his kneecap, and he winced.

Episode two unfolded before Steve's appalled gaze, Granny performing her art on the second subject. The lad's right knee was swollen and damaged. Steve rubbed his own in empathy, unconsciously attempting to wipe away Granny's imprint.

Someone hitched the boy's foot onto the table top, quite close to Steve's now empty bowl. The view and smell of the filthy sock gave Steve some small satisfaction as to Granny's choice of working order. He might not have been able to finish his meal had the foot appeared beforehand.

Granny repeated the prayer/incantation with some variations. It seemed a bit longer this time yet finished with the scraping of the sign of the cross on a terrified forehead. A bead of blood showed at the junction of the two lines. Whether this was intentional or not, Steve had no guess. But the appearance of the droplet elicited seemingly pleased commentary regarding the potential success of what was to come. The lad seemed rather more fidgety than his friend, probably due to insight of what was in store for him.

The procedure which followed the chomping of the leather strap appeared to be more complicated than the shoulder intervention. Granny stuck her index finger into a tear above the kneecap, fishing about inside the skin. Muffled screaming erupted from her victim. Still, after a few minutes of this unorthodox surgery, a loud popping noise burst from the boy's knee, and Granny proudly held-up a fairly large piece of metal in her bloody fingers. Once again, she turned to Steve with a proud smile on her face, nodding toward him as if to say: "See what I did? Isn't it wonderful?"

The undigested stew roiled about in his stomach, threatening to reappear, unbidden, on the tabletop next to the filthy, twitching sock. Steve swallowed it down, turning to the older man standing behind him near the door, looking for help from some quarter. The man patted Steve on the shoulder, keeping his words to himself.

Very little talking was done during the second episode of sewing. Barring the groaning of the patient, the proceedings were carried out in a relative hush. After all, it was well past dark and the curfew. Sound might have alerted the patrols.

Steve respected this hush, although his curiosity and concern for his future spawned dozens of questions now that his fate seemed firmly lodged behind the red painted door.

#

He spent the night in the kitchen on a cot near Michel and Guillaume, the two groaning chaps who'd been tended to by the knife wielding Granny; Michel being the lucky one with the shoulder injury. Steve didn't sleep much. He learned he was to accompany the two to join the resistance camp once they were well enough to travel.

When birdsong warned of the coming dawn, the three men moved upstairs to an attic. The wounded were tightly wrapped in blankets and covered with quilts as there was no heat in the attic, and autumn had settled in long ago with its gusty winds and drizzling skies. The elderly man warned them to keep completely silent, a difficult request to honor considering the great pain the lads were in.

When they attempted to relieve their bladders, moans of pain escaped their clenched teeth. Steve held the chamber pot for each, allowing them to turn a bit to one side while still lying on their cots. It looked as though Guillaume would have trouble with his knee for some time to come. It had swollen under the bandages to an impressive size and was now inflamed and purple.

When at midday the middle aged woman appeared at the top of the ladder with warm food and a jug of much awaited spirits, the boys guzzled more than they ate. Steve finished the food, leaving the alcohol to keep them company in their misery. The afternoon was much quieter, hard drink having worked its magic, bringing on a deep sleep.

Steve rested as much as he could, his boredom finding no other relief. He thought about what the future would bring, wondering if he were a step closer to freedom or not. It seemed like years had passed since he'd climbed into the cockpit of his plane in England. It also seemed as if he'd flown across the channel not only to Dieppe but into a more remote history, as he took into account last night's healing ritual.

Steve had never before been witness to such proceedings. A Methodist by his parent's wishes, he didn't hold anchored religious beliefs. Steve was influenced by his Grandpa, who was a doctor, relying more on scientific know-how than superstition, and who owned a large collection of medical journals piled on the shelves of his office. Steve had thought Ginette's somewhat unhygienic ministrations were quaint, but they appeared positively modern when compared with Granny's incantations and finger surgery. Steve deduced that a sort of pagan witchcraft mixed with religion had been put to use, the sign of the cross displayed to bear a certain validity to the rest.

Granny herself could have stepped off the stage of a performance of Shakespeare's 'Macbeth'. She was a bizarre mix of harmless little old lady and witch, the likes of whom he hoped never to meet up with alone on a moonless night. He feared childish nightmares peopled with her macabre grin would follow him for the rest of his life.

He spent part of the afternoon pondering life in a country where such ancient practices were carried out in the back kitchen of a pharmacist's shop. He felt far removed from home and his mother's spotless kitchen, geographically of course, but in an evolutionary sense as well.

Understanding he was in the old world now, he realized he must adapt to this world's practices if he were to survive. For now, all he could do was wait until the boys were well enough to take him to their camp and hopefully from there to freedom.

Throughout long days in the freezing attic and evenings passed in front of the kitchen hearth with the three generations of the pharmacist's family, he heard many horrific tales of the war. He also got a vivid explanation of the noise he'd heard before arriving at the red door.

He listened with incredulity at the whispered story told in turn by the boys, whom he now viewed as youthful idiots. Apparently they'd tried to steal a quantity of petrol from a German supply tank in the village when they'd been seen by a patrol. Gunfire had hit the barrels they were hauling off with a hand truck, igniting the petrol and burning the lads while they dodged the bullets. Luckily, they'd found somewhere to hide before making their way to the safe house, showing up unexpectedly just before Steve.

Amazed that a responsible adult could send two unarmed boys off to attempt such a brazenly stupid act of thievery, Steve voiced his misgivings about the good sense of their commanding officer. His soldier's training put an emphasis on efficient use of manpower, not attempting operations doomed to fail. His opinion reaped sardonic commentary regarding the luxury of planning from afar with abundant weaponry, resulting in blatant failure nonetheless. Steve pursed his lips in grudging agreement. The raid on Dieppe had been a well-planned disaster. He kept the rest of his opinions to himself, knowing first hand how things could go frightfully wrong, with no one in particular to blame.

As the boys recovered, they regaled him with tales of their other exploits, sometimes stifling hilarity when they'd succeeded at pulling off some caper against the Germans. They obviously enjoyed ridiculing them with useless pranks just as much as succeeding at more strategic aims. There was a worrisome element of fun infusing their story-telling which bothered Steve, reminding him of the immaturity of the boys, especially knowing he would be accompanying them to their camp.

Once again he wondered if he wouldn't be better off taking his chances surrendering to the Germans. Officers were supposed to be well treated in accordance with the Geneva Convention. He evaluated his chances in both cases. Neither was substantially more attractive than the other, but there seemed to be a minute chance to return to duty if he stayed with the resistance fighters. Any soldier would prefer a shot at escape if it could lead back to the Allies. Only time would tell if he should have taken his chances as a prisoner of war.

#

During this period of increased activity on both sides, Paulette and Heinrich were even more careful not to be seen together, even in casual conversation. They had to broach the subject of pregnancy, for the safety of Paulette who couldn't risk such a thing at this time. Precautions were taken but neither one of them could reconcile themselves to the idea of giving up on one another. Their bond was a true one and its mettle was being tested for endurance.

Paulette's mother suspected something had changed in her daughter. She had become quieter and more prone to pensiveness. Granted, during such uncertain times, worry was normal, but young people possess a resilience of spirit allowing them to continue living in the face of incredible odds, with hope for better days intact. Paulette, even as a child, had the gift of happiness, finding pleasure in small things, humming at work, always ready to smile and laugh. This trait had become less and less noticeable as time went on, for Paulette had begun to despair of ever being able to share her feelings with her family.

She was unhappy to hide her love from her parents, but more fearful of their reaction. When the locals caught women known to have physical relationships with Germans, their heads were forcibly shaved in public. Paulette was frightened of the repercussions of her feelings.

She was also subconsciously aware of the difference in their giving of one to the other. Hers was a sacrifice, given with the promise of a heavy price to pay.

His was a joyous sharing of a moment, with little or no fear for the future. He wanted her for his own. It was simply a matter of time before he could claim her as his chosen. His parents wouldn't take much notice of his wife's social status, since he wasn't the all important heir to the family fortune. His brother would have to choose from a select group of young ladies of appropriate background, who came with a substantial dowry, as his father and his father's father had done before him. As second in line, Heinrich wasn't counted on to fulfill these obligations and thus enjoyed a small measure of freedom.

During one of these stolen moments when they lay in each others arms, damp with spent energy, their difference in outlook broke the charm of post-lovemaking repose. Heinrich was dreamily describing his family home, explaining what she could look forward to as his wife, without having thought to ask her opinion on the matter beforehand.

As she listened to him ramble, exasperation took over and she pushed out of the sincerely cherished but now stifling, circle of his arms. "And just what makes you believe I want to move to Germany to be your wife? No matter what the outcome of this war, I don't think we'll be safe either here or in Germany. You will always represent the enemy to my family, just as I will also seem so to yours."

He was taken aback by her reaction, having assumed by her desire to see him and partake of their love-making, that she was truly his to possess. He was after all, a man and as a soldier of rank, used to a certain amount of compliance to his requests. He didn't quite know what to reply.

Seeing his face register blatant surprise that she might possess ideas contrary to his own, only served to infuriate her. She sat up and gathered her clothing about her, creating a wall between them in the straw. Momentarily, she chose to forget his gentleness and concern for her in every situation, and allowed anger to take hold of her tongue.

"How can you just sit there and think that everything will turn out just fine for us? *You* come to be with me and enjoy yourself, while *I* fear every second that I spend with you and hate every minute that I can't! How can you not care enough to be worried about us? I'm scared witless and you're planning on how I'll teach your mother French cuisine! You're a blind idiot! A... A man!"

She hurriedly threw on her clothes, not taking care to hook straps and buttons, or tuck and smooth. Her hair was a riot dressed with bits of straw and tears dribbled along her nose. She struggled to her feet to make an escape, from him as well as from her own contradictory feelings.

"He wants to marry me! What could he possibly be thinking?" she railed as she stormed off, stomping down the ladder from the hayloft.

She charged out of the barn, straight into one of the soldiers with whom Heinrich shared the room formerly owned by the young *demoiselle* of the manor. He caught her in his arms as she stumbled, her tearful countenance giving cause for misunderstanding in his mind. Turning quickly, he shouted to another soldier, whose coat was off, head stuck under the hood, working on one of their trucks, commanding him to hurry and alert Colonel VonEpffs immediately, never releasing a babbling Paulette from his grasp.

Heinrich, in the meantime, hearing a commotion but not identifying its cause, dressed with some care, hoping to be able to stroll out of the barn looking normal, and avoid being involved in whatever was happening outside. When he reached the barn door, he immediately knew they were trapped.

His friend and roommate turned on him with furor in his eyes, the accusations ripping off his tongue like so many bullets shot from a machine gun. The soldiers had noticed Paulette and few were free of daydreams concerning her sweet innocence. This young man was particularly infuriated that Paulette could have fallen victim to Heinrich's unwanted attentions and his desire to protect her reigned supreme, though heavily tainted with a certain disreputable form of jealousy.

Rape was not acceptable on our farm. Colonel VonEpffs was very strict regarding conduct toward the females working on and about the domain. He greatly prided himself on being a man of honor. While he entertained women himself, they were of the sort who offered themselves to him willingly, arriving in the wake of officers who, most often out-ranking the Colonel, showed up to be entertained in the manor house. They enjoyed my hospitality and the wonderful food produced by the conflicting culinary interests fighting it out in the basement kitchens. These women were compliant guests. Never before had any plundering been done, other than of the strawberries, by his contingent of soldiers.

The Colonel arrived at the scene at once, gently taking a shivering, panicked Paulette by the arm. He sent someone to look for her father, before sitting her down on a stone bench in front of the barn next to the paddock gate.

Flynn meandered over to stick his head through the wooden fence posts to pull on her hair. She automatically reached up to pat his nose over her shoulder and realized she had left her kerchief in the straw. She quickly reviewed her list of clothing, hoping that in her haste she hadn't forgotten a more accusatory article, such as an undergarment.

Her mind whirled as the situation spun out of control. Perfect misunderstanding displayed by the Germans condemned her to a private hell, when their only goal was her protection. The language difference wasn't a problem, anyone could take in the view and jump to a half-dozen conclusions each more disastrous for the protagonists than the other. She looked around her for a possible avenue of escape, but the indignant soldiers had effectively surrounded her. She was trapped by people trying to help her, when the only thing she needed was to flee. She was a prisoner, although no questions were asked of her until her parents showed up.

Her father had been shaving and cleaning up before dinner. Flecks of homemade fatty soap were still in evidence near his nose and ears, like bizarre globs of white jewelry, in stark contrast to the raw red of his freshly scraped skin. This red turned pale before developing into an even more livid crimson when his sweeping glance took in the scene before him and his imagination supplied him with details he didn't want.

Heinrich asked to speak. Paulette turned a terrified face to him, silently begging him not to reveal their liaison. She turned away from him and stood up addressing Colonel VonEpffs herself.

"This isn't what you think. I...I was in the barn...and I fell," she babbled, "from the uh... the hayloft, when Hei...er...this soldier came in." She pointed vaguely in the direction of Heinrich, restrained by his friends. "He helped me up and was sending me home when the other officer caught me coming out of the barn." She rambled on about maybe having sprained her wrist.

It was a pathetic untruth, devoid of imagination and conviction, but she hadn't had the time to think up anything more convincing.

Paulette's father looked at her closely, examining her face and asked "Why are you protecting this young man?" He could see her lie.

She wasn't terribly good at it. She couldn't look back at him.

His pain was evident. She was his child, not by her birth, but few were privy to that detail. He considered her to be his daughter and as such, would always be his baby. He correctly guessed rape wasn't exactly what had happened. Paulette wouldn't have jumped to Heinrich's defense, had it been the case. So, in addition to his distress, he was disappointed by her conduct.

As realization dawned amongst the spectators, for the initial shouts had roused quite a few, almost everyone in the yard seemed to be embarrassed as well as ashamed of her, with the exception of Heinrich, who watched each of them in their turn, formulate unspoken judgments against her. Extraordinarily enough, they forgot to be angry at him. His pride couldn't let any young girl and most certainly not the one he loved, bear the consequences of his actions.

Just as the ensuing silence seemed about to burst, Heinrich spoke up, directing his words at Paulette's father.

"Monsieur, I am very sorry to tell you under these circumstances, but I must inform you that I am in love with your daughter."

A collective gasp reverberated around the paddock and returned to lodge in Paulette's heart, as she watched her life being taken possession of as if she were no more than a pawn on a chess board. Heinrich forged ahead, undaunted by the frowns which now graced practically every face, both French and German, differing only in their intensity.

"I should have spoken with you sooner, but I am aware that my cause is a delicate one, given our presence here, and not likely to meet with your approval. My cowardice in not being frank with you has led directly to this situation. Please accept my apologies and be kind enough to consider my case. I wish to marry your daughter as soon as possible. I intend to request permission from my commanding officer as soon as I finish my request to yourself. I have reason to believe that your daughter has some feelings for me as well."

The hush following this eloquent speech was pregnant with surprise, frustration, indignation and finally anger, all of which danced in sequence across Paulette's blotchy face.

As Heinrich noticed her obvious furor, he felt lighthearted, having freed his conscience of its burden. He made a move toward Paulette with a hand partially out-stretched as if to grab her and march off into the sunset with her tucked under his arm, but his gesture was unexpectedly punctuated with a small cry as Paulette's mother sank to the ground in a faint.

This faint, as every real faint does, left Liliane sprawled in an awkward position in the mud. Her skirts were askew; snowy underpants on display. She looked like a broken doll, tossed to the ground in a childish fit of temper. No one had caught her and there was a short instant when all eyes had turned to her, but all movement was paralyzed.

The first to reach her side and crouch down was, unfortunately, Colonel VonEpffs. He attempted to pull her dress down to cover her white pants, but was knocked over by Paulette's father, who thundered as he landed on

Colonel VonEpffs back, pummeling him with his fists, legs and arms flailing.

"You rotten son of a bitch! How dare you touch my wife! This is all your fault! First my daughter and now my wife!"

All hell broke loose in the yard, as the soldiers immediately tried to restrain an out of control father, a screaming daughter and a crazed St Bernard, who barked and growled furiously at anyone who tried to approach Paulette's prone mother, still in a dead faint, face down in the dirt.

So much adrenaline was diffused by the participants in this scene that I can still smell the faint stench of tainted sweat produced by so expended energy. Human perspiration is quite different under duress than it is when produced by hard work. This odor causes animals to become aggressive and Polka and Flynn were displaying its effects admirably.

The dog bit Heinrich and Paulette slapped him.

Paulette kicked Lieutenant Bierdorf, the young man who had caught her and raised the alarm, on the shin and tore at his earlobe after he punched her father who continued to assault the Colonel.

Paulette, as she thus entered the fray, was rewarded with an elbow to the left eye which knocked her to her bottom in the dirt next to Polka and her mother.

Flynn was kicking the paddock bars and rolling his eyes while screaming, as frenzied horses are prone do, causing the other horses to stampede around the paddock and raise more dust and mud with their flying hooves.

All in all it was a scene depicting havoc, worthy of a Delacroix painting.

Incapable of bringing any one of the actors to their senses myself, I watched as a fortuitous small drizzle began to fall, making the ruckus in the mud become sufficiently unpleasant to calm things down a bit and wake Liliane from her faint. She halted the fighting herself, simply by opening her eyes and starting to cry as she remembered the reason she was on the ground in the first place.

"Do you love him? Did you give yourself to him freely?" she asked Paulette.

Paulette could find no further reason to lie about it, as it was common knowledge now anyway.

"Yes, but I couldn't tell you, I'm so sorry!" she blurted while swallowing a sob, "I was so afraid that you and Papa would hate me for getting involved with a soldier…I just couldn't bear to tell you!" It was her turn to cry now, which was about as many crying females as a contingent of soldiers from any country can handle when combined with a drizzling sky.

They stood around looking sheepish and growing damper by the minute.

The only solution was for Marthe to herd them all into the warm, dry kitchen, patch some cuts and chip slivers from the chucks in the icebox for the lumps and bumps while passing around shots of *calvados*. Her German foe-ally, Franz, helped with her efforts at peacemaking by creating an underground safe zone out of the kitchen.

Conversations resumed, the unavoidable topic being the young couple's intentions and prospects. With so many people from both sides getting involved and offering suggestions liberally peppered with warnings, Paulette and Heinrich found themselves to be a sort of communal project in the warmth of the brick lined kitchen.

Towels filled with ice circulated amongst the bruised and battered, while earthenware cups of *calvados* followed close behind. It took a large edge off their fears, calming tempers to the point where a festive atmosphere developed amongst the men, with no small thanks to the alcohol.

Still, a line was drawn just short of the couple in question being allowed to exhibit any sort of affection. Paulette was uncomfortable in their new position of being affianced, and afraid to look at her betrothed, much less display anything other than grief at being found out.

It was an unusual way to celebrate an upcoming wedding, resembling the arranged liaisons of old, when neither of the participants had much say regarding their fate. Feeling once again like a pawn on the chessboard of war, Paulette looked across the room at Heinrich in dismay.

He grinned back at her like an idiot.

CHAPTER 15

October 1991:

On the morning following her aborted escape to Cabourg and disappointing return home, Debra rose early, took a shower and insisted on accompanying Philippe to Patricia's to retrieve the girls and drive them to school. When they knocked on the door in a village some fifteen miles away, Patricia opened with a smile suggesting nothing unusual had taken place. They were invited in and niceties exchanged over coffee while uncomfortable minutes dragged around the face of the clock. Debra was impatient to escape and relieved when she could extract herself from Patricia's company, a daughter in each hand.

The girls were excited about having spent the night in a new place and chattered happily in the car. When Debra walked them up to the schoolyard gate, Susanna lifted both arms to give her a fierce hug and whispered into her ear, "Will you be here to pick us up after school, or will it be Francoise? I like her, but I don't want to go back to that other lady's house, her husband talks mean about you."

"What did he say about me, sweetie?" Debra was suddenly worried. Luckily Philippe had stayed in the car and was oblivious to this exchange.

"He said it was too bad those men didn't do what they were supposed to do to you when they had the chance." The little girl stopped, looking slightly ashamed of something.

"He said that to you? What else did he say?" Debra put her daughter back on her feet, searching the child's face. She was confused about this comment, and tried to fit it into a context which would make sense, but found none.

"I listened at their bedroom door. I know I shouldn't have, but I wanted to run away and come home to you, and they said I couldn't because you weren't there, and probably wouldn't come back!" She grabbed her mother lacing both arms around her thighs, holding tight and burying her face in Debra's jeans.

"I told them you would too come back. And you did!" She smiled up.

Debra crouched down and took Susanna by the shoulders, their faces close and her voice low. "I won't ever leave you. Don't you worry, if I have to go away, I will always come back for you. I just got home late last night is all." She sighed and chewed her lip thoughtfully before questioning the little girl further.

"Do you remember if they said anything else about Mummy?"

The child was distracted by a group of her friends passing by. She turned to watch them, and answered as an afterthought, "I went to listen at their door until they fell asleep, so I could go away and they wouldn't know, but I had to wait for such a long time that Victoria fell asleep and wouldn't wake up, and I didn't want to leave her there alone, so I laid down for a little bit and fell asleep too. But I didn't want to stay! I wanted to come home to you! Say you'll come and get us after school, I want it to be you!" She clutched at Debra in a desperate way.

Debra knew she wouldn't get much more information from a child who was obviously upset at having been made to leave home and spend the night at a stranger's home. She thought quickly about what course of action to take, realizing that for the time being, the safest place for the girls was at school. So, she tried to reassure Susanna, promising her to be there at 4:30 when the children were released for the day.

"What was that all about?" Philippe asked when she returned to the car.

"Oh, nothing. She wanted to have a girlfriend over for a sleep-over this weekend," Debra hoped her voice sounded offhand, surprised at how quickly she had been able to produce the lie.

"Ugh!" he groaned. "You know I don't like all that squealing and running around the house. I hope you said no, the weekends are the only time I can relax." He'd swallowed her lie, enough to act peevish at the prospect of several five year olds disturbing his peace.

"I told her I'd take her to the park on Saturday and that maybe we could take her friend with us. She's fine with that." Debra hooked her seat belt up before continuing. "Just drop me off at the gate and I'll pick up my car. I have to go to Fécamp this morning".

"Well, no. I've had Patricia cancel your appointment, since we didn't know if you were planning on coming home last night or if you were going to be able to go to work. Instead we've got a different one this morning. Together." He glanced across the car at her, a stern look on his face.

Debra turned in her seat to stare at him, trying to guess what was in store. She blinked twice and shook her head before launching her interrogation.

"Since when have you started visiting customers on the road? That's why you made me start working for you. You said you couldn't be away from the office so much."

"I never *made* you start working for me. Don't try to deny you love your job. Anyway, we're not going to see a client. We're going to see a psychologist. For you."

Had he hit her over the head with a blunt object, she couldn't have been more stunned.

"What? Why? I'm perfectly fine! And who gave you the authority to judge my state of mind? I mean...isn't it *normal* for a woman to be angry with her husband when she catches him having sex on his desk with a secretary?" She gaped at him, incredulous, before crossing her arms over her chest. "I won't go in, so you can just turn the car around, right now!"

"Oh yes you will, if I have to drag you inside myself!" he barked.

Seized by a sudden, uncontrollable panic, she tried to open the car door even as they were tooling down the road at a relatively high speed.

"Stop that! You know the car doors can't open when were driving. And just what are you planning to do, throw yourself from the car and commit suicide? Control yourself or we'll go to the emergency room and they'll calm you down with a shot!"

Debra was horrified to feel tears of frustration seep from her eyes. Turning to face the window, the last thing she wanted was to give him the satisfaction of seeing her cry. She was submerged with the helpless feeling of being taken prisoner. She knew she had to calm down or her panic would work against her. Slowly releasing her grip on the door, she clamped both hands onto her knees to keep them from shaking. Deep breathing helped to clear her head and slow her heartbeat.

She would have to be very careful. She glanced at him from the corner of her eye without turning her head, half expecting to see a monster of some sort sitting in the driver's seat. What she saw was the monster who'd been hiding under the skin of the man she married. He was wearing a grim, determined expression but as yet, hadn't grown any horns, or long teeth which would give him away. He looked rather like the nice man she'd thought she was married to, which was more dangerous yet, because it dawned on her that's what others would see too. The monster didn't appear to everyone, just to her.

They drove on in silence.

#

When they walked into the doctor's office, Debra had regained some measure of self control though tainted with indignity at the prospect of having her sanity evaluated by a psychologist. They took a seat in the waiting room, Debra still refusing to look at Philippe. He sat stony-faced, ignoring her as well, their mutual distaste wafting around them like the pungent smoke from a cheap cigar.

After just a few nasty minutes of waiting, the receptionist ushered them into the psychologist's office, happy to remove them from the outer office where they were polluting the atmosphere in spite of the tinkling oriental music piped from speakers hidden behind the potted plants.

The woman who greeted them was someone Debra knew by sight from the gym where she attended aerobics classes once a week. Relief flooded her, then froze solid as the woman smiled at them both cordially, but with no sign of recognition for Debra.

Philippe opened the conversation as he shook the woman's hand.

"I was expecting Doctor Gourdain...is he busy? Or off sick? I specifically made an appointment to see him...not that I'm not pleased to meet *you,*" he added, along with a flirtatious smile. "Had I known there was another doctor we could meet with who's more pleasant to look at than that old rascal Hervé, I would have asked for an appointment directly!" His smiled warmed his eyes as he poured charm all over the desktop.

Debra stared at him as if he were morphing into Mr. Hyde.

'Docteur Lamartine, Sylvie' as her name tag labeled her coat, filled the awkward silence following this display. "Well, I'm sorry to tell you that your...friend?...Doctor Gourdain, has taken a leave of absence. I'm surprised he didn't tell you, if you were set on consulting him...?" The doctor let her sentence trail, leaving space for Philippe to respond; to set the record straight about his knowledge of her absent colleague.

"Er, well you see, it's been quite some time since we've run into each other. Old school chums, you see." He nodded his head with a knowing wink at Doctor Lamartine.

"I see," said the Doctor, "however, you must know that it is extremely rare for a *psychiatrist* to attend to a patient with whom he has a social relationship?" She glanced at Debra before continuing, who choked on hearing the word 'psychiatrist' in lieu of 'psychologist'.

"It's easier for both parties to be objective about any concerns we'd be dealing with. I'm sure you understand this, Monsieur..." here she glanced at the card on her desk, searching for his name, "Monsieur...Dubois" She smiled at him, tilting her head, visibly tossing the ball back to him.

Debra regained her composure and stifled a smile.

Philippe did not. His face was stuck in its last position of dazzling smile, which was wilting in place, trying to stay put and look genuine, and not succeeding.

Debra tried not to laugh out loud as she watched his struggle to stay amiable, piping up with a lighthearted tone of voice, "So, you're not really a marriage counselor, then?"

"No. Although since you're here, it might be a good idea to talk about exactly *why* you're here, no?" She looked at Philippe, gesturing toward the chairs facing her desk. "Let's all have a seat, and we'll get to know one another. Could I get you some coffee, or tea?"

"Tea would be lovely, thank you, Doctor. Philippe? Would you like a coffee?" Debra smiled pleasantly at her enemy, watching him as he took stock of this unexpected set of givens, and feeling distinctly pleased at his discomfort.

"Well, yes, if you're having some Doctor, I'd very much like coffee." He pulled out Debra's chair for her after helping her out of her coat, the perfectly attentive husband facade back in service. Debra remembered with bitter irony, how his impeccable manners had so impressed her when they first met, realizing now that they were automatic and had nothing to do with her at all. Here he was, dragging her to the lions and politely holding her chair for her. It was ludicrous. Still, she sat on the offered chair, nodding to him in thanks, the obligation to keep up appearances keeping her from treating him with the disdain she felt.

Coffee and tea were distributed. The doctor sat at her desk observing them, and after a sip or two, launched the battle.

"So, what is it that brings you here today?" The innocent question sounded rather like an H- bomb to Debra.

Philippe gave a wry smile, shaking his head with a deep sigh. "Well, my wife, Debra..." he moved his raised cup in a sort of salute in Debra's direction, "has been having hallucinations." The proverbial pin dropped quietly to the plush oriental rug.

Debra opened her mouth to protest, then decided shutting up was best. She scrutinized the depths of her tea cup.

Doctor Lamartine waited a moment, then seeing that no other explanation was to follow unless she dug for it, asked, "What makes you think she has hallucinations?"

Philippe hesitated as if ashamed to reveal some terrible skeleton hidden in Debra's closet, and then leaned forward to respond in a quieter, secretive voice.

"She sees things. I've caught her talking to herself or to someone who isn't there and I'm afraid for the welfare of our two small children."

"Could you describe the things she says to the person who isn't there?"

"Well, sometimes she curses in the most vulgar manner, at some very inopportune times. She was using shocking language just the other night, when we...well...when we were...having sexual relations..."

Debra's teeth hit the side of her teacup, rattling the spoon on the saucer.

"I beg your pardon! What did you just say?" she hissed, just above a whisper.

He stayed facing the desk, ignoring Debra's astounded expression. "Yes, and she has been requesting some unusual things as well. Hmmm...how should I say this?...in the bedroom."

With enormous difficulty Debra remained seated and silent, waiting for more bullshit to be deposited on the rapidly growing pile in the middle of the desk.

"Monsieur Dubois, sexual preferences in individuals are hardly matter for psychiatry, that is, as long as neither of you have been physically hurt by your practices. Curiosity regarding the plethora of ...positions, is quite common, especially after a few years of marriage. The need to shake things up a bit is after all, quite normal."

"Well, Doctor, I'm not an adolescent, and not meaning to boast, but I've had my share of experiences throughout the years, and I can affirm to you, that her behavior is not *normale*. She's been making scenes at home and out in public. She picks a fight and then throws herself on me begging for sex, in a *violent* sort of way. I...I just don't know what to do!" He put his right hand to his forehead partially covering his eyes, mimicking distress.

"Hmmm..." said the doctor, "but, you mentioned hallucinations. What makes you say that?" the Doctor asked, swinging the conversation away from the alleged wild sex and back to his initial accusation.

'Two points for the Doctor!' Debra thought, 'and he seems to have met his match, under different circumstances this would be interesting.'

"Well, I've heard her talking to ghosts, at home, or imaginary people. She was asking if we were allowed to use the furniture that had been left in the attic. I was in the hall and stopped just outside the living room door, thinking maybe we had visitors. But I looked in and she was talking to a *chaise*."

"Were there any other incidences you could describe to me, of hallucinations?"

"Yesterday, she came to my office and had a fit, shouting that she had seen me in a compromising position with one of my employees. It was very embarrassing, bad for business and quite inappropriate for employee relations. Nowadays, you can't just go around accusing people of wrongdoing in the workplace and not worry about repercussions. I had to smooth things over with the young woman in question who was threatening to take the matter up with an agent from *L'inspection du Travail!* Very bad for business!"

"I see. And her *hallucination* as you put it was...?"

"Well, obviously I was not having carnal relations in an office full of people!" he snorted in ironic laughter. "And a while ago, she made up some story about burglary and even got the police involved. As to be expected they found nothing, for there was nothing to find. It made us look quite ridiculous to the police." He was on a roll now, babbling. "You know the story of Peter and the Wolf? Well, I'm afraid that if we ever really did need the police for anything, they'd be reluctant to come, knowing my wife is such a liar."

Debra took a deep breath, biting the inside of her lower lip with such indignation that she drew blood. It left a pink mark on the outside of her teacup as she gulped a much needed swallow.

She searched her mind for a motive for this speech, and found none. What was he trying to do here? Why discredit her like this? Did he hope to have her declared insane? If so, why? What would he stand to gain? Surely he wouldn't claim custody of the girls if he were to file for divorce. He hadn't even wanted to have children in the first place. She turned the why question over and over in her head, while watching the Doctor absorb this long line of crap served up by her husband. Anger drowned her self control and she stood abruptly.

"Okay, I've listened to about as much as I can. I'll be outside waiting for you, Philippe. Madame Lamartine, it's been a pleasure meeting you. Goodbye." She grabbed her coat and handbag from the back of the chair as she turned to the door.

The doctor's voice stopped her retreat. "Madame Dubois? Actually, I would like to have a word with you, in private if I may. I've heard your husband's side of the story and I'd like to speak with you. Please give me a few minutes of your time."

Philippe stood, sputtering a bit, "But I want to hear what she has to say for herself!"

"Monsieur Dubois, if we hope to make any progress, I feel that it would be better if your wife speaks in confidence to me. She didn't say a word in front of you, and I can see that she doesn't intend to. If you want my help, you'll have to give us a little privacy. You'll be comfortable in the waiting area just outside. Would you like another cup of coffee in the meantime?" she asked, as she moved to the door and opened it with a clear invitation for Philippe to remove himself from her office.

As the leather embossed door shut firmly on a disgruntled Philippe, the Doctor turned to Debra, "Would you like a glass of water?" she asked, touching Debra's forearm.

"Actually, I think I'd like a shot of whiskey!" she countered, with as much good humor as she could muster.

"Hm!" the Doctor chuckled, "I can see why. How about some water instead? Sounds to me like things aren't going along as you'd like in your marriage, am I right? I didn't want your husband to know that we took aerobics together, so I apologize for ignoring you at first. And it is my job to listen to both sides of every story. So, let's have it, what's going on?" she asked in a familiar manner as she handed Debra her glass of water before returning to her seat.

"Well, good grief! I have no idea what this is all about. I think he's trying to get people to think I'm crazy, but I can't figure out why."

"Tell me what you've noticed lately..." the Doctor offered gently.

Relief flooded her veins as she began to empty her heart, feeling pent-up stress flow from her mouth and free her tensed muscles. The story of the past few years as Philippe's wife tumbled out and Debra found herself realizing as she recounted everything, that little signs of strange things seemed to link together, giving her clues to some sort of plot playing out against her. The Doctor was mostly quiet, taking notes and nodding, though

Page | 240

sometimes asking for clarification. Debra explained the attempted burglary, and then remembered as an afterthought to mention Susanna's comment about what Patricia and her husband were discussing behind closed doors in their home.

When Debra had finished, both women sat quietly for a moment, lost in their thoughts, before the psychiatrist finally broke the silence.

"I have a nasty habit of observing people, even outside of the office. I guess it's a tool of my trade. I have noticed you, and up until today when you walked into my office, I had you pegged as someone who seemed happy and well adjusted. I would never have guessed you were living with someone like your husband." She took a sip of water before continuing, "He's very smart, but I think you already know that. He's probably fooled quite a lot of people in his day, which explains his over confidence. I need to know what your plans are regarding him. Do you want to stay with him and try to maintain a life as his wife?"

"I hadn't thought about it before. I didn't have any idea that he had plans to discredit me like this. I don't know why. It's all so sudden that I'm a bit lost right now. Of course, I'm so angry at him that I would like to never have to look at him again, but he is the father of my children, and I need to think about what's best for them more than anything."

"That's a reasonable response. Your thoughts and the way you express yourself prove to me that you are going through an ordeal which has been sprung on you, and that it's not something of your own making. However, I feel that I must impress upon you the precarious nature of your situation. I'm not certain your husband will accept my help, so I'm going to ask you both to come together for a series of appointments, under a role of marriage counseling. Let's hope he accepts this proposition, although I will present it as ultimately helpful to you. I'm going to give you my mobile number on the back of my card, and I want you to call me whenever you want to." She reached across the desk handing the card to Debra, yet not letting go of it.

"I'm worried about the dynamics between the two of you and I want you to be very careful from now on. Until you know more about his motivations, you could be in some sort of danger."

As she released the card, she took Debra's hand in both of hers, smiling into Debra's eyes while wishing her *bon courage*. "I'll be asking him to come in and speak with me alone now; 'his turn' sort of thing. You understand?"

Debra nodded and opened the padded door.

Philippe rose slowly, looking pointedly at them both before saying in a voice loud enough to be heard by all those present in the waiting room, "Just try and stay calm while you wait, we don't want anymore outbursts, now do we?" It was all she could do to refrain from kicking him in the shin as he walked by her into the office. She dropped her coat and purse onto the chair he'd vacated, slumping exhausted into the one next to it.

Ten minutes later, the door re-opened and Debra was ushered back inside the office once again. Philippe's face wore a smug Doctor Hyde expression. Debra couldn't even guess what else he'd made up during his second chance to have at her, this time behind her back.

True to her word, Doctor Lamartine suggested a series of appointments to them both. Philippe hadn't expected this and started to protest, but thought better of it. "If you think it would be helpful to my wife, then I can't refuse. I'm very worried about her, and I'll do anything to help," came the condescending response.

The appointments were noted on a card which Philippe slipped into the breast pocket of his blazer.

They left and Philippe drove them to his office. Debra wanted to go home directly but he insisted he had a few urgent phone calls to make before driving her to get her car.

They entered the building and she accompanied him through the outer office where she felt several pair of eyes drilling into her. She had to face a pink cheeked Sophie, and while she refused to respond to her timid greeting, neither did she jump up and rip out Sophie's hair. She felt proud of her self-control, although it was drawn from a fear of providing more ammunition to Philippe's arsenal of lies.

As she sat in the hall, Philippe and Sophie entered his office, leaving the door open this time, while she briefed him on his calls. Debra felt like a student sitting outside the principal's office waiting for punishment to be doled out.

It was humiliating, but this time she drew strength from the knowledge that she was on to him and understood that this humiliation was part of his ploy to destabilize her.

She just needed to find out why.

#

After eating lunch together in the stony silence of a truce, Debra begged off work for the afternoon as Philippe rose to return to the office.

Alone at last, she settled in the depths of the chintz covered chair with a cup of tea to mull over the events of the last few days. I embraced her there as the helter skelter thoughts exhausted her and she slipped into a fitful doze.

In this half sleep, images of people Debra didn't know the names of danced beneath her eyelids. She recognized them somehow, though they were dressed in clothing speaking of different times than her own. A common thread seemed to link them to her, as if they'd been family or friends that she'd not seen in many years.

When she woke later, stiff necked from sleeping sitting up, the flitting pictures made no sense at all. She felt as if she'd been watching several period films at once, where the characters and sequences had been edited in a non-cohesive fashion.

I knew she'd communed with their souvenirs, that in her distress the others had tried to whisper of their own to her open heart.

CHAPTER 16

Winter 1943:

Paulette's family decided to keep quiet about the small civil ceremony performed one winter morning in my sitting room. A German Lutheran military chaplain summoned from Rouen officiated.

Paulette's parents would have preferred a Catholic husband, with a Catholic mass, in a Catholic church. Instead they settled on a German Lutheran son-in-law, no church and a not quite legally binding ceremony, as they doubted the validity of a union blessed by a chaplain whose jurisdiction was questionable.

However, their biggest worry was for the safety and happiness of their daughter, neither of which were assured by her choice of groom.

I've seen many unhappy in-laws in my time. So many in fact, that I've come to believe that a daughter's choice rarely, if indeed ever, meets the approval of the parents. If one set of parents appear contented the other set most likely is not. Quite possibly in this case, the other set, as yet still ignorant of their son's newly attained status, would be just as disheartened with their son's decision as Paulette's parents were with hers.

Still in all, I have found that when children do abide by their parents' wishes concerning match-making, the final outcome is rarely one of marital bliss. There appears to be no sure fire recipe for success. However, Paulette was blushing and lovely and Heinrich looked at her with open adoration and pride. Watching their faces during the unpretentious ceremony left me with brimming with hope for their happiness.

They were to come live with me in the big house, occupying one of the servants' rooms on my top level near the attics. This was intended for Paulette's safety, giving her extra protection from any repercussions from the local populace, in the case they discovered she'd married a soldier, which they eventually would. News travels fast in the country, word of mouth being extraordinarily efficient. Especially when gossip was as juicy as this.

Their cohabitation was somewhat lacking in privacy as the adjacent rooms were home to Heinrich's soldier friends, and this proximity was a source of considerable embarrassment to Paulette, knowing the other occupants of the house were well aware of what went on once their bedroom door was closed. In the mornings, she was so self-conscious about facing several pair of knowing eyes that she couldn't bear to have her breakfast in the dining room with Heinrich. On their first day as man and wife, she slipped out the back door to have her morning meal with her parents, where familiar surroundings could provide a reassuring antidote to an unfamiliar situation.

The evening meals were easier, although getting up when it was over and bidding goodnight to the Colonel and the other officers turned out to be quite an ordeal. The first evening, Colonel VonEpffs quickly squelched the initial whoops and catcalls brought on when they rose to take their leave from the wedding supper table. This was partly in sympathy with her parents' misgivings and partly in compassion for Paulette's flaming cheeks.

As time went on, she took to helping clear the table, allowing her to escape to the kitchen. Never did a young woman so appreciate washing dishes after supper, for when finished she could slip up the back staircase to their room unnoticed. Of course no one was duped, but it safeguarded her pride to camouflage the obvious. She was eighteen, and while very mature in some ways, she was also justifiably immature in others. Heinrich was somewhat disconcerted by her behavior, but any misgivings were quickly set aside as he held her in his arms every night.

Dining with the German soldiers every evening put Paulette in the uncomfortable position of being privy to information concerning the interaction between the locals and the army. As the wife of an officer, she was assumed to be sympathetic to their cause and while she didn't specifically wish harm to come to their particular unit, for by now she knew them all, she couldn't give up her innate allegiance to her own country.

It was in this manner she heard of the parachuted pilot who had been taken in by the covert resistance group harboring Michel and Guillaume. No one else at the table knew that her brother and his friend had joined up with the same group, their disappearance having been linked instead to a group of refugees headed south.

When their absence was been discovered and revealed to the Colonel, he had assured Paulette's mother that he had no news of their capture, but that he was certain the boys had headed into the southern *zone franche* and from there perhaps off to foreign climes. Paulette's family was happy to have him believe this and thus relieve some of the pressure of possible discovery.

The pilot in question was Canadian. Apparently he had been receiving help from some locals, having eventually made his way inland after the raid on Dieppe this past August. The Gestapo had been searching for him since then, his body not accounted for amongst the wreckage of his plane. Two other aircraft had been found with their pilot's bodies strapped in place, riddled with bullets. The wreck with an empty cockpit gave rise to a man-hunt which had turned into somewhat of a wild goose chase.

Unfortunately, the Gestapo's methods of retrieving information from people being brutally efficient, someone's testimony under torture had finally led them to Yvetôt and thus much closer to their prey; rather too close to Paulette's little brother for her peace of mind. She was doubly uneasy listening to Colonel VonEpff's casual speech at the dinner table one evening.

"And so, the Gestapo is sending a special contingent of men trained in tracking, to our area," he told them while munching *camembert* on crusty *baguette*. "I'm afraid we'll have to entertain them for an evening or two and replenish their supplies before they continue onward to Yvetôt. They plan to solve the missing pilot problem once and for all." A sip of wine brokered a pause. "I would rather they stay somewhere else, but their path westward from Beauvais leads them straight to our door. In general, they're rather unpleasant fellows, but I don't have a choice in this matter. So, everyone must be prepared to make some room to accommodate them for their hopefully short stay here."

He brandished his fork around the table to point it at each of the officers in turn. "I also expect you to be on your best behavior and to be as helpful to them as possible. We all wish for our present pleasant working conditions to continue, so there must be nothing done to give the commander cause to believe we aren't doing our very best for the Fuhrer."

His warning was of course in German, but there were more and more words Paulette recognized and the ones she heard gave her to understand that the Gestapo were on to the path of the Canadian pilot currently being housed in the same camp as her little brother. She would have to warn her parents.

Sitting in silence, smiling whenever someone spoke to her or looked her way, she never gave away her limited understanding of their conversation. Whenever someone addressed her directly, it was always in French and out of politeness, any banal conversations about the weather or the crops were carried out in French as much as possible, but always the German language reappeared when the content was of more importance. Of course, she aimed her nose toward her plate, pretending to be interested in her food at these times, while acutely listening to pick out familiar words. More and more words became familiar doing just that.

It has always been said that immersion is the best way to learn a language and Paulette had unwittingly immersed herself as deeply as possible, marrying into this foreign language and dining amongst native speakers at least once a day. She feigned ignorance and never once let a German word slip from her mouth, not even the tender words Heinrich taught her during their warm nights together, but listened more closely to the words being spoken around her in their everyday context, absorbing their meaning through her observation of the situations they accompanied, much like a child learns his own native language. Dinner was an excellent opportunity for this particular exercise.

The positive side of this dining arrangement, other than acquiring new language skills, was that Paulette found herself in a position to request new tires for the bicycle. She wisely placed her request the evening following her wedding, while the Colonel was still feeling not a little responsible for this last event and was received with a promise to try and obtain them from the supply stores in Dieppe the very next time he went there.

Paulette looked forward to supplying the new tires to Emile and to everyone else whose bottoms would enjoy the renewed comfort of a well cushioned ride. Maybe it would help them to forgive her for her apparent defection from France to Germany as the wife of an enemy officer, regardless of Heinrich's worth as an individual. She could possibly regain a small measure of esteem.

For in spite of her love for Heinrich, she felt rather guilty, as if she had personally let her compatriots down. Of course, those who knew her well were more worried about the consequences of her love for this man and therefore concerned for her safety, but bore Paulette herself no hard feelings. Instead they considered her to be rather unlucky to have succumbed to a foreigner.

There were however, those who were always quick to criticize. Some of them had sons of an appropriate age and regretted that their own son hadn't been swift enough in plucking Paulette themselves, for her parents were hardworking and well respected. She would have made a nice daughter-in-law and borne many healthy children: French children to be specific. Her choice of a *Boche* over their sons was somewhat of an affront. The clucking of tongues and shaking of disappointed heads stopped just short of whispering words of accusation such as: *traitre, espion* and *putain.* Or at least most of the time.

Paulette was far from guessing that even if she were to supply new bicycle tires for the entire village, it would never stop the gossip or lighten the judgment that some had made against her.

#

The next evening after the warning put on the dinner table by Colonel VonEpffs, concerning the arrival in their midst of the Gestapo, Paulette rummaged through her brain in an attempt to come up with a diplomatic way to question her husband about the conversation she had witnessed in German. She was afraid to ask outright what had been said, understanding that her unique position could be of real assistance in saving her little brother from capture if the Gestapo uncovered the location of the Resistance camp while searching for the Canadian pilot.

I found it quite unfortunate that her loyalties were being put to the test so very soon after her wedding, and watched her struggle with her conscience while brushing her hair, preparing to slip between the sheets next to her husband.

"*Mon amour*, I have to confess something to you," she started out cautiously, once she'd tucked herself under his right arm, laying her cheek against his chest. "I think I understood that the Gestapo will be arriving here to stay, and I'm afraid of them and what they could do to us."

"*Mien Liebling*, you have nothing to be afraid of, especially now that you are my wife. Never would I let anyone harm you, you must be sure of that. Now come here and give me a kiss, I've missed you, and have been thinking about getting you here in my arms all day long."

She turned her face in the direction of his mouth, but the stretch was too far for more than a peck. He shifted their position so that he could access her kisses with ease.

"Before we were married, you were never far from my thoughts and I looked for you around every corner, but now that we're married it's even harder not to think about how you look when I'm making love to you. In fact now that I know what loving you is like, you've become even more of a distraction for me. I'm afraid my work is suffering!" His voice was smiling between his kisses just as much as his lips were. He was a happy man.

Her question was teased away and she wasn't sure how to be insistent enough to obtain an answer, yet not so much as to arouse any uncomfortable suspicions about her concern.

"No honestly Heinrich, I'm scared of them. Just the name: the *Gestapo* makes me shiver. I've heard so many horrible stories of things they've done. Why are they coming *here* of all places? We've been doing exactly what Colonel VonEpffs has asked us to. What business do they have coming here?" The sincerity of her tone brought him up on one elbow to peer down at her before covering her cheeks, eyes and neck with more kisses.

"*Ma douce*, they're not coming here to check up on any of us, nor on any of you. No one has done anything wrong. They're simply stopping over here on their way to somewhere else. You have nothing to worry about." He continued kissing her, causing little noises to escape from her parted lips and taking her far off the track of her previous train of thought.

With a considerable effort at self control, she pushed back slightly into the pillow to better aim her question into his half opened eyes, seeing there a drowsy impatience with the interruption.

"I'm worried about my family and friends. You have to understand my fears. They say that the Gestapo are monsters who have no regard for human life or suffering. I'm scared of them, and I think I should be."

He pushed himself back onto both of his forearms, still hovering about her lips, but conceding the point. "You're right, I'm not happy to say that they are cruel," he punctuated this with a tiny peck at her neck just beneath her right ear. "...and they do use torture as a means of getting what they want. Things have taken a turn for the worse in our plans, and their methods are at least very effective. But, you're with me now and you have nothing to worry about. I promised to take care of you, and I will." He smiled at her again, before bending to resume a far more pleasant task.

She was far from satisfied with the outcome of her questioning, but to press the issue any further might give rise to an argument, so she held her tongue. Instead, she chose to listen to the blood dancing through her veins, singing the song of the coming spring, her body sensitive to the awakening of a season ripe with promise and sensuality.

I looked away with a smile of my own, as her heart and body opened to her lover, setting aside any worries about what a visit from the *Gestapo* would hold in store.

#

The Gestapo showed up a week later, plowing into the yard in their convoy of two sleek black cars and one large truck. Six pair of shiny black boots emerged from the cars, dressing the legs of six immaculately dressed officers, complete with braid, stars, arm bands and caps with equally shiny black brims.

They were frightfully impressive. Even Colonel VonEpffs looked shabby in comparison when offering his greetings, including the unavoidable salute to the

Fuhrer. Several of the newly arrived officers looked at him as if he were a lowly goat herd, before deciding, with a somewhat eloquent moment of hesitation, to respond with just the slightest of acknowledgments, while scanning the house, barn, outbuildings and yard with critical eyes.

I felt scrutinized, dissected and analyzed for my worth and usefulness in their grand plan, with the final verdict of coming up rather short of their expectations. I found their judgment quite unpleasant, as though they would just as gladly reduce my frame to ashes if they hadn't needed a dry roof for the night. Their entire demeanor was offensive to me and my sense of grandeur took a blow.

Unpleasant group of fellows, indeed! I found myself wishing I could control the weather in order to bring about a sudden downpour or better yet, to pelt them with hailstones and mess about with their tidily uniformed selves. Fortunately for them, I could only hope to blow chilly air over their denuded buttocks throughout the night in revenge for their pompousness. I vowed to remember to be unpleasant later on.

The locals stayed out of sight, busy at tasks which didn't involve being in the yard while the Gestapo officers were milling about. It was a wise decision on their part and I saluted someone's good sense.

#

Paulette was at her mother's, in essence, hiding out while mending shirts and darning socks belonging to the soldiers. Both women were rather uneasy and ran to the window at the signal of crunching gravel and purring motors, to take a furtive peek at the new arrivals, hoping to get an idea of what they were in store for.

A better view was to be had from her former bedroom window, and they were observing the greetings from this vantage point when Heinrich was suddenly engulfed in an exuberant embrace by one of the officers. It was difficult to tell if it was a friendly exchange or an assault.

The shocked expression on Heinrich's face didn't dispel the feeling of alarm causing Paulette to gasp in fright. She was torn between fear for herself and a feeling of loyalty urging her to run down and rip her husband from the man's obviously powerful grasp.

The large fellow let out a sonorous booming sort of snort, which apparently corresponded to a manifestation of good humor, as he turned toward his fellow officers with a huge grin while pounding a bit too hard on Heinrich's back. Poor Heinrich took an involuntary hop forward under the impetus of the back slaps, a grim smile on his face while attempting to salute the big fellow's comrades. Not that Heinrich was a little man, but he was dwarfed by the other, as much in size as in presence. The other officer simply took up much more space than Heinrich, in a physical sense and in a commandeering sense as well.

"Who could that possibly be?" Paulette asked her mother. "Heinrich obviously knows him, but doesn't seem very pleased to see him. He's a monster of a man and so loud!"

"I don't like the looks of him either," her mother stated. "But it's probably because of the uniform. He does look huge next to Heinrich! And we know that he's a member of the Gestapo, that's scary enough in itself...and that black hair... and those heavy eyebrows make him look sinister enough even without that strict uniform." She let slip a sigh and a small shudder.

Paulette was astonished to see her mother react so strongly to someone. Usually she was quite close lipped about her impressions of people, always willing to give them a second chance when their initial behavior left something to be desired. She frequently advised her daughter to be careful of making hasty judgments about people, a fault that Paulette couldn't seem to overcome.

"Well, I've got a bad feeling about this. But I don't want to go see Heinrich just yet. I wish I could stay here and have supper with you tonight. I'm not looking forward to being at the table with *them* at all. I wonder how I could get out of it?" she mused, half directing her thoughts to her mother, half directing them down to the yard at Heinrich, who was turning, being escorted into the house tucked under the larger man's arm.

The yard cleared of the officers, but the truck was spewing more men and cargo: camp beds with sleeping rolls, weapons and crates of who knows what. These were being carried into the barn, where apparently the soldiers were to bunk down. There would be no visiting of Flynn for awhile and Paulette felt slightly uneasy about this, as if the horse could somehow be in danger with the Gestapo for roommates.

I listened as new boots trod on my terra cotta tile floors and huge voices resonated from my beams, feeling a little uneasy myself and not very hospitable toward these newcomers. They didn't feel quite right, as if they were casting shadows over my windows from the inside outward.

I found myself not wanting them here. At all.

#

The dinner hour was approaching and Heinrich came in search of Paulette, only to find her tucked into the open fireplace on one of the settle benches flanking each side of the small blaze. It was a pleasant place to work, warm and bright, with the oil lamps hanging from the mantle overhead. The sun had set early. The promise of spring warmed the afternoons but the evenings still held a pronounced chill. He stuck his head in the door, but held his breath until she looked up at him, appreciating the peaceful snapshot of the vision before his eyes.

Firelight warmed the color of her hair, changing it from a light sunny blond to a warmer strawberry tint. Her profile, while she bent over the sock she was mending, wore a slight frown as she worried her upper lip with her bottom teeth.

He must have made a slight noise for she looked up and saw him standing in the doorway. She hesitated a moment, watching his expression before putting down her darning ball and needle, hoping to catch some clue as to his mood, for she was increasingly uneasy about the evening to come. Rising to greet him, she crossed the room and kissed him lightly, trying to hide her discomfort and breaking the spell of silence the evening had cast.

"*Bonsoir mon amour*, how have you spent your day?" she purposefully tossed out the loaded question knowing he would have quite a long story to share with her concerning the large officer who had crushed him in his arms earlier. That is, should he choose to tell her the whole story.

She was apprehensive about what she would discover, never having connected him with an organization as horribly notorious as the *Gestapo*. The possible folly of having married someone with such acquaintances had hit her earlier in the day and left her preoccupied. She'd been fighting back these feelings which she considered disloyal to her husband all afternoon, hoping he could dispel her worries, while carrying certitude buried deep in her heart that he would not.

Her eyes hadn't deceived her. She was afraid that he was one of them, and not only her beloved Heinrich. The two roles seemed irreconcilable. She watched his face as he turned his answer around in his head before letting the news escape from his lips.

Heinrich pulled her into his arms as he said: "I'm going to introduce you to my brother this evening." He waited an instant, thinking she would make some sort of surprised exclamation, then continued as she looked away from his face toward the hearth seat and her mother, understanding the dismay he read there before she could turn away completely, camouflaging it.

"As fate would have it, he is among the other officers who arrived this afternoon. He'll be the first person to welcome you into my family. He's very much looking forward to meeting you and I'm am very proud to show off my lovely wife!" He picked her up and twirled her around, hoping to give an atmosphere of lighthearted delight to the situation.

She couldn't hide her disappointment. It was written in the slump of her shoulders, the way her face was turned away from his, drooping off to the side, and in the way she let her body drag, pushing against his shoulders as he executed his swirl. Her skirt made a pathetic little effort at a swish but he felt her stiffness and set her back on her feet, letting her escape from his embrace, to turn her back to him.

Once again the fire teased the highlights in her hair, but the circumstances had changed so drastically in the last two minutes that he didn't take notice, instead feeling her disquiet at his news, in fact mirroring his own.

He had no desire to see his brother step out of the car. He had thought he was engaged in the North African desert with Rommel, far enough away to be of no nuisance to him.

He should have guessed that Rolf would be inclined to find a role which would give free reign to his mean streak. Heinrich knew too well that Rolf was not to be refused, not to be questioned and especially not to be crossed. The *Gestapo* was perfect for him. Wielding power, intimidating people and crushing them to bend to his will would be exactly the sort of role at which Rolf would excel.

Heinrich remembered with sadness, a scandal which had taken place, proving just how heartless a businessman Rolf could be. He had overheard an argument between Rolf and his father one evening long ago, taking place in the study after dinner. His father's voice resonated in shock as he reprimanded Rolf for having pushed someone too far. Apparently, the poor man had taken his life as the direct result of Rolf calling in some debts, threatening to reveal the problem to the man's family. Rolf's intransigence had pushed him into bankruptcy. Heinrich would never forget Rolf's flippant attitude towad this sorry event, providing yet another reason to escape his presence when he enlisted in the army before the onset of the war.

Now here he was, back in the same house as Heinrich, dominating the very air around him as if breathing in his presence was something he possessed the power to allow one to do, or not, as he wished. To make matters worse, Heinrich was obliged to introduce his young wife to this brute he called brother, while searching for a way to keep her safely away from him as much as possible.

He wished their stay would be short one, effectively adding his wishes to a rapidly accumulating pile of identical wishes, echoing from most of the other hearts beating throughout my domain.

CHAPTER 17

Paulette clamped tight onto Heinrich's arm as they descended the front staircase into the drawing room where the usual soldiers and the new guests were indulging in drinks before dinner.

She had changed into her best frock- a flowered cotton shirtwaist with a short, royal blue matching jacket. A ribbon wound around her chignon matched the blue satin belt at her waist. On her feet were high heeled Mary Jane pumps which had grown a bit tight since she had bought them three years earlier. Discomfort was set aside. Putting her best foot forward to meet a member of her spouse's family did not include going barefoot or wearing her stout, brown leather everyday shoes. She looked her best but she felt awful.

The patent leather Mary Janes mercilessly pinched her toes with each step, dread of the evening to come pinching her heart as well. What a contrast to the last time she'd worn this outfit at her wedding just a few weeks ago, when her heart was filled with excitement, pounding with each step, oblivious to the tightness of her shoes!

Paulette hesitated an instant at the door to the sitting room, hovering one step behind Heinrich before

Colonel VonEpffs leapt from his spot on the settee in front of the fire to greet her, gallantly kissing her hand.

"*Ma chère*, you're looking particularly lovely this evening and I wondered if you would sit across from me at dinner so that my meal will be graced with your beauty." His warm smile was a gift bestowed, proof that he'd correctly guessed her misgivings about the evening she was forced to spend in their presence, as well as an offer to be her ally. Relief clearly registered across her features, bearing a timid smile in its wake.

"*Monsieur*, it will be a pleasure for me to see your friendly face across from my own, as usual." Her answering smile was genuine, her appreciation for this man authentic, for the gentle respect he had shown herself and her family since his arrival here, as much for the kind heart kept tucked away beneath his dress uniform.

This exchange of pleasantries was barely finished when a larger than life voice boomed across the room from the black haired giant leaning nonchalantly against the mantelpiece. He spanned the room with three strides to plant himself in their path, blocking out the Colonel, who was left with no choice but to return to a seat near the fire.

Heinrich stepped forward, making a sweeping gesture toward the impressive fellow, while keeping his right hand at the small of Paulette's back.

"*Ma chèrie*, I would like to introduce you to Major Rodolphe Maximilien VonZeller VI, my brother. Major, may I present my wife, Madame VonZeller?"

Before Paulette had the time to extend her hand to say she was pleased to meet him, his response crashed over her like a shock wave.

"So here she finally is! It's no wonder you've kept her hidden all afternoon! And what a fine looking little thing she is!" He walloped Heinrich on the back once again, causing him to flinch, before bowing from the waist in front of Paulette.

Upon rising he stopped midway, on a level with her face, the Major offered Paulette a leering wink while exclaiming, "My darling girl, you must call me Rolf, and may I use the lovely name your parents bestowed on you as well? Since you're my sister now, I hope my brother wouldn't object to me welcoming you into the family officially!" Taking her by surprise, he punctuated this innocent speech with a hairy, distastefully wet kiss planted on her unsuspecting lips.

Paulette shoved herself off his chest with both arms with such enthusiasm that they were both caught off balance, and only Heinrich's hand at her waist kept her from toppling over backward. Her eyes flashed anger and disgust as she recovered her wits, biting her lips to hold back the scalding insult which good sense warned her she might regret later. He was after all, a Gestapo officer.

Heinrich spoke on her behalf. "Well, actually a handshake would have been more appropriate, Rolf. In France, kisses as greetings are reserved for the cheeks, never on the lips and only then among very close friends. I should think that it will be some time before my wife allows you to get close enough to try that again. Not the best way to make a friend out of your new sister-in-law! Mother would be rather ashamed of you, I should think. Paulette will believe we've been very badly brought up, and that would make both Mother and Father quite upset." His tone of voice was casual, but his expression very stern, a clear warning to his older brother to keep away.

"Now, now, aren't we getting huffy about nothing? I should hope my little sister will forgive me if I've offended her in any way. Isn't that so, my darling?" He winked at her once again before turning back to the fire and a smattering of snickers from the other Gestapo officers, in contrast to the disapproving murmurs emanating from the resident officers. He swaggered as he walked, demonstrating pride in his little joke.

The others frowned, dipping their noses into their wine glasses. Paulette had been adopted by Heinrich's comrades. Her pretty face had been such a welcome addition to their mealtimes that they felt quite protective of her, and none of them appreciated the way this large, loud fellow seemed to display such disrespect.

She correctly perceived Rolf as a person to be avoided at all costs; finally understanding the reasons for her mother's rules about keeping away from the soldiers and not attracting their attention. Unfortunately, she had become the unwilling target of one of the most dangerous men she had ever met and this through no fault of her own. No amount of kerchiefs could protect her from him.

It was unnerving to think that such a man was now part of her family, and she feared he would represent a continual threat. To have a brother as a foe, in lieu of a much needed ally, was a great disappointment, so strong was her sense of family. She realized how correct she had been that evening in the barn when complaining to Heinrich regarding her fears that their families were destined to be enemies. At the time, she hadn't suspected it would be based on her new brother's character, instead of imposed on them by politics beyond their control.

Observing the brothers from across the room as Heinrich poured her a glass of wine from the decanter on the sideboard along the opposite wall, she was struck by their differences. Heinrich was tall and rather slim through the shoulders and hips, with thick curly blond hair and bluish gray eyes. His brother was massive in height as well as in the breadth of his shoulders, his muscular thighs and large calves stuffed into tall boots. Rolf had black curly hair, a large mustache begging to be trimmed and heavy black eyebrows, joined together above an aggressive nose bearing an unusual bend halfway down the bridge.

Evidently, someone or something had once violently imposed itself on Rolf's nose, breaking the smooth line so natural to Heinrich's appendage. Paulette wondered who would have been brave enough to hit Rolf, breaking his nose, and then wondered with some unease, about what damage had been done in return to that foolish soul. She must remember to ask Heinrich about it later on.

I was just as curious as Paulette about the answer, and wished I could have witnessed that particular episode.

The young couple took places on the settee opposite the Colonel, hastily vacated for their use by two of Paulette habitual dinner companions. They made small talk about the upcoming meal, the weather, and the progression of the plowing and spring sowing. It was a short lived respite.

When Marthe came in to announce the eminent arrival of dinner, Paulette rose to assist her, happy to escape the strained atmosphere of the drawing room. Before she could reach the door, Rolf snatched her arm.

"My dear, you must allow me to escort you to your seat, for it seems I have to make up for my lack of good manners. We wouldn't want the little brother to go writing home to Mother about me and complaining I've made an oaf of myself, now would we?" Her elbow was imprisoned by his great paw. The covering of black hairs lent some doubt as to the cleanliness of the skin.

As Paulette was dragged unwillingly away from the others, she realized that he reminded her of a huge black bear: large, furry, and most likely, surprisingly vicious. She attempted, unsuccessfully, to wriggle out from beneath his paw.

'Good choice for a brother-in-law. Sure to keep the family gatherings exciting!' she thought with bitterness. 'What will the rest of the family be like?' she wondered, creating a new worry to nibble away at her lower lip and peace of mind.

For the first time, she addressed him head on, in a polite but courageous voice without much of an accompanying smile. She had come to the hasty conclusion this afternoon when looking out of her bedroom window, that she didn't like this man, brother or not. Never again would she regret instantaneous character judgments.

"Do you have a wife of your own? Heinrich hasn't spoken much about his family and I'm sorry to say I don't remember him mentioning a sister-in-law." She kept her face trained straight ahead when speaking to him. She sensed he had bent his head closer to her shoulder than strictly necessary, and she chose to avoid having her face come into the dangerous proximity of his own.

"No, and I have just recently discovered why I don't. I do believe that the prettiest flower has already been plucked by my rascal of a brother. What pickings are left for me? I may have to stay a bachelor for the rest of my life! I do believe Mother will be very upset with Heinrich for marrying you, since it will keep me from ensuring the continuity of our family line. If I don't marry and produce an heir, who will inherit the family heap of stones?"

I was shocked at his referring to his family seat as a heap of stones, and I could tell Paulette didn't care for being categorized as anything pluck-able. I grumbled and shifted, letting the wind moan through the eaves in protest. How distasteful I found this large fellow! If I were his family 'heap of stones', I believe I would have done my best to frighten him as a child, at least enough to make him believe in ghosts. I decided to provoke a nightmare or two while he was here, out of solidarity toward his most certainly noble home. What a dreadful man!

He heard my protestations, and added "Do you hear that? I think this house must be even noisier than our own! Another example of faulty French architecture! Even our ancient pile of rubble doesn't shift as much as this one does!" The paw on her arm caressed the skin on her wrist. He looked at it with interest as he continued his architectural musings.

"I've been thinking I might have our old manor house demolished and replace it with something much more modern, something pleasant to live in. These huge old places are sinister, not to mention drafty. What do you think, my dear: a new, brightly lit home with lots of windows and modern features, or crumbling old houses where everyone spends their nights shivering in the drafts?"

Paulette's sincere reply was immediate. "Personally, I prefer knowing that a house has been lived in before me, as though I'm sharing something with those who came before. It's a bit like shoes actually. Some are beautiful, but how nice it feels to take them off and put on old ones that are lived in and comfortable. The others are just for show, and you're happy to put them away. My parents live in a little cottage that my grandparents lived in and theirs before them. It's almost like they watch over me in my sleep and protect me from harm. I have sweet dreams there."

She glared at the hairy paw and wriggled her wrist away from his touch which she was finding increasingly unpleasant. His hairy fingers had rough, broken nails. She tried to concentrate on her answer, ignoring the insistent stroking of the vein running from her wrist up under the edge of her sleeve. The nasty forefinger slid underneath the hem, making her feel undressed. Jerking her arm from his grasp as she reached her chair, Paulette firmly planted her hands on the back of it.

She continued with her commentary, free from his bothersome touch. "Since we've been married, Heinrich and I have been sharing a room in this house and it's just the same here. I've played in the kitchens and the garden since I was a child and even if I wasn't sleeping in the big house before, I feel like I'm part of this place because my ancestors have always been a part of it."

I purred with pleasure at her response. He laughed, and I could tell it was in mockery.

Frowning at his reaction but feeling a bit braver, she changed the subject as he pulled out her chair, placing himself in the spot next to her own, on her right hand side, the chair usually occupied by her husband. "Heinrich told me you don't have any sisters, it must be lonely for your mother with both of her sons gone off to war. Do you write to her often?"

He let out a large guffaw before spreading his hand wide open, covering the width of her empty plate. "My sweet, does this hand look like it would do well holding a fountain pen? Heinrich is the one who's good at words and writing letters. I should think he's probably written *you* some love letters at least: probably swayed your poetic little heart with flowery phrases and declarations of undying devotion. Or did he excite you with promises of what he would do to you on your wedding night?" The leer was back in place as he turned in front of her to aim his words directly into her eyes, watching for her reaction.

Paulette flushed with surprise at his rudeness and pushed back her chair in an attempt to escape just as Heinrich placed his hand on the back of it while sitting down at her left. "What's wrong, *ma chérie*? You look rather flushed." His concern for her took into account the smug look on Rolf's face, who was pouring himself a brimming glassful of red wine, slopping bloody spots on the snowy table linen.

"I'm afraid I don't feel well. I'm not certain I'll be able to stay at the table." Her eyes begged him to relieve her of the obligation to stay sitting next to such an awful person.

Heinrich bent and whispered, "I know he's bothering you, but if you run from him now, he'll think you're a coward and won't ever leave you alone. I know you've got more spirit than that. Just answer back when he says something to displease you and he'll soon get the message that you're not a timid sheep to be toyed with. I'll be right here at your side, don't be afraid."

"At least let me get up and help with the serving, I feel so uncomfortable having others wait on me!" she begged, hoping to get away from Rolf, even for a few short minutes.

"Please believe me; you're safer sitting down than serving him directly. Just stay put this once, for me? The cook will forgive you, if you explain to her later."

She fidgeted in her chair, trying in vain to reconcile herself to an evening of small talk and eating dinner seated next to a bear, and a crude one at that.

Turning her upper body slightly away from him, she leaned left, toward her safe haven.

Marthe and Franz had outdone themselves on orders of the Colonel, who was hoping to ingratiate himself with the officers outranking him. Paulette realized how uncomfortable the situation was for the Colonel, his choice of elaborate menu proof of his disquiet. How ironic that their contingent of the occupying army was in turn being occupied by another more powerful contingent!

She didn't feel any sort of satisfaction about their discomfort, just pity that even amongst themselves, there was a struggle for power and affluence. She found herself wondering exactly what their world would be like if this war went on forever. Will the occupying forces come to them in waves, each more heartless than the last? How could there be a return to normality if the nation of people who intended to impose themselves on France and the rest of Europe couldn't agree on a line of conduct amongst themselves? Only chaos and disaster can come of it and the highest price to be paid will certainly be shouldered by the conquered: herself, her family and the rest of her countrymen.

The meal dragged on and the conversation changed from French to German and back again, depending on the subject matter. She listened intently when a change in language took place, knowing that any clues regarding plans to hunt down the Canadian pilot would have a direct link to her brother's resistance camp. There was some talk of the pilot, but she couldn't be sure what was said. She picked out names of towns mentioned and all of them were very close to Yvetôt, from where the last news of her brother had been delivered via the channels of the black market.

There was a bit of excitement around the table when Rolf mentioned something about a new project to be set up across Normandy, something involving missiles or planes and England. Her frustration was overwhelming at not being able to better understand what was being said, especially because it seemed as though Rolf was to be involved and it would take place in the vicinity.

When the conversation was in French for her benefit, she let her mind wander, observing the new officers tucking in to their dinner with gusto, trying to evaluate their positions in respect to Rolf. She didn't need to pay much attention when they were speaking French, since she knew nothing of any importance would be said.

During a slight lull in the conversation, Rolf chose to embarrass her once again in front of the group.

"So, Paulette, tell me, do you have a sister? I would like to meet her if so, but only if she is as delectable as you are. Heinrich, just think how furious Father would be if I came home married to a little French peasant girl, just like you are. What would happen to the illustrious line of VonZellers if we both chose to mix in a healthy dose of poverty with our pure blue blood? I do believe the old man would finally have an attack and die. Just might be the thing to do after all! What do you think?"

Rolf was leaning past Paulette, in order to better get a view of Heinrich's face when she pushed back her chair with some violence, slamming her elbow into Rolf's chest as she went.

Standing, she scanned their surprised faces, all eyes watching her obvious fury, before turning to Heinrich. The officers stood, as was customary when a lady rose from the table, but they weren't sure what to expect from this furious young woman. They waited patiently, in awkward silence. Paulette drew a deep breath, attempting to calm her angrily pounding heart, before speaking to her husband. Her words poured forth on the flow of expelled breath.

"Heinrich, I am very sorry and I do hope you'll forgive my bad manners, but I must say that I'm very glad to have met your brother, if only to reassure myself that you are indeed a wonderful man. I'm very happy to have married you, especially now that I've had an evening to compare you to your brother, who, in my opinion is about as different from you as possible and seems to me to possess not even one of the qualities which make you such a gentleman." She turned and gave a curt nod to the others seated around the table.

"*Messieurs*, please excuse me from dessert, I suddenly feel incapable of swallowing another bite. Colonel VonEpffs, please accept my thanks for another delicious meal. May I bid you a good night?"

The Colonel stood still as she was addressing him, smiling a sad little smile while returning her good night wishes. As she turned from him, she bestowed a lengthy, furious glower at Rolf, silently daring him to open his mouth once again.

Instead of showing even the smallest measure of shame at having insulted herself and her family, he grinned and clapped his hands in applause.

"Well done, little sister! I'm quite happy to have you think that I'm a cad, for I've always found that attractive women grow quickly bored with a man who has good manners, they much prefer the more exciting company of a scoundrel: which means there is hope for me after all! I will be most happy to prove my theory to you in time! *Bonne nuit, ma belle!*" He raised his glass of wine to her in a mocking salute.

Paulette turned a dismayed face toward Heinrich before kissing him on the cheek, and whispering to him: "I'll go help Marthe clean up in the kitchen if you'll please excuse me. I'm very sorry, but I can't stay here a moment longer." She turned on her heel and stalked off, snatching an empty serving platter from the sideboard as she went.

Behind her as she left the room, Heinrich's raised voice resonated, obviously berating his brother's odious behavior in their native language, once again proving that sometimes one didn't need to be fluent to understand what was being said.

#

Paulette descended the stairs to the kitchen where Marthe was busy serving up the fruit tart for dessert.

"I see you managed to escape in one piece, *ma petite*! Not an easy thing to have to dine in the midst of lions, is it?" Marthe remarked looking at Paulette's fallen face. "And you got yourself all dressed up for the occasion as well, I see. Well...no matter, I can always use your help. First, cover that pretty frock with an apron," she said pointing to the hooks behind the door.

As Paulette tied the strings behind her back, her head drooped on her chest, listening to the cook, while observing the flagstones paving the kitchen floor. She let out an eloquent sigh, punctuating Marthe's attempts to brighten her view of the future.

Marthe waved the pie server upward at the ceiling, adding: "Now don't worry yourself about those men, Franz has told me they'll only be staying here for a day or so, and then you can forget all about them. They'll soon drive off to bother someone else. You've got yourself a nice one, not at all like those others. You'll see, it'll all work itself out in the end. Now fetch me the pot of cream in the icebox and we'll finish this up."

As always, busy hands kept Paulette from wasting too much time letting her thoughts chew away at her. The work calmed her tormented heart and cooled her flaming cheeks. By the time the meal was over and the kitchen returned to normal, all surfaces scrubbed down and the copper pots and pans hung shining on their hooks above the big table, Paulette was tired enough to climb the back stairs to the third floor and to bed.

Each step pinched her toes and she looked forward to prying the Mary Janes off of her aching feet and settling under Heinrich's right arm. When she reached their room, it was disappointingly empty. Sitting on the bed, she removed the painfully attractive shoes and wiggled her toes against the cool floorboards. It wasn't enough.

She needed comfort from her husband, to hear him assure her that everything would be alright, and that Rolf was indeed a nasty fellow and that she was justified in disliking him, even if he was her husband's brother, as well as a load of other things about which her young heart needed reassuring. She was no longer tired; certain that sleep would elude her until she had spoken with Heinrich.

She paced the room for a few minutes before curiosity got the best of her and she went in search of Heinrich. The tiles on the steps of the main staircase felt wonderfully cold and soothing to her throbbing toes. She stood on the last step, enjoying refreshing relief under her feet, while listening for voices to follow in hopes of coming upon Heinrich.

Turning toward the west side of the house, she approached the door to the library where she spied a gleam of light stealing beneath the closed door. She tiptoed to put her ear to the oak, listening for Heinrich's voice, and attempting to identify the others in the room before opening it.

The voices were low, the hushed conversation shared by at least four Germans, still Paulette wasn't certain that Heinrich was one of them. She could hear from the urgency of the tone of pronunciation, that this wasn't a banal discussion of the spring planting. Curiosity piqued, she hesitated before placing her hand on the door handle, turning it as quietly as possible, edging the door open just a crack.

She peeked through the slit with one eye and saw Colonel VonEpffs, Bierdorpf, and the two other men who used to be Heinrich's roommates. She pulled her eye back from the crack and stuck her ear close as they seemed to be expressing serious concerns regarding Rolf and the project he had mentioned at dinner involving some sort of air base to be set up nearby.

Her eves-dropping was interrupted when shouting erupted in the yard, followed by screaming. Paulette jumped back from the door, melting into shadows farther down the hall. As the library emptied, she sped soundlessly on bare feet, down the back staircase tucked beneath the main stairway and into the kitchen.

She tore across the half darkened room toward the servants' stairs leading back up from the kitchen to the upper floors. She knew she couldn't afford to get caught listening at closed doors. After running up the smaller twisted staircase to her room, she stuffed her feet into her worn leather everyday shoes, before clattering down the main stairs; this time officially in search of her husband, wondering what the ruckus outside was about.

#

The human inhabitants of my walls spewed into the yard, some wisely carrying lanterns to light the midnight gloom. The remaining shadows did little to conceal the horrific scene of a young woman in shredded clothing, lying on the gravel in a pool of dark liquid.

The workers' cottages emptied simultaneously and the two groups of people milling about on opposite sides of the scene resembled the opposing teams of a soccer match waiting for play to recommence. They held their hands on their hips, shaking their heads as if in criticism over a bad call from the referee.

Paulette pushed through the crowd of uniforms on her side of the fray to get a better look. Colonel VonEpffs knelt on the ground next to Guillaume and Manon's parents. Bare legs protruded from the torn skirt, one of them swathed with blood. They belonged to Manon.

Paulette let out a gasp of recognition as she collapsed next to the Colonel. Heinrich caught up to her just the gravel bit into her knees. He steadied her with a firm grip on the shoulder. The sight was a gruesome one.

Manon's eyes were open. A vivid lump above her left eye reflected the flickering lantern light. Her teeth chattered as her hands clutched frantically at her mother's blouse. A large gash dribbled above her lip, but most of the blood seemed to be coming from beneath her skirt. The older woman held her daughter's upper body across her knees, rocking her to and fro, while murmuring little endearments, the words diluted by silent tears coursing down her cheeks.

There was absolute confusion as to what had happened. No witnesses had seen anything, or else they had chosen to stay quiet about it. Manon was incapable of coherent speech. Emile explained in desperate circles that he had come upon her like this when he called for Polka who had failed to return to her bed by his fire. He'd found the dog whining and standing over top of the poor girl lying in the stones. There was no question of the dog being responsible for Manon's current state. Dog bites had not produced this condition.

They gently carried Manon off to put her in bed at her parents' home, while Emile, accompanied by two soldiers was dispatched for help from Doctor Hervieux in Bacqueville.

Paulette and her mother stayed with the anguished parents, the women shutting themselves in the bedroom with basins of warm water and clean toweling, before removing what was left of the young girl's clothing in an effort to determine the extent of her injuries. She seemed to have lost rather a lot of blood from an internal injury. Her arms showed early signs of bruising, welts rising around the wrists. There seemed to be no doubt that her injuries were the result of an attack by someone, or several people.

"Who could have done this to my baby? Why would anyone want to hurt a child?" Her mother intoned this pair of questions over and over in a pathetic litany. No one provided an answer. They tended Manon as best they could and waited for the doctor to come.

Outside, questions were asked, Manon's father holding the Germans to blame and not swaying from his position.

The problem was: how did she end up in the yard? There was no trail of blood coming from any direction, leading Colonel VonEpffs to deduce that she had simply been dumped there when someone had finished with her. He was reasonably certain the doctor would indicate she had been raped in a horrific fashion and in his heart, he was also certain it wasn't the work of the soldiers under his command.

He approached Rolf, who was leaning on a fence post smoking with some of his comrades, his position nonchalant as if watching a circus side show.

"Major, may I have a private word with you?" They moved a few paces away from the other men, before the Colonel continued, "I would appreciate it if you would authorize me to interrogate your men. I'm afraid that otherwise we'll never get to the bottom of this and it could cause great unrest among the locals if we don't do our best to discover the identity of the author of this heinous crime."

Rolf tilted his head in speculation, looking at the Colonel amused interest. "If you insist, Colonel, be my guest, but I have to say that one less French whore, here or there, doesn't really have any effect on our purpose here. You seem to forget we're in the middle of a war." He flicked the ashes from his cigarette to dust the Colonel's boots, before taking a long draw from it.

Laying an arm along the Colonel's shoulder with a grip on the back of his collar, he spoke quietly. "These people are peasants and if you fear repercussions from them, then I'd guess you don't have control over the situation that you've been put in charge of. I'd be very careful, Colonel, about what you report and who you implicate. Your position as commander of this garrison could very easily be put in question." Releasing the collar of the Colonel's jacket, he stepped in front of him, brushing away imaginary lint from the lapels. He stopped to fix his gaze on the Colonel's stricken face, smiled, adding as an afterthought, "but by all means, question away!" He dropped the butt of his spent cigarette to the ground, crushing it with his boot heel.

The Colonel was struck dumb. He froze, evaluating the warning, before returning to Heinrich and Lieutenant Bierdorf. They organized a rapid interrogation of those present, in hopes of coming up with a plausible explanation, yet knowing from the Major's attitude that they would find none. It was clear the Gestapo officers were responsible and that the unfortunate girl must have been in the wrong place at the wrong time. Whether she went looking for trouble or not was irrelevant.

Doctor Hervieux arrived in time to give a calming draught to Manon's mother and put her to bed. The poor woman had held her daughter as Manon bled to death. The girl never regained control over her shaking incoherency to say who had hurt her. A young life slipped away in a stain blooming across the bed linens.

Paulette, her mother, Marthe and several other women stayed to clean up the vile mess. Manon was washed, dressed in her best frock and laid on a blanket placed on the kitchen table of the cottage.

Emile dragged the ruined mattress out to the brush pile and immediately set it afire.

The doctor distributed sleeping powders to Manon's mother and to anyone else too shocked by this event to stay calm before returning to Bacqueville, escorted by the two soldiers who had gone to fetch him.

Manon's father was plied with shots of *calvados* until his furor was obliterated by extreme drunkenness resulting in a vacuous stupor.

Their friends organized themselves into groups who would watch over the parents and keep the dead girl company in the kitchen until she could be buried in the churchyard.

Dawn was breaking as my group of exhausted, heart-broken, and bitterly angry inhabitants fell into their beds, many of them crying themselves to sleep, measuring the brutality which had arrived in the yard, dressed in black boots.

Colonel VonEpffs was in the library, doing his best to drink himself to oblivion. His position was in jeopardy. He would lose the goodwill of his French charges if nothing was done, no justice meted out. He would lose his position of commanding officer in a heartbeat if he accused Rolf of involvement in the murder of a local girl. His superiors would allow him no leeway to judge the Gestapo. He found himself in the frustrating position of having his hands tied while his moral code was trampled by one man. He watched the fire burn low in the grate, inspecting the reflection of the glowing embers in the amber liquid in his glass, and finding no answer there.

I hoped the perpetrators and the accomplices who accepted their behavior, would forever burn in hell.

CHAPTER 18

March 1943:

The following morning the Gestapo left.

As the remnants of vehicle exhaust dissipated into the clear morning air, the putrid smell of arrogant men lingered: men who were immune to the repercussions of their actions, no matter how dreadful the tally of their deeds. The devil had shown up amongst us and none could claim indifference. Fire and brimstone scorched our nostrils as a glimpse of hell branded itself into terrified brains. The nationality of the victims of this vision was mixed.

The Gestapo turned right on the road leading to Yvetôt in hopes of capturing the missing Canadian pilot, whose whereabouts were whispered by those hoping to win some sort of favor from the occupying forces.

To be fair, the majority of this information was doused with stale sweat, tears and blood. These revelations were pathetic as well as useless. Requests for compassion once the details were retrieved were almost never honored. For such impassive brutality, happily incomprehensible to most mortals, was rarely accompanied by any sense of obligation to bargains struck. It was an easy thing: convenient for the men wearing the Gestapo insignia to leave a trail of destruction in their wake. It served as a visual warning to all.

We had expected to breathe a sigh of relief when they disappeared down the drive and out of sight, but no relief was to be had. A corpse lie on the kitchen table of Manon's cottage. Hearts were overrun with grief and accusations weighed heavily upon the Colonel, who had no antidote that could begin to ease the strain.

No one believed he was to blame, but the locals couldn't absolve him of some measure of responsibility. His uniform shouted his affiliation with those who had done so much damage.

He tortured himself with his cowardice, for his hesitation in reporting the event to the commander in Dieppe. Then as time passed, he found himself incapable of doing so, justifying his inaction with the understanding that we were better off if he stayed in command of the farm, fearing what a replacement might be like should he be removed from his post. Imbibing his guilt with *calvados*, he managed to convince the golden liquid in his glass that he was doing the right thing by not reporting Rolf to the *Kreiskommandateur*. Fear and disgust had soured relationships between the Germans and the French, the French and the French and the

Germans with the Germans. There seemed to be no hope of erasing the image of Manon lying crumpled in the drive, no diluting the picture she had left stamped in every soul.

Paulette and Heinrich endured the strain. She and others, held his brother accountable for Manon's death. During the two days during which Manon was laid out in her cottage—waiting for a funeral to be hastily organized by the village priest, *Père Lemarchand*—Paulette spent her time with Manon's mother, comforting her, helping about the cottage, cleaning and cooking for the family, hoping to ease some of their pain by shouldering everyday concerns. The parents were left free to weep, mourning their loss.

By spending her time away from her husband, Paulette very efficiently avoided discussing the role her brother-in-law played in this disaster.

I observed Heinrich, who was horrified to think Rolf could have had a hand in this brutality. He knew that Rolf, at his very best had likely turned a blind eye to the actions of others. Having never displayed a tendency to support the weak and fragile, Rolf wouldn't step out of character to bring any of his men to call over this event. He would find it easier to ignore the entire affair.

Heinrich prayed this was the case, the worst option being the unbearable one. Rolf might have played a first-hand role in this tragedy. Heinrich tried not to consider it, hiding his head in the sand each time the accusation reappeared above his left ear, taunting his tortured conscience.

Heinrich would have preferred to explain his feelings about his brother to Paulette, in hopes of dissolving the bubble of discomfort hovering between them. But, he didn't know how to go about it. His shame at admitting Rolf capable of such horror was countered by a certain honorable sense of family loyalty. He'd witnessed the close knit bond in Paulette's family and felt as if he should stand behind his brother in all circumstances. He regretted not being able to do so. Cringing at the thought of Paulette equating him to his brother, his greatest fear was that she might doubt his integrity because she believed his brother capable of the worst.

At night, I saw his sadness at her decision to turn away to sleep as soon as her head hit the pillow. Attempting to dissolve the silence between them, he spooned his body to her backside, repressing as much as possible the desire that her warm shape provoked in him. He knew she could feel his unsolicited reaction to her, but since she took no outward notice, he waited patiently, hoping that sooner, rather than later, her own desire would get the better of her and the stalemate might end.

A mountain of unfortunate information to assimilate loomed between them. There could be no arguing that his brother was an arrogant, distasteful fellow, who had treated her in an unpleasant fashion. Secondly, this same brother could possibly have been implicated in the rape and murder of one of her family friends and his rank allowed him to saunter off without being held accountable. Thirdly, these events brought to the forefront a fact that they had been doing their best to ignore; the couple belonged to opposing camps, at least until peace was had. Hope for that peace was infinitely more fragile today than before Manon's murder.

I listened for two nights, as he tried to count sheep, to say the alphabet backwards, anything to get some rest. I watched as he examined the cracks in the ceiling above their bed. He was lonely holding his wife in his arms, feeling cut-off from her even while their bodies remained tense, his front glued to her backside.

I melted sorrow over the pair of unhappy lovers. This loneliness was far more distressing than the more basic kind, the sort caused by the physical separation of two people in love. I wished I could help them find each other once again, but I knew Paulette's heart was a good one. I hoped she could remember how to use it, to excuse an association for which Heinrich carried no responsibility. She must learn that one couldn't choose one's family, but that she could choose to return his love. Or not.

#

The morning of the funeral assembled the French in the yard, dressed in dark clothing and ready to follow the fragrant apple wood coffin, hastily manufactured by two of the men who worked alongside Manon's father in the fields. The priest, accompanied by choirboys carrying incense loaded balls swinging from chains, preceded the coffin in a flat wagon drawn by Maurice. Manon's parents and little sister followed behind. The workers and their families fell in step.

Colonel VonEpffs and the soldiers under his command, dressed in their cleanest uniforms followed the procession to the gate, but out of respect stopped there, preferring to avoid potential conflict by accompanying the body to the churchyard. Instead, they busied themselves until the French returned from the ceremony, helping to lay out planks on trestles: improvised tables for the post burial meal prepared by Marthe and Franz. The weather was pleasant and the wake would take place outside. Heinrich stayed behind, not certain that Paulette wanted him present at her side and rather afraid to ask.

Two hours later, the group pushed open my gate under a warm noonday sun, unusual for the early spring, but welcome; the family's cottage couldn't accommodate so many people. The neighboring villagers had swollen the ranks of mourners, eager to participate. Manon's virtues were touted and exaggerated by many in hopes of being invited back to eat. A good meal was hard to come by for most of them. Marthe and Franz had been given free rein to feed the masses, a product of Colonel VonEpffs' guilty conscience.

I mused at how often the deceased are posthumously clothed with qualities that during their lifetimes, they didn't have the good fortune to possess. Although Manon had spent her young life as a selfish, manipulative child, she was suddenly blessed with a pure, innocent heart and a generous nature. No matter all this, because as a victim of viciousness, she deserved these bowers of praise. Sadly, they could in no way make up for the missing balance of her life.

The afternoon wore on and when the hard cider was replaced by *calvados*, the proceedings took on the allure of a party. Numerous toasts were made in memory of the defunct and contented belching resonated amongst the assembly. The sun dropping from the sky brought the party to a cool closing. As the uninvited tottered off down the road to their hamlets, the soldiers and the

French dismantled the trestles side by side, before turning in to their respective quarters for an early evening.

With a sigh of weariness of soul as much as of fatigue, Paulette untied her apron strings after giving a last glance around the now spotless kitchen. She climbed the stairs to the dining room, unable to avoid taking her place at her husband's side. Cold leftovers had been laid out for an evening meal should anyone feel the need, although very little eating was done and most of it was once again in carried out respectful silence.

The soldiers were wary of getting in Paulette's way, fearing her reaction to their presence. Aware that she was testing her allegiances, each hoped to do nothing to aggravate her dilemma. Instead, they were constantly leaping up to help her in whatever way they could. She found this exasperating and eventually lashed out at Lieutenant Bierdorf who knocked his head against her own as they simultaneously bent to retrieve a fallen napkin. "Will you *please* get out of my way?" Her voice exploded a bit louder than she'd intended, the pitch higher than usual and sounding rather frenzied. Frozen in a crouched position, Bierdorf looked up, a horrified expression on his face, worthy of a little boy who had disappointed his beloved mother by farting at the table or some other shameful deed.

Paulette had intended to berate him further, but when she saw the look on his face, she burst out laughing instead. The sight of this adult man in uniform kneeling at her nineteen year old feet wearing such an expression of remorse, struck her as ludicrous and her natural sense of humor won out.

The rest of the men in the room paused in shocked silence at first, fearing she had at long last lost control of her emotions and veered off into hysterics. Bierdorf hesitated, then chuckled in response. The rest of the room breathed a sigh of relief, as the balloon of tension emptied itself of stale air. The fire in my grate cackled merrily in agreement with the changed atmosphere and a welcome relaxation of tensed muscles. Harmony had been reclaimed.

Heinrich let hopes of a warmer reception in bed this night drench his heart. He volunteered to help carry the empty plates down into the kitchen for a last bit of washing up. When they finished, he reached around her back to untie her apron strings, letting the checked cloth slip to the floor as he kissed her instead of aiming for the peg behind the door. She didn't push him away and her timid response was enough.

The apron was left in a crumple as he lifted her in his arms and carried her up three flights of stairs, passing Bierdorf and his roommate on the way. They executed a mock salute and removed themselves from Heinrich's path, causing Paulette to blush prettily and bury her face in Heinrich's shoulder. He picked up his pace and kicked open their bedroom door in no time at all.

There were happier vibrations spreading through my rooms this evening, a moment's respite amid the choppy waves of uncertainty.

#

Michel and Guillaume crept through the woods near St Catherine's spring, a week later, aiming for home. They had received word of Manon's death and left in a fury, disregarding their commander's admonitions to stay put in Yvetôt. Attempting to avoid the *Geheimefeldpolizei* patrol they heard marching toward them, they had sidestepped into the woods before reaching the farm. They hid, crouched in the little stone hut covering the spring—up to their bottoms in freezing water—as the patrol took the path cutting through the clearing. It was dark and the earlier warmth from the sunshine had disappeared with the setting sun. The clear sky made the temperature plummet and the boys' legs numbed as they waited for a last soldier in the patrol to finish urinating and packed up his pants before catching up with the others who hadn't paused in their march.

When there was no sound other than gurgling water as it escaped over the rocky stream bed and out into the deeper forest, they cautiously crawled out from the hut, crossing themselves in thanks to Catherine for her protection. A measure of lightheartedness at having once again escaped capture took over their young hearts.

"That was a close call! Any longer in there and my nuts would have fallen off, frozen for good!" whispered Guillaume while they took off their trousers to wring the worst of the water from them before struggling back into the sodden material.

"Hmmph, your nuts are just for show anyway, you'll never get close enough to a girl to use them, seeing as how you're so ugly," bantered Michel, ducking to avoid the light handed punch, which he knew would be offered in return.

The numbness of their legs made dressing more than difficult, putting on wet trousers being a tricky business in the best of times. This was not the best of times. Guillaume's leg was permanently crooked, after being shot in the knee, making him less than graceful. Any unusual noise could bring the patrol back to investigate.

"We'll both be better off if you shut up and stop talking about my nuts, which happen to be very attractive ones, in comparison to your own little grapes! Now let's get home in one piece, before the Krauts get back here."

Walking through the woods in wet boots added a squishing noise to the slap of wet material against their legs. The only way to avoid this noisy concerto was to do an unusual tiptoeing hop with their knees spread far enough apart to keep the cloth from slapping together and their heels from hitting the soaked insoles of their boots.

Any spectator would have wondered if they weren't dancing through hot coals, instead of trying to slip soundlessly toward home. The kilometer separating them from us would seem much longer under these conditions. Still, having traveled this far, the familiar area already felt like home.

#

When the boys reached the fence separating the back of Guillaume's cottage from the road, Polka was there waiting, tail wagging like a flag, for she had heard their approach a good five minutes beforehand. Lucky for them she wasn't much of a barker and she recognized these boys as her own, having spent many an hour playing with them when they were younger.

"There's a good girl!" Michel whispered, ruffling her fur in welcome.

"You know who your masters are, don't you, girl? No speaking German for you!" Guillaume added before turning back to Michel, "You're going to have to help me climb this apple tree, so I can reach the window upstairs, my damned knee won't be of much help here. Give a hand, will you?"

Guillaume heaved himself onto the lowest branch as best he could using only the one leg. Michel favored his left shoulder, shoving on Guillaume's bottom to help push him onto the next branch up, before swinging himself up using his legs for leverage against the tree trunk.

The window into Guillaume's bedroom had a broken latch, and memories of past nocturnal escapades came in handy. Coming and going up the apple tree, conveniently growing near the window was second nature to the boys. It was the perfect avenue to slip in quietly and make their presence known to the family without causing a stir which might alert the Germans in the manor house.

Guillaume decided to wake his little sister and send her to their parents' room, knowing she would be the least likely to scream if wakened from her sleep. "Lizzie! Lizzie-belle, wake-up! It's me, I need you to go and wake *Maman* and Papa and tell them that I'm here. But don't make a fuss about it. Be quiet for me, alright?"

The child rubbed her eyes, not surprised that her brother had appeared at her bedside in the middle of the night and staggered out into the hall toward her parents' room, still more than half asleep.

Waiting, the boys sat on the little girl's bed, looking about the room as if they'd been away for years and years. Suddenly quiet, they remembered the girl who should have been sharing the bed with Lizzie and remembered why they'd come, their euphoria at being home falling to the floor in a puddle around their damp, muddy boots.

Michel remembered a goodbye kiss and it took on an importance that it didn't have at the time. Tears came to his eyes as he looked about him, searching for some trace of Manon lurking in a corner. Guillaume was thinking much along the same lines and coughed a bit to disguise his emotions.

The door burst open and his mother threw herself at Guillaume who hadn't had time to get up from the bed to catch her.

"*Mon bébé ! Mon fils*! You're home! Are you alright? You came home!" she sobbed her happiness and her pain at finding one child safe, while another was gone forever. Guillaume's father hovered in the doorway, as

Michel rose to embrace him in the traditional fashion with a kiss on either cheek.

"It's a wonder to see you boys," the father said, shaking his head as if to dispel a bad dream. "Did you hear about...what happened?"

"We came as soon as we could. *Capitaine Martin* didn't want us to, but we came anyway," Michel said, leaving an arm about the older man's shoulders.

Guillaume's mother cried with no attempt at self restraint, these fresh tears matched by Guillaume, who had also given up trying to hold his emotions in check.

"Who did it? Do you know who's to blame?" Guillaume choked out.

"No one will say. No one saw anything, or they won't tell for fear of what will happen. There's no way to find out. VonEpffs says that he's sure it wasn't one of the permanent soldiers. We had the Gestapo here for a few days. It was probably one of them. But there's nothing to be done about it, and nothing to be done to bring your sister back to us anyway... so don't be getting any foolish ideas into those heads about revenge. Your poor mother couldn't stand another thing like this happening... I hope you've not come home thinking to cause more trouble!"

"But Papa, you can't just let this go as if nothing's happened! Think about Manon! We can't just pretend like she never existed!" Guillaume's voice was louder than intended. His little sister was fully awake now and clinging to her father's leg, half hidden behind him, eying the boys as if they were strangers.

"And what about the rest of us? Do you think it will do us any good for you to come here to raise a fuss? You'll just get caught and hauled away to a German work camp, and how do you think your mother will feel about that?" Guillaume's father pushed frustrated hands through his bed-tousled hair. "And would you put little Lizzie here in danger, by doing foolish things to get us all in trouble? Just coming back here is irresponsible of you... even if I am happy to see you safe and sound...You just have to accept things without making them worse."

His speech ended with a strangled sob of frustration. He drew a deep breath, gathering the strength to continue, "God knows it's hard for me to get up every morning and not look for Manon to come down, to sit next to young Elizabeth, all grumpy about something or other... but I'm happy to say that Elizabeth is still here... and you're safe as well... and your mother is too."

His voice broke, swallowing back smothered tears. "I can do nothing to change that Manon is gone. I miss her every day, but I need to keep the rest of us safe, and I can't let you do anything to put the others in danger, just to satisfy some selfish need for revenge. It won't bring her back, but it could send us all to join her. And I won't have that if I can help it." The stern resolve in his voice warned Guillaume to keep still, even though its tone indicated a man broken by pain. Guillaume extracted himself from his mother's stranglehold and rose to embrace his father.

They held each other in silence for a long moment, before Papa pulled back and slapped his son on the back. "You have a lot to tell us, I suppose? What are those marks on your face? Did you see Michel's parents yet? Who else knows you're here?" Once started, the flood of questions poured out, each more important than the last. No answer could be fast enough to stem the flow.

"You're so thin! You must be starving," *Maman* broke in. "You'll tell us everything over some food. Henri, did you fasten the shutters on the windows and the door downstairs before coming up to bed? Can we go down without anyone seeing us?" she asked her husband.

"Everyone is used to us staying up late and not getting any sleep anyway, but I'll go down and draw the curtains shut as well. Just give me a minute." He left them while their mother tried to tuck the little girl back into bed.

"*Mais, Maman!* I want to hear where Guillaume and Michel have been, too! I want to hear their stories! I can't go back to bed! It's not fair!" Little Elizabeth balked at being treated like the child she was.

Guillaume bent over her and kissed her forehead. "I'll come back up when I've had something to eat and I'll tell you some stories, just for you, ones that no one else will hear, alright? You just wait for me right here and I'll come up later on. You promise you'll wait for me?" Lizzie nodded her head and rubbed her eyes.

They left the room, moving quietly down the stairs to the kitchen where *Maman* gathered the makings of a cold meal for the boys.

"You'll have to hide upstairs until we can warn your parents that you're here, Michel. I don't want you running about the yard tonight risking being caught. You know that Paulette is married now, to one of them? She's staying up in the big house with her husband. He's a good sort of fellow though, her husband is. For a German." Henri describing Heinrich in this fashion was about as glowing a compliment as could be expected given the circumstances.

The young men devoured the food, still possessing the appetites of growing boys, equivalent to that of a pack of wolves considering the wreckage on the table when they finally pushed back, stomachs full for the first time in quite awhile.

"So, Paulette was the one to tell you about the Gestapo leaving for Yvetôt to hunt down Steve? We probably should get right back there and help out, what do you think, Guillaume?" Michel asked his companion.

Guillaume's mother cut in before the words finished tumbling out of his mouth. "You boys won't be going off anywhere until your mother and father have had the chance to see you for themselves! And it's no use going back there right now, you'll just be caught and lead those beasts directly to your encampment. They'll be especially vigilant about comings and goings and you're sure to be seen. It'll do more harm than good, so you'll just stay put for a while until we find out more about the capture of this 'Steve' person." She finished off this little speech with some menacing shaking of a wooden spoon in their direction, in memory of the days when she took after them with it, when they were up to mischief.

"*Maman*, put your spoon down, after facing the Germans practically every day, we're not afraid of the spoon anymore! We're grown men now." Guillaume gently teased her.

"Grown men! You're just foolish boys! And you'll be wise to listen to me. I'm your mother and always will be, no matter how big you think you are. And this spoon can still sting your backside! That's something for you to keep in mind too, Michel! Your mother would thank me for giving you the spoon if she could hear you talking about running back into danger. I'll tell her myself tomorrow!"

Her cloth hair curlers bobbed about her ears, showing exactly how irritated she was by the thoughtlessness of these young men, who would always boys in her heart. She glared at them with the singular regard of a mother watching her authority wash away with time, and not understanding how this could happen so fast. Spoon or no spoon, they were going to go against her wishes and get themselves into some awful kind of trouble and she couldn't stop them from running headlong toward it.

In a fit of frustration, she flung the wooden spoon into the fire Henri had stirred up in the grate, before dropping herself onto the bench across from them, with an air of defeat. Tears returned to her eyes and Guillaume reached across the table to pat her hand.

Henri put his arm loosely around her slumped shoulders while addressing the boys. "Don't you think this Steve fellow can take care of himself? It's surely not up to you to be his protectors?"

"*Non*, Papa, it's not like that. We stay alive because we work together to watch each others' backs. If we know something, it's our duty to make sure that we pass that information on. Otherwise we'll be no better than traitors to our group. We have to at least send word. Is Emile going to the market in Bacqueville tomorrow? We could send a message with him to the pharmacist, he could send it with some medicines to the pharmacist in Yvetôt. I know that they know each other. When they took care of us in Yvetôt after we got hurt, they told us so. Do you have some paper?"

Much deliberating took place as to how to word the message, so that no one but those who should understand it, would. Henri promised to give the missive to Emile first thing in the morning, before he left to the market with the butter, milk and eggs that they traded for cloth and tools and the other things which they didn't produce.

This commerce was strictly controlled by the Colonel, who always sent two soldiers with Emile, but enough time had passed that there was no suspicion about Emile running an errand or two for the locals while he was in town. A trip to the pharmacy could be easily explained. Manon's mother was expected to depend on sleeping powders.

CHAPTER 19

December 1991:

During the days and weeks following the interview with Doctor Lamartine, Debra lived on pins and needles. She pretended to be oblivious to the continual tiny jabs Philippe threw at her, apparently hoping to provoke an explosive reaction. It was an exercise in self-control. He went out of his way to annoy her. She knew, and ignored it, aggravating Philippe all the more.

He had a phone installed in her car and called her constantly to find out where she was and what she was doing. He insisted Sophie make her appointments with clients. Those *rendezvous* taken by Debra, when she was with a client planning the next visit, must be listed every day and relayed to Sophie. That way Sophie could work around them, planning Debra's schedule.

Of course, Debra voiced her resentment. No woman would want her rival to have any sort of control over her life. Philippe's insensitivity made her furious.

Still, she did her best to maintain a calm facade for fear of feeding his still incomprehensible plan. The harder she tried to feign indifference the more effort he put into finding ways to provoke her. Their life together was extremely difficult. The vibrations sent out when they were together were so negative that my air soured. I began to regret my last owners, finding this animosity too much to absorb.

He postponed a family ski holiday to the mountains. He refused to allow her to take the children to the States to visit their grandparents. He invited people over without consulting Debra, and more and more often, the guest list included Patricia and her husband.

This went against his standing rule of social contact with their employees. He reprimanded Debra when she'd confided in Patricia, saying that it was never a good idea to be too close to the personnel. Debra struck back at the time: accusing Philippe of a relationship with Sophie and remarking that having sex with employees apparently didn't count as 'close contact with the personnel'. But now, it seemed as though he was foisting her off on Patricia. Debra found his attitude odd, but held firm to her resolve to avoid conflict as much as possible. It would have tried the patience of a saint. Sadly, Debra's character didn't place her on the Pope's list of beatification.

Christmas came along. Philippe invited Patricia and her husband to share their Christmas Eve dinner without clearing the invitation with Debra.

Traditionally the French celebrate on Christmas Eve, opening their presents at midnight. In previous years, she and Philippe had let the girls go to bed, and open their presents on Christmas morning, allowing Santa to drop off the gifts while they were asleep. Theirs had been a typically American ritual: the kids sprawled on the floor in their pajamas, surrounded by ripped wrapping paper and toys. It was chaotic, but fun. Then at noon, they would enjoy a typical American turkey dinner.

This year he changed everything. Philippe insisted the girls stay at the dinner table from 9 pm until midnight, reprimanding their fidgeting during the heavy five course meal. He blew Santa out of the picture by bringing out their gifts for the girls himself at midnight.

By then the children were unruly and crabby, having stayed up far past their usual bedtime. Philippe had turned Christmas into an ordeal, instead of a special family day. Debra did her best to keep the girls in line in front of the unwanted company, and Philippe did his best to aggravate her efforts. It was disastrous.

Debra was especially displeased when she opened her gift from Philippe. Debra felt Patricia watching her closely as if particularly interested in Debra's reaction as she unwrapped a heavy sweater made of an ugly shade of khaki wool, embroidered with bears and squirrels and other woodland creatures. It was shapeless, unfashionable, and downright ugly.

She was rather surprised at Philippe's choice of gift since he usually displayed good taste, until Patricia finally burst out, inspired by too much champagne, "I'm so pleased you like it! I thought you would, Philippe and I had a hard time finding something that would suit you."

Debra was floored. They'd been shopping together? The barely veiled insult didn't escape her notice either.

Patricia gurgled on, unstoppable, "Men just have the hardest time shopping for their women! It's a good thing I was along to help!"

Debra squeezed out an unwilling smile as she set the gift aside, "I'm sure you're right..."

Patricia's turn was next as she opened a package from Philippe containing a royal blue silk blouse. Debra had no idea there would be gift giving between these people and her husband either, although someone had signed the accompanying card in their names.

Debra politely asked to see the confetti decorated gift card. The handwriting on the card was Sophie's. Evidently he had taken her shopping as well. Too bad

Sophie hadn't chosen this gift for Debra: the blue silk blouse was quite pretty.

The evening dragged from bad to worse. Once she'd succeeded in calming the girls down enough to go to bed, she cleared the table and went to the kitchen to attack the dirty dishes. Philippe had gone to bed as soon as their guests departed, complaining of indigestion. This suited Debra. She needed time alone to wash this horrid evening from her heart even as she scrubbed Patricia's coral lipstick from the crystal stemware.

She'd observed Patricia's husband this evening and during previous meals they had shared. He was a rather nondescript fellow, smaller than his wife and much quieter. He sat and smiled, a drink in hand, letting his wife furnish their share of the conversation. Debra remembered Susanna's remark about what she had overheard that night outside their bedroom door.

What had he meant when he'd spoken about the men and what they were supposed to do? The bland image he projected and the tale Susanna told didn't quite mesh. The discrepancy chewed at her peace of mind. Susanna had been genuinely unsettled by what she had overheard. Try as she might, Debra could make no sense of it.

#

Throughout January they faithfully kept their first three appointments with Doctor Lamartine, but the rapport between Debra and the psychologist never reappeared. The Doctor spent more time interviewing Philippe than she did Debra, and in spite of herself Debra was annoyed at this lack of attention. After the promise of their first meeting, she'd thought she'd found an ally in Doctor Lamartine.

One week, when the Doctor didn't show up at aerobics class, Debra called the private number on the back of the card she'd taken that first day.

A young woman answered the phone. "No, I'm sorry; Doctor Lamartine isn't here right now. In fact, she'll be off for some time. Can I reschedule you with another her replacement?"

Debra pushed the issue, "I'm sorry, I thought I'd called her private number."

"Oh you probably did, but since she's been in the hospital, all her calls have been transferred to us," the receptionist replied.

"The hospital? Is she ill?" asked Debra, coldness seeping into her veins.

"Well, I shouldn't say..." the receptionist hesitated, "you know: not nice to talk about someone behind their back, but since it's in the news and all... and you have her private number... I guess you should know." The receptionist's voice betrayed her eagerness to chew over the exciting gossip once again. "Last week she had a terrible car crash, almost died! The police are doing an inquest because it seems the brake lines on her car had been cut!"

"Good heavens! Do they have any idea who could have done it? Or why?"

"No, they've asked us for all of her client lists. You're one of her clients aren't you?" the receptionist asked, then added without waiting for an answer, "Most likely you'll be hearing from the police yourself, since they seem to be questioning everybody."

Debra took leave, slowly hanging up the phone. Poor woman, she thought, to have an enemy capable of trying to kill you, it sounded like the script of a Hollywood B movie. She shuddered at the thought of a psychotic patient on the loose, ready to do in the Doctor.

#

Winter dragged its heels, refusing to release its cold gray hold to a timid spring. I felt as if I was harboring a cancer, developing into a festering tumor of unpleasantness hidden just beneath the surface of Debra and Philippe's marriage. Their arguments became more frequent and to my great surprise, I found myself to be the subject of unpleasant remarks from Philippe.

He kept complaining about my defects. My floors were crooked, my windows let in too many drafts, and my plumbing was noisy. I was greatly offended by these attacks and did my best to react accordingly.

When he would try to light a fire in the grate in the sitting room, I would snap my flue shut and puff smoke in his face. Every time he took a shower I purposefully changed the rhythm of the hot and cold water gushing from the shower head, annoying him by forcing him to fiddle with the faucets in an attempt to obtain a homogeneous flow at a stable temperature. He would shout at Debra about these things and she could only reply that she never had any problems, which was of course, absolutely true.

All trickery aside, it was a difficult time for everyone. The atmosphere of antagonism was stifling. They were very unhappy together and it was permeating my entrails. I was uneasy and developed leaks in the roof and let mice chew on my wires, feeling myself wallow in the muck of their distaste for one another.

#

Later that week, a police car pulled into the drive in the early evening darkness, the siren off but roof lights flashing through the dark yard.

Debra grabbed a furiously barking Elsa by the collar, opening the door to two men in dark suits, who'd shown their badges to her through the locked window. Two uniformed officers stayed outside on the terrace.

"Madame Dubois? I'm Inspector Lavoisier and this is Inspector Simonin. We've been expecting you to come to the police station for the past week following our summons. Since you didn't show up, we decided to come to you. You know...if the mole hill won't come to the mountain..." He gave her an ironic smile, but it was obvious that he wasn't pleased to be there.

"I'm sorry, but...a summons? I've had nothing of the kind."

"Uh, sorry to contradict you, Madame, but isn't this your signature?" He pulled a yellow slip of paper from his pocket. It was from the post office, the kind which accompanies a registered letter. He handed it to her to inspect but didn't release the paper.

Debra looked down at the yellow slip, widening her eyes. "Well, you're right. It does *look* like my signature. But it's not. I've never seen this paper before."

"Hmmm, and you've no idea why we requested you to come down to the police station either, I suppose," Inspector Simonin remarked with audible sarcasm.

"No, and I wasn't expecting to see you in my yard either. If you'd stop playing cat and mouse with me, we might get somewhere. What do you want to speak with me about?" Their insinuations that she was lying about something made her snap.

The dog growled, perceiving her mistress' rising anger.

"Would you lock up that dog somewhere?" Inspector Lavoisier asked in a tone of voice which couldn't be mistaken for a request.

"She's fine right where she is," Debra answered. "She just trying to protect me against some threat she can feel coming from you, and I'd like to know what it is, too. Now if you'll tell me what you want, I can let you get on with whatever important things you should be doing tonight." Her invitation to leave and be out of her house was clear.

"What were you doing on Thursday, December 18th, Madame Dubois?"

"Well, I don't remember off the top of my head, but let me get my appointment book and I'll tell you." She left the room and they followed her from a distance up the stairs to her bedroom, where she grabbed her purse from the closet door handle. She brushed past them on the way back down the stairs, glowering as she lead them back into a room more suitable for receiving guests, remarking on the way, "Did you think I was going to jump out an upstairs window and flee, for God's sake?"

"Just doing our job, Madame Dubois."

The sarcastic answer brought Debra to a halt. She turned to face them. "Now, just a minute, I don't know what you think I've done, but I really don't like your tone of voice, or your attitude. I'll be happy to answer any of your questions, I have nothing to hide, and I've done nothing wrong, but please just tell me what you want with me?"

Susanna and Victoria chose this minute to appear in the kitchen doorway, "Mummy, the video's done!" Susanna said in English, the language she always used when speaking with her mother. The girls stopped, suddenly shy and visibly impressed by the two dark suited strangers. They hid behind Debra's legs.

Inspector Lavoisier, the shorter of the two men, squatted down to speak with Susanna in heavily accented English, *"You speeek Angleesh, leeetle gurrl? Whaat ees you nam?"*

Susanna looked at him as if he were a Martian, and refused to answer.

"She speaks perfect French, Inspector, and her name is none of your business, unless you've come to question her." Debra was very angry now, having had just about enough of playing games with these two not so friendly guys in her kitchen. "Can we just get back to it?"

She opened her agenda and recited her appointments for the Thursday in question: one in the morning in Beauvais, an afternoon appointment in Doullens and then finishing off in Abbeville. Her aerobics class was penciled in for 6:30pm at the bottom of the page.

He jabbed his finger at the evening aerobics class entry. "You take aerobics at the *Maison des Sports?"* he asked.

"Yes, for the past three years. Why?" she countered.

"Do you know Sylvie Lamartine?" he asked point blank.

"Of course I do, she's our marriage counselor. And she attends the aerobics classes at the *Maison des Sports*. Is this about her accident?" A light of sudden understanding switched on in Debra's brain.

"We thought you might know something about that," Inspector Simonin said with a wry smile.

"The only thing I know about it, is what her receptionist told me over the phone when I called to confirm an appointment." The lie was a tiny one but she didn't feel obligated to give away the personal nature of her phone call to the psychiatrist, still it must have shown on her face.

Inspector Lavoisier squinted in her direction, evaluating her answer. "How well do you know the Doctor?" he asked.

"Not very well at all. We have a doctor-patient relationship, so we don't speak to each other at the gym ever, except to say hello. It would be a bit awkward, otherwise."

"And your husband, how well does he know her?" asked the other inspector.

"I would think even less than I do, seeing as he's not much one for aerobics."

"Cut the crap, Madame Dubois. We know that your husband has been seeing Madame Lamartine without you. On the side, shall we say? Don't you know anything about that? His secret appointments for lunch, and after lunch entertainment?" he needled.

"If you'll excuse me, I'll go put on another video for the girls. I think this sort of conversation should be kept to adults." She took the girls by the hand, as she left the kitchen to go into the library where the TV lit the room with a vivid blue screen. The inspectors followed her, and she shut the door in their faces.

"What do you want to watch now, sweeties? How about 'the Little Mermaid'? That's a nice one, with all those fish and dolphins. Remember?" she chirped. "Mummy will be in the kitchen talking, and when I'm done, I'll come back with some milk and cookies and we'll watch the rest together, alright?" she kissed each girl on the forehead, and slipped out the door, bumping into Inspector Lavoisier, who'd obviously been listening.

She sighed, as much with aggravation at his sneaking about following her, as with disgust at the entire situation. She let them tag along behind her and the dog into the kitchen once again, far enough away so the girls wouldn't hear unflattering things about their father.

"So, I'm to understand that my husband has been having an affair with our marriage counselor?" she asked as she sat down on the bar stool at the counter.

"And you had no clue?" one or the other asked, she didn't bother to listen which. She was weary of this subterfuge and of Philippe's lying, cheating, sneaky behavior. Suddenly, it was just too much for her.

"No, I was still back at the last chapter where he was having sex on his desk with his secretary. I guess I should have tried to keep up." Debra's wry response reflected her resignation and exhaustion.

"He's a runner, is he?" asked Simonin.

"You've got the proof, I just have the suspicions. You do have proof don't you?" she asked, suddenly disoriented by the conversation.

"Yes, Madame, and we need to know if you've had anything to do with the cutting of Sylvie Lamartine's brake lines. Did you cut them? Angry at her for sleeping with your husband?" he asked in a more gentle tone of voice.

"No, I did not. I had no idea they were... that they had... well, that they'd been seeing each other for personal reasons. I thought he wanted me to see a psychiatrist because he was planning on having me declared insane and locked away or something crazy like that. We've been having some rough times in our marriage and I've been considering divorce, but was hoping that Madame Lamartine would help me when the time came by giving evidence in my favor. I guess I was completely out in left field about her motives."

Debra was broken and her shoulders were heavy with the weight of deception. She ran her hands over her face, rubbing her forehead, where this new information was pounding itself into her brain.

"So now what? You're planning on arresting me for attempted murder?" she looked up at them from under the hand massaging her throbbing forehead.

"No, but you have to understand that we have to question everybody she knows, even against her wishes. She spoke very highly of you, and didn't want us to summon you in for questioning. But that in itself was suspicious, and then when you didn't show up. Well, it looked bad for you. But I don't think you're a very good actress, Madame Dubois, and we already tested your signature against the one on the receipt for the summons. The expert says they're not the same hand," he admitted.

Now she was furious again. "So you came out here and treated me like a suspect of some kind, scaring me and my daughters, when all along you knew I was innocent? What the hell is wrong with you?" she sputtered. "That's enough of this bullshit! You are free to leave now, or arrest me, but at any rate you'll leave my house!"

"Listen up, Madame Dubois, you might not like our methods, but we get the job done, you were a loose end that needed tying up, that's just what we did. You'd be amazed what people will say if they think they're in trouble. Most of the time they point the finger at the guilty person, just to save themselves. Not new stuff, the collaborators did it with Nazis during the war."

"And you're modeling your behavior on the Gestapo? Good choice, I hope you're proud of yourselves for frightening a woman and two little girls. Now if we've finished here, goodnight gentlemen." She rose and headed toward the door, opening it wide, the dog at her feet.

"Well, as they say in the movies, don't leave town in case we need to speak with you again. Good evening Madame Dubois!"

She slammed the door, leaning against it, her hand on the dog's head, a question repeating itself over and over in her brain: What in the hell is going on?

CHAPTER 20

It was a Tuesday in April. School would soon be out for a two week holiday. Debra had gone against Philippe's wishes and booked plane tickets for herself and the girls for a much awaited visit to the States and her parents.

He had been furious in spite of her patient explanations. She wanted to see her family and the girls needed to develop a relationship with their grandparents. She felt it unfair of him to question her right to visit. He knew she had family in the States, and while he seemed happy enough to have them visit—which they did once a year—he always found a reason to refuse her visiting them.

At first she had bowed to his wishes, for they always seemed to be well founded. He couldn't get away just then, or lately it had to do with her responsibilities at work. It had taken her a long time to realize that there would always be a reason, valid or not. It had taken her even longer to overcome her misgivings and go ahead to book the tickets in spite of his protestations. He would never be ready to accompany them, so she had to resign herself to going without him, whether he wanted her to or not. So she went ahead and bought the tickets: three in all.

Ever since the day two weeks ago, when she had informed him of her purchase, he alternated between being furious and nasty, to wheedling and whiny, begging her to reconsider, offering an alternative holiday family to some place in France. After the canceled ski trip this past winter, she knew not to fall into that trap.

It was too late. She was aware of his ploy to force her to change her mind. This time she would not. She'd stashed the plane tickets in the glove box of her car, afraid that if he found them, he might rip them up.

She'd chosen not to confront him about the police visit and their revelations regarding his personal link to the Doctor, although the knowledge reinforced her decision to go home for a while. She thought that when— for it seemed unavoidable now—she filed for a divorce she would use that as evidence in her favor.

Debra swallowed the facts like nasty medicine. Doctor Lamartine was still recovering from her accident, which had never been elucidated, and Debra never saw her. She did her best to set aside all thoughts of Philippe and the Doctor, concentrating on daily routine until she felt ready to proceed.

Work, the girls and their activities and avoiding contact with Philippe, filled her days. She lived the empty life of a zombie, pretending to the world that all was well.

It was not as difficult as it would seem, the children were her refuge. Philippe avoided arguing with her in front of them, so it was with the girls that she spent most of her time. They were a shield, and she gladly hid behind them.

Today, she'd finished work very early, having phoned her afternoon clients from the car to beg off as she was feeling slightly under the weather. The tremendous stress of living a lie was taking its toll. Philippe was clearly trying in any way he could to make her change her mind about the upcoming trip to see her parents. She hadn't been sleeping well. Enticing visions of a nap drove her home.

When she was a half mile from the house, driving along the two lane country road they lived on, she crossed paths with Patricia's car. She braked, while looking in the rear-view mirror, but the other vehicle seemed to speed up putting too much distance between them for Debra to be sure.

When she arrived home, she was surprised to see not Francoise's car in the drive, but Philippe's. She stopped, parking close to the road instead of approaching the house. She walked up the drive after plucking the mail from the box on the gatepost.

She stopped as she came inside; listening carefully in the downstairs hall, before going straight upstairs, where shuffling noises seeped from the master bedroom.

Pausing before the half-open door she observed Philippe as he turned around their bed. He was changing the sheets. The interval filled itself with missing details pertaining to the reason for a mid-day sheet change. Debra's imagination supplied vivid images of Philippe and Patricia mussing the bed she'd tidied before leaving that morning.

He turned the corner of the bed, tugged on the comforter and looked up.

Debra said nothing.

His face showed disgust at having to come up with some plausible explanation for his occupation, with no previous warning.

As usual, he chose to become angry in the face of her calm. "So now what?" he shouted, "I can't even count on you to keep your appointments any more? It's no wonder our business figures are down this month! I would think that since you've gone and spent all that money on those extravagant plane tickets, you would at least hold up your end of our bargain, and respect your work responsibilities!"

Debra remained calm at his outburst, overwhelmed with crushing sadness by the change in their rapport. She used to run to him for a kiss when she saw him at the end of the day. Now as he shouted, the missing kiss took on an enormous importance. Its absence summarized their marriage. Her only desire at that instant was to speak with him, to bridge the rift between them by talking about what they had become, to try to figure out why. She wondered how to get back to where they had come from.

Her voice overflowed with regrets, "Could we sit and talk about what is going on here?" Her hand made a timid gesture as if afraid to point at the half made bed.

"Oh! And here we go again! *Madame* is jumping to conclusions and confabulating about my sex life! You know what? You must be pretty obsessed with sex yourself to always be accusing me of having it with every woman I cross paths with!" he continued shouting, not even remotely resembling the dignified man she had once been in love with.

"No, I just wish that we could have an honest conversation about our marriage and what seems to have gone horribly wrong with it. You must be dreadfully unhappy with me and I want to know why."

"Why? Don't you know why? Can't you guess why? Don't you know what trouble we're in? I've tried, time and again, to make you understand that we can't stay here; I can't continue to pay for your whims. You keep buying new furniture. You're continually re-painting or wall-papering the rooms, buying new curtains, spending a fortune on a new espresso machine! Buying more clothes than those kids could ever wear out! You think money grows on trees and that I should just provide, provide, provide for Madame Dubois, and spit out money for plane tickets and ski holidays!"

Debra was aghast. Mouth dropped open in shock, she watched him advance on her, swinging his arms in a fit of rage such as she had never witnessed before. With remarkable difficulty, she recovered her senses as well as her tongue.

"I had no idea we had any financial problems. I have access to our accounts and see the balances all the time on the monthly statements from the bank. There was never any indication that we had troubles! Why haven't you told me you had worries about money? We could have come up with a solution of some sort, to save the house. But wait a minute, just what has that got to do with you sleeping with your employees in our bed in the middle of the afternoon? Forgive me, but I can't see the connection!" She had almost been diverted by the enormous reaction he had to seeing her standing there unexpectedly, but remembered what she had seen before his diatribe started.

He wrenched open the *armoire* door and took out his shotgun and three cartridges, starting to load it even as he approached her.

He spoke in lower, more menacing fashion. "I had thought that you would be afraid to live here after the break-in. It's a shame those idiots I paid believed you, when you shouted about getting the gun and phoning the police. But you get what you pay for, they were cheap labor, and not surprisingly, very stupid. It would have been the perfect way to get you out of this house, and get this debt off my back! But no, you wouldn't leave here for anything, would you?"

She backed into the hallway onto the landing as he continued toward her, an extra cartridge in hand, having loaded the first two.

"No, you were too self absorbed, living the high life, imagining yourself to be the reincarnation of some countess or whatever other crap you make up in your pathetic head, spending all your free time visiting castles and trying to make this big old hunk of building worthy of your status. All you Americans want to give some imaginary luster to your family tree. But you went overboard, spending all my money trying to make people believe we're some sort of modern nobility."

Debra was face to face with someone in the throes of temporary insanity, and having no clue how to deal with it, slowly started to back down the stairs one at a time, keeping her eyes on the gun, now pointed at her chest.

Philippe kept talking, as if now that the floodgate of truth was opened, emptying his reproach was necessary before emptying the barrel of the shotgun. He moved toward her, in rhythm with her backtracking, following her path. He was now at the top of the steps and she eased down the steps, just before the turn on the halfway landing.

"...and when I tried to get help from that stupid woman, she refused to declare you incompetent! If she had I would have been able to claim the insurance policy on you as a lost asset to the company, it would have given me some breathing space. But you wheedled her into believing that I was the one with a problem and not you! Stupid creature! I couldn't even get through to her in bed. She wouldn't listen."

He took another step toward her, waving the barrel of the gun in punctuation, no longer aiming at anything at all.

She glanced behind her, judging the possibility of making a run for it, backward down the stairs while his rant carried on.

"... and now, here you are, trying to push me even further into debt, buying plane tickets and jetting around the world like a movie star or something." He took another step forward and she took another step backward starting down the second set of stairs from the landing, her hand on the wall to brace herself.

"It just has to stop, Debra, and I don't know of any other way to make it stop. You have to go. It's as simple as that."

She opened her mouth to try and reason with him just as he stopped in front of the door to the attic at the top of the second set of stairs. He carefully lifted the sights of the gun to his right eye, taking aim.

Elsa bounded up the stairs barking, sensing danger.

#

I couldn't let this drama take place. Debra loved me, and Philippe resented me. It was in fact, a very simple thing for me to burst open the door to the attic, knocking Philippe forward off of his feet.

As he pitched headlong down the stairs, Debra instinctively crouched. The dog hurtled past her toward Philippe as the shot cracked.

A sharp yelp rang out. A great chaotic tumbling of the three of them: Elsa, Debra and Philippe, still clutching the shot gun. Hindered by the barrel, they slammed down the staircase breaking out railings as they avalanched, entwined together to the bottom.

Debra cracked her head on the floor when she hit the tile flooring at the foot of the steps and passed into oblivion, her last vision being the third cartridge as it rolled slowly across the hallway floor to hide beneath the portmanteau.

CHAPTER 21

April 1943:

   Outside it smelled of worms. Spring had brought heavy rains and the sudden sunshine, doing its best to dry my sodden lawns and evaporate the puddles which had accumulated in my yard, amplified the earthy odor of mud. Normandy in spring could be alternately glorious or disheartening, according to the weather.

   Farmers spent their free time musing about it, discussing the probability of its effect on every crop imaginable. If one were to delete conversations regarding the weather, not much else would be discussed. This concern was shared by generation after generation of the families whose job was to produce some of the best food available on earth. The ground was fertile and ambient wetness made germination a sure thing. What wasn't so certain was the steady growth of the plants, for lack of sufficient sunshine.

   This year was exceptional. Spring had come early and was dry. The recent rain had been a blessing, until it lasted for a week, causing concern about the drowning of the newly sprouted plants. Yet today, the sun shone bright and the animals grazed in fresh green pastures. The sheep munched away, contented, entertained by the gamboling of the newborns, some with white faces and legs, the others with black: the black legged ones looking as if God had run out of matching wool coats when dressing them. The lambs took no notice of their differences, playing with their mothers under the apple trees between snacks.

Most years, spring worked its magic on Paulette. Warm breezes made the blood dance in her veins, coordinating with the rivers of sap swelling the buds on the trees. She loved tending the sheep in the spring, when the first bluebells appeared, adding a purplish blue fuzz to the grassy spots in the orchard.

I heard her singing disjointed little tunes in a charming, yet discordant voice. She only sang when she was alone. If someone overheard her, it was accidental, for she knew that her singing voice was nothing like that of the lovely peasant girl she'd seen in the first animated feature movie by the American, *Monsieur* Disney. Nonetheless, sing she did. Although unlike *Blanche Neige*, her warbling was never known to attract admiring birds or wildlife.

To the one who loved her as his own, this lack of tunefulness was an endearing quirk, which caused him some surprise the first time he'd witnessed the unexpected creaking of its illogical assembly of notes. He thought at the time that she was deliberately wreaking havoc on the ditty that he finally recognized with some difficulty as *'Au Clair de la Lune'*. He'd chuckled at her ingenuity at so successfully rearranging the score.

It was only when he heard her efficiently massacring a second children's song, that he realized with some amazement that she must be completely tone-deaf. Somehow finding she wasn't perfect in every way encouraged him to initially seek her out in the garden last summer. To his disappointment, he hadn't heard much singing lately.

This year, she was quieter than usual. Pensive, worried expressions popped up unexpectedly on her face when she thought no one was looking. She had taken to chewing on her bottom lip, leaving it pink and a little raw. Heinrich took care when kissing it.

#

Paulette had a secret. I knew what it was but she was incapable of sharing it with anyone else.

She had wrongly assumed that Heinrich was more careful than he obviously had been, for I heard her praying in vain for her monthly cycle to resume.

Having grown up on a farm, she'd witnessed animal coupling on a regular basis. She understood what it took for pregnancy to occur, but had carelessly pushed that thought from her mind when her bodily needs squelched her common sense. They had discussed it, deciding it was much too early to become parents in the uncertain times they were living in and Paulette firmly believed Heinrich when he assured her of his capacity to push away from her in time.

He had professed a dislike for the 'French coats' supplied to the German soldiers in their kit. Funnily enough the French referred to these items as 'English bonnets', the reference to outerwear belonging to the enemy camp seeming rather ironic. It appeared as though neither side liked them much, preferring to attribute their invention to some other nationality. She would have preferred now, too late, that he had gotten over his distaste for their protection, regardless of who'd invented them. I knew that they were English, although the English thought they were of French origin. I wondered what the Americans thought of them and where they imagined they came from, but couldn't ask.

She waited another month until her breasts became tender and swollen. It was then that she knew for certain. Once again, she found herself in circumstances which should have been accompanied by celebrations and congratulations, but were instead, a source of anguish. In her heart she knew that it was very wrong not to be thrilled by this news and her heart rebelled against her reluctance to be joyful.

She was afraid to tell Heinrich, afraid to see disappointment on his face, when she deserved to see joy. She worried her bottom lip with her teeth when they were together, the words stuck in her throat, refusing to exit beyond the swollen lip.

#

It was Colonel VonEpffs who first guessed the reason for Paulette's worried countenance. He discovered her napping under an apple tree just starting to bud out in deep pink, with Polka's head resting quietly on her abdomen.

As he crossed the orchard, he gently cleared his throat, showing his presence. In response, Polka let out a low, warning growl, though never lifted her head from the spot she was protecting. Paulette stirred, rubbing her eyes with one hand, while shading them from the sunlight filtering through the branches with the other.

The Colonel drew a deep breath of moist spring air and put an arm out to lean against the tree she was resting beneath. He looked at the pristine sky, taking a moment for himself before speaking with a note of nostalgia in his voice.

"At home in Germany, I once had a female Bernese mountain dog. I named her Olga. The race is quite like the Saint Bernard in temperament." He paused. "I loved that dog and she loved me, but when I was fourteen-years-old, my mother became pregnant with my youngest sister. One day I found my Muti asleep on her chaise in her room, with my dog curled at her side, and her head posed upon Muti's round stomach. You can imagine my surprise when my dog growled at me, much like Polka is doing now." He looked kindly down at Paulette at the end of this little speech, watching her reaction to his comment. It was immediate.

"I don't know who to tell!" she burst out with such anguish, that he saw at once, just how young she really was. Her tears were great blobs of water, like raindrops accumulating on leaves before their combined weight causes the stem to bend, releasing them to fall to the ground. She lay still on her back, her hands covering her face as if she could disappear behind them.

"Well, my dear, you've just told me. Why haven't you spoken to Heinrich about it? Weren't you certain before now?" He squatted next to her, his elbows resting on his knees, with his head tilted to one side, in the attitude he adopted when he didn't wish to frighten a small child. "Surely he'll be crazy with pride at such wonderful news. I'm certain that he loves you very much.

You know, his work has never been the same since he met you. In fact, I should be rather upset at you, for having caused his head to turn so completely." A smile in his voice, he was hoping to tease her safely away from the fears that had brought on her shower of tears. They'd had enough rain for at least another week.

She spread her fingers open and chanced a look up at him.

He gently pulled her hands away from her face, took a handkerchief from his shirt pocket and dangled it in front of her nose. "I hope that you realize the news will break rather soon. This sort of thing isn't easy to hide for very long." His accompanying smile was tender and a bit remorseful.

She nodded quickly, wiping her tears and blowing her nose.

As she sat up, he sat down.

"So what are we to do? Now that I know, you're not alone with your secret. I'm guessing that you are relieved to have someone know, even if it is only me. Am I right? So, together we will talk. And you'll tell me why you are sad, and I will convince you that you should be happy instead. Then, if you like, I'll take you to see Heinrich or your mother, or anyone else you wish to share this good news with. How does that sound? See? Polka thinks this is a good idea, she's thumping her tail at me instead of growling." He looked at her with a nostalgic sadness in his heart, moved by her youth and dilemma, before continuing.

"When I was younger, much before the war started, I hoped that I would stay in Germany and grow grapes on my family estate. I had met a young woman, much like you actually. She was very young and beautiful. I fell in love with her and she promised to wait for me when I enlisted to make a name for myself, before coming back to the estate. While I was gone, she fell in love with someone else. So, I had to forget my dreams of being a wine-producer, with my Bridget at my side, sipping our wines on the back porch and looking out over the sun setting on the fields. We could have had lots of children, with a daughter much like you, kind and innocent." He patted her hand but withdrew it after just a minute, afraid of his gesture being judged improper.

"Now, here I am in France, an old man, with no wife, no children, and no vineyard. So, you see, my little sparrow? Life can be good to us. Or not. But what counts, is what we do with the situations it throws at us. Whether we rise to the occasion and try our best to make what we want of ourselves. Or whether we give up and join the army."

She smiled at this, a tiny giggle sliding out of her constricted throat.

She looked at him differently, with a new perspective. It showed on her face and he was pleased to see her regard him as a man for once and not just an enemy uniform.

"Do you think it would be best if I spoke to my parents first, or Heinrich?"

"Well, I don't want to scare you. But we are at war, and Heinrich is still enlisted. I don't think the Fuhrer will let him leave the army just now," he added, a bit of sarcasm tinting his voice. "Things are going to become much more complicated before they become easier. Heinrich will do everything in his power to protect you and you may also count on me to help, but I do fear that there will be many dark and dangerous days in front of us, before this situation is resolved, one way or the other."

He frowned at the thought of an uncertain future. "You have someone else to think about, not just your parents or friends or even Heinrich. You are carrying in you the most precious being that you'll ever know: your child. You must keep safe, even if it means being separated from Heinrich, or from your family, at one point in time. You must let that be your first preoccupation: keeping yourself and your child safe. No matter which side wins. No matter where you have to go to make that happen. Do you understand?" His voice held a note of urgency and Paulette looked up at him with alarm in her eyes.

"Do you know what is going to happen? Is something awful about to take place? Should I convince my parents to leave here? Where should we go?" Paulette rose to her knees in front of the Colonel, begging him to give her the information she needed to keep her family safe.

He had frightened her.

"Oh, my dear girl, I am sorry to have alarmed you after all, but I just wanted you to realize that you must take care of yourself first, because of the baby." He turned to scan the field with his gaze, and then gestured with a hand.

"I think these sheep look just fine. I don't see any wolves hanging about, do you?" He was teasing her again, hoping to back away from the fright he'd given her. "Let's go see your mother. Will you let me accompany you to find her? What is she busy with today, do you know?"

He rose, held a hand out to Paulette who got up, brushing bits of grass off her skirt and blouse. He tucked her hand under his arm, a gentleman strolling with a lady, as he brought her to her parents' cottage, chatting amiably about inconsequential things, and avoiding their previous dangerous topic of conversation.

He made a mental note to be more careful about giving away clues as to his commanding officer's plans for the region, even if he simply had her safety in mind. It wouldn't do to be accused of revealing top secret information.

#

Michel watched this little parade and if he had possessed fur, it would have risen in anger at seeing this German officer—who had been leading them all around by their noses for three years—walk his sister off as if she were his girlfriend. His hiding place was too far away to hear their conversation, though his imagination supplied him with details enough, erroneous details, but plentiful nonetheless.

He practically growled in anger, jumping down out of the tree fifty yards away from them, before sprinting off toward the barn, running low to the ground and hiding behind trees as he went, to avoid being seen.

He found their father there, hitching Maurice to a wagon. Michel hissed to catch Papa's attention before slipping into the tack room. His father looked up in surprise, scanning their surroundings to ensure that they were indeed alone and followed Michel inside.

The late morning sun slanted through the window, lighting the shiny leather saddles and harnesses. It glinted off of the metallic bits and pieces, giving the impression that they were new, although they were not. On the contrary, Marcel was continually repairing the harnesses; using bits and pieces of old belts and other leather goods: leftovers from the days of the last owner when money was readily available to replace whatever accoutrements were needed to keep Maurice firmly attached to his load.

While Marcel was a frugal sort of man and sincerely enjoyed finding an inventive, economic solution to any problem, it also was a point of pride for him to do his best not to ask Colonel VonEpffs for anything at all. He perfunctorily accepted what was offered to help facilitate his work, but if no one noticed that something needed to be replaced, he did without as much as possible. Some of this was a grudge held over from their scuffle in the dirt, the day he found out that Paulette had been going about with Heinrich and part of it was his Gallic pride: not asking for help from the enemy. He'd been disappointed that Paulette had asked for the bicycle tires and refused to ride it.

In this instance he was ready with a harsh word on his tongue for his insubordinate son, regarding the obvious disrespect for the rules set out to keep him and the rest of them safe from the repercussions of hiding two fugitive young men. Nothing could keep them from being shipped off to German work camps if their presence were to be found out.

"Just what in the devil do you think you're doing, running about in broad daylight? Might as well go right up to the front door, knock on it and ask the Colonel to haul you away!"

Michel snorted impatience at his father, brushing aside his admonitions, to blurt out as fast possible his news. "I think we should both go and knock on the front door and slit the Colonel's throat! He's walking about with Paulette now, as if she's one of his trollops come to warm his bed!" He stood still, fists clenched in anger, waiting for his father to have a volatile reaction matching his own.

He waited a bit longer than he thought necessary, so he decided to throw a bit of extra oil on the fire. "I'll bet he's taken her up to his room right now, to spend the afternoon with him while everyone else is busy working to keep his ass in clean sheets! I saw them go in that direction and she was fawning over him like a little whore, all sweet and clingy" He executed an ugly imitation of their stroll, while aping a light skirted hussy.

Papa reached over and slapped Michel's grimacing face.

"She's your sister, no matter who she's married to and you'll do good to remember it. These are hard times and family is what we've got left to hold on to. You'll respect that."

"So you've sold her off to be a whore, just to keep plodding along, doing their bidding? I didn't ever think I'd believe my own father to be a coward!" Michel spat at him, angered by the sort of slap he'd received as a child and thinking he deserved to be treated like a man.

In truth, he'd rather have received a punch in the nose, an adult blow, worthy of a man to man confrontation. It would have been easier on his pride. Instead he was insulted by the gesture used for mouthy children. His words reflected his desire to insult his father in retaliation for the insulting slap. However, once the hurtful words were out, floating around, irretrievable, amongst the dust motes twinkling in the sunshine, he regretted them and stammered as he saw shock register on his father's face.

"I...I just get so angry at everyone not doing anything!" He kicked at a wooden saddle horse, in a gesture that illustrated quite effectively, his childish frustration. "How could you give up our sister to the enemy like that? And why doesn't she see that she's acting like a cat in heat? Aren't you ashamed of her?"

Michel's father unclenched angry fists and took a deep breath, remembering once again, just how young this impudent, idiotic boy was and forgiving the meanness of the words spoken just seconds before.

"You think I'm a coward, do you? I'm doing my best to keep my family safe, but that's a man's job. I don't expect a child to understand it, but I'd like you to keep your tongue to yourself until you've found yourself in a similar situation. Then you can pass judgment on me, just as God will when I have to answer to my actions before him. Until then, shut up." Marcel turned away, feelings hurt, in spite of understanding Michel's lack of clairvoyance, and in spite of his knowing that those words weren't truly reflective of his son's thoughts.

"Papa! Wait! I...I'm sorry. I didn't mean what I said. I just don't know how Paulette could bring such shame on us all, and no one seeming to care about it, except me. She's sleeping with a dirty kraut right under our noses. And...liking it!"

"Michel, once again, stop judging people until you've found yourself in similar shoes. Paulette loves this man, no matter what his uniform is. She's married to him, and because of that, this 'dirty kraut' has become your brother and my son-in-law. Give the man a chance. He's not the devil." He paused, placing a hand on Michel's slumped shoulder.

"His uniform is the wrong one, granted. But, he's part of our family now, whether you like it or not. You'd best learn to live with that, we've had to. You can't just come running back here and dictate what's right to the rest of us. You're young and full of grand ideas, but war isn't grand. Or glorious. And to die for ideals is a luxury that I can't afford. I have to take care of my family, your mother, and Yves and your little sister, Roseline. What good would I be if I were to go pick a fight that I know I couldn't win, and ended up dead? Would I be a hero? I think I'd just be dead. And then there'd be no one left to protect my family when they need me." He half turned toward the harnesses hanging on the rack, fingering them as he spoke.

"You must learn to chose your battles and only undertake ones that you have a chance of winning, and only sacrifice yourself when your life could save another. I'm hoping that you'll understand that, and that you don't throw your life away for no reason. But when I listen to your thoughtless words, I'm afraid that I've done something wrong, bringing you up with a faulty sense of honor." He shook his head, as if to straighten out his thoughts and make them come out more easily, expressed in words his son could absorb correctly.

"I'm afraid that I've done wrong by you, and not taught you what it really means to be a man. I'm sorry for that. But if you don't listen to me, there's not much else I can do. I've tried to set an example for you all my life, and you only see me as a coward." This time he did turn away, his shoulders hunched over, much older than ten minutes before.

He slowly left the tack room, walking down the alleyway of the barn, back toward Maurice who was waiting patiently for his task to begin.

Michel sat down hard, thinking, questioning his father's words, turning them in his mind before swallowing them in a large lump that brought boyish tears of frustration to his eyes. He swallowed those back as well, making for a throat full.

He had disappointed his father, of that he was sure, but he didn't comprehend how. He'd thought they would be proud of his ideals, and of his courage in the things he'd done to provoke the Germans. Instead, his father had more or less informed him that he was a stupid child. And that hurt.

As he sat, his pride crushed, he swatted at the dust floating through the air, slowly at first, then again and again, trying to make it disappear. It didn't work. More particles came to flit about his face in spite of his swatting, faster and faster, until his arms ached with the flinging movement. Knowing it was a lost cause, he continued slapping at the dust, in spite, in anger, in frustration and in fury, until he wore himself out with the futility of it.

So, he got up and went to find something to eat.

#

In the interim, I listened to Colonel VonEpffs knock on the door to the cottage occupied by Paulette's family, keeping a hesitant Paulette from escaping off into the distance in a cloud of dust, by maintaining a firm, yet gentle hold on her elbow. Her trembling heart sent out the rapid vibrations of a small bird trapped behind a window.

She was plagued by fears of her father's reaction to the Colonel getting involved, while knowing that her mother would most likely cry. She didn't want that.

Liliane opened the door, a startled look on her face. After all, no one knocked around here. They'd lived in a communal fashion for generations and usually a shout outside the door before opening it directly was as much warning as anyone was given before being strode in upon.

"*Bonjour Madame Fournier, Comment allez-vous aujourd'hui?* I was wondering if you had a moment to spare? I'd like to speak with you about something important which has come up." The Colonel ushered Paulette into her parent's home as if she too, were a guest.

Paulette's mother stepped aside, unable to do anything except let them in, while wiping her hands on the apron protecting the front of her worn frock.

He steered Paulette toward the offered chair, before taking the one next to it, settling in as if they had been invited to a tea-party.

I absorbed the heavy air of anticipation.

Liliane perceived it and looked warily at the pair of them, disconcerted by this unusual behavior. Clearly remembering her manners, she asked: "Could I offer you something to drink?"

The Colonel politely declined, although asked Paulette if she would like something herself.

Suddenly, Paulette found the whole charade suffocating. She turned to her mother and dove in head first. "*Maman*, the Colonel has accompanied me here today, because he fears that I'll run off without confiding in you once again." She marked a pause even more pregnant than she was.

"I've been afraid to tell anyone, but now that I'm certain..." she dragged on once again, the words sticking horribly in her throat. Looking down at the table, she scanned its surface, searching for the courage she needed to drop the words out of her hesitant mouth before looking up with an expression of anguish, directly into her mother's eyes. "I'm expecting a child."

There. It was out. The much mulled-over news squatted in a small pile in the middle of the table glaring at them. They looked at the spot where it lay, waiting to be commented upon, dissected, cried over, and finally...inevitably, for that was the sort of news that it was, accepted.

What could be said? Not much that was useful. What could be done? Again, not much that was useful, except for the offering of the gesture that the Colonel had bet on when coming here.

Liliane's hand slowly reached across the table toward her daughter and Paulette grabbed onto it as if it were the lifeline saving her from drowning in a sea of despair.

The Colonel looked at his own clasped hands placed not far from the pile of news, then smiled down at his lap.

There were suddenly so many words coming from both women, that even native French speakers could have become confused by the flood of phrases piled high on top of each other and running together, helter-skelter. The Colonel chose to stand and leave them to it, knowing his role had been fulfilled.

They didn't notice him go, so tightly were their hands entwined on top of the pile of news, the size of which was shrinking fast.

I was warm all over. It was the sort of announcement that should come with the spring. We would have a baby!

#

Rolf VonZeller leaned back against the black leather of the Mercedes driving him back to us and twisted his mustache, exactly like any villain worthy of the name would do. So predictable, he never realized that his gesture was a bit too theatrical or stereotypical. Of course that could also be because he didn't perceive himself in this role. He was simply too self-centered to take into account what anyone else thought of him. So he twisted and twirled the black hairs over his lip until one side molded to a point.

He'd been doing this ever since had grown the hairy thing and was surprised every morning when he saw himself looking rather lopsided in the mirror. He continually trimmed the one side since it refused to lie down during his morning inspection, having been pulled on so much over time that it could no longer comply with his wishes. Even though the fashion of the day was for a much smaller tightly clipped mustache, Rolf kept his own somewhat bushier, unconsciously fueling the need to pull on the left side of it. Admittedly, a shorter one would be more difficult to fiddle with.

He did this whenever he was thinking.

Today, he was looking forward to being the fly in his brother's soup once again. It had never been easy to exasperate Heinrich. The sly bugger always seemed to be one step ahead of Rolf, but now... now, he had an Achilles heel.

He would be much easier to annoy. All Rolf had to do was have some fun with his little blonde. Rolf was indeed, looking forward to another evening in her company. Of course, Paulette was attractive, in an idiotic, naive sort of way. She reminded him of a small rabbit, ready to flee once the petting got too rough. He was ready to assume the role of the cat, happy to play with his prey before devouring it. He twirled away in anticipation. Just a few more miles to go...

I had no way to warn anyone.

Paulette was busy with Liliane. Marcel was arguing with Michel. Heinrich was in the cellar, once again supervising an order for more *calvados* for the warehouse in Dieppe.

The horses were nervous and the dog knew that danger was afoot, but humans tend to take little notice of the clues that animals leave in forewarning.

We were left with the unacceptable option of waiting and watching.

CHAPTER 22

"Where do you want us to put the prisoner, Major VonZeller?" A uniformed officer stood frozen in the salute to the *Führer* as he addressed Rolf with fearful respect. Rolf surveyed with a cold eye, the unloading of a bloodied, shabby looking fellow who had obvious difficulty keeping to his feet.

Unloading was a generous word, I should say that the poor chap, evidently the worse for wear, had been chucked off the back of the open lorry which followed the Mercedes transporting Rolf back to us, welcome or not.

Rolf responded without so much as a glance at the junior officer left standing with his arm stuck out at odds with body. "Lieutenant Schmidtz, I should think that you would be able to handle such a decision on your own. After all, you must have earned your rank somehow. Did that involve proving yourself capable of thinking on your own? If so, do it once again. If not, remove the stripes from your uniform and demote yourself to the rank which you are capable of assuming."

Rolf's sarcastic smirk was met by a stoic face, although colored bright pink, a click of the heels and a murmured response of "Yes, Major. Of course Major.

Right away, Major," before the flustered Lieutenant turned away, silently inventing obscenities aimed at the Major and at his own stupidity for not second guessing his superior's reaction.

That was something of a tall order for anyone, Rolf being so very unpredictable in this sort of situation. Sometimes he would upbraid a soldier for asking his wishes and other times would thunder against those who didn't ask for his opinion before taking action. To take initiatives, or not? That was the question.

I'd noticed that inconsistency was one of his most consistent character traits. He enjoyed keeping his inferiors on their toes, dancing attendance on him before smiting them with cruel, sarcastic commentary. As could be expected, he wasn't much appreciated by those beneath him in rank. However, those above him couldn't find fault with his results, not caring much about the means he employed to achieve them.

Rolf turned, stalking off toward the house, suddenly hungry and thirsty. Meanwhile, Schmidtz stomped over to the fallen man, kicking him out of spite as he struggled to rise, hands tied behind his back and feet hobbled together. "Get up! Be quick about it!" he shouted at the prisoner who lie face down in the dirt.

#

Steve turned his head to the side to draw a deep breath, making another attempt to rise without the use of his hands. He ached all over. He had bruises all about his head and was certain of at least two cracked ribs.

Now he was sure that it had been a grave mistake to give himself up to the Gestapo who'd come looking for him. But when the resistance camp was warned they were at risk, he had simply walked off toward town on the main road and let them find him on purpose. Plucking him off the road, they beat him senseless, although his hands were raised in surrender and he was unarmed. Instantly regretting his decision, he was by now reasonably sure that he would soon feel as if he would be better off dead. Obviously, these men were capable of cruelty unaccounted for in the Geneva Convention and had no qualms about respecting the premises for the treatment of prisoners enumerated in it. No one questioned their actions. Indeed, they seemed to be accountable to no one.

There was no reasoning with them, either. No possibility of requesting even the most basic things such as a drink of water or the freedom to urinate without his hands tied behind his back. They laughed when by accident his urine had stained his pants, since he couldn't use his hands to direct the stream away from his body. At the time he was grateful that one of them at least, had shown him the courtesy of unzipping his pants before he started to relieve himself. Unfortunately, he soon realized the inevitable consequences of peeing with his hands tied behind his back. The soldiers thoroughly enjoyed his discomfort at the end result, laughing heartily at his expense. He was getting a first hand taste of what the word "misery" truly meant.

He mulled this over as he drew on his reserve of strength, built up over the weeks of convalescence with the Duchemin couple and their pigs, then again during his stay with the resistance organization in the forest south of Yvetôt. Finally, he succeeded at rising to his knees, and then to his feet before the German could kick at him once again.

While he approached the barn under the impetus of rough shoving, he thought in an instant of somewhat ironic happiness that he would be better off in the company of animals and would gladly stay there forever, knowing that even the meanest of beasts would be a better companion than this particular group of men had proven themselves to be.

Hurled into a dark space, the last stall along the row of stalls housing the horses, this one's walls reaching all the way to the ceiling, Steve fell to his battered knees. There was no window, the only light filtered through the cracks between the planks making up the walls and the door. The room was piled high with sacks of grain of some sort and the cobbled floor was bare, except for a thin layer of old straw. It looked like heaven to Steve, who'd been jolted along in the lorry for two hours, his wounds and bruises aggravated by the bumpy ride.

Content to stay on the floor as he had fallen when chucked inside, he was exhausted to the point of not being able to move. He kept his eyes open though, listening for telltale sounds indicating they were coming back for him. The horses were brought back into the barn and he identified the noises of someone bringing them feed and water. He listened to the French voice speaking gentle words while brushing down the horses and its slowly rocking cadence brought relaxation and finally, sleep to the extenuated Canadian.

Sometime much later, the door creaked as the hinges were undone, swinging open from the wrong side. Steve turned on his side to see who was coming in. It was dark now, and he couldn't distinguish much through the shadows.

"Pssst!" said whoever had undone the hinges. "Are you awake? I've brought you some food and water. Please tell me that I'm not too late and that you're not dead," said the feminine voice whispering in soft French through the darkness.

#

Paulette had escaped from the kitchen where she was supposed to be helping Marthe clean up after dinner. She had begged off the meal upstairs with Rolf and his men. Heinrich covered for her, remembering her distress after the last dinner she had shared with his brother.

Rolf and the other Gestapo thought she was sick in bed. Heinrich was certain she would be in the kitchen while he shared drinks and cigarettes with his brother and the others. He'd thought it sufficient to warn her to use the back staircase to their room and to go to bed early to avoid crossing paths with any of the Gestapo. He didn't guess that she had no intention of listening to his warnings.

When Michel came in to their parents' cottage earlier in the day to find some food, Paulette saw surprise register on his face, seeing her speaking earnestly to their mother, hands clasped on the tabletop. He sat with them to listen, saying nothing and looking glum.

Later they were looking out of her former bedroom window in her parents' cottage when he recognized Steve being thrown off the lorry bed into the dirt. Their father had been obliged to practically tie Michel to the bedposts to keep him from charging out into the yard to try and save Steve. Paulette wondered what Papa had done in order to restrain Michel now and hoped that whatever it was, it worked.

The visions of the prisoner being savagely kicked around in the dirt had run through Paulette's head throughout the afternoon. She knew where they would lock him up; it could only be one of two places. There were only two locks on any of the storerooms on the whole estate, one on the spirits cellar in the cider house and the other on the feed store in the barn.

She had correctly guessed that the feed store would be their first choice. Arrogant men that they were, no one had even taken pains to guard the poor man, assuming he wouldn't have the strength or the capacity to get out of his bonds and demolish the store room walls to gain escape. They were right. His wounds and his bonds had kept Steve exactly where they'd dropped him.

Paulette remembered seeing her father take the iron pins out of the old hinges on the door, on one occasion long ago, when he had forgotten to fetch the key from its peg in the study in the big house, effectively opening the door from the wrong side, while leaving the padlock in place. She had thought the whole idea of the lock completely silly that day and laughed and laughed with her father, who asked her never to tell anyone what he had done. It was their secret. Since then, she never considered the door to be truly locked and wondered if everyone else knew that the padlock was a sham. Obviously the Gestapo hadn't thought to examine the ancient hinges before securing their own padlock on the old door.

Paulette lit a single candle, settling its small holder on floor in a space carefully cleared of straw. Steve sat up with some difficulty, as she crouched beside him, lifting the tin cup to his cut and swollen lips for a much needed gulp of water. The edge of the cup pushed on the cut and he winced in pain.

She let out a small cry of regret at having hurt him and pulled the cup away.

"*Non, Non, Mademoiselle, s'il vous plaît!* Don't stop! I'd like more water please."

She held the cup up once again and he drank, rather sloppily, before licking away the fresh blood pearling on his lip. She dipped a clean cloth in the jug of water, dabbing at some of the other cuts on his face.

"Where else are you hurt?" she asked. "If you show me, I can see if I can help you somehow."

"I hurt just about everywhere that I can think of, but if you have some food. Please. I'm very hungry. I can't remember when I last had anything to eat."

"Of course. I can't get you out of those bonds on your hands, so I'll have to feed you myself, if you don't mind?" she asked, suddenly shy.

"*Mademoiselle*, I can't think of anything more pleasant."

She smiled sadly at his attempt at gallantry, in spite of the horrible bruises on his face. It was impossible to see whether he was a handsome man or not, but the charm in his voice made her think he must be, for he was sure enough of himself to flirt with her.

"Then stop talking, because we have work to do and I can't stay here very long," she scolded gently, putting a spoonful of mashed potato with spiced minced beef in his mouth.

Steve groaned with pleasure when the simply perfect mixture of the *hachis parmentier* landed on his tongue, commenting that the finest dish of lobster couldn't have tasted any better. It was warm and perfectly satisfying, so he swallowed quickly, opening up for more like a starving baby bird. He enjoyed his meal in silence for a few minutes before starting up conversation once again, asking Paulette where he was.

She told him.

"I've heard of this place," Steve said, "I think I know two boys who worked here before. In fact, I had quite an unusual meeting with them, unforgettable actually..." He proceeded to relate his crash landing, his stay at an unnamed farm, as well as the strange goings on behind the red door at the pharmacy in Yvetôt.

The conversation was one sided, although Steve, having warmed to his subject didn't notice Paulette's resounding silence. He was simply happy to talk to her, happy to have her company, happy for her attractive feminine presence, as well as welcoming the warm food.

As he chatted at her, Paulette listened with shock written eloquently all over her face, her mouth hanging slightly open. She now knew that Guillaume and her brother were in serious danger, as were the rest of them. If this man were to be tortured he could give them all away, and nothing that Heinrich could do would keep her family safe from harm if Rolf were to get involved. Should he find out that they were harboring two resistance fighters and that she was helping out their prisoner. The Gestapo would be capable of executing her father, as his role as hostage dictated, and quite possibly Michel and Guillaume, along with anyone else who tried to intervene.

She clamped her mouth shut again, sitting back on her heels still looking at him in horror.

"You must not say these things! This can't be the same place. You must be mistaken!" she blurted out in terror. She began tossing her things into the basket, preparing to take flight, at once horribly aware of the risk she was taking. Although she had come to him with her heart full of compassion for the straits he found himself in, she quickly weighed the danger to her loved ones against her pity for a stranger and the imbalance between the two was very clear. She must abandon him to his fate. Now.

The horses smelled her fear, and shifted uneasily, snorting in their stalls next door.

"Miss, what's wrong? I'm sorry. I didn't mean to frighten you. You won't be in any danger from me, I promise you! Don't leave yet." Steve voiced dismay at her volatile reaction.

"No! I have to go. You don't know how much danger I'm putting my family in!" She gave him another gulp of water before flinging the tin cup in the basket with the rest of the things she had brought with her, forgetting to pick up the cloth she had used to wipe the blood from his face.

She was backing out of the door when she backed straight into someone sturdy, standing behind her, and froze.

"What in the devil do you think you're doing?" Heinrich hissed at her. "Have you completely lost your mind? Do you have any idea what Rolf would do to you if he found out that you were here? I thought that you were smarter that that!!" He seized her by the arm, spinning her around to face him, but keeping such a tight grip on her that she twisted her upper body in pain.

"Let go! You're hurting me!" she cried out a bit too loudly.

Steve made an attempt to intervene, not understanding the relationship between the two. "Hang on, now! You leave her alone!"

By now, the horses were stomping and snorting through their nostrils. Flynn let out a high whinny. Polka heard Paulette's cry and started to bark as she ran across the yard from Emile's cottage toward the barn. Shouts were heard coming from the house as the soldiers were alerted to something unusual happening outside.

"Hurry up and climb that ladder to the loft, right now!" He shoved Paulette out into the alleyway of the barn, before sticking his head into the grain room to tell Steve "and you! Not a word about her being here or you'll regret it!"

He pulled back, shut the door and slid one of the iron pins back into place just as the first two soldiers arrived in the barn, lanterns held high. He slipped the other pin into his pocket as he turned to respond to their summons.

"It's only me; I came out to see the horses before going to bed, like I usually do. I don't know what got into the dog...must have seen a rat or something. Not to worry, everything is fine."

He started walking slowly toward the soldiers who were moving to the grain store room to check and see if the prisoner was still safely locked away.

Rolf and Lieutenant Schmidtz showed up in the doorway to the barn before Heinrich could reach it.

"Really Lieutenant, I don't think you'll keep your bride happy very long, if you prefer to keep company with animals instead of taking her to bed." Rolf sneered sarcastically. "Do you need some help with her? I'd be happy to oblige, and let you continue consorting with the sheep." He laughed at his joke, while everyone else held their tongues in horror at the insult, clearly intended to provoke his brother.

He was still laughing, his eyes tiny slits of mirth, when the punch landed squarely on his already crooked nose.

#

A fight is often a source of entertainment on a slow day such as today, and I chose the side I wished to root for just like the other spectators in the barn.

More soldiers arrived, but stood back giving the contestants room to scuffle about in the dust and bits of straw stirred up by their rolling around on the floor, arms and legs locked in the oddly disgraceful embrace of men wrestling. It was obvious that this wasn't the first time these two had gone at each other. The spectators, although they were German, were all rooting for the one and against the other. Yet half of them couldn't admit to which side they'd chosen. Their common interest in the outcome made an informal circle take shape as they watched in surprise while a lieutenant dared attempt to throttle a major.

It should have been a largely unequal contest, since the two men were quite badly matched in size. But for some reason Rolf didn't appear to be winning. Heinrich apparently had forgotten his gentlemanly ways and was playing rather dirty and thus, was coming out slightly better than his brother, whose weight and size slowed his movements. I felt a budding respect for Heinrich.

Since the attention of the soldiers was fixed on the skirmish on the floor, Paulette seized the opportunity to slip silently back down the ladder from the loft. She then sidled around the fray toward the door, unnoticed, before letting out an intentional scream bringing eight faces jerking around toward the sound of her shrill voice.

She elbowed the spectators aside and landed a swift kick in Rolf's testicles, while shouting at them both. "You stop this right now! Both of you!"

She aimed again, this time at Heinrich, before he scooted out of reach of her foot. The momentum of her kick, reaching thin air, brought her other leg from underneath her and she landed squarely on her bottom on the hard cobblestone floor.

Her spinal cord sent a jerk of electric shock up through her body toward her teeth and she bit her tongue hard, drawing blood and bringing tears immediately to her eyes. Four of the eight spectators rushed to her side to help her up, being the Colonel's men and her usual dinner companions. The others stood by, still rather stupefied by what they had just witnessed.

Rolf lay on his side cursing, holding both hands over his sore parts, his rapidly swelling eyes screwed shut in agony.

Heinrich looked at her in surprise, wiping blood from the corner of his mouth, bent over with one hand on his knee, as she started to berate him in a shrewish fashion, about acting like a child, fighting in the dirt with his brother.

Just then, Colonel VonEpffs came in, alerted a bit too late, by the noise coming from the barn.

Paulette leaned over Rolf with a concerned look on her face, asking him if he would be alright and if she could help him, while apologizing for having kicked him accidentally in the wrong spot.

No one present entertained the slightest doubt that her gesture had been intentional. Still not one of them chose to question her declaration of innocence. She continued to fuss over Rolf, begging him to let her help him to his feet and to forgive her.

"I'm so very sorry, brother, I was trying to get my idiot of a husband to stop behaving like a child and missed and caught you instead. Please forgive me!" She gave him such a concerned look, her face awash with tears that even Rolf with his insensitive nature had to buck up and act as if it were alright. His obvious concern was to keep his men from thinking he was going to be mad at a mere girl for hurting him. It would make him look like a sissy.

I chuckled at his dilemma.

"You have a good leg on you little sister! I won't ever have to worry about you taking care of yourself!" he admitted through teeth just starting to unclench, as he stood up as straight as possible and hobbled toward the exit.

Paulette put her arm around him, letting him lean on her, leading him to the house with promises of ice and a shot of *calvados*, the handy Norman cure-all, so useful in the aftermath of squabbles.

As they passed close to Colonel VonEpffs, he held out his arm to stop her, looking her straight in the eye. Rolf's head was still drooping, so he didn't notice the defiant look she shot the Colonel, warning him to keep his quiet.

The Colonel let go and let her pass, listening to Paulette murmur kind words to the man that he knew she absolutely hated. He turned an inquisitive eye to survey the rest of the scene.

Heinrich was brushing himself off and his usual colleagues were patting him on the back, partly in silent congratulations and partly in sympathy at discovering that he had taken such a shrew to wife. The lesser Gestapo officers were milling about uneasily, although Lieutenant Schmidtz shook Heinrich's hand heartily, a wry smile on his face, before rounding up the others to follow Rolf and Paulette into the house, always ready to partake of spirits when the offer arose.

There would be many hushed conversations to follow, commenting on the fight and its unexpected outcome. The Major had been brought down and all because of a girl!

Colonel VonEpffs was silently thoughtful. He approached Heinrich, speaking softly near his left ear. "Quite a wife you have there, my boy, quite a woman, indeed. You'll take good care of that one, she's worth the effort!" He stepped back, looking Heinrich straight in the eye, "You heed my words, she's worth the effort," and nodding at him, turned with a thoughtful expression still painted on his face, to return to the house and a shot of his own, leaving Heinrich alone and free to slip the last iron pin in the bottom hinge of the door to the grain storeroom.

Heinrich, in turn left the barn, shutting the main door a few minutes later after trying to collect his thoughts about what had just taken place. Unable to decide if Paulette had simply lost her mind or if she had a secret agenda that he hadn't dreamed of up until now, he headed back to the house. He planned to seek her out, hoping to be able to shake her until some of her normal good sense returned to her brain and before her irresponsibility got them all in serious trouble.

No one had thought to check on the prisoner and Steve was dying of curiosity about what he had heard through the chinks in the door.

So proud of Paulette's quick thinking that I was about to burst, I creaked with excitement, wishing I could talk with someone about the extraordinary wits this young lady possessed.

I vibrated with joy, hoping Rolf's testicles would ache for days and days on end.

CHAPTER 23

Heinrich was astounded to hear laughter coming from the lower level as he descended the half flight of steps leading to the kitchen. He paused midway to listen, to link names to voices before joining what sounded like a celebration in full swing.

The scene playing out before his eyes did nothing to temper his initial reaction. He caught sight of Paulette as she raised a cup to her lips in tune with the cheering encouragement of a crowd of Gestapo officers.

Red hot anger rose; scorching his face and aggravating his throbbing lip, head and damaged eye socket. He had come to the kitchen in search of an ice chip to soothe his lip, and a bit of sympathy from his wife to soothe his weary heart. He was ashamed at having come to blows with his only brother. Considering her present activity, he guessed that his wish would not be granted.

Paulette stood, hair mussed and skirt rumpled, leaning on the table in the middle of the group of soldiers. Two bottles of *calvados* were open, one rolling empty on its side, and the other well on its way to following suit. Nine earthenware cups raised in salute to her as she threw back the contents of her own, much in the manner of a swaggering sailor on leave after months at sea.

"What in the devil do you think you're doing now?" The shout escaped him, louder than he'd intended, causing the ten revelers to turn and look in his direction. Now the center of attention, his anger bubbled over, out of control. He elbowed a path through the circle to plant himself in front of her.

"Isn't it enough that you tried to kick me...in...in my privates...while I was involved in a fight? You distracted me from what I was doing! That could have been dangerous for me and for you! Never, never intervene in a situation like that!" The finger he aimed at her nose thrust closer and closer to its target. She lifted her eyes to his, her facial features arguing amongst themselves as she stifled a mischievous, inebriated grin.

A pregnant silence from the Gestapo broke as Rolf blurted out in a drunken guffaw: "You're the lucky one, little brother, she did kick me in the balls! She missed yours!" All around mirth exploded as gulps of fiery apple brandy lifted the spirits of the participants to a new high.

Even Paulette laughed at the absurd conversation, though her laughter soon veered off toward the hysterical sort caused by fear and tension washed down with strong alcohol. She hiccupped and choked while Rolf pounded her on the back, keeping time with the general hilarity running away with the lot of them.

Heinrich stood aghast at the camaraderie facilitated by a liter and a half of *calvados* consumed in short order. He was the odd man out, the last to arrive at a full blown *fête*, and it was a disagreeable sort of feeling.

Paulette's participation in this singular party ended rather quickly as the thumping on her back brought up her dinner in a rush, and she vomited onto the flagstone floor at Heinrich's feet. This gift was greeted with another round of laughter and applause from the Gestapo, by now well into their cups.

"Good for you, little sister!" shouted Rolf, a toast lifted in her honor. "Just another sip to wash away the bad taste and off to bed for you!" He presented her with a brimming cup, dribbles of overflow splashing to the floor, and she willingly slugged it back in tune to a chorus of hoorays.

"She's yours now! Take her up to bed. Though I think she'll be passed out before you can get her undressed! But, she's a tough little trooper, she is! Good luck with her!"

The young couple exited the kitchen on a wave of applause. Paulette turned to salute the assembly behind her, bringing on more cheering, before leaning heavily on Heinrich's arm, as they took the back steps one by one, all three and a half floors of them, up to their bedroom.

Heinrich felt Paulette drop her guard and deflate under his arm with each step. They kept silent until the door shut firmly behind them. However, once inside Heinrich could no longer contain himself.

"What were you thinking? Breaking in to free the prisoner! Don't you realize the danger you've put everyone in? And coming down out of the loft to get involved in a fight! You could have been seen and how would you have explained that? And kicking Rolf! He has a horrible temper; he could have killed you for embarrassing him like that!" Once again, he waggled his finger at her nose, scolding her like a child.

"And if that's not enough, you tell me you can't stand being around him and within ten minutes you're drunk in the kitchen, carrying on as if you were old school chums! What kind of behavior is that for my wife?...And..."

His rant ground to a halt as her eyes obviously lost focus on him. She swayed and lurched in the direction of the chamber pot, a hand plugging her mouth.

"My God! Just how much did you have to drink before I came in? You were only there for a short time..." He exclaimed as she gagged over the pot.

"I don't think that's what the problem is..." she mumbled miserably between retching noises.

"Of course it is. You're not used to drinking such hard stuff. Whatever has gotten into you?" His voice was a bit gentler now, pity having finally caught up with and surpassed the anger dictating his words earlier. He reached behind her and gathered her hair in two hands to relieve her of its burden and to keep it safe from the flood of vomit she couldn't seem to stop spurting.

"You have!" she blurted. "This is all your fault!" This declaration took him by surprise, hearing the tables turn on him as she looked up, green-faced and bleary-eyed. "I'm pregnant!"

He dropped her hair, speechless.

#

Steve realized after quite some time that he was indeed alone with the horses and that no one would be coming back to check up on him that night. He slept, tormented by dreams of blond-haired angels and nightmares of physical struggle, alternately with the

Gestapo and then with the granny in Yvetôt, who kept trying to sew his mouth shut. He woke immediately when the hinges came off the door once again, rough hands shaking him before clamping over his mouth to prevent him crying out in surprise.

He recognized Michel and Guillaume. "Get up! We've come to set you free!" Michel whispered as he sawed at the ropes tying Steve's hands behind his back.

"We've brought you different clothes, water and some money, but you'll have to walk to Bacqueville and reach the pharmacist's shop before dawn. You've only got about an hour and it's close to three miles. Do you think you can do it? You'll have to stick to the woods and keep away from the road as much as possible, so we drew you a map."

While Guillaume was outlining this plan, Steve stretched his stiff muscles and changed into the offered clothing.

Michel was quietly pulling nails and using a wedge to dislodge the planks making up the side wall of the stall. "It has to look as if you broke yourself free. They won't accuse anybody else that way." Michel explained. "We'll leave the cut ropes and tools on the floor. Then, we'll replace the hinge pins and be out of here."

All in all it was a fairly simple plan, if they could get out of the barn and off the farm as soon as possible. They made a quick detour as the boys left a note for their parents, knowing that a thorough search for Steve would be carried out and they couldn't remain hidden safely anywhere nearby. The price of Steve's freedom was their disappearance.

Steve took stock of their sacrifice to save him, grateful of their decision to risk compromising their loved ones. He shook hands with the boys in thanks and silent *adieu* and once again they were off, swallowed by the night.

#

Paulette woke with her brain thumping about in her skull like a tennis ball bashing off an expert's racket, similar to the match she'd watched on the lawns in Dieppe. Each bounce was more painful than the last. Her throat was burnt raw from bile and her tongue tasted of acid covered in a film of dust. Her hair smelled of vomit, her bum was bruised and her husband was mad at her.

Thinking that today was as good a day as any for staying in bed and dying, she screwed her eyes shut tight against the ray of sunshine annoying her face.

The urge to get up and use the chamber pot kept her from fulfilling this death wish. However, simply thinking of the chamber pot brought to mind vomiting once again, which she did before peeing into it. She landed in a heap on the braided rug after successfully completing both of these tasks without making a mess.

The smell from the pot, although of her own making, was enough to bring tears to her eyes, for she knew that she would have to carry it down three flights of stairs to dispose of it. There were no maids or other kindhearted souls to care for her, in spite of this being the maid's room from long ago, when there were maids. She realized with a tiny glimmer of humor that she would most likely have been the maid emptying the pot for someone else anyway. She got to her knees, but the bent over position only served to bring up more bile.

Quietly she cried out for her mother, as most young girls, turned too quickly into women, do when the road gets a little bumpier than they had planned. *Maman* was far enough away not to hear her, as is often the case. So, Paulette sat on the rug and tried to pull herself together, that being the only thing to do.

Little more than a half hour later, feeling weak and subdued, Paulette appeared in the doorway of the kitchen, covered pot in hand. Marthe took one look at her, went to put the teapot on, and started the preparation of ginger root tea, helpful in reducing nausea.

"Are you feeling poorly for the reason that I think, *chèrie?*" asked the cook in a compassionate voice, while patting Paulette gently on the shoulder with one hand, and feeling her forehead for a fever with the other.

"You heard about the *calvados* then?" asked Paulette, without looking up, feeling that if she moved her head any more than was strictly necessary, the whole business could quite easily start up once again.

"No, I wasn't talking about too much drink," Marthe replied.

The questioning tone caught Paulette's attention at once, "Oh, so you know about that too? How did you find out? My goodness, can you tell already?" Vanity took over and she wondered if she already looked as if she were getting fat.

"Don't be a silly duck; it's just that it's normal for this sort of thing to happen to young marrieds. Didn't you give it a thought before now? Surely your mother warned you!"

It dawned on Paulette that Marthe feared she'd gone into marriage a true innocent.

"*Bien sûr que oui!* And anyway, I grew up here on the farm tending the animals, I knew all about that side of things long ago." She remembered in vivid color the day her father and several other men helped Maurice to mount Flo, resulting in Flynn's birth some months later. It had been an exciting day, in a hot uncomfortable sort of way and Paulette hadn't been able to look away as the usually calm Maurice showed a wild lack of restraint when his encounter with the mare in heat was imminent. The sight of the two of them was intriguing and slightly scary. Paulette stayed out of the path of the enormous Percheron as he screamed and snorted, dancing an equine tango with his mate. The memory of the coupling brought an embarrassed flush of color to her pale face.

"*Alors*, is your man pleased with the news?" Marthe asked, in a tentative tone of voice. It was quite clear that this wasn't the very best of things that could happen in such uncertain times.

Paulette thought for a moment before realizing that she didn't remember him commenting about his pleasure at all. She had been rather sick when she told him. She recalled him saying he would leave her in peace for the night, before escaping out the door from her retching, and she hadn't seen him since.

She did vaguely recollect throwing him a nasty look when he, and very stupidly she'd thought at the time, asked her how it could possibly have happened, once she'd blurted out the news of her pregnancy. After all, it was a very foolish question for *him* to be asking. If anyone were to ask it, it would be more logical for *her* to throw it in *his* face. Maybe the glower she'd bestowed in response to the ridiculous question had chased him from their room. Or maybe it was the vomiting.

It was rather early, but he hadn't even checked on her. She was at once miffed at his cavalier attitude. She'd saved him from getting beaten up and had even gotten drunk with his horrible brother, just to dampen the repercussions from the fight. Then, when she told him what he'd done to her, he'd run. The transformation from wretched to rankling took about twenty seconds.

"You know what? I don't think I really care what he thinks about it!" she declared, suddenly feeling strong enough to empty the offensive pot into the water closet.

Marthe stretched her eyebrows as Paulette rose from the table, but called out to her as she climbed the stairs leading outside, "Come on back here as soon as you're done, the ginger tea will be ready, and then you must have some breakfast!"

Paulette waved her hand without looking back as she stomped up the worn stone stairs, pot at arm's length and a renewed liveliness to her step.

#

Heinrich poked his head around the door to their bedroom looking for Paulette, noticed the empty bed and the remains of the foul smell, and opened the window to let fresh air wash away the stink.

When he reached the kitchen, Marthe looked up with a wry smile, and pointed him out the door toward the latrines. "If I were you, I'd be very careful what you say to her this morning. She's not feeling so well, if you know what I mean..." She tossed him a meaningful blink.

He let out a weary sigh and his shoulders dropped of their own accord. "Do you have anything for my head? My eye is killing me and I don't think I'm ready for another fight just yet." He was miserable with his face all swollen up, dried crusty blood pulling on the skin of his lip.

"Alright, you just sit yourself down here. She'll be back soon enough from her chore. I've made her some ginger root tea, I can make you some willow bark tea and you'll both have some breakfast. Nothing like warm tea and warm food to make things look a little brighter!"

The cook's recurrent recipe for problems appealed to Heinrich. So he straddled the bench at the long kitchen table, cradling his thudding head in his hands.

#

Paulette came back and found him hunched over, head in hands and shoulders slumped. Her heart jumped in her chest, and I felt her concern for his well being douse her anger. She approached, but Marthe heard her before Heinrich did.

"You sit yourself down, *Mademoiselle*, and start sipping this tea before you start feeling woozy again. Here's your own, young man. Just sit and sip and no arguing until you've both finished your tea and eaten. I'll have your porridge in no time."

Marthe turned her back to them but her ears were focused like a cat's, catching any noises coming from behind her at the table. She and I smiled into the pot of boiling water, as she threw in several handfuls of oats while stirring vigorously. They seemed to be heeding her words, so they really must be feeling poorly. No matter, the porridge was on the way.

The couple sat quietly, looking as if they'd been punished by the schoolmaster, but sipping dutifully at their tea, facing each other but avoiding eye contact. I thought their behavior ridiculous.

Heinrich glanced up at Paulette's pale face across the table and tossed the proverbial olive branch in her direction. "I think we need to talk about what happened yesterday..."

Marthe nipped this conversation in the bud while still stirring their porridge. "Yes you do, but not until you've eaten, and not in my kitchen! You'll go somewhere private, later!"

They chuckled at this and Paulette saluted Marthe's impressive backside, feeling some measure of complicity return to the air.

That was partly my doing. The pleasant atmosphere of my kitchen as the teapot whistled and the pot simmered with the timeless activity of food preparation had comforted many a soul before these two and would be a haven for many more to come, or so I hoped.

Marthe deposited two bowls of warm porridge drizzled with honey and cream before them and they tucked into it, letting the goodness seep into their bones, relieving some of the tension between them.

The cook pottered around making up platters of food to be carried upstairs to the dining room, a comfort for the soldiers who most likely had the same sort of morning look about them as these two did, considering the empty bottles abandoned on the kitchen table this morning.

Things seemed to have a more normal feel to them, at least for now. I was curious about what today would bring. Each passing day revealed itself to be more eventful than the last. I was full of hope that Heinrich would step up to the task and give Paulette the reassuring support she needed to cope with a pregnancy during wartime.

I wondered what Rolf would make of their news. Would he find some small glimmer of kindness in his heart toward Paulette and his brother now that she carried his nephew or niece? Surely family bonds would win out now that he'd tested Paulette's mettle and found her to be in possession of more strength of character than he'd previously thought. Maybe he would be a bit kinder to them both.

I mused while my kitchen was humming with activity, but of a peaceful sort, as two hearts reconciled over their porridge.

It was a short lived pause.

Just a few moments after the porridge was consumed, while second cups of tea were being quietly sipped, turmoil galloped down the kitchen steps, dragged in by the boots on Bierdorpf's feet.

"I've been looking all over for you! VonEpffs is arguing with your brother out in the barn right now! I think they're going to come to blows! The prisoner's escaped and the Major is saying that it's our fault! You'd better get out here right now!" He was tossing the words in Heinrich's direction while turning and running back up the stairs two at a time, obviously anxious to get back to the confrontation.

Heinrich leaped to his feet to follow. Paulette did the same. The sudden movement made her wobble, bracing her hands against the chair back to steady herself.

Marthe made a move toward her just as Heinrich barked out a stern warning to Paulette: "You! You will sit back down and not get involved in this! Make yourself scarce, but do not go anywhere near the barn. I'll be back to speak to you as soon as I can. Do I make myself clear? I refuse to have my wife getting herself into any more trouble!"

His warning was just a bit too harsh and a bit too clear, for a young pregnant woman who hadn't yet had the time or the luxury to be happy about her present state. He was gone, up the stairs after Bierdorpf before the tears pooling in her eyes could spill over onto the table.

The pleasant humming stopped as I listened, disappointed with Heinrich's apparent insensitivity.

Marthe was at her side in the blink of an eye and she sent one of the newly arrived kitchen helpers to run over to the Fournier cottage to ask Paulette's mother to come to the kitchen for a bit. She patted Paulette on the shoulder while guiding her back to her chair.

I wished I could pat her shoulder too.

"*Chèrie*, you mustn't take his words to heart so, he means to protect you, not to scold you. It's only because he wants you and that baby to stay safe. He's just a man, you know... and they don't always say things the way they mean them. Believe me; I know how men can be thoughtless when they're talking to their women."

Marthe cut off there and Paulette looked up sharply at her. This ageless woman who had dominated the under ground of the big house for many years, was a forceful person, never letting anyone ruffle her feathers, even when the Germans showed up and Franz had been imposed on her.

Marthe's presence had always been a given in Paulette's life, sometimes criticizing her actions and scolding her when she dropped things or served something up with a less than perfect presentation.

Everyone who ran into her, feared her tongue, but also knew that under the bluster, you could count on her for help under any circumstances. But never had Paulette's imagination paired the cook with a man, and she was surprised to hear her mention them as if she knew something about the opposite sex first hand. Her curiosity did much to dry her tears.

I knew that everyone has a story to tell. I was chock full of their anecdotes. So, I settled with a contented sigh to absorb the telling of another.

A frustrated Paulette began, "But, he doesn't seem to realize that I only wanted to help him yesterday. I was so sure that Rolf would kill him if I didn't do something to stop that fight. With everyone looking on, I was afraid that Rolf would try and teach a lesson to Heinrich, just to prove a point in front of his men. And all he thinks was that I was enjoying drinking with his brother! How could he be so stupid?"

Marthe answered after a moment's reflection. "As I told you, men just don't think like we do. And they say things thinking that we'll understand just how they mean them, but we don't. We understand other things they haven't said. And most of the time, we put thoughts into their heads that aren't even there at all. They're much simpler beings than women are. We're the ones who read too much into what they say and sometimes we twist their words into something completely different..." Her eyes took on a faraway wistful look tempting Paulette to fish for crispy details.

"How do you know so much about men? Does it come with being older, or do you have a secret lover that I don't know about? It's not Franz, is it?" Paulette let a note of teasing come into her voice to soften her outspoken question.

"No, it's not Franz, for heaven's sakes! Although he could turn into a halfway decent chef if he would just stop leaving the meat cook for too long. But no, not him." Her reverie took over her eyes once again; softening them and making Paulette think that she might have been quite a handsome woman at one point in time.

"The problem with you young people is that you think us older ones have never had a life before, and that we've always been old. I was just as young as you once, and I remember being in love, and how scary and exciting it can make you feel. Can't think straight...nothing else seems important but him...and seeing him...and what he thinks...and how he feels about you. Completely takes over your life, love does. And when it goes away, it leaves you empty."

I looked back in time to conjure Marthe in her prime, pent up desires bursting from her short, slightly rounded frame of youth. She had been the sort of young woman whose beauty came from voluptuousness, a promise which didn't go unnoticed by several young men who took to hanging in the kitchen for any reason imaginable. She simmered like the soups she made to keep those men happy although I suspect they had hoped for more than soup.

By now Paulette was all ears, her own problems temporarily flown the coop as she urged the older woman to give up more of her past: "I never knew that you'd been married, Marthe. What happened to him? Who was he? What was he like?"

"Oh, so now you're curious about an old woman like myself, are you? Well, let's just say that love is sometimes very difficult. In fact, it almost always is. Very few people that I know have a simple love that just goes on and on as smoothly as a river with no rocks to break up the flow. Most times it's very rocky. Your mother could tell you something about that, what with her first love being the lord's son."

"What? My Mother was in love someone other than my father? When was that?" Paulette's curiosity was by now so intense that she wriggled on her seat with impatience, Marthe's revelations not coming out fast enough to suit her.

"Oh my! Well the cat's out of the bag now! I might as well tell you the truth before someone else puts you in the wrong about it...your mum was very lucky to have your father there to fall back on after the young man she fancied was shipped off to school." Marthe wiped her hands on her apron before reaching for a large skillet hanging from the rack above the table.

"You see, she'd fallen in love with the master's son, and he with her, or so she thought, but the master intervened right away and sent him off to school and your mother never saw him again, until it was too late. She was lucky enough to have your father come courting her right away afterward so she could forget him. Then she ended up with you all and didn't have time to do anything else. She's only seen him once or twice since he went away. You see the old master made sure that she was married and set up with you children born before he let his son come back here for a visit. By then it was too late for them to get into any trouble together."

Marthe was bustling around preparing food, slicing ham, clanging pots and pans, generally keeping busy while talking, as was her habit. I changed my mood to accommodate confidences shared. A warm complicity set the stage.

"And I do think that your mum is better off today for it, because he was a stupid young man, the son was. I don't think he ever did understand the difference between love and lust. Just look at the wife he chose. Now there's a useless piece of work if I ever saw one! If he can get along well enough with her, than your mother's much too good for him. The silly creature's always complaining about this and that not being like it is in Paris. Grew up in the city and you'd think it was paradise, to listen to her tell. Anyway, she's not made for living in the country, doesn't like the smell of the animals, she says. Every time she was here, she kept her windows closed even when it was summer! Because of the smell of outside! Like I said...useless woman. No wonder they ran off south when things started to get a bit difficult here. Wouldn't like to see her dealing with what's been going on around here since those nasty Gestapo fellows arrived! She wouldn't have the brains to handle them." She punctuated this with a knowingly mischievous wink in Paulette's direction.

Paulette answered this with a sheepish little grin then added: "But wait, I don't understand. My mother loved this other man, the son, so why would she agree to court my father? Wouldn't she have waited anyway, for the son to maybe come back for her? I would have, if I truly loved him, and he loved me. I wouldn't even look at another man!" Paulette's voice held a pleading note in it, not thinking about her father, just feeling sorry for her mother's disappointment at being dropped, and surprise that her mother should give up so easily on her love.

"Oh, well, she didn't have any doubts about how his family felt about them being together. The master sat her down and her parents with her and told them straight out that if she didn't forget about his son all together, then they could all pack their things and leave Bout L'Abbé for good. Don't forget that times were tough then. We were just coming out of the Great War, and jobs were hard to come by. I'm thinking your mother had to put her parents' luck in place of her own, she couldn't have them turned out from their home, and sent off to who knows where with just the clothes on their backs. So, she let your father woo her and she's settled here now and I'll imagine as happy as she could hope for. I know how happy she was to have you! When you arrived she was just as pleased as any woman ever was, to have such a lovely baby. For you were just as sweet a darling as they come, always smiling at anyone who looked at you. A real charmer you were!"

Paulette smiled at Marthe's flattering memories of herself as a baby, and put a hand on her own belly, hoping for the same sort of child to have for herself.

Marthe noticed her gesture and reached out and patted Paulette's other hand.

"Now don't you worry about the one you've got in there. It will surely be just as sweet a baby as you could ever hope for. You've made him with love in your hearts, how could he be any less than perfect? Or she, for that matter...could be a baby girl..."

"But you didn't tell me about your love, Marthe. You said that you've known what love was like. Who was your beau?" Paulette wheedled, trying to get the cook to come clean.

"Well, you see, I wasn't as lucky or as smart as your mother was. I had feelings for a young man from the village. He went off to the Great War and came back many years later, long after it was finished. Seems he had seen some awful things, and he just wandered all around France when it was over, not knowing what to do with himself, but not able to come back home either." Her voice softened and her eyes grew misty with remembering.

"It was like he was afraid to see us. Or maybe to see me. I don't know. He never really could explain it to me so that I could understand. We all thought he was dead, but never got the news of it, so when he finally showed up in 1923, five years after it was over, he was wearing a priest's collar. My heart broke all over again, because he never told me that he didn't want me for his wife, but instead just turned himself into the one thing that could keep him from me. He didn't even ask how I felt about it, or if I still loved him. He just came back and started preaching here, as if I had never existed."

"You were in love with *Père Lemarchand*?" Paulette asked, incredulous, "and he with you? All he ever does is preach to us about the sins of the flesh and how we should devote our love to God, and forget what our bodies urge us to do! I can hardly believe it!"

"Well, I can hardly believe it myself, because before he left for the eastern front, he was having some trouble keeping his hands off of my flesh!" Marthe admitted, rather coyly. "...and I can't say that I really wanted him to either. You have no idea how handsome that man was when he was nineteen!" She sighed and shook her head, as if to disperse the overwhelming memories.

"I felt so lucky to have his attention, to think that he could want me so much, that he found me so irresistible. What a feeling that was, to be swept away by such a wanting..."

Her voice faded to a whisper overflowing with nostalgia. Paulette was embarrassed by the intimate images appearing in her own mind, images of stolen moments with Heinrich when she'd forgotten that same priest's advice about the sins of the flesh, and forgotten without a moment's hesitation. She blushed with her memories, ones that brought a tingle to her insides.

They were both silent for a moment, lost in their thoughts.

Marthe was the first to shake herself out of the fog of her recollections. "The worst part of it is the hurt I caused to someone else. When everyone assumed that my Jean-Pierre was dead, Emile Levasseur brought me some of his cabbage roses and told me he wanted me for his own."

She waited patiently for Paulette to ingest this last tidbit of news.

"Emile? Old Emile Levasseur, from the garden? He was in love with you?" Paulette's mind ran erratically from one eye-opening revelation to the next, thinking that porridge in the kitchen with the cook should be taken more often.

It was a rare moment of secret sharing, one of the moments I loved most.

"Yes, there was enough age difference between us then that I was offended by the very idea of it and told him so, in no uncertain terms. You see he was thirty when I was seventeen, and I thought he was very old already. But he told me he would wait and let time see if I would change my mind. Every few weeks he would bring me more flowers and ask me once again. After a few months of this, it made me so very angry, his asking if I was still in love with Jean-Pierre that even when later on, when I knew that we could never be together I still said no to Emile, just because his asking annoyed me so much. He stopped asking about ten years ago, just bringing me the flowers without the asking, and I think I miss it."

"He still brings you flowers?" Paulette asked, trying to imagine Emile as a young man in love, superimposing the image of that young man over top of the old man, Emile, who was her friend, who'd taught her so much about the plants he devoted his time to.

"Every few weeks, I'll find a bouquet in front of my bedroom door in the morning. I've tried but I've never been able to catch him, putting the flowers there. You'd think he knows of a secret way to get up the stairs without them creaking."

Marthe smiled at Paulette, whose face was no longer sad, but wore a peculiar look of happiness, mixed with sadness, digesting with some incredulity all she'd learned that morning.

She took the spot vacated by Heinrich across from Paulette before continuing, "You see, if I've told you all of this today, it's so you'll know what's worth fighting for...and what's worth fighting over...and what's worth forgiving...and what's best forgotten. When you get that straight, you'll be happy. You just have to get that straight, is all. Get your important things on one side of the fence and the other bits and pieces on the other side of the fence, then keep yourself walking along the right side of it. Forget all that nonsense about the grass being greener...it's just not."

Paulette got up and came to stand behind the older woman, leaning over her shoulders and putting her arms around Marthe's neck from behind. She placed her head on Marthe's left shoulder and kissed her on the cheek. "You've been very kind to me; you always have been, but especially today. I've never thanked you for taking an interest in me, but I do now. I just didn't know how to say it before. But thank you...now...and for then too."

Marthe patted her arms and brushed away the sudden tears brought forth by this simple, yet sincere speech. "Now, just don't worry yourself about your man. He loves you; I can feel it. I wonder what's keeping your mother? But, while I'm thinking of it, it would be best if you didn't let on that you know about her story now. She might be angry at me for telling. You'll promise me?"

Paulette straightened up from her bent over position with one last kiss on Marthe's cheek. "Of course, but I won't be able to forget it, I'm afraid. I just can't imagine her kissing anyone but Papa; they get on together so well. I would never have guessed that he wasn't her first choice."

"Life sometimes doesn't let you choose, it just happens to you. It's up to you to make the best of it. I don't think I did, but I guess I'm happy enough, taking care of feeding all of you. Lord knows, it keeps me busy! But enough chatter!" she said, once again all bustle and bluster, her hands active. "I've got to get on with it; those men are going to want to eat soon enough. But I do wonder what happened to our guest out in the feed stall..."

Just then Paulette's mother came down the steps from the garden. "I just heard about the prisoner's escape, and your father and I found this note from Michel. He's gone and done something stupid once again. He and Guillaume have let the prisoner loose and run off themselves!"

She plopped herself down on the bench only recently vacated by Marthe, and covered her forehead with one hand while hiding her head the crook of the other arm "I just don't know what to do with that boy! He's going to get himself killed and probably your father along with him!" she declared from beneath her arm. Her muffled voice had an oddly wooden echo to it, reverberating off the table-top.

Paulette scanned the note quickly. "This says that they're returning to their camp, but that Steve has been sent to Bacqueville. They're not together, *Maman*, so it won't be as dangerous. They'll just get back to where they were before. They found their way here with no problem; they can find their way back to the camp from here as well. I can't say the same for that poor Canadian fellow, though. He has no idea where he's going. He's the one we should worry about. If he gets caught, he could tell the Gestapo about us all, and where the camp in Yvetot is located."

Her mind skipped back to the role she had played last night, in coming to his assistance, and the ensuing argument with Heinrich about her behavior. Her cheeks flushed pink once again.

"Who could tell who, what?" Heinrich asked as he came down the stairs on the tail end of Paulette's sentence.

The mood swung around again, like a gate askew on its hinges and I mirrored the feeling of something going wrong.

The three women looked up in shock, realizing what he could possibly have heard and seeing his German uniform as if for the first time, without taking into account whose back it was on. He was, all at once, an enemy soldier who posed a threat to their son/brother/comrade.

The uniform spoke: "What are you hiding behind your back, Paulette? Give it to me at once."

She wasted not an instant and ran to the open fire in my hearth tossing the note from Michel into the heart of it, before she turned back toward him, cheeks flaming and eyes spitting defiance at his uniform. "It was nothing to concern you. That's all."

He was in front of her immediately. "You little idiot! Did you have anything to do with helping that man escape? Tell me this instant!" He grabbed her by the shoulders and began to shake her.

Marthe tapped him on the shoulder with the end of a long handled warming pan, one of the sort filled with hot coals used to warm sheets at night. It was made of copper and could effectively be used as a club when the need arose. Marthe looked quite capable of doing just that.

"Pardon me lieutenant, but I'll thank you to remember that you're speaking to your *wife*. She's pregnant with *your* child, you're shaking her around in *my* kitchen, and you're doing it in front of *your* mother-in-law. I won't have it and I'm sure that she won't let you continue on with it, either." She glanced at Paulette's mother who had in the meantime, armed herself with a broom.

I applauded Marthe's good sense and bravery. Paulette could use every ally available.

Heinrich let go of Paulette's shoulders, coughing to cover his embarrassment at having lost his temper in such an ugly fashion. "I do beg your pardon, ladies. Paulette, please forgive me." he said in a rather tight voice, as he released her from his grasp. "It seems that they've found a kitchen towel covered with blood in the feed stall where he was locked up, as well as a hammer and wedge. I'm afraid that my wife has lost her mind...that she has provided these things to the prisoner, allowing him to escape and therefore casting suspicion on all of us here! The Gestapo doesn't look kindly on helping prisoners to escape and I'm afraid that whether or not Paulette is my wife won't be of much help if they find out that she was responsible for his getting away."

"I know for certain that Paulette was not responsible, but I will not say who was. You'll just have to come up with something yourself, Heinrich." Liliane said, chin lifted in a personal declaration of war, and still brandishing her broom as if Heinrich were a bug to be crushed on the stone floor. "Paulette, if you need to, you can always move back into the cottage. If your husband isn't capable of standing up for you, I will." Liliane's maternal instinct charged her with angry energy and she bristled at Heinrich like a hissing feline. Her words, spat of her mouth at Heinrich, intending to shame him, had the desired effect and more.

Adrenaline drenched the air and soaked into the wooden table and oak ceiling beams. I drank it in, storing it for future use.

It broke on Heinrich and he sat down looking exhausted, pulling Paulette toward him and burying his bruised face in her skirts at level with his child, as yet, too small to be noticeable. Still, Heinrich was aware that he was in there, watching his father act like a lunatic and being brought back to his senses by two women armed with housewares. He was quite simply ashamed, but also at a loss as to what possible course of action could stop their headlong rush toward certain disaster.

I was thinking that it was about time for yet another cup of tea. So I made the kettle whistle, breaking the silence which had descended so quickly after the wind was taken out of Heinrich's sails.

CHAPTER 24

The next legs to descend the stairway to the kitchen were sheathed in shiny black boots, stomping in an ominous fashion. Heinrich, Paulette, Marthe and Liliane waited in an expectant hush to see whose body was attached to them.

I'd been hoping to continue monitoring the conversation uninterrupted for a few more minutes before any intruder broke in on us. These hopes were dashed when we recognized the worst possible choice of legs, those belonging to Rolf. My attempts to shake his self-assurance hadn't yet been successful. The devil slept like a baby.

"Well, well, what have we here? A little meeting of like minds?" His mustachioed sneer roved over each of them in turn, raising the hair on the backs of necks and provoking acute discomfort. I noticed Paulette begin to bristle with self-defensive anger.

For if in her heart she knew that she was guilty of conduct this fellow thought was wrong, she also knew that she had followed the dictates of her conscience, and was therefore justified in the eyes of God in disobeying the Gestapo. Any person who knew right from wrong would have done the same. She'd only been trying to ease a fellow human being's suffering.

This self-righteousness was about to vent itself via her tongue, when Heinrich, who had been observing these same thoughts display themselves in successive waves across her features, decided to cut her off before she could hang herself.

He stepped in front of her.

"I came to look in on my wife, who was feeling rather ill this morning. Not surprisingly so, considering the drink that you were shoving at her last night!" He voiced spousal jealousy, as well as disapproval, aiming to turn Rolf's thoughts away from the escapee.

"Oh really, Heinrich! I feel like I'm speaking with Mother! You look just like her when she gets to nagging. Your *wife* was just having a little fun last night. And, I must say, she was rather entertaining. How *do* you feel this morning, little sister? A bit blue about the gills?"

Chin lifted in response to his ungentlemanly comments referring to her drunkenness, Paulette answered: "I'm feeling much better now, thank you, Major. How are you today? You seem to be standing a little taller than last evening." She tossed the indiscreet observation across the tabletop in his direction thinking, *'Voilà*, you beast! The ball's in your court now...'

I was proud of her spirit, although I knew it might get her into trouble.

His bushy eyebrows flew upward. He paused, his eyes fixed on hers, taking the time to think of a suitable jibe while twisting the left side of his mustache. Paulette flushed bright red under his scrutiny as we waited, holding our breath, for his response. He was a dangerous man to toy with, and we were afraid to discover at our expense just how dangerous he could be.

"Obviously, you're better at drinking than I assumed. I would have thought you'd be quite dispirited this morning, and here you are, all full of spunk. You definitely are quite a little woman. Well, my dear, to answer your thinly veiled question, my testicles are quite fine. Thank you for worrying about them. But never fear, they're ready to get back to work whenever I should choose to put them to good use. You'll let me know if I can be of any service to you, won't you my sweet?" He smirked in pleasure at the horrified looks reaped by his self proclaimed witty repartee.

I was not alone in judging him to be a disgusting chap, and once again wished I might do something to replace the snide look on his face with one of acute pain.

The three women in the kitchen sucked in sharp hisses of breath at the vulgarity of his response. Heinrich drew himself up, indignant and offended at the crudeness of his brother's remarks and at his obvious pleasure at their shocked faces.

"You will apologize at once to my wife, sir. No one will speak to her in such a fashion!"

"Get down off your high horse! You look like you're about to challenge me to a duel! Good grief, man, your wife was concerning herself with my balls! You should be angry at her, not at me! She was the one who kicked me! Teach her good manners yourself, if you don't want men treating her badly. No *lady* would think of getting involved in a brawl. Do your job and keep her in line, but don't be angry at others when they have to do it for you. If you're not man enough to handle her, leave her to someone who can!"

These were fighting words. Having just diffused one argument with a teapot full of goodwill, I scrambled for a solution which could work a charm on Rolf, and found none. I would have to let them hash it out themselves. Marthe intervened for me.

"Now Major, you'll be wanting some breakfast, I should think. Where is that Franz? Paulette, could you please see if you could find him? I think he's in the garden searching for early berries to go with the cream. Just run out and get him to come in here to take care of the Major."

She shooed Paulette out the door and out of Rolf's reach, while patting Heinrich gently on the shoulder, sending him a silent message to keep quiet. "We'll have you something fixed up in no time Major. You'll be wanting to eat with the Colonel in the dining room, I'll expect. I was just on my way up with some *oeufs à la coque* and ham. Would you like to go and get seated? I'll carry these up to you."

Not relishing the prospect of another confrontation in her kitchen, Marthe very adeptly herded the men upstairs to my formal dining room, where the other officers were already milling about eating warm bread. Ruffled feathers smoothed flat with the magical perfume of steaming ham as it wafted about the protagonists, taking their minds off each other and redirecting thoughts to stomachs, now rumbling in response to the delicious smells of breakfast foods.

Regrouping was done, punctuated by chewing. Plans were rehashed regarding the transportation of the Canadian once they caught him again as they were sure to do. Lieutenant Schmidtz had set out immediately with a team of soldiers to chase him down as soon as his disappearance was discovered. They should send news any time now.

Heinrich played shadow to the Colonel, planning the days' activities and leaving Rolf to keep company with his own problems.

Colonel VonEpffs was doing his very best to ignore the Gestapo, festering at Rolf's insinuations regarding the blame for the pilot's escape. He had made himself very clear in the barn earlier, when they were arguing about what had happened. His men were not responsible in any way. They had a specific job to do and they were doing it. Rolf's preoccupations and orders were his own. The Gestapo should have posted a guard on the man if he was such a precious prize. VonEpffs had other things to occupy his time. Cooperate, yes. Be held responsible when things went wrong, no. As soon as he finished his toast and tea, he took refuge in the library where he had set up his office, followed by Heinrich who was, as always, ruminating thoughts of Paulette.

It seemed preferable to avoid contact with Rolf. The humans sometimes succeeded. I however, could not, having the misfortune of being privy to the seething nastiness entwined amongst his intestines. His sour nature left a putrid smell in each room he occupied. He was the epitome of flatulence personified, or as Michel would have simply put it: a nasty fart.

#

I took a silent inventory of my protagonists, reaching out to feel their whereabouts through their thoughts, for even those who leave me physically send their energy back to me when they think of me as their home or as a safe haven.

Steve had made it to the pharmacist's and was hiding in the cellar, waiting for nightfall once again and wishing Paulette would miraculously show up with some *hachis parmentier* like the previous evening. He would have liked to get to know her better. And he was hungry.

Michel and Guillaume were lying low in a barn loft, asleep, a good ten miles away from us and about fifteen miles from Yvetôt, also awaiting nightfall. They planned to make their way in stages, traveling on foot at night, from here back to their camp, eating and sleeping over in houses belonging to other members of the resistance, by now becoming better and better organized.

Paulette and her mother went back to their cottage and started the laundry, filling large galvanized steel tubs with hot water and scrubbing spots off the soldiers' whites with the strong lye soap which chewed the skin off their hands. Both women were quiet, lost in their thoughts, both worrying about what was to come, and both afraid to talk about it too much, as if not speaking could somehow dissolve the stains of fear.

The Colonel was in the library scribbling numbers, losing himself in the busy work of inventory tallying, Heinrich assisting him in a companionable silence, each battling their demons side by side.

#

For many agonizing days, Paulette and her parents had no real news of either the boys, of the prisoner, or of the contingent of Gestapo who had left so hastily to track down the escaped Canadian. When news finally arrived some days later, I wished it hadn't.

Rolf had been biding his time with us. He often disappeared to spend a few days in Rouen, always returning with rolled documents and plans under his arms. Otherwise he passed his days roaming the area in a black Mercedes, accompanied by a man with a photographic camera. It was obvious that they were preparing something important. I couldn't guess what it would mean for us.

He was rather jubilant one evening, throwing news out onto the dinner table, in French this time, while closely observing Paulette's reaction to it.

A resistance camp had been found, and destroyed. Many prisoners were taken, including the Canadian pilot who had slipped out of their grasp through the barn walls.

Paulette choked on the bitter taste left in her mouth by the usually delicious cabbage and carrot soup. The pounding of her heart hammered a message to her brain and rebounding from the dining room walls, over and over again, in a staccato of doom. Her brother had been caught. Her brother had been caught. Her brother had been caught.

She did her best to pretend to be engrossed by her soup, and to be insensitive to the conversation buzzing around her like frenzied flies on carrion. She flushed, feeling weak, her thoughts making her physically ill. Finally she could bear no more. Leaning close to Heinrich's ear, she whispered her request to be excused, feeling faint, using the pregnancy as an alibi. They made their apologies to the others, both of them leaving the table to retire for the evening.

Once they were safely ensconced in the relative privacy of their room, Paulette's fears plowed out of her mouth in an avalanche. She confided in Heinrich about her brother and Guillaume.

"So, you've known all along where they had escaped to a year ago?" her husband gently questioned.

"And it was they, who had brought the tools to the Canadian to allow his escape?"

Paulette lifted frightened eyes to her husband, now divested of the uniform which had the power to transform him into the enemy. Naked he was her husband, lover and best friend. "You must help me! If they've been caught, I can't let Rolf harm them!"

"But Paulette, surely you must understand that even though he's your brother, he's a man and is responsible for his actions. You can't help him, and neither can I," he added, his voice low with regret. "It's not that I would do anything to hurt you, or your family, you must know me well enough to believe that. It's just that I can't put a young fool's best interests in front of yours. He has done that. He didn't measure the repercussions his actions would have on you, or on your parents. His selfishness has created this situation and I can't put it right. He'll be punished, most likely sent to a work camp in Germany; they're filled with your resistance fighters."

The 'your resistance fighters' crashed around the bedroom catching her attention. The rift yawned wide between them, separating the two lovers with a sea of politics. An immense weariness gained control of her, the breath escaping her lungs in a sigh of defeat, as that defeat settled its weight deep inside her.

Paulette's thoughts turned to her mother, measuring how it would feel to watch a child be imprisoned and driven away to an uncertain future and how it would most assuredly break her heart. Heinrich watched her face and felt the heaviness of her body droop with a despairing resignation to helplessness. No courage or fire was left, just the bleak hopelessness.

It was a horrible thing to see. I saw the light extinguish in Paulette: hope for the future snuffed out like a candle. And it left a smell of dried up love: powdered and musty.

"I'll have to be with them. You know that. I can't stand beside you and watch your brother drive mine away, a prisoner. I won't be your wife. I can't." She turned away, already taking her leave of him.

I felt the familiar despair of breaking hearts, and wondered how love could carry such a variety of emotions for humans: how it could be ecstatic, joyous, silly, impetuous, heated and dejected without even a change in partner. I came to the conclusion that love was, after all, a contradictory state to find oneself in, and maybe not all that desirable. Still humans ran into it blindly, thoughtlessly and abandoning all restraint. Maybe it was like drunkenness. As I watched their intimacy slip away, each folding back into themselves like morning glories closing with the night, I wondered if drunkenness wasn't preferable.

He held her, having no words to change what was about to happen to divide them once again. Very little sleep was had. It was pitiful.

The next morning he awoke to empty arms. She had already left their bed. He found her, about an hour later, standing between her mother and father watching the trucks roll into the yard, dumping out the prisoners, most of them wounded and all of them tied together in a long line of single filed dejection. I smothered myself with the emotions of the prisoners, a wet blanket of apprehension.

The older ones were quiet in their movements, more resigned to a certain fate. The younger ones were skittish with nerves and fear of the next minutes; not at all sure of what was to come, still thinking an escape might be possible. Steve was amongst the resigned, quiet ones.

Guillaume was alone. He was limping on his bad knee, but was also holding his right arm askew, the sleeve colored a dark brown: the unique shade of dried blood on blue cotton.

The Fournier family watched the line of prisoners, searching for Michel. They looked on as Henri Quesnel held back his sobbing wife Aimée, as she struggled to rush to Guillaume's side. Paulette's parents clamped onto young Yves' arms as he squirmed, trying to escape, desperate to ask Guillaume for news of his brother Michel.

I bore a sorry, silent witness to yet another drama.

Paulette had an arm around the skinny shoulders of little Lizzie Quesnel and around her own sister Roseline, as they pressed their young faces into her waist, hiding their eyes from the awful parade in front of them. She looked in vain for Michel. When he didn't get off the truck, instinctively she knew not to be relieved with imagining he'd escaped the raid.

Paulette caught Steve's eye, winging a silent inquiry across the yard. He answered with a sideways shake of his head.

Tightening her grip on the little girls, she looked away, eyes dry, unable to face her parents, realizing that Michel: hot-headed, overly courageous, imprudent Michel wouldn't be getting into any more trouble. The understanding of his absence leapt like a vicious, unchained monkey from her guts over to her parents.

A second later, she heard her mother's keening lament, muffled by the shoulder of her husband, and wondered in a distant way, if *Maman* had married her first love, if any of these things would have happened. If that one detail could have changed the course of events leading them to this place, to this moment of abomination.

It was a strange thought and Paulette half resented her mother for it, as if these events were her fault. Her mother could have been safely evacuated to the south of France, living a life of relative peace and luxury, instead of losing a son to the misery carried forth through time by having been convinced to stay here. Paulette was suddenly angry with them both: her mother for giving up on love too soon and her father for stepping in too quickly to provide an alternative.

Feeling an inescapable desire to leave the yard, she turned away and took the girls into the cottage, sat them down at the table and started a pot of water to boil: for what reason, she had no idea. It was instinctive. People always boil water when things go badly: sometimes for tea, sometimes for sterilizing instruments for cleansing wounds, sometimes to clean up after accidents. It was a busy activity and she felt it needed doing. She moved about in a dazed fashion, her mind numb.

The little girls sat quietly, watching her, waiting for something to do, some directives to be given, some chore to be done, some sense of normality to be supplied by an adult. Until someone could take over, they sat very still, waiting to be told just how to get on with their lives.

#

Paulette stayed with her parents that night, and the next.

However, there was to be no sneaking away to bring food or any other comfort to the prisoners locked away for the night. The troops relegated to the guard were well armed.

The frustration at knowing their wounded son was locked away, so close, yet so completely inaccessible, was more than Henri and Aimée Quesnel could bear. They paced the floor of their kitchen, worrying the terra cotta tiles on the floor, restless, yet dreading the daylight. No amount of tea could help them.

Having lost an adolescent daughter to the brutality of these men, they allowed themselves no hope for their son's fate. Watching the Gestapo's treatment of him was indescribably difficult. Refraining from rushing to attack the soldiers with fists and verbal venom was an exercise in self control which devoured their hearts. The futility of such an attack weighed even more heavily on them, the sense of helplessness that it brought was physically unbearable, leaving them incapable of anything aside from restless pacing.

Henri realized how silly he had been to think that not knowing what happened was worse than knowing. He had been very wrong. Bearing witness, while being helpless to intervene, was much worse than ignorance. Ignorance at least, allowed some small space for hope, while knowing did not.

The dawn brought new movement as the prisoners were loaded up and driven away to the east and to Germany, in relative silence.

The tears and crying had been done yesterday. Today was despair and it was mute.

#

In the quiet that settled over us, following the last faint rumbling of the trucks as they drove down the road and turned at the corner, gone away from here, the assembled people of the two different factions found themselves staring at each other across the open space that had been occupied by the trucks. Once again, two opposing teams were faced off across a soccer pitch, waiting, as if a time out had been called by an invisible referee.

Time had stopped, and no one was able to move for a long moment.

A very different future than the one each person had taken for granted, was to start at this exact instant and no one knew how to go about commencing it. What were the correct words? What were the appropriate actions? How were they to go about starting this different life, living it together in close proximity, one camp to the other, knowing what they knew? Someone had to make a move. Someone had to say something, or they would go on suspended in time forever.

The Colonel was the one to take charge. It was his duty.

VonEpffs crossed the yard, seeking out the workers and assigning them tasks not common to their routine. Work needed to be done, to occupy the fists clenching in spasmodic frustration.

So, he decided that whitewashing was to top off the agenda, as it involved no tools which could be useful in a moment of foolish bravado. The stucco between the timbers making up the upper floors of the manor house, the barn, the dovecote and the cider house as well as most of the buildings on the property, was to be whitened, the pretext being an imminent visit by some authority or other. This chore would take a few days. VonEpffs hoped it would be enough time to dissipate some measure of the intolerable tension. It was the best he could come up with on such short notice.

He sent them off to fetch pails, brushes and brooms and set about their task. They would digest the events they'd witnessed, while keeping their arms busy. Each avoided looking at one another, doing their best to ignore the sighs, or occasional sobs breaking the slurping noises of dripping paint brushes. Sniffles could have just as easily been caused by the smell of the whitewash, the turpentine or by repressed tears. Grief was a personal thing and it was too dangerous to share openly. Rolf didn't need to know any more about who was upset, about what, or why.

So when young Yves Fournier went off on his own, no one took much notice, except me.

Yves had been given a job two years ago. He was responsible for moving the four nanny goats kept for their milk, from one area to the other. These goats were wonderfully efficient mowing machines, keeping the grass from growing too long and evolving into weeds in the yards surrounding the house. They wore collars and ropes and were pegged in one spot, mostly away from the flowers and no where near the vegetables. They were milked every evening and one of the women made small white cheeses with the fermented milk.

Rather intelligent creatures, they knew Yves well and always called out a welcome to him when he came to move them around or to gather their ropes together to lead them off to milking in the evening. Theirs was a mutual friendship, he was happy to scratch around their stubby horns and rub their hairy chins and they pushed up against him, bleating contentedly, thanking him for his attentions.

Shortly after the painting got underway, a distressed sound coming from one of the nannies rang out across the yard. The shrill bleating was obviously that of an animal in pain. Emile was closest to the sound, and he stopped weeding the green beans and ran to see what was about. When he found the goat, she was still pegged and covered in blood, lying on her side panting heavily. He examined the goat quickly and turned to see Yves, crouched on the ground crying, a heavy branch still in hand.

Emile looked at the boy, shaking his head, before going to the side of the barn to retrieve a brick. He bent over the nanny and brought the brick down hard on her skull, cracking it open, killing her. He left her lie and lifted the little boy to his feet, shook him hard twice, before folding him into his arms like a baby.

"You little man, you mustn't take out your anger on others for what was done. It won't make you feel any better! Poor nanny. She was your friend and now look at what you've done to her." He patted the hiccuping boy on the back, and continued.

"Never be cruel to animals, they look to you for their care, and reward you with their milk as well as their friendship. Never kill in anger…you must be kind to those who are weaker than yourself. Even strong horses like Flynn and Maurice are weaker than you, because they depend on you to care for them. So, in spite of their strength, they're the weaker. Now, you and I will go get a shovel and we'll bury our friend, we won't take her meat nor her hide, for you killed her and she should be buried as she is. You'll be punished for the loss by your father. But you won't be angry at anyone for it. It's a lesson to be learned, and a hard one at that. It's a terrible thing you've done."

Yves struggled with himself when it came time to lift Nanny off the ground and put her small, bloody body into the hole he had dug under Emile's watchful eye. He balked when he was forced to touch her limp shape still warm from a lost life. He looked away from her crushed head, and cried into the blood left on his hands when she fell disgracefully into the hole.

I disliked the smell of blood and felt sorry for Yves as he rubbed his hands on his pants trying to relieve himself of the metallic odor.

He took a deep breath before reaching down into the hole, realigning her head with her body on its side, so that she looked as much at rest as possible. He covered her with dirt and smoothed the ground over with the shovel, before throwing it on the ground in a fit of anger once again.

"You'll stop your tantrum just now!" Emile warned him. "We still have to go and tell your father what you've done and tell the Colonel as well."

Yves looked up in surprise at Emile. "I can't go to the Germans! They killed my brother! I won't go and say I'm sorry to them!" He exploded angry tears once again.

"You will, I'll make sure of it. Too bad if you don't like it, but Nanny wasn't to blame for your brother. The Colonel isn't to blame either, but you've killed an innocent animal the Colonel is responsible for and he'll say your punishment."

He pulled Yves to his feet and picked up the shovel, before herding him off toward the cottage in search of Marcel.

There was some surprised cursing at the little boy's actions followed with a few quietly exchanged words on the stoop of the cottage, before Papa grabbed Yves by the collar and carted him off toward the big house, Emile following along, shovel still in hand. The sooner this was dealt with the better.

Marcel possessed a measure of pride which clogged up next to the frustration plugging his throat, begging to be swallowed before reaching my door to ask for an interview with the Colonel. It was going to be very difficult for him to look a German in the eye just now.

However, they were lucky. Rolf had left for the day. At least they didn't have to see him.

The Colonel came outside in his shirtsleeves, to stand in front of Yves, his hands folded behind his back. The boy hung his head in shame, his brilliantly reddened ears proof of the extent of his embarrassment.

"Why did you hurt that goat, young man?" the Colonel asked in a stern voice. No answer came from the boy. Marcel looked as if he were about to answer for him, but Emile put a restraining hand on Marcel's arm, nodding toward the boy.

"I'll have an answer to my question, please." He reached out and lifted the boy's chin. "Why did you do it?"

"Why did you kill my brother?" the child hurled defiantly at the Colonel, jerking his face out of the Colonel's hand. "He didn't do anything to you, why is he dead?"

"Yves, you must listen to me. Look at me," the Colonel grabbed the boy by the shoulders, but standing straight to tower over Yves with an authority he couldn't afford to lessen just now. "I did not kill your brother. I regret that he was killed, but I had nothing to do with it, nor did any of the soldiers under my command. I understand that you are angry and very hurt by what has happened. But I think that your brother was in the wrong place at the wrong time. You must look at it as an accident, and you must be very careful that you don't ever put yourself in that position. But none of that is a good reason to kill a goat. You hurt her deliberately, and that's a very different thing. You know that you must be punished for her loss. What do you think I should do with you?"

The Colonel waited for the anger to subside a little from Yves' young face, worry taking its place. "I think that you should be made to cut the grass in the fourth spot that the goat would have kept trimmed every day, gather it up and give it to the horses to eat. That way part of the work that the goat provided will be compensated for. Now, what about her milk? To make up for that loss, you'll learn to milk the other three goats yourself, and carry the milk to the lady who makes the cheese and help her in her task. You also must pay for a new goat to replace this one. How do you propose to find the money for that? Is there some sort of job that you could do for me that would merit some pay, which you could use to buy a new goat? Think about it and you'll let me know tomorrow what job you have found for yourself. If you don't, I'll be obliged to find one for you myself."

Yves looked up at the Colonel during his sentencing, expecting worse, but still rolling his eyes in the typical manner of a boy made to do a chore not of his choosing. He scuffled his feet in the gravel in moderate rebellion. His gesture brought a small twitch to the Colonel's mouth.

VonEpffs kept his hand weighing heavily on Yves' shoulder, while turning to Marcel. "Monsieur Fournier, I am truly sorry about your son. I wish I could have done something to keep it from happening. We must all do our best to keep this one safe from harm. I think Monsieur Levasseur will assist us with this as well?" he half asked, half stated, turning toward Emile.

"Thank you for taking care of this problem for me, Monsieur Levasseur. I'll let you get back to your work." He turned to go back up the steps into the house, after nodding his respects to each of the men, and clapping Yves on the shoulder once more. It was a sad day indeed.

#

Rolf, however, was in his element. He was preparing to get the ball rolling on a project that would end the war, so brilliant a plan it was. Quite a lot of time had been spent, roaming the area's woodlands, searching out and surveying well camouflaged sites to start the installation of the launch ramps for the V1 airborne missiles which would fly, unmanned, toward England to demolish the morale of the Allies. For once, destruction of their homeland would snuff out the pride of the English.

Rolf thought that the Brits had successfully played at war on terrain belonging to other countries during the last war and up until now in this one. Even the Blitz wasn't enough for them. Well, they were about to get a good taste of what it was like to see their women and children hurt. It would bring their participation to a halt, Rolf was certain of it and he would be commended by his handling of the weapons that would end the war in their favor. Glory was in his sights.

He was proud of these missiles. They were technological gems. They'd been tested since December of 1942, the first missile launched by a ramp only flying the insufficient distance of three kilometers. Since then other tests had proven much more successful and by now they were flying over two hundred kilometers. The beauty of the project was in the potential for no risk on behalf of the Germans. They would launch the missile from a protected site set in a copse of trees. A mixture called perhydrol would cause a chemical reaction diffusing enough heat to create twelve kilograms of pressure per square centimeter, enough to bring about the explosion necessary to send the missile hurtling out of its catapult toward the English coastline.

The projected debut date for these sites was slated for the end of the year, and Rolf was very busy. Trucks were rolling in from Germany with heavy materials and Russian prisoners to be taken to the construction sites for assembly. Rolf had left his position with the Gestapo, having received a promotion putting him in charge of the sites in this section of Normandy, which meant that he was to be around for some time yet. He knew that he would enjoy the time this gave him to torture his brother.

#

Paulette was able to avoid Rolf, ignoring the occasional knowing looks and trivial remarks about her rounding shape, for she had stayed at her parents' side, at first to help, then in solidarity at their shared loss. And now because she didn't know how to come back.

She told herself that many women had raised children without the help of the father. War brought about a large quantity of orphans, the widows simply having got on with living, using the welfare of their children as a screen to hide their grief. She tried to prepare herself to do the same, but seeing him across the yard, looking at her with such a forlorn expression and tired set to his shoulders made it even harder. She was not a widow and she was having too much difficulty grieving for someone who was so obviously alive and waiting for her, watching her for any kind of sign.

Initially, she hadn't planned on never returning to the attic room she shared with her husband, but the first night spent at her parents' turned into a second and so on, as she let the division between herself and Heinrich widen into a gorge, the depth of which had become impossible to traverse.

He wasn't responsible for what had happened to Michel and while she knew it, she still couldn't force herself take the first step to returning to his arms and bed. The feeling of disloyalty submerging her whenever she entertained the thought of sleeping in his arms was so overwhelming that it was easier to pretend that she was indeed, alone. She battled with her thoughts and emotions, never one winning out over the other.

Her head reasoned with her heart, arguing that raising a child alone could be too hard on the child. Then her heart would disagree, refusing to betray the memory of her brother and his death at the hands of the Germans. Other times her love for Heinrich would battle with her head, pleading for her to forget who was on which side and return to the father of her child.

No part of her could agree on what plan of action was the best, so she waited, miserable because she loved him and wanted him.

Her parents watched without taking part in her inner conflict, for they also lacked an answer to her dilemma.

#

Heinrich observed his wife from across the yard, her belly growing with each passing week. He had hoped that time would help Paulette accept his innocence and bring her back to him, but time seemed to be turning into an adversary, working against his cause.

Her absence in the house and at the table was noticed, remarked upon and criticized. It became the object of merciless commentary on behalf of Rolf, underlining his brother's obvious incapacity to keep a woman in line. Nasty remarks were heard about the wearing of trousers or skirts. These remarks were largely ignored, their source not being the most popular person living under my roof.

Weeks passed in a miserable fashion. Summer stretched before them, bringing the usual amount of hard work harvesting the fodder, the grains, the vegetables, the flax and the multitude of produce we were relied on for supplying. Kicking multiplied in Paulette's belly. There was no hiding what was about to happen anymore.

Late in September the cider press was turning, harnessed to Flynn for the first time, crushing apples. The juice ran from the trough into the vats where it would be stored before filling the fermentation barrels. It smelled divine.

Paulette was watching Flynn, whose nostrils were twitching at the bewitching smell of the natural sugar he loved so much. He was often treated to some of the left over mash when his work was done at the end of the day. In the meantime, his work seemed to be quite easy for him, and he walked in an effortless circle, head high, acting pleased to be driving the enormous wooden screw drawing the press downward, crushing the apples into a fragrant pulp.

When the screw reached the bottom, he was unhitched, the press rewound and the pulp was shoveled out of the bottom, to be spread in the fields for the cows to enjoy. Another load of apples was chucked into the wooden slats of the press and Flynn was hitched up to drive the screw downward once again. All in all it was easy work for the handsome, powerful Percheron gelding. Paulette watched him with a sort of motherly pride at how fine he'd grown.

He became skittish at once when she squeaked in response to the unusually nasty cramp sending warm liquid rushing down her thighs to pool on the floor between her feet. She sat down rather quickly, clutching with both hands at her belly which had come to life, heaving upwards before it seized up hard as a rock. She hadn't expected this to happen so fast. She cried out but Flynn was the only one to hear over the groaning of the wooden press as it did its work. When he stopped walking, the noise stopped and her father heard Paulette's second cry.

Flynn looked over to her at the same time her father did. Much later she remembered noticing that the horse looked just as surprised as did Papa, their two faces turned in her direction, side by side, eyes widened alongside long noses. It would have been comical, if she had been able to laugh at the time. However laughter was quite impossible, as the breath squeezed out of her once again by an evidently impatient baby.

#

Paulette was carried off to the cottage by several men and someone had the brilliant idea of sending for Heinrich. It was, after all, his baby causing this ruckus.

I was hoping for another little girl, just like her mother: blond and cheerful.

We hadn't had any babies for the longest time. War seemed to put life on hold. It continued ending but there was very little beginning. So, it was all the more comforting for me to have another life to look forward to sharing, to hear singing and giggling and small dancing feet running in my hallways and playing in my yards.

I think I liked girls best because they spent more time with me. Little boys were continually running off to play in the fields or the woods. As children, I would see the girls more often. It wasn't until the boys turned to men, that I could share the calm evenings of *calvados* and cigars in front of the fire.

It seemed too long to wait. Yes, I definitely was hoping for a girl.

CHAPTER 25

April 1992:

Philippe lay twisted in a macabre fashion on the tiled floor of the downstairs hall. His eyes were open, targeting Debra, and while he was no longer breathing, she knew he was still present behind them, observing her, not yet gone to his eternity.

Her heart swelled, bursting into great wrenching sobs as it broke. She'd thought he couldn't hurt her again. She'd believed that he had destroyed the love she professed. She'd imagined that his infidelity had hardened her soul, thickened her skin, built a wall around every part of her that was tender, or sensitive.

How wrong she had been! This man, the one she'd loved beyond all others, for whom she had changed her life: separating her from her family and her country in the belief that her love for him could be sufficient compensation, was leaving her. Debra retched with the loss, floundering amid regrets she would carry for the rest of her life, wondering what she had done wrong, when it had seemed to start out so right.

Their marriage had been a white canvas, and someone had painted it chaotic. Was it her? What should she have done differently? Should she have chosen red instead of blue for the bedroom walls? Should she have respected his wish not to have children? Should she have had sex more often, or differently: under the kitchen table or in the yard? Should she have found a job on her own, in a field unrelated to his work? Would he have felt less trapped, less financially burdened, having even a small income coming in from an outside source? What had she done to push him to the desperate decision to want to be rid of her so badly, that he felt he must kill her?

Questions pounded through her brain: a stampede of angry elephants, opening old wounds and inflicting new ones with heavy footfalls. She didn't notice when the light in his open eyes went out and he left, absent forever from the pathetic twisted form, inert on the floor.

Elsa whimpered and Debra crawled over to the dog lying on the floor bleeding, in a canine replica of her master's pose. Elsa lifted her head and licked Debra's hand, thumping her tail on the tiled floor.

Delving her hands into the thick ruff of fur at the dog's neck, the strong pulse she felt there comforted them both. She realized she had to take action and picked up the kitchen telephone to dial 17. Her voiced sounded wobbly and strange to her ears, asking for help.

"There has been an accident."

It could never be anything else. Her children could never know their father tried to murder their mother. She needed to refine her lie quickly, to repeat it out loud several times in order to remember each detail without hesitation. She must repeat the same story so often she would come to believe it herself, this alternate tale being easier to live with than the truth. Her husband could never be tagged a murderer, just as she couldn't bear the weight of being the wife he had tried to kill.

Elsa had to survive. The girls adored her, and Debra didn't want them to believe their father had killed the dog even accidentally. They would have more than enough to assimilate in the days and weeks to come. Debra made a second phone call to the vet. Concentrating on the life left to save, staunching the bleeding from Elsa's side with towels, she averted her eyes from the other body on the floor.

She wanted to cover him, but realized she shouldn't touch him if she didn't want to raise suspicions against herself. Looking at the gun stuck under his chest, her first instinct was to make it disappear. The object was incredibly offensive, but a grain of good sense told her she must keep to her story.

She must not be accused of foul play, and she knew she'd be the prime suspect. She had to keep her wits about her: not an easy task for a woman who had just been shot at, by the man she was married to. This litany of good sense repeated itself in her brain, holding her on the correct side of sanity. It was a tenuous hold, and just along the precipice of panic, but the reassuring murmurs I breathed into her ear reinforced these useful gestures, passing the time until help arrived.

The siren on the lone patrol car turned off as Debra threw open the front door and ran outside, recognizing the officer who'd stayed with her on the evening of the attempted break-in.

"Madame Dubois, we've been told there has been an accident..."

The phrase was cut short when Debra's strength abandoned her, substituted with shock as she fell to her knees in the gravel. The policeman helped her to a sitting position before carefully pushing open the front door. She heard the static from his hand radio echo in the hall as he requested help.

He came back outside and squatted down in front of her in the gravel putting his hand on her shoulder, gently asking if she was injured. She stared up at him in shock, her face ravaged by tears, eye make-up washed in swirls all over her cheeks. The side of her head was throbbing as a breeze needled a damp spot in her hair. The officer carefully looked at the wound on the side of her head parting her hair at the spot, making her wince with pain.

He retrieved a blanket from his patrol car, and wrapped it around her shoulders, while they waited for the others to arrive.

#

Administrative procedures would be fulfilled, questions would be asked and Debra's life would be chaos for the next few hours, gradually decreasing in intensity over the next few days and weeks, to eventually dwindle back into nothing but routine.

I'd seen the unique grief of sudden violent death dealt with many times before. There would come a time when I would be of help, supplying a focus for small activities to keep hands busy while her head and heart adjusted themselves to a new life as a single mother.

But while we waited for the chaos to begin, the silence in the yard was broken by birdsong and a sighing wind whispering through the trees, swaying the daffodils planted at their bases. Debra and the police officer gazed at the perfectly blue sky, listening as bees hummed in cadence with the planet turning on its axis and normality pervaded.

It was a pleasant afternoon, and in a surreal fashion, they noticed.

CHAPTER 26

May 1992:

An inquest was held within the month. The witnesses included some of Debra and Philippe's neighbors, although most of them lived far enough away to be of no use at all.

In spite of her innocence, Debra was wrought with anxiety at what would be determined, chewing her thumbnail down to raw skin.

I helped in the only way I could, drawing soothing energy from stored away happy memories of calm moments shared by mothers and sleeping babies, lovers satisfied with each other and companionable evenings of embroidery and newspaper reading before a warm fire. This quiet energy can be just as powerful if not more so, than the electricity given off by argument, and easier to use. It produces a peaceful hum which lulled Debra's nervous heart to sleep at night when the thoughts galloping through her mind should have kept her awake. I could see to that at least, if feeling rather useless to help in any concrete manner while we waited for the verdict to fall.

The police questioned Philippe's employees, including Patricia and Sophie. Their testimonies were bland, both of them pleading ignorance as to any problems existing between the Dubois couple which could have justified Debra seeking revenge.

I think that they both felt guilty enough to wish for the police to forget them, and that they silently shared reasons for wishing to forget the Dubois couple and their former jobs. A lesson learned was the most I could expect, and while I sincerely doubted any true remorse on either woman's behalf, I could hope they regretted the dramatic end result of their scheming.

I'm not above wishful thinking from time to time.

It was the testimony of the accounting firm who did the official bookkeeping for Philippe's company which made mention of the obvious financial difficulties on their ledgers. Still, the life insurance policy taken out recently by Monsieur Dubois was for Madame Dubois, with himself named as beneficiary of the half a million euros to be paid out in event of her death, or several hundred thousand if she was incapacitated and unable to work. The policy on himself was for a small amount sufficient to cover burial expenses and included a small trust for each of the girls in view of their education, but could not be considered an extravagant sum.

The other insurance policies were the mandatory ones, taken out through the bank when loans for the business as well as the house had been signed. These policies insured the full repayment of the loans to the bank, in the event that the primary breadwinner was to pass away before the loans were paid off. Philippe had been the logical person designated as the primary breadwinner. This was standard procedure and therefore not cause for speculation.

Thus the probability of Debra's culpability was eroded. However, because of these insurance policies, she found herself in full ownership of the house and their business, and as thus, debt free.

The psychiatrist was in the end, unexpectedly helpful in clearing Debra's name. She testified in her favor at the inquest, stating that during their consultations, in view of saving their marriage, Philippe had shown himself to be unstable and perfectly capable of bizarre behavior. Her role as his onetime lover was never revealed and the woman never directly contacted Debra.

The inspectors who'd shown up at the house to accuse Debra were not present at the inquest, which was of some comfort to her. They had been so anxious to implicate her, she was sure that they would invent some reason to hold her responsible for Philippe's death. She'd been dreadfully afraid that someone would accuse her of shooting Philippe or pushing him down the stairs herself.

Of course, she and I, and the dog knew this wasn't true, but neither I nor the dog were of any help as witnesses for her defense.

I breathed a sigh of relief when the judge ruled that his death was accidental and that the insurance companies could proceed with the settling of his estate. Debra finally gave up chewing her nails.

The helpful police officer who'd answered her call for help on two occasions had guessed the truth, except for the part involving my assistance in Philippe's topple down the stairs was concerned. Given the drama of the circumstances, he chose not to give voice to his belief that the accident had taken place while Philippe was in fact, attempting to murder his wife, in hopes of collecting the insurance money, thus getting himself out of financial difficulty. There seemed to be no valid reason to stir that particular pot of stew, as it would be of benefit to no one. So he kept it to himself.

He arrived on my doorstep to return the gun to Debra one afternoon just shortly after the inquest was closed. She opened the door to see him standing there, holding the gun in a plastic bag and another containing the clothing Philippe had been wearing that day as well as the contents of his pockets and wedding ring.

Debra wasn't prepared for this, and seeing those items mocking her grief through the transparent plastic bags brought on a fit of uncontrollable shaking. The officer accompanied her to the kitchen where she lit the gas flame under the tea kettle, all the while gently speaking to her much like he had on the night of the attempted break-in.

Elsa settled herself with the deep sigh of old injuries laid to rest on the cool tile floor under the table. The dog had come very close to passing that day as well, but the speedy appearance of the vet, and an emergency surgery had left her not only with a limp and a scar, but with a strangely intensified sense of protection toward Debra.

The dog refused to leave Debra's side, dragging herself upstairs at night to sleep outside Debra's bedroom door. After the first few times Debra woke to find her curled up on the other side of her door, she took to leaving it open, and Elsa had moved inside to sleep at the foot of the bed on the rug.

However, this gave free reign for the cat to take up nocturnal residence on the bed, and Debra was so well surrounded that she was struck by the sad realization, that she didn't really miss the other occupant of the room at night, and actually slept rather well.

She had forgotten that he'd tried to kill her. She played the role of widow and believed it.

Her grief was authentic, well maybe not quite for the *real* Philippe, but at least for the Philippe she had thought to love and be married to. During the second half of their marriage she had discovered that she was married to a stranger, which didn't keep her from loving the man she'd thought she had married, in spite of daily proof that he didn't actually exist. It was as though he had gone off on vacation and his nasty twin had moved in. Now the twin was gone as well, and she could miss the nicer version, with sincerity. It helped the girls to have their mother share in their sadness at missing their father, and the three of them spent some evenings looking at photos and being sad together.

But the shock of seeing the blood on the clothing and the gun brought back a multitude of horrible details, reminding her exactly of that day's events. She sat for some time in the kitchen after the kind police officer finished his tea, leaving her with many entreaties to phone him if she needed help of any kind.

There was a small tint of friendly interest involved in his kindness, and Debra caught on to it, but chose to pretend she didn't, having absolutely no desire for romantic involvement of any kind. The officer didn't persist much, realizing it was rather soon after a horrible experience, and that time might make his case for him. He hoped she would find some cause to call for his help in the future. She hoped that she would not.

Looking at the gun propped against the oven door, she pondered what to do with it. She had an aversion to firearms of any type, and most obviously to this one.

Debra couldn't stop herself as she wheeled back in time, remembering the feel of the cold tile on her cheek when she'd fallen and cracked her head open. She re-lived the fall down the stairs. Philippe's calm voice pronouncing that dreadful sentence resonated in her ears over and over again. "You have to go; it's as simple as that." His face bearing quiet resolve as he aimed the gun at her appeared clearly before her eyes. She blinked several times to erase the vision when she remembered the lost cartridge, got up from the kitchen table and went into the hall.

Lying down on the floor more or less where she had fallen, she squinted the eye closest to the floor, to peer beneath the portmanteau. She couldn't see a thing so she went back into the kitchen and got the broom. She lay down once again and slipped the broom handle underneath the portmanteau sliding it from left to right.

The cartridge rolled out the side stopping just short of Debra's nose, confirming her worst fears. She hadn't dreamed it all. It was true; her husband had hated her so much that he had decided to kill her.

She stayed on the floor, rolling herself into a ball, crying without stopping until she fell into an exhausted sleep. Elsa joined her on the floor, lying alongside Debra, keeping her warm on the cold tile until she woke an hour later.

#

When Debra woke, she decided that doing anything was better than doing nothing.

She resolved to never again lie on the hall floor crying, ever. It solved absolutely nothing. It screwed up her hair and her make-up, it wrinkled her clothes and gave her a headache. She had to forget how to wallow in self-pity, for it could become self-destructive and that would be harmful to her children.

Elsa accompanied Debra outside with the gun, the cartridge, and a shovel. When they reached an outbuilding once believed to be a chicken coop, Debra laid the shovel and the cartridges on the ground.

Taking a firm hold on the rifle with both hands, she swung it with all of her force, bringing it to crack against the stone foundation of the chicken coop. She did this again and again, until finally the barrel of the shotgun was slightly bent, and the wooden parts of the gun were broken to bits.

She jumped on the top edge of the spade with both feet to break the ground along the south side of the chicken coop, thinking as she dug that this would be a good place to plant some irises, once she had cleared away more of the weeds growing there unchecked.

Carried away with the idea of the flower bed, she decided to work along the wall all the way, clearing brush as she went. This physical activity did much to raise her spirits, as she worked up a bit of a sweat, digging deeper than strictly necessary, but enough to worry the stubborn roots. At the very end of the wall her spade hit something, making a strange thump.

On her hands and knees she rummaged around in the soil, expecting to find a large rock. Instead, her fingers caught the straight edge of something.

She ran back to the cellar and grabbed her basket of hand gardening tools, filled with enough excitement to rival Nancy Drew. Using the small hand trowel, she gently dug around the perimeter of a square object wrapped in a ragged piece of oilcloth about eight inches long on each side. Then, gently digging beneath one side, she managed to loosen the cube from its resting place. She extracted it like a stubborn tooth, with a heave that left her on her bottom in the grass, but with wrapped package in hand.

Unfolding the remains of the cloth, she held a carved wooden box. The lid was fastened with a tiny lock. She dug around a bit more with the trowel hoping to find a key, but to no avail, and decided to complete the task she had initially set for herself.

It was into this deeper hole, formerly containing the box, that she deposited the bits and pieces of the gun. She used the tip of her trowel to pry open the left over cartridge, emptying the powder into the dirt, before throwing the shell in. She covered the lot using the trowel, and then stood to smooth over the entire area with the shovel.

Elsa followed her back into the cellar where she carefully washed off the tools before drying them on a rag and hanging each one in its spot. She used the moist rag to scrub off some of the dirt encrusted on the box, using an old tooth brush to finish off the cleaning job, gently brushing around the ancient looking leather hinges and key hole.

Her curiosity took her into the house where she grabbed the phone book to look for a locksmith in the village. As she described the box and the lock to the locksmith, he suggested she take it to a specialist in Dieppe, whose area of expertise involved antique clock repair. He could surely help her get the box open without damaging it.

Debra resolved to go the next morning after dropping the girls off at school. Glancing at the kitchen clock she realized it was just about time to go and pick them up, which she happily had been doing ever since they had returned to school ten days after their father was laid to rest in the tiny village cemetery.

She'd been allowing herself the luxury of being there after school let out every afternoon, since she no longer had a job. The business had been sold and she was living off of the proceeds of the sale. All of the debt Philippe had incurred having been covered by the insurance policies linked to the bank loans, she found herself free and clear with a modest profit at the sale of the business. Eventually, she would have to find a job, but she could take her time looking for one, and enjoy spending the necessary time with the girls, hoping this might help put the disaster of Philippe's death behind them.

Destroying and burying the shotgun was the first step toward that goal. The girls needn't ever see it. It was a violent reminder of a tragic accident. Feeling unexpectedly more lighthearted, she hopped in the car and drove the two miles to school to pick up her kids, anxious to hear about their day, and eager to show them the old box she had found.

Of course, I knew who the box belonged to, why they had put it there, as well as what it contained. I felt confident that Debra was the right person to find the box and was happily anticipating what would unfold when she finally looked inside.

CHAPTER 27

September 1943:

Paulette found the whole business rather alarming.

Considering the multitude of birthing she'd seen on the farm, the pain part of it was much scarier than she'd imagined it to be. Animals seem to get on with it without much groaning. Granted, there is some snorting and heavy breathing but they don't seem to cry out much.

Paulette was having quite a lot of trouble not screaming until her lungs burst. Pride kept her from letting on that she was as scared as she was, for fear of looking like a sissy. Every woman did this. They all, well... most of them, got through it and she would as well, yet she was running through just about every curse word she could conjure up while struggling to hang on to that goal: surviving the day.

Hanging on to any thought at all was becoming difficult as she fought off rising panic. Maybe she wasn't capable of doing this! Was she doing something wrong for it to hurt so badly? Where was the doctor?

#

She wasn't the only one asking those questions. Heinrich was relegated to the kitchen, where he was treated to a variety of sounds wafting down the stairs from the bedroom. They were terrifically scary sounds.

He hadn't realized she possessed such a diverse vocabulary of cuss words. At one point he was curious enough to inquire about one or two with which he wasn't familiar. As a learning experience, it was a bit unorthodox, but at least he gleaned a few new expressions, not ones that could easily fit into normal conversation, but interesting enough on their own.

Heinrich had some difficulty imagining that those colorful expressions were erupting from the mouth of the sweet-hearted Paulette he was married to and not issued by a fishwife from the docks of the seediest quarters of Marseille. Even her voice, under the strain of her *travail* was unrecognizable. He was ashamed to be relieved he hadn't been allowed in the room, thinking that if every thing else was transformed for the worse, then maybe he was better off not actually seeing her at work.

But where the devil was that doctor? Walking in from Bacqueville? It was only a few miles down the road, so what was keeping him?

#

Paulette knew Heinrich was in the kitchen and at first she wanted to see him, then she changed her mind. Her mother and the other women flat out refused his presence, insisting that it was bad luck for the father to be in the room.

It was traditional for women to be involved, while the men sat in another room drinking themselves silly. Most likely, this handy bit of superstition kept the men from forming unfavorable opinions of their women. Still, Heinrich and Paulette had some unfinished business, even though talking about anything at all was quite out of the question right then. More important things were happening.

In spite of Paulette's uncontrolled verbiage, there was bit of a party atmosphere in the bedroom where the ladies had gathered, each giving advice, sipping tea, and telling stories about previous births. They got in as much of this as possible before the doctor arrived or before things began to speed up. He would shush their chattering soon enough, being known to prefer the silence needed to listen for the baby's heartbeat through his stethoscope. I enjoyed the story telling part and was looking forward to greeting the baby's arrival and sending out a warm welcome to my newest charge.

I also sat in on a very different sort of party going on downstairs, with the men grouped around the table eating bread with jam and drinking *calvados* while commiserating with the mostly miserable father-to-be who was not eating at all, instead drinking his anxiety into a mushy mass.

Every so often one of the women would come down and put more water on to boil, leaving the men wondering just what they were scalding upstairs, but not truly wanting any more details than were strictly necessary. The alcohol kept their squeamish thoughts at bay. Women's business it definitely was.

The children were playing in the yard and sometimes the older girls would stop when they heard a cry of pain and look knowingly at one another, thinking ahead to when they would be old enough to swear their heads off without fear of having their mouths washed out with soap. It was a unique sort of occasion, when young women were permitted all kinds of oddities and were immediately forgiven for it. Although it didn't sound like much fun at all.

#

Colonel Von Epffs was in the libarary, waiting impatiently for news to filter back to him about the safe arrival of the child. He'd heard the frantic knocking on the front door, listened to the urgent request for Heinrich to get himself over to the Fournier cottage. He'd stopped Heinrich as he was rushing out the door, rolling down his sleeves and putting his uniform jacket on.

"This might be the opportune moment to set things right between the two of you," he advised. Heinrich nodded at him, already turning away in a daze of excitement. "No, Heinrich! Look at me! Now is the time! Get it right! Once and for all, son, get it right this time! If you don't, you'll lose her forever!" He was gently shaking the young man by the shoulders until Heinrich focused his eyes correctly once again.

"She's having our baby!" was all Heinrich could say. The Colonel knew it was hopeless to try and give more advice to this young fellow in the state he was in just now. All he could do was wait and hope for the best.

So, with a resigned sigh, he shook his head at the young man, adding: "Go on now, but make sure she knows that you're there, and that you're staying there. Don't be coming back here until she comes with you! She's your wife, and that's your baby. Don't let any of them doubt it!" He clapped Heinrich on the shoulder while pushing him down the front steps and off across the yard toward his loved one, soon to change into plural.

#

Well, plural loves it would be.

When Doctor Hervieux finally trotted into the yard and dismounted his horse, having had no available petrol for his old car, things had already progressed nicely both upstairs and down. He burst into the kitchen, greeted by drunken cheering from the men, before being excitedly ushered upstairs by an impatient matron carrying yet another basin of hot water and an armful of clean toweling.

"Well, my dear," he said to a red-faced, straining Paulette, "isn't it a bit early for this? I was under the impression that we had almost another whole month to wait." The answer he received did little to enlighten him, except to confirm that someone had been wrong in their calculations.

She let out another long wailing cry, punctuated with additional colorful expletives.

"Oh my!" exclaimed the doctor, eyebrows raised in the direction of the bed. "Alright, things look just about right, so I'm going to ask you to breathe deeply and when you feel the next contraction start to build, you may push as hard as you can, from your belly." He turned and washed his hands with strong soap. "Ladies, you may help her to sit up a little so she can push easier, if you will."

He turned about the room, inspecting the preparations. Finding them satisfactory, he returned to the foot of the bed, peering through his spectacles beneath the sheet to see what was happening.

Paulette's mother and Aimée Quesnel hoisted Paulette to a reclined yet almost sitting position as her breathing puffed stronger and faster. "It's time to push now, *chérie*, as hard as you can. You can do it!" The women had a hard time keeping hold of Paulette's fists which were crushing their hands as she strained against their hold, pressing against their arms, crouching forward from what used to be her waist, but was now a rock solid mass of heaving agony.

This next cry started out as a low growl, building slowly, gaining power as well as momentum. It didn't end, but was simply suspended while excited voices encouraged her to breathe, then to push more. "We can see the head, sweetie! Keep at it...that's it...PUSH!"

A strange slurping noise was heard before Paulette's growl changed into a triumphant shout. *"Gottverdammt, Hurensohn und Sheisse!!"*

Downstairs, all eyes turned in surprise to
Heinrich. Clearly, none of them had been responsible for
teaching her the words pronounced in this last outburst of
vulgarity. The short pause dissolved as they clapped him
on the back, hysterical laughter uniting them once and for
all.

The ladies laughed as well, then let out a
collective sigh of relief and exclamations of "It's a boy!"
followed by "Oh look how handsome he is!" and "What
a fine looking baby!" Finally, the doctor, looking rather
pleased with himself, held up a tiny, purple, squirming
package to present to the stunned mother, saying:
"Congratulations, my dear, you have a fine looking son!"

The cord was cut. The child was examined,
washed and bundled before Paulette eagerly reached out
her arms to clutch her child, face wet with tears of joy,
incapable of looking at anything but his tiny, squashed
and wrinkled face. Liliane's arms encircled the shoulders
of her daughter and grandson, the new grandmother's
tears dripping unheeded into the daughter's hair.

Much cooing and generally tender, motherly
sounds came from the women gathered around the bed,
admiring, touching and sighing with happiness at a
successful delivery.

This vision was one of the sorts engraved in memory, forever transcending time, sending out rays of warmth and contentment for years to come.

I was drowning in happiness, feeling the hearts around me burst with pride, joy and great quantities of love. I swallowed it up in large gulps, enough to hold me over through rougher, unhappier moments.

The news was carried downstairs to much cheering, laughter and many congratulations to the father and grandfather, who were clapping each other on the back as if they had done the birthing themselves. More drinks were had in celebration.

Upstairs, just as some of the ladies were packing things up and the others were cleaning up the new mother and changing her bedding, one of them called out to the doctor in alarm. "Doctor, come quickly! Look at this!"

Paulette was very quiet of a sudden; her breath cut short, eyes round with surprise and pain. "Oh no! What's wrong now! Ohhhhhhh!!!" Her voice climbed the scales to a fever pitch; pains once again ripping through her tender insides.

"Good heavens!" shouted the doctor. "Get more towels over here right away! It looks like there's another one!"

The agitation reverberated alarming noises back down the stairs causing a shocked halt to the celebrations below, as all ears strained to make out the cause for the noise when there should only have been calm. Long minutes passed, drinks forgotten on the table as worried minds were swiftly peopled with nasty imaginings of things gone bad. Blood ran cold in anxious hearts, fearing the worst. Frightened faces turned toward the stairway when the next footsteps descended to bring the news of yet another successful birth.

Marguerite followed her brother Thomas by about a half hour.

I would have my girl after all!

Ecstatic cheers rang out and the general unbridled euphoria was contagious.

The doctor insisted on proudly explaining to anyone who cared to listen, although most did not, that he had been right in his calculations after all, since twins were always known to come earlier than single births. "Simply not enough room, you see!" he would add a little blearily, as he partook of celebratory drink himself. He purposefully forgot to mention that he hadn't thought to check for multiple heartbeats during his previous examinations of her. But no one thought to ask, either.

This time, the exhausted mother, clean, but giddy with happiness, looked up with hope and love in her eyes as Heinrich timidly opened the door to the upstairs room.

I'll leave to you to imagine what went on, once the door was shut.

CHAPTER 28

December 1943:

The holidays were approaching. Not that there was a lot of celebrating going on, but for us, there was a moment of quiet, rather like the calm before the storm.

Over the months since the summer I'd been gleaning bits of information vital to half of those occupying my rooms, tidbits which undermined their foundations of security. The Third Reich had been increasingly confronted with issues destabilizing the tenuous hold Hitler struggled to maintain on his positions. In May, Nazi forces surrendered in Tunisia, which was now completely under Allied control. In July, Anglo-American forces had landed in Sicily, causing Mussolini to fall from power, thus eliminating Hitler's strongest ally in Europe. The Nazi submarine fleet had been forced to withdraw from the North Atlantic due to serious losses and the Allied bombing campaign on German cities and military arms manufactures was taking a serious toll. Hitler's hold on the Eastern front was slipping and he was withdrawing troops from the line holding Leningrad. In addition, German forces were massing as much as possible along the western reaches of Europe in preparation for a rumored invasion of Allied forces along the coast of northern France. The Fuhrer was losing ground and frustration was high amongst those Germans who cared about the outcome of this seemingly endless war.

Of course, they were numerous. There were however, a good deal of them who feared and greatly so, that Germany would be crushed once and for all if this war too, was lost. Others were concerned that the continued destruction of her infrastructure, while desperately trying to maintain the war, would be just as bad as surrendering now. There were others who only wished for peace, no matter what the outcome. However, it did appear as though a turning point must be approaching.

It seemed to be increasingly urgent to move the western campaign forward and to actively attack England. The rumors circulating about the existence of an Allied plan of attack on northern Europe reinforced the necessity to act aggressively. The Germans were anxious, in particular Rolf, to commence the V1 operation before anything more could happen.

Rolf was furious that things weren't going along as planned. The sites should have been in service by now.

Looking over his shoulder, I saw that this project had been in the works since the building of the technological facility situated in the secret military base of Peenemünde, 100 kilometers from Berlin, in 1936. Employing more than 12,000 people, it was the most modern arms development site in the world. Working out the kinks in this particular weapon was taking much longer than had been originally planned, which wasn't doing much good for Rolf's abnormally short temper.

In fact, he was chomping at the bit like a race horse, ready to begin his offensive. The relative calm we'd enjoyed while Rolf was busy hunting for sites and starting construction was over. His hands were now idle, waiting for key components to arrive on site. There was nothing useful for him to do. Luckily, he turned his energies to some useless pleasantry.

He spent increasing amounts of time in Rouen, carousing with fellow officers and dawdling with the ladies who constituted the inevitable camp followers, present in any long term war. Women, who gave themselves in exchange for an easier life as the kept woman of an officer, were everywhere.

As city dwellers, the scarcity of food and the general privations of wartime were the best fertilizer to spread on an urban population in order to harvest a large crop of desperate women. They sprouted in *cafés* and on street corners, as well as in the more traditional docklands. A gluttonous man like Rolf could change companions every evening and never run out. There would always be a different female ready to sacrifice her integrity in exchange for a hot meal and the chance to spend the night in a bed, regardless of what else went on in it. Each of them hoped to catch his fancy enough for a longer term relation to develop, possibly obtaining a place to sleep and regular funds to live off of.

That particular thought never crossed Rolf's mind. He profited from their desperate efforts to convince him of their worthiness as a mistress. He invariably paid them for their troubles and walked away without sparing these ladies a further thought. At least it mostly kept him away from us.

#

The babies were ten weeks old and growing nicely. Paulette wasn't getting much sleep, nursing the two of them several times per night. Heinrich wasn't getting much sleep either, cuddling the other, attempting to keep the crying to a minimum, while waiting for a turn, as the first suckled greedily. Twins seemed to be disproportionately more work than just one child. They were both exhausted.

During these first few months, they stayed at the Fournier cottage, Heinrich included, enjoying the extra help provided by Liliane and Roseline during the daylight hours. When the sun rose, he would wash and dress, before staggering over to the main house for some breakfast. The work day would begin and once more his mind wandered continually back across the yard to the cottage to linger with his new family.

He was increasingly preoccupied with thoughts of what was yet to come, being privy to morsels of information concerning the unfolding of events on the front. He also knew of the project Rolf was setting up and could only be worried for the security of his tiny family, if it were to come to fruition. Such installations would be at the top of the list of targets for Allied bombing raids and he was well aware of the limited accuracy with which these raids were carried out.

Once again, he was in a position where he was hiding details from his wife and her family with whom he spent all of his free time, hoping to keep them from leaking any information to the resistance. This would, instead of helping their cause, put these same people, now his extended family, in grave danger from those seeking to help them. It was a no win situation which provoked even more sleeplessness, if that could be possible, considering the crying babies whose room he shared in the cottage.

#

The Colonel was the first to notice, seeing Heinrich's shoulders slump over his ledgers while at work.

"Finding married life a little tiring, are you?" he chuckled kindly while patting Heinrich on the back one afternoon. He had come asking for details concerning their projected wool production that winter and found Heinrich propping his head up on one arm, as if it couldn't stay upright on its own. "You look as if you've not slept for a week."

"Sir, I'm afraid that I don't even know how to sleep anymore!" Heinrich admitted with shame written on his expression as he jumped to his feet surprised, not hearing the Colonel's approach. "I never imagined what it was like for people who had twins. They're wonderful and I'm so very happy to have them. I find myself smiling all the time when I'm with them, but they never seem to sleep at the same time!" He shook his head slowly. "I thought twins did the same thing all of the time: two identical babies. But they're so contrary to one another, in everything they do. Never anything at the same time. One eats while the other is sleeping, then one cries and wakes the sleeping one! It's exhausting!"

"And how is the young mother coping?"

"She's got some help from the other women who all seem to be happy to lend a hand. But, the feeding is her duty. Not much anyone can do to help there! Except they've started talking of using some of the dairy milk now, since it could help to keep the babies asleep a little longer. They're getting old enough to have some now. The doctor said they're fine and healthy. I guess that's what counts even if we are both wretched with sleep loss!" He smiled, rubbing his swollen, red eyes.

"Will you be bringing them back over to us soon? We all miss the young lady, especially at dinner time. Eating is so much more pleasant when she's about. The news is so depressing from the eastern front that we all need a reason to talk about other pleasantries and she's a wonderful excuse to not hash over our Führer's plans at dinner. Do you think you could come across the yard one evening for a visit?"

"I will ask her this evening. Thank you for your kindness. Paulette often asks me how you are getting along and if Marthe is treating you well." Heinrich bowed in thanks to his commanding officer, extending his hand to his friend, these being one and the same. This done, he continued in a more worried tone of voice. "Sir, I feel that I can presume upon your kindness to ask you for some advice, if you have a minute?"

"Of course. What can I do for you?" The Colonel stepped back, crossing his arms behind his back while scrutinizing the younger man's face, just now clouded over with a frown.

"I know that I enlisted as a single man, but now...well, I was thinking that for the future it would be better for my wife and our children if we could lodge together...here," Heinrich paused looking at the Colonel, during a hopeful pause.

"I'd like to request the use of the room next to the attic room I shared with Paulette before the twins came, in addition the old attic room. If that's possible, that is. It would simply involve removing a partition, and bringing in some cots, but I would feel much better if they could lodge here instead of in the cottage." His voice drifted off toward an uneasy silence, waiting for a refusal. None came.

"Don't you think her family would object to having her taken away from their protection once again and this time with the babies as well?" The can of worms was opened.

Words rushed out in relief at feeling understood. "That's exactly what I'm worried about. I would prefer *my family*...to be with me. So that I may protect them. I fear for the future and the line drawing which will most certainly take place, probably sooner than later. I want them to be on the same side of the line as I am. As it stands now, they're on the other side of the yard, but also, on the other side of everything. I need to be able to pack them up and take them with us if we have to go. With your permission of course, sir..." Another rather uncomfortable pause stretched between them.

"It seems you have a bit of a dilemma." The older man strode about the room, walking and thinking aloud, as if the problem laid before him, was of the most delicate strategic importance.

"You stole her away from them at first, and then you went to join them. You capitulated. It seems as if they've accepted you, as one of their own. But now...now, will they let you take all three of them away? I'm not so sure. You're asking for their surrender." He stroked his chin in a thoughtful manner. "You've got your own tennis match going on here...bouncing back and forth across the yard. But I suppose you're in the right, wanting to get it clear before the time comes and she'll have to make a decision in haste."

He stopped his pacing and came to stand in front of Heinrich.

"You can have the two rooms. It should be easy to place a door connecting them. Talk to that young soldier whose father was a carpenter, get him to organize it. But fix it up *before* you go get them. Use some of the furniture in the attic, as well. There are some nice ladylike things packed up there. She'll feel better about it if she's got some nice things to use. No sense not being ready, before you ask her. Waiting could just give her some time to change her mind. Fix up a nice surprise for her. You just might win." He smiled at the relief flooding the young man's face.

"Sir, your generosity of heart is greatly appreciated. I'll go tell Paulette at once!"

"No, man! Did you listen at all? Get it all done first, the door, the furniture, all of it! *Then* go bring her to see and ask her once you've got her alone in the newly furnished rooms, once she's seen the surprise you've made for her. You have to *tempt* her away. Don't know much about how a woman's heart works, do you lad? Hmmm..."

He sighed at the frustration he felt at not being young once again himself, yet realizing at the same instant, that when he was a young man, he most likely made the same sort of foolish mistakes. Probably how he had lost hold of his Bridget, now that he thought of it. What a shame that experience was only had with age, when it was so much less useful. Wisdom and youth were two contradictory qualities, it seemed.

Still musing, he watched Heinrich go off to find the men capable of setting his plans to work. Thinking still, that the young fellow had better learn to do things in the right order, he laughed. Backward planning had gotten the chap married at least, which was more than the Colonel could say for himself.

"Youth and wisdom, indeed!" He smiled a sad little smile while rummaging about through the forgotten papers on Heinrich's desk, searching for the inventory of last year's wool production.

#

So it came about that a hole appeared in my attic wall, reinforced with an oak door frame, and new plaster and whitewash were applied to the nursery walls. A good sized baby cot was retrieved from the attic, as well as a large, comfortable arm chair covered in flowery chintz fabric. A cherry wood chest of drawers topped with a lovely mirror carved with swans, and a large carpet rounded out the furnishings, while the same flowered chintz hung as drapes over the small window.

The rooms and furnishings were dusted, polished and swept. Good use had been made of the young Mademoiselle's belongings which had once graced the large upstairs room formerly occupied by Heinrich and his companions.

For men, they had arranged things surprisingly well. My attic rooms were given a new life. As for myself, not minding the sawing and hammering over much, I was looking forward to embracing those babies in my heart and making sure their dreams were sweet ones.

#

Heinrich had convinced Paulette to come across the yard to supper with her former dinner companions for a bit of a change in routine. The young mother relinquished the twins to their grandmother's care after their feeding. She changed her dress, carefully fixing her hair before joining her husband at the door to the cottage.

They were contentedly strolling across the yard, Paulette's hand tucked under Heinrich's arm as if they were young lovers walking out for the evening. In spite of the winter cold, their insides were warm with being together, outside, away from the twins' overwhelming presence. It was a welcome diversion and they both felt quite free and lighthearted.

The smells of something wonderful had permeated my entire ground floor, drifting out to tickle their nostrils as soon as the front door opened. Marthe and Franz had been busy. Most likely the combination of both talents accounted for the delicious perfumes bringing appetites to a peak. They breathed in deep with a pleased sigh, laughing at their identical gestures before heading to the door to the sitting room, where Paulette's former dinner companions had gathered for an *aperitif,* the traditional before dinner drink so readily adopted by the Germans.

A unanimous cacophony of greetings met their arrival. The officers rose and came to shake Paulette's hand, each with a considerate question regarding the twins or a compliment on her loveliness. She blushed at their kindnesses, smiling, genuinely happy to speak to them. The Colonel hung back a bit, waiting his turn. She finally had an instant to draw her breath, turning toward him.

"My dear," he said, as he stood in front of her. "I'm so very happy to see you looking so well. We've been rather lonely here without you. Do promise to never leave us alone again for quite so long!" His smile reached his eyes as he took both of her hands in his and kissed the backs of each of them in turn, before offering her a glass of wine.

"Tell us about the children then. Have they started to get teeth? Are they rolling over now, or already walking and talking? I'm certain that they'll be prodigies, the both of them, what with the extraordinary parents they have! Although, I should think that they must sleep quite a lot if they take after their father. I've been finding him asleep on the job every day lately!" He winked at Heinrich and a goodhearted laugh turned about the room.

The fire crackled in my grate, and a layer of snow carpeted the yard, dressing the darkness in a coat of white, covering the gray of the autumn mud. It would soon be Christmas and although there wasn't a decorated tree or boughs of holly and evergreen gracing the doors or mantle pieces, authentic good cheer reverberated amongst these unlikely companions, friends in the face of conflicting politics.

#

Emile Levasseur froze, listening for another noise to follow the thud which had halted his pencil midway along the sketch pad spread over the oak tabletop in his cottage. Polka lifted her head to do the same. She growled and silence answered. But this silence was pregnant with something that both Emile and Polka recognized as needful of an investigation. Emile slipped into his ragged coat and lit an oil lantern. Polka rose from her bed by the fire to accompany him.

They stepped into the night with caution, Emile's eyes adjusting to the starlight before dousing the lantern. Closing the door of the cottage behind him cut off the inside light source, bringing the shapes of the garden laid out in front of him into the peculiar focus of moonlight across snow. The shapes of ordinary objects distorted by blue shadows took on dimensions and grandeur not afforded them by ordinary sunlight.

Cautious eyes inventoried the area directly in front of his window. Emile easily identified the clay pots on the window sill, the stone bench near the door to the walled kitchen garden, the well head, and the wheel barrow near the tool shed. He didn't recognize the square shape on the ground next to the bench. Polka spotted the cube as well and set off to sniff it. The box shook in response to her prodding muzzle.

"What have you got there, girl? Let's have a look." Emile crouched to examine the wooden box. Hearing the rustle of wings inside, he hastily scanned the yard to check for signs of anyone else who might have heard the thud of its landing. Stepping away from the crate, he hesitated. 'Should I do this? How involved should I get in their affairs?' The answer came swiftly. Emile snatched the box, and kidnapped the carrier pigeon.

Once inside, he carefully removed the band from the bird's leg. He placed a saucer of water inside the crate, before sliding it under the table with useless admonitions to keep quiet.

He unrolled the small paper square to read the inscription.

"Honni soit qui mal y pense". The motto in antiquated French rang true beneath a drawing of the arms of the Order of the Garter. Emile remembered the design from childhood and his favorite stories by Alexandre Dumas. Visions of swashbuckling, sword-bearing heroes defending the honor of princesses and homeland sprung from the paper.

On the reverse side was a tiny map. Emile recognized the layout of the villages of Bertreville, St Ouen, Auppegard and Omonville. Contemplating the miniature map, he toyed with the pencil he'd used for his sketch, and poised it carefully above the forest on the western edge of Bertreville. Several minutes of indecision passed before Emile drew a deep breath as he brought the pencil down and circled a specific spot, not far from us. Carefully he re-rolled the tiny paper and slipped it into the hollow *cartouche* on the pigeon's leg.

Once again, he spoke to the pigeon. "You'll be careful not to get your feet wet. It might ruin the map. And fly high, stay away from planes, and be brave." He opened the door to the cottage, with the cooing bird tucked warm against his heart beneath the jacket. Polka followed as he walked to far edge of the walled garden, to the gate leading to the north facing fields.

He was in shadow here as he opened his coat, kissed the pigeon and tossed it into the air. "Fly true," he whispered into the moonlight as the disoriented pigeon circled to get its bearings before winging it off toward the trees on the hedgerow separating the fields to the north.

Emile wondered if it would rest the night before heading back to England and its usual roost. He patted Polka on the head, turning back to the cottage where he broke the crate into bits before feeding the pieces to the greedy fire.

#

"Are your eyes really closed? Not cheating are you? If you are...we'll go back and you won't get your surprise!" Heinrich teased his wife as she giggled like the girl she still was, in spite of growing up a bit faster than anyone had expected, due to circumstances, some of her own making, while others were not of her choice.

Paulette was joyous with wine and with the pleasant evening she'd just spent, truly welcome among her husband's friends and colleagues. She displayed just the tiniest bit of tipsiness. Heinrich found looking at her pleasure intoxicating.

"Hurry up! Or I will peek! Where are we going?" She laughed her words instead of speaking them as he carried her up the stairs in his arms, hoping to keep their destination secret until he might open the door.

"Patience, patience. Didn't your parents teach you the virtue of patience?" he teased. He let Paulette's body slowly slide back to her feet along his own as they stopped in front of the door, careful to keep her facing his chest so she might not yet guess that they were standing in front of their former bedroom door.

"Eyes still closed?" he queried as he opened the door with one hand. "You may open them now," he said, stealing a kiss as she looked at his chest, then up into his face, her backside at the now open doorway. She was just too tempting. Still, he pulled back as she was carried away by the kiss, keen to forget the promised surprise in the tasting of his mouth.

It had been a while since they had the time, the energy or the freedom to love each other as they had before the pregnancy, before Rolf spoiling things between them and before the babies took up the bulk of their time. To complicate things, Heinrich had serious qualms about enjoying her company in her parents' cottage, where the tiny rooms left little privacy. She obviously felt deprived as well, but still, he was impatient to please her heart, before tending to the rest of her.

"Apparently they didn't teach you patience!" he laughed. "But, that wasn't quite the surprise I had in mind. However... if you'd rather do something else...we can leave the surprise for another day!"

"No! No you don't! I want to see my surprise! I'll do my best to control myself, sir. Just stand back a bit! A safe distance and I'll be good. I promise!" She sparkled with their flirtatious banter, reveling in the familiar feeling of being young and in love.

He turned her around and gently shoved her through the doorway.

Oil lamps had been lit, giving their old room a cozy glow. Another lamp lit in the new room beckoned Paulette through the open doorway. She followed it, stopping in her tracks at the threshold.

She felt it. She felt me.

She connected with the others who had left their memories and emotions buried in the materials making up these furnishings. The feeling ran up her legs from the floorboards, radiating through her torso and out to her fingertips, which she used to caress the smooth wood of the crib and the dresser. The vibrations reversed themselves from her fingers and tingled their way through her body back into the floor, before starting all over again, a wave of intense well being, coming and going through her flesh and bones. A sense of belonging somewhere. To me, in fact. She felt overwhelmingly, at home. Her heart was warm and comforted, and at peace.

Heinrich felt it as he watched her absorb this benevolence, taking in his share, but mistaking it for his love for her. He was enthralled by the expression on Paulette's face, fascinated with the movements she made as she toured the room, fingers lighting on each surface, touching the fabrics, sliding a hand along a freshly painted wall. She had no words. None were needed.

It might seem contradictory. It might seem impossible to imagine. But at that instant, the war didn't exist. Everywhere, on all of the different fronts of conflict, there was a moment of respite. Paulette's well being traveled around the earth in that split second and everywhere, humans and animals alike froze their gestures for a few heartbeats, breathing deeply of her peace and tranquility, without knowing why.

It lasted only an instant before those who shared it shook their heads and took up their paused activities, keeping only a small ounce of hope that not all was wrong in the world.

They moved in the next day.

CHAPTER 29

Winter 1943-1944:

It was starting.

Late one evening between Christmas and the New Year, a large black Mercedes rolled through the gate and crunched the gravel path, pulling to a halt in front of my main entrance. Three men in uniforms decorated with excessive braid and insignia stomped across the threshold into the Colonel's study.

Anxious faces peered through the sheer curtains of neighboring cottages into the night. Aside from the shadows of the naked tree limbs dancing across the snow covered lawn, not much else was to be seen. Long minutes of hushed conversation dead ended with unanswerable questions. The curious finally resigned themselves to forced ignorance until morning broke with welcome gossip. Although they slid under warm eiderdowns back into bed, their whispering echoed throughout the remaining hours until dawn. The something that was starting was perceived by all, yet escaped identification.

Until the crunching of the gravel, our lives flowed in the ever constant rhythm of rural life. Seasonal changes necessitated tasks appropriate to the weather: overseeing the birthing of cows and sheep as well as the sowing and harvesting of crops.

Elsewhere, the war stumbled on. Men died and desperate families were starving in the cities. However, we would look to the sky in the morning and the evening, speculating on the weather, the only unknown which could alter our daily routine.

Even when air raids dropped bombs, farm workers would rise with the sun and go outside to tend to the animals, working around the danger. It was commonplace to see airplanes rumble across the sky above a plow, the man driving it tucking his head between his shoulders and cringing, stopping only for a second or two before clucking to the horse. Even the horses skittered less when droning airborne engines silenced the birds.

Time rolled on, dragging the living in its wake. Creatures of all types adapt to danger when escape isn't an option, especially now that Hitler had invaded the southern part of France. News crackled over the radio, leaving us guessing what it meant for Normandy.

The south had originally been a 'safe zone', unoccupied by the German army and under the control of a proxy government rooted in Vichy. But when the Allies invaded North Africa, taking a permanent hold there, Hitler told the Maréchal Pétain in no uncertain terms that their bargain would not be respected. The south was no longer free. The few people who wished to seek refuge there at such a late date, now had nowhere to go.

I wondered about the family who should have been here, running their domain. They had thought to escape the war by fleeing to Menton. Now they were trapped in a region which was doubly dangerous. *La Résistance* was firmly implanted in the south, carrying out frequent attacks on German army installations and supply convoys. This activity enraged the Germans, engendering horrific, retaliatory attacks on civilians.

Here at home, north of the demarcation line, we had come to ignore the constant air-raids. My people expected to hear explosions. In fact, quiet days were a surprise. Not much energy was wasted worrying which targets were hit or missed, but the certainty that at one time it might be our turn was perched on every man and woman's left shoulder, a squawking crow that could only be ignored to a certain degree.

Although the bovines appeared oblivious, munching away in spite of the noise, on days of intense aerial activity there was less milk to be taken. They felt stress much as we did. The abundance of snow this winter cloistered the animals inside for long days, substituting hay for the grass which usually stayed green throughout the mild Norman winters. The noise was thus slightly diminished. Still the milk was thinner than when the cows were roaming grassy meadows.

Still the babies thrived, giving a much needed rest to Paulette's over-extended personal milk production. She nursed each child twice a day in addition to the supplementary cow's milk, and the difference showed on her features and in the renewed shine of her hair. She was recovering easily from the strain of feeding two healthy babies. Better quality sleep made a difference as well.

Her nights with me were calmer. I could see to that. The babies woke less frequently, dreaming in tune with my soundless lullabies hummed in their ears, inaudible to those for whom they were not intended. I was pleased to weave a nest of comfort around this precious little family, relieving some of their burden.

There were however, events over which I had no control whatsoever. No magic of mine could stop the inexorable rolling of time toward the culmination of this conflict. Peace was held at bay until it might be reached, but over the next few months, I suspected we would be holding our breath.

#

Rolf, our willing carrier of disastrous news, stomped into the drawing room one evening, possessed by a rage of the type we had all feared him capable. An installation under his control near Auffay had been destroyed by an Allied bombing raid in October and just now, another near Pommereval had been targeted and irreparably damaged. It would take months to reconstruct the heavy cement storage facility protecting the volatile chemicals used to ignite the missiles. The launch ramp was incapacitated, as well as the cement housing structures meant to protect the missiles themselves, not yet arrived from Germany.

Certain that an insider was behind the leakage of information allowing the Allies to pinpoint the well camouflaged sites; he intended to discover which reckless tongue had betrayed him.

He paced the room before throwing himself onto a sofa. A fortuitous glass of plum liqueur arrived close to his clenched fist. Although he spoke in German, he fixed Paulette as he raged between gulps, scrutinizing her face as if his words were meant for her alone, looking for recognition of their meaning to alter her expression.

"There is no possibility the English could have discovered the location of the site from the air. It is camouflaged from view by the surrounding trees. The only opening in the tree cover is the exit of the launching ramp parallel to the ground, and so, invisible from above. It has to be someone who has access to my documents who has given the coordinates to the enemy. When I discover who that person is, and I will, they will regret their decision to cross me. No one sabotages my work and walks away!"

His words skittered across the low table separating the opposing sofas, the other holding Paulette and Heinrich, each with a child tucked in their lap. The menace ricocheted from one person to the next, bouncing off guilty hearts hidden behind carefully arranged, and unreadable faces.

VonEpffs had received the nocturnal visit of a group of officers sympathetic to the mounting plot to depose the Fuhrer and replace him with someone of less radical ideology, someone capable of bringing the war to an end, thus ensuring the safety of their homeland. The movement to mount a *coup d'état* was gaining momentum and the Colonel's contingent was ready to participate, excluding Rolf of course, who would be arrested as soon as the code word "Valkyrie" was announced over the teletype, signaling the arrest or death of Adolph Hitler. Thus, most everyone present in the room was guilty of disloyalty to the cause championed by the Nazis. Rolf unknowingly found himself in a minority.

The previous night, while Rolf distracted himself in the arms of a dismal woman in Rouen, Colonel VonEpffs welcomed the visitors who were carefully questioning officers throughout the whole of the army, identifying those who would admit to disagreeing with the Fuhrer's course of action.

As a rule, they looked to those hailing from old German aristocracy who were weaned on ideals of patriotism, seasoned with a strong sense of honor and not Germanic supremacy at all costs. Numerous were the officers who understood that the Fuhrer had embarked on a path of destruction, his personal desire for power and glory having completely discolored his vision of Germany's best interests. They squirmed at tales of conditions in the prisoner of war work camps, as well as at the rumored extermination of the minorities using gassing chambers.

I had listened to the hushed conversation in the study the previous evening as another shocking chapter of Hitler's grand plan was dissected. The promotion of white protestant supremacy achieved by a campaign of genetic hybridization was being implemented in Germany. The concept of blatant manipulation of natural selection was morally repulsive. That a group of generals should pick and choose men and women to procreate amongst themselves in order to induce visible genetic traits in their off spring, such as the finest stud horses were bred with the finest mares to produce sturdy horseflesh, was quite simply revolting. While 'blue-blooded' alliances had been the rule of thumb throughout the European nobility for centuries, it was in a quest to benefit the financial or social standing of a family tree. To see such principles applied to the common man, with hopes of weeding out unacceptable genetic traits while reinforcing typical Aryan coloring was disgraceful.

They felt he must be stopped.

The Colonel had, in silence and for quite some time, held serious doubts about their leader's mental stability and was thus, in wholehearted agreement with the project to depose their misguided Fuhrer. Heinrich followed in his footsteps and swore his support before our guests drove off into the night, silencing the whispers from behind the curtains.

Rolf hadn't a clue as to their defection from the grand plan.

#

Ranting and raving, accompanied by suspicious scrutiny of the listener's faces, brought about no admissions of guilt. Rolf was clever enough to realize that he wouldn't trap the culprit so easily, unless of course it had been his little ninny of a sister-in-law, who had such trouble disguising her thoughts. No, he would have to be subtle in his investigation. But, pride made him secure in the knowledge that he would ultimately succeed.

It was easy to trick a group of idealists. His brother topped the list of dreamers, out of touch with the reality of the power Rolf held. He would find out what he needed to know and the guilty would pay for their stupidity in trying to trip him up.

Rolf decided to change his attitude for the rest of the evening and adopt a more pleasant demeanor, hoping to encourage relaxation of spirits and the loosening of tongues. A bit of a drinking binge would be just the thing.

#

The children were put to bed and Paulette had come back downstairs to share her meal as usual with the others. Dinner unfolded in a more relaxed atmosphere.

Rolf had calmed down and become noticeably more pleasant, his conversation turning back into French, including Paulette, relating anecdotes about the time he had spent in the city. He plied them with conversation and plum brandy, adopting an uncharacteristically charming attitude.

Paulette noticed the Colonel humored Rolf, laughing at his stories with the rest of them, but with a certain reserve which Paulette had come to recognize as a sign of wariness.

The evening wore on as Rolf played the clown, entertaining them while distributing glasses of last summer's plum brandy. At one point, during a long story told by a slightly inebriated Lieutenant friend of Heinrich's, Paulette discreetly excused herself from the group to use the water closet.

Along the way to the drawing room she glanced into the dining room, still littered with dishes and glasses. She decided to help out the kitchen maids, most likely long gone off to bed, by gathering the plates, scraping the remains from each plate onto a single one, and piling the cutlery on top. As she started down the stairs toward the kitchen she was halted in her tracks by Rolf, who was climbing up, coming from below.

He stopped, facing her.

Paulette tried to take a step backwards up the stairs, but loaded down as she was with ten dirty dinner plates piled high with the accompanying silverware, her position was difficult. Her arms were aching from the weight of the porcelain and the silver, but before she could turn away, Rolf caught her about the waist making her lose her balance. She plunked down on the stone step behind her, keeping the dishes from crashing to the floor.

She could have dropped her load and taken to her heels, but her frugal upbringing instinctively made her protect the china. So she sat on the step with a pile of dirty plates in her lap, her brother-in-law three steps below her, breathing fumes of brandy uncomfortably close to her face.

Keeping her eyes lowered, she focusing her attention on the cutlery balanced on the plates, listening for any movement from him, and avoiding his eyes. Her heart thundered in her chest, suffocating her, yet she stayed still, like a small animal trapped between cat's paws.

He observed her, still and silent for a long moment, before gently taking the dishes from her lap and placing them on the step next to her feet. She started to rise, hoping to escape up the stairs, but he quickly grabbed her hands, helping her to her feet, though certainly not in a gesture motivated by gallantry. Their respective positions on the stairs placed her face level with his and he seized the advantage. Her evident discomfort titillated his already firm resolve to have her, for Paulette was far too lovely to be left alone much longer. His patience in the role of the cat teasing his prey came to an end.

A wet mustache landed on her mouth, his tongue invading her lips as she opened them to protest. An overwhelming taste of alcohol drenched her taste buds. Using one huge paw to pin both her hands behind her back, he used the other to fumble inside her blouse, groping her breasts heavy with milk.

She wanted to scream. She wanted to cry. She wanted to run.

She decided to bite.

Blood from his tongue flooded her mouth as she chomped down on it like a piece of steak. He screamed in pain and jumped back, sending the entire pile of dishes and cutlery toppling down the remaining stone steps to explode into shards on the floor below. She was gone, back up the stairs in a flurry of skirts. One hand struck out to catch her ankle, bringing her crashing onto the stone steps above her, face first.

Bellowing echoed in her ears from far away as her vision blurred and she tasted blood again, this time her own. Her last thought was an urge to laugh as she understood that she could identify a difference in taste comparing his blood to hers. Then the pain around her left eye thudded, drowning his voice as she lost consciousness.

#

Sometime later, Paulette pried open her right eye, to see the Colonel looking down into her face. She saw his lips moving and imagined she could hear a voice but chose to not attempt understanding it. The throbbing came back, muting all other sounds. Her hand moved to touch her head, instinctively seeking out the source of the pain. The thumping of her heart echoed with a second's delay in the space above her left eye. A goose egg bulged her forehead. Touching it was almost a necessity. The hurt forced her consciousness to reside in her body once again. The pain grounded her flighty head as the agony of the goose egg produced a groan.

"She's back!" crowed the Colonel just as Marthe's face appeared over Paulette's right eye before obliterating the bleary view with a cold cloth. She could clearly hear them now, as chaotic murmurs deciphered themselves into comprehensible speech.

"Here you are, *ma caille*," crooned Marthe's voice, "this should help your head. Colonel, would you help me sit her up just a little so she can sip some of this willow bark tea? She'll be feeling the pain just now that she's started to moan. It'll help fast enough."

The Colonel slid an arm behind Paulette's back, propping her up enough for the scalding tea to slide along the back of her throat. She swallowed twice before he lowered her onto the extra pillow Marthe slipped beneath her shoulder blades. She groaned again.

"You'll feel like you've been trampled by a horse for a day or two, *ma douce*, there's nothing to be done about that except for you to drink up this tea, and as much of it as you can," said the cook.

The Colonel added: "Yes, but at least she seems to be able to focus her eyes...er... well... her eye."

"That goose egg is a beauty, and she'll have a nasty shiner, but I think she'll be just about fine by tomorrow. We just need to get her to talk to us; to be sure she's not addled her brains with the fall."

This comment shocked the Colonel, and his relief that she would be alright took leave as quickly as it had come.

"Addled her brains?" he questioned Marthe.

"Well, yes Sir. When you take a fall and crack your head like she has, sometimes your brains get shook up and you're not right anymore. Sometimes it goes away after a day or two, sometimes never. We'll have to keep an eye out for vomiting. Usually they vomit when the brains are shook up too much."

"Good heavens!" he exclaimed, as he uncovered Paulette's right eye and peered into it. "My dear girl, are you there? Can you hear me? Please say something; we're very worried about you. Paulette? Please, dear..."

She felt like she had a mouth full of dirt dampened by the metallic taste of blood. Her tongue stretched to her lip to pronounce a word, hoping to reassure those above her who seemed so worried, but as she did this she felt an unusual hole: one left by a missing tooth!

Fury seized her: her feminine pride offended at her certainly wrecked smile. She had nice teeth. She kept them clean, knowing her smile was one of her best features. And now it was destroyed, and by the fault of that hideous man! She tried to push herself up off the pillow, anger supplying the necessary energy.

"He bwoke my foooff! The bathturd! Where ith he! I wanth thoo kill him!" she slurred around the hole in her mouth, which kept catching her tongue and scraping it across the newly rough edges. More blood oozed into her mouth and she turned her head looking for somewhere to spit.

"Well, I don't think she's addled," pronounced Marthe with obvious relief, as she placed a cloth in Paulette's hand to catch the spit blood. "She knows exactly whose fault this is and she wants to kill him. Seems to be thinking straight enough to me! We'll have to watch her closely for a few days though, just to be sure." Marthe turned away, hiding a smile of mirth in reaction to Paulette's slurring tirade, but not wanting to offend by outright laughing at her.

The Colonel sighed with relief once again, looking down with a benign expression at the furious, disfigured girl he had come to love as if she were his own daughter. "You should have some more tea, my dear; it will help take the hurt away." He held her up and put the cup to her lips once again. "Try and drink more of it this time, it will wash away the taste of blood, too."

She drank a large gulp, the tea having cooled down a bit more. "Wherth my huthban?" she asked him. "How are thhe babieth? Whoth thaking care of tthem?"

"Everything is just fine. The babies are with your mother in the other room. I'll get her for you."

"I'm right here, *ma cherie*," called Liliane from next door. "The babies are fine. I'm just feeding Marguerite now. When I'm done I'll come in to see you."

"Thoo? Wherth my huthban?" she demanded, the right eye sparking anger and frustration, even at those who loved her.

Marthe and the Colonel looked at each other and Paulette instantly suspected a conspiracy of silence.

"Thell me now! Where ith he?"

Liliane called out pleasantly from the nursery. "Docteur Hervieux is sewing him up just now, dear, down in the kitchen. He beat up Rolf again."

#

Docteur Hervieux had his hands full attempting to reposition Rolf's nose in the spot the good Lord had intended. Granted, it had been a bit crooked before this time, but now it sat at an odd angle sloping down on a diagonal from the small space between his heavy eyebrows, aiming for the left side of his mustache.

The good doctor's healthy sense of self-preservation kept him from the brutal wrenching required to correctly re-set the broken appendage. Rolf's bad temper was common knowledge in the area and the position he occupied, with connections in the much feared Gestapo was hampering the doctor's technique.

Finally Rolf lost patience with the timid prodding at his throbbing nose and shouted for someone to bring him a mirror.

"Oh my," stammered the panicking doctor, "I think you should wait, at least until I've finished my work, Major."

"Scheisskopf! I don't have all night to sit here while you diddle about, not solving anything! Now, bring me that mirror!" His tone of voice escalated from a low growl to a shout in the short space of ten words.

A mirror appeared on the table adjacent to his left fist, although the bearer removed himself from the proximity of the fist so quickly that no one knew exactly who had supplied it. The spectators instinctively took a few steps back from the table as Rolf scowled at the image reflected back at him, assessing the damage caused, once again, by his younger brother.

A bellow of rage accompanied his right hand as it grabbed the crooked nose and jerked it back toward its place of origin. The resulting crunching, grinding noise made the observers unanimously cringe, the sound more horrific than fingernails dragged across a blackboard.

A bubble of blood oozed from the offended nose, dribbling into the heavy mustache. The Doctor reached a cloth out to dabble at it, but his hand was slapped away as Rolf stood up.

"You won't get any payment from me for your pains, you lily-livered piece of turd! See if you can tend to my brother instead. He'll most likely let you pet and fawn over him. You're of no use to me!"

Rolf grumbled something about the French being little girls when it came to pain, as he swayed on his feet, before crashing to the floor, bending his nose out of shape once again as it hit the table leg. Rolf was out cold when the doctor rolled him onto his back and unceremoniously wrenched the nose back into place, displaying a somewhat self-satisfied smile as he did so.

Doctor Hervieux stood up, dispensing instructions regarding care of the nose over the next few days to the unfortunate soldier who had drawn the short straw and whose job it would be to look after Rolf during his convalescence. Rolf was hauled up the stairs out of the kitchen to his bed, luckily for those involved, still unconscious.

The doctor turned a wary face toward Heinrich who had been patiently waiting his turn for medical attention, a cloth full of ice on one eye, and another drenched with blood stuck to his ear.

"Erm...well Lieutenant, will you allow me to have a look at your ear?" he asked tentatively, fully aware that Heinrich and Rolf were brothers, yet hoping their genetics would prove disparate enough to avoid another nasty scene.

Heinrich mumbled something indistinguishable, a drop of blood pearling at the corner of his mouth, his tongue the worse for wear after a blow to the chin.

He peered at the doctor, who appeared quite unsure of himself, and removed the bloody cloth from his ear. A resounding 'ouuughh!' from the company in the kitchen eloquently punctuated the view of a missing ear lobe.

"Oh my," said the doctor once again. Never before had he seen two brothers inflict such vicious damage on each other in spite of his thirty years of medical experience.

"Urm...I'll have to sew that up a bit, if we don't want it to get infected."

Heinrich was aching all over and wished he could go lie down somewhere to sleep, but resigned himself to letting the doctor get on with his business. Although smiling acquiescence at the doctor through one eye, the blood covering his teeth and the missing lobe were so garish that the effect of the whole package brought about another 'ouuuggh!' from the spectators. His smile was misconstrued as a menacing grimace.

"Go ahead, Doctor," was the general consensus among the soldiers. "He's not like the other one at all..." piped up Lieutenant Bierdorpf. "he doesn't bite!" The bad joke caused a certain amount of snickering while Heinrich shook a good humored fist in Bierdorf's direction.

The nervous doctor breathed a sigh of relief as the atmosphere in the kitchen unwound. He busied himself preparing the sewing kit.

#

Later, when Heinrich made his way slowly up the stairs, each step causing an ache in some spot or another, he wondered if he wouldn't be doing the world a service by committing fratricide. Of course, he promptly regretted the thought, knowing his mother would be shocked beyond comprehension at seeing her sons in the state they were just now, and knowing they had done it to each other.

He couldn't consider murder, although he harbored a tiny, misshapen toad of a wish, that someone else might relieve him of the responsibility. Some people seem to cause too much pain and anguish to validate their presence on earth. Still, he was raised as a Christian and revenge was highly condemned by his upbringing. He sighed with the moral struggle of ambiguous feelings for his brother. Reaching the landing, he turned left and opened the third door on the garden side of the house.

"My sweetness? Are you asleep?" he whispered as he gently cracked the door.

"Oh, my GOD!" they exclaimed when they caught sight of one another.

He rushed to her side. She sat up in bed.

They reached for each other, but physical contact brought stabs of pain to various spots, and they flinched in unison.

"You look awful" they blurted. Laughter bubbled between them as they looked into each others single valid eye.

Their mirth was short lived since it split tender mouth and lip wounds, drenching their tongues with the tang of blood. Swallowing with a grimace, Paulette handed Heinrich a glass of water, the side of which had her bloody lip imprinted on it. He shook his head ruefully, took it and drank deeply, leaving his mark next to hers.

He lay down beside her, and tried his best to position himself so that he was touching her without causing any pain. They promptly fell asleep.

#

"Now this should fit just fine," said the dentist, as he wriggled the gold tooth deep into Paulette's gum, pushing it into the empty space left by wrenching out the remainder of the broken tooth. A gush of blood was washed away with harsh stinging as the dentist forced her to swallow a gulp of *calvados.*

"It will give you an even brighter smile, my dear," he said as he stepped back to admire his handiwork.

She was woozy with pain and with alcohol as well. Her head no longer hurt, if only she could refrain from touching it. But in an inexplicable way, her hand rose of its own volition to prod the remains of the goose egg, as if that hurt could relieve the new hurt born of having a foreign object jammed into gums, newly raw from excavation.

The Colonel had insisted on paying for a new tooth and found a dentist who was absolutely thrilled to do the job, as orders for gold teeth had become extremely rare during the war. No one had enough money to indulge in a new tooth, even a lead one. An order for a gold tooth was practically unheard of.

This *largesse* made the dentist wonder about the relationship between the young woman and the older German officer. 'Probably his mistress,' he thought to himself, and clucked his tongue in disapproval. 'Still,' he mused, in prudent silence, 'mistress or not, he paid cash, and it's never wise to look a gift horse in the mouth.' He supplied a bottle of tonic with which to rinse her mouth and instructions about what to eat over the next few days, so as to not dislodge the new tooth, before ushering them through the door of his office.

Outside on the street, Colonel VonEpffs, guided Paulette by the elbow down the sidewalk, toward the *rue du Gros Horloge*.

They had come to Rouen by car to find a dentist who could take care of the offensive hole in Paulette's smile, and in spite of everything, she was excited to be out in the city. It had been so very long since she had gone anywhere at all. They'd waited until her bruises had faded enough to not attract attention, but her happy curiosity about the sights and sounds she took in as she strolled along on the Colonel's arm brought an attractive pink flush to her cheeks.

Passersby looked at her, noticing her fresh prettiness before drawing conclusions similar to those of the dentist. She didn't guess their thoughts. Instead a timid smile answered each and every glance thrown in her direction, accompanied by a polite nod of her head.

It was now early February, and in spite of the cool temperature, spring sang in the air, just a few weeks away. They walked along the narrow street, lined with shops, some of which had nothing much in their windows and others with discreetly curtained facades, leaving curious eyes dissatisfied.

As with any other town in occupied France, one could obtain just about whatever you desired, *if* you had cash. When this was the case, the curtain was drawn aside and an abundance of goods were on display. It was silly trumpery. Everyone knew about it, especially those who had instigated the rationing in the first place. They were the first to disregard their own quotas, but the laws were kept in place just the same. Those who had no ready cash were not allowed to look and scraped by, selling up possessions in order to buy food for survival.

The discrepancy between those who had and those who had not, was heartrendingly evident to Paulette who looked at skinny children hiding in doorways, hardly dressed enough to cover their bare skin, let alone stay warm against the cool breezes of a Norman February.

None of their apparel seemed to fit, obviously hand-me-downs from some unknown source. Some of the boys had pants that were too big, held up by a worn out belt tightening the extra material into baggy shapes, while others had pants that were too short by far, revealing dirty ankles left bare by ragged stockings. The girls were in general a bit cleaner, but often their droopy stockings bore the marks of so much mending that the original knit was almost nonexistent. The children hung together and chattered, sometimes smiling at Paulette when she caught their eyes. It was horrible.

She hadn't realized the position of privilege that her family enjoyed living on the farm. It used to be that farmers were looked upon as peasants, not particularly fortunate to live amongst the animals or tend the earth from one season to the next. During the war, the tables had turned and Paulette looked to be exceptionally fortunate to those children, who watched her pass, dressed in her mother's woolen coat as if she were a fairy princess.

It was a shock to her as she passed them by, wishing she could scoop them all up and bring them out to Marthe, to see them fed bowls of warm soup and eggs, to scrub them free of the grime on their clothing and skin and to knit them soft sweaters and stockings of lambs wool. She imagined her own children, growing up under these circumstances and turned tearful eyes to the Colonel.

"Please, let's go back to the dentist and have him remove this tooth! I can't bear to think that I've got enough money in my mouth to feed all these poor children! Please, Colonel VonEpffs! I'm so ashamed!" She choked as the words crashed against the gold tooth, still so foreign in her mouth. Her vanity was stifled with shame. "I don't need it!"

He patted her gently on the arm and guided her to a *charcuterie*, entered and bought up a large quantity of meat filled pastries and handed the box to her, with a nod of his head in the direction of a group of children in the open door to a paved courtyard serving as entrance to a set of flats above the businesses lining the street. The children hesitated but an instant before standing in an orderly line to take the *friands*. Amazingly enough, there were three left over as the group of children turned away after thanking her politely for the food.

The Colonel took one and asked Paulette to take one herself. "This is all the lunch we'll be having I'm afraid. I have some business to take care of, and then we'll be off toward home. It's a bit of a drive, and I'd prefer to get back before nightfall."

She nodded her assent, carefully biting into the pastry filled with pork *paté*, using the half of her mouth that hadn't been dug about in this morning. They made their way to the Hotel de Ville harboring German headquarters.

Climbing the staircase inside the building, they turned to the left along a hallway filled with open doors, revealing a flurry of activity. There were women sitting at desks clattering away at typewriters, while others were answering telephones. Soldiers rushed in and out of offices, depositing sheaves of papers on each others desks. So many papers, so many people, so many uniforms, so much noise. It was quite exciting.

"Paulette, would you be so kind as to sit here and wait for me? I have to speak with someone. I shouldn't be too long." The Colonel smiled at her and she nodded her head as she arranged herself on a wooden chair in one of the rooms.

Across the room was a desk occupied by a young woman, who'd stopped working and was looking Paulette over, head to toe. She had short black hair, cut in a bob with a spit curl artfully arranged so that it was almost touching her eye, an eye that was adorned with cosmetics. She had black lines painted about her lashes and brilliant red lipstick. Paulette noticed the make-up and wondered why the curl was placed so low. Surely, it must impede her vision.

Realizing she was staring and knowing it was rude, Paulette shuffled a bit on the wooden seat of her chair making its legs rub on the tile floor, producing a sort of belching sound.

Embarrassed, Paulette looked down at her skirt, feeling quite frumpy with her hair fixed in a simple bun with a ribbon twisted around it. Her shoes were scuffed and they pinched her toes. She wished she could take them off and rub the aching parts, but that would draw even more unwanted attention to the Mary-Janes and their over-used condition. Paulette was feeling so self-conscious that she could barely look up from her lap, the scrutiny from across the desk crushing her previous excitement. She hoped the Colonel would be quick about whatever business he had.

Just at that moment, the young woman spoke, and in French. Paulette was startled.

"*Alors*, where did you find him? He's a nice looking one, and he seems to like you well enough. How much does he give you?"

She tilted her head to one side and Paulette understood the spit curl. It gave her a sly, coquettish allure. Holding her chin rather low allowed the young woman to look up and out from beneath the curl, through heavily made-up eyes. Paulette could imagine a film star using that technique in a flirtatious conversation with a handsome leading man.

Paulette felt somewhat envious of the other woman's allure and wondered if any amount of artifice could ever make her feel as sure of herself as this other young woman appeared to be.

Then she realized with a jolt, what the question asked of her, still hanging unanswered, implied.

She opened her mouth to protest but was handicapped by a lack of coherent speech. Very much aware of the glint that her new gold tooth must give off, she tried to hide it by biting her lips shut. Paulette blushed furiously.

"No need to tell, sweetness. Just be careful and make sure he pays you enough. I know girls who manage to get five thousand francs a day. Don't let him take advantage of you. It will just make it harder for the rest of us, if you give it away! Us girls have to stick together you know!" She smirked at Paulette's obvious discomfort and shook her head while mumbling something uncomplimentary about silly creatures who shouldn't be getting into business they knew nothing about.

A matronly woman came in just then, throwing a severe look about the room. "Véronique, where is Marie-France?" This question was of the kind that demands an answer, and right away. No silliness or hesitation would be tolerated.

Paulette found herself sitting up straighter, as if she herself were under the authority of this stern older woman. Paulette hoped not to be seen, willing the woman to remain facing Véronique and leave before noticing her. Paulette wasn't keen to explain her presence. But, as often happens, the desire to remain anonymous attracted the woman's unwanted attention.

She turned and Paulette held her breath.

"And who have we here?" asked the matron in a voice that held a forced imitation of benevolence.

"Uhmm...My name is Paulette VonZeller, *Madame*," replied Paulette with quite a lot more dignity than she could actually afford. She lifted her chin, forcing her eyes to keep steady hold on the older woman's face. "I'm here accompanying Colonel VonEpffs who has an appointment."

"Oh!" said the matron, slightly taken aback by the names dropping at her feet. "Well, I'm sure you would enjoy a cup of tea while you wait, Frau VonZeller. Véronique, go get Frau VonZeller some tea." She used the impatient tone of voice tyrants reserve for slow witted underlings on a wide eyed Véronique, who was by now remembering her previous indiscreet remarks aimed at intimidating Paulette.

Véronique rose, blinked twice, tilted her head and looked at Paulette more closely from beneath her spit curl. As she crossed the room, her eyes narrowed and her expression changed. The girl obviously thought Paulette was lying, and she pursed her lips as she went out the door, giving Paulette the nasty impression that she had just made two enemies of these women.

The tea was consumed in silence. The matron stayed in the room conversing with Véronique. Well, actually picking apart whatever it was Veronique had been working at. It was obvious they both wanted to see who would come and retrieve the little country mouse who'd given herself such grand airs, adding the illustrious VonZeller name to her very ordinary French moniker.

They waited for some time. Tension in the room caused the minutes to crawl by for Paulette, as if waiting for a condemnation to be issued forth regarding her imminent be-heading. Paulette realized that Marie-Antoinette must have found the time to be horribly long as she whiled away the months preceding her execution. She hadn't really done anything wrong either. She also was being judged by her compatriots, a judgment which was always more severe.

"My dear?" said the Colonel as he entered the room, extending a hand to Paulette, who rose to her feet with an audible, irrepressible sigh of relief. "Are you ready to leave, my dear?" he asked politely. "I do hope you haven't been too bored during this long wait, I'm afraid it took rather longer than I had expected. But I see you've had company...?" His remark held a polite request for the woman to introduce herself, not quite an order, but clear enough just the same.

"Yes Colonel, your...friend?...has been taking some tea with us while she waited for you. I trust that the lady has been comfortable during your absence. My name is Madame Delarue. I am head of the secretarial pool here." Her tone was pompous and self-assured, yet held an obligatory respect for higher authority.

Paulette was swamped with relief that the dreams of her youth, to come to Rouen to find a position as a secretary had never come true. She raised her eyebrows at the thought of working under such a woman and felt a minuscule morsel of sympathy for the person of Veronique. But it didn't last long.

"Well, thank you, Madame, for taking care of my niece for me." Paulette looked up at him, surprise at suddenly finding herself to be part of his family sending her eyebrows once again rushing upward trying to reach her hairline, but she said nothing. "Her husband would thank you himself, but he was too busy to accompany us to the city today."

The Colonel had correctly judged the dynamics playing out amongst the three women, who inexplicably had developed a rivalry during the course of his absence. Women would never cease to amaze him with their cruelty toward one another. Quite different from men, they were more cunning and nasty, less capable of bloodshed, but not to be underestimated nonetheless. He took charge of Paulette, extricating her from an obviously uncomfortable position.

"Well, my dear, we'll be on our way home. It's quite a drive back to the *chateau*." He gave a polite smile and a nod to the ladies as he turned and steered Paulette by the elbow. "Good evening, ladies." And off they went, sailing down the hallway like royalty, knowing full well that the women had their heads stuck out the door, watching them go.

"When we get outside you'll have to tell me what that was all about..." he whispered to the top of her hat once they were sufficiently far away.

"Of course, *Tonton*!" she giggled. "Onward to the *chateau*!" she chimed as they made their way out of the building.

They enjoyed the drive home, talking continually about the day's events, and what they'd seen. The Colonel laughed at her story of the nasty women, explaining to Paulette that he had sadly guessed at once at what assumptions the secretarial pool had come to regarding their relationship. She affectionately teased him with the *tonton* nickname for uncle and giggled while accusing him of snobbery about the use of the term *chateau*. He agreed that putting those two nosy women in their place felt deliciously naughty and that sometimes a tiny lie was worth the confession in church the following Sunday.

They also spoke, with some gravity, about her distress regarding the poverty and deprivation she'd witnessed, regretting that the strife of war was always felt most by the innocents.

Paulette removed her shoes and rubbed her toes with a grimace.

He smoked and listened to her chatter, inwardly wondering what the consequences of his meeting would be on this young woman and her family, while wishing he could protect them. It bothered him to think of it, so he turned his concentration to her voice.

#

I helped Marthe and Franz prepare for their arrival, in celebration of the new tooth. They prepared the food while I prepared the atmosphere, feeling quite relieved to think of a nice evening spent in peace.

We could have more of those now, for Rolf had received orders to move to the officers' quarters provided at the nearest V1 site, just a mile from us, but still a mile was better than just down the hall. Because of his absence, the celebration could be had in genuine, with no fears of fighting and snide remarks. That was enough to celebrate in itself.

And to crown it all, spring was on its way.

CHAPTER 30

Spring 1944:

The bird song took on a completely different meaning. The change from carefree musical whistles and chirps to the staccato chatter of warning was noticeable to all who cared to listen. It was an unpleasant sound meant to deter a predatory attack.

Alerted, the Colonel examined the view from the window next to his desk in the study. It was a deceptively pleasant one. Danger was lurking somewhere, hidden in the bucolic scene stretching across the other side of the mullioned glass panes.

He swept his gaze from left to right, looking for the cause of the frantic chirping. He saw the greening tended lawns trimmed short by goats, reaching to the fence beyond, defining the edge of the orchard, itself dotted with fat brown and white splotched dairy cattle, the size of which never failed to amaze him. While German milk cows were healthy and productive, grazing the pastures of his homeland, these cows were enormous. They were also disproportionately gentle and endowed with an inextinguishable curiosity.

He amused himself when no one was about: moving toward a fence at the far end of whichever field they had been parked in for the day, counting the minutes it took for the first cow to look up and commence the inevitable exodus provoked by his presence. It usually took about ten minutes for the entire herd to line up at the fence directly in front of him, like soldiers mustering for roll call waiting to pass inspection, although this inspection consisted of a bit of scratching between the horns.

Many a half hour had been completely wasted by this activity. The Colonel hoped never to be brought to account for his behavior in these circumstances, having no viable explanation. He was slightly ashamed of the satisfaction it brought him, knowing the war was tallying victims on its abacus while he was dallying with dairy cattle.

I was amused by this ritual and strangely moved to tenderness regarding him because of it. Later, some psychologist might define his actions as symptomatic of some disorder or another. But I knew he was in quest of an instant of peace, to justify his grudging acceptance of the horrors he couldn't control elsewhere, out of his direct line of sight, yet never out of his thoughts.

It took a minute but he spotted her, as had the birds. The young female cat's teats were hanging limp under a thin belly. Her litter of spring kittens had been hidden away in the loft of the barn; horses and cats cohabiting in good humor.

It must be hard for her to abandon her young in order to hunt, he thought, realizing the dangerous trade-off imposed by nature on young mothers. She had to feed if she were to provide sustenance for her offspring, yet leaving put them in immediate danger. What terrible decisions life obliges one to make, he mused, distracted by the tail twitching signaling an imminent attack. All the chirping in the sky couldn't keep the huntress from her offensive.

She pounced and death sang in the ears of her prey, a small blue-tit, not yet apt for efficient takeoff. A fluff of feathers spurted from the grass where the young mother settled down to dine, with the merciless gusto linked to survival. This was a trade-off the Colonel could understand, even though he felt sympathy for the mother blue-tit who had chirped so desperately to her fledgling, fallen victim to the mother cat's hunger.

He stopped to consider how she could dine with any sort of satisfaction, knowing that during the course of her meal she could lose one of her own offspring to a hungry rat or pine marten. Foxes mostly stayed away from the barn, preferring the hen house, or better yet, the wild nests that some vacant minded chickens chose to construct in the bushes, away from the relative protection of the buildings. Even discounting the foxes, there were enough other species happy to choose a defenseless kitten as a tasty meal.

She finished eating, licking her whiskers quickly, already on the move. The birds, seemingly shocked into silence by the loss of one of their young, watched along with the Colonel as the cat trotted off in the direction of the barn. She would drink from one of the horse's water pails before her acrobatic ascent to the loft and the nest of straw. Before settling down to expose her belly to her hungry youngsters, she would subject them to a frantic inventory, poking her nose into each of her offspring, checking its scent, and ticking each one's unique odor off her mental list. He hoped she would find them unscathed and clamoring for her milk until her next forced departure for food.

The cat looked pathetically thin. Obviously the decision to feed herself must come far behind the importance of standing guard over her young. He wondered if lately she had felt an additional threat to their safety from an unusual predator. He made a mental note to bring a dish of bread soaked in milk up the ladder to the loft later on.

Interfering with the natural selection of survival somehow made him feel unfair: the predators also need to feed their young. What criteria caused a man to prefer the survival of a cat over that of a fox? Where was the justice in that stance? Feeding the mother cat would give her an unfair advantage over a mother fox for example, and thus upset the natural balance of things.

However, none of these takings of life were brought about with any spirit of vindictiveness. Nature's motivation was the survival of all species, through a complex scheme of give and take which could only be unbalanced by human intervention. Death is a part of the circle of life, sacrifices begetting new lives. If only humans could learn from that and conduct themselves accordingly, he mused, suddenly frustrated by his philosophical considerations.

The Colonel refocused his attention to the map the map spread across his desk, the map he had kept hidden, the map which could earn him a spot against a wall, facing a firing squad. The indications on it, written in pencil could be erased if given enough advance warning. Each time he had made a mark on it he had consciously chosen a pencil over a fountain pen, while knowing full well erasing would never take place.

If he were found out, he would die. If not, he held the opportunity to help thwart a horrific project ready to take the lives of so many. This taking of lives bore no resemblance to the natural process causing the murder of the tiny flightless bird. These victims would be innocents as well, but their deaths would serve no purpose, and would not bring honor or glory to his homeland.

The price tag of Nazi victory over the rest of Europe had risen too high. No one could force him to choose the Fuhrer while disregarding the dictates of his conscience. He had a strong sense of patriotism; still he saw the obvious detour from the path of the common good of Germany. The path they had embarked upon led directly to the personal gratification of Adolf Hitler.

Now that he had taken concrete measures to aid the plot to overthrow the acting Nazi regime, his repose was deeper and more satisfying. He was amused by the fact that having put his life in grave danger by signing on to the German resistance, rampant among the occupying army stationed in France, he was more at peace with himself than he had been in a very long time.

His previous visit to Rouen had been a meeting behind closed doors of like minded officers plotting to bring down the Fuhrer by assassination. He had learned with some surprise that many plans had been hatched over the years to thwart the Nazi game plan by taking the Furher into custody and deposing his commanding officers. However, each time a proposed visit to Paris was to take place the man invariably changed his mind about showing up. It seemed as if Hitler had some personal inkling of these plots which kept him from an appointment with destiny. Since official plans for his visits to France were never respected, the plots never came to fruition. As their frustration grew, the would-be perpetrators altered their plans to remove him from power by taking his life.

Now that VonEpffs was involved in the movement headed up by Claus von Stauffenberg, he was prepared to carry out the necessary sub-plots by removing the remaining local chain of command still sympathetic to the Nazi cause. He, as well as his contingent of soldiers under my roof, were to be part of the alternate armed forces deployed under the code name 'Valkyrie'.

Never in his wildest dreams as a young man, would he have contemplated murdering one of his army superiors. Yet now, in his forties, though pride prevented him from classifying himself as old just yet, he found himself plotting multiple murders and sleeping soundly because of it. A wry smile was brought about by the realization that he had succeeded in manipulating his moral code to fit his dedication to this cause.

He wondered if Judgment Day would find him side by side with the Fuhrer, each begging for an interview with God, hoping to explain why they both felt justified in killing. Poor Saint Peter, the ruckus he would face if that happened! He expected God might have to recruit extra help for the necessary triage under the circumstances.

Who would be pardoned? Who would be condemned? Would every single weapon bearing man be sent straight into the flames of hell, regardless of his willingness to participate in the games of war? Or, would God consider each and every case, weighing the circumstances of each man and meting out punishment accordingly? 'Thou shalt not kill'. It seemed clear enough and straightforward. He would therefore, most certainly be heading downstairs instead of up, because his conscience, if not his religion, was shouting at him to plan and commit these murders. The Colonel had decided to listen.

If Rolf never caught on to his deceitful stealing of information regarding the geographical locations of the V1 sites in the upper Normandy area, the Colonel would continue passing that information on to Rouen, bringing about the destruction of as many sites as possible before they could be put to use.

Of course, obtaining that information was more complex these days, since Rolf had officially taken up residence in the cement dormitories built on site, down the road in the forest. It wasn't as if they were friends, close enough to justify a visit to the site to rifle through

Rolf's personal documents. Still, he could supply the coordinates for this site and pray that the air-raid would be precise and not destroy the surrounding area.

He had become much too attached to these people, whom they had invaded and occupied for the past four years. Bonds had been formed, and while it was completely against his military training: this fraternizing with the enemy population, it was equally impossible for him to ignore his feelings.

An enormous sigh pushed itself out of his chest, leaving only a small space for his heavy heart to continue beating. He folded the map, took another long look outside and finding nothing to catch his attention or deter him from his task, he stood up and slipped the map into the inner breast pocket of his uniform jacket. This action reinforced his resolve. He was doing the right thing.

One more trip to Rouen to relay the information pertaining to the location of the site where Rolf resided. After that, he was disposed to follow any orders given to him requiring his assistance in planning and carrying out the assassinations of those in command of the local garrisons loyal to the Fuhrer.

Later, he hoped to be able to enter into negotiations with the Allies, to help cease the destruction of this country and prevent the crushing of his own. He simply wanted it to stop. Any means would justify that end, even murder.

The disposal of information regarding the exact coordinates of the V1 site in the neighboring woods could at least help avoid unnecessary loss of civilian life. This could be a bargaining point in future negotiations with the Allied forces. The alternate army had shown their good faith in providing this top secret data. Some credibility could be gained by this eagerness to stop Hitler's retaliation against innocents.

His conscience was in a much better state than that of his Lieutenant.

#

Heinrich knew his brother would be in immediate danger. His personal distaste for Rolf didn't enter into the battle he had with his conscience. He knew that if Allied bombing were accurate, Rolf would most likely be killed, along with the contingent of soldiers guarding the site and those who would be working there: prisoners of war taken from the eastern front, most of them Russians.

He also knew that thousands of innocent civilians would be murdered in England if the bombing raids were not accurate, because the site was ready to start work, waiting only for the arrival by truck convoy of the sections of V1 missiles, to be assembled on site.

The weighing of the value of many lives over the sacrifice of a few, including his brother or not, was obvious.

That is, when he could step back and be objective about it.

That is, when he could ignore the memory of his mother's voice, begging him to try and get along with his older brother, for her sake, to try and forgive him, since he was the only brother he would ever have. Heinrich wondered if the opportunity would arise to look her in the eyes once again and he wondered when the time came, if he would be able to do so.

#

April 1944:

The Colonel had received the news of Allied air strikes on Rouen, about the same time as had the *Kommandateur* in Dieppe. The Fuhrer had given orders to stay put, to hold tight to their positions in Normandy, in spite of the increasing frequency of the Allied bombings. This last raid on the bridges connecting the northern and southern sides of the Seine River was aimed at effectively cutting off any attempt by the occupying army to retreat toward Germany.

That city's local population had heard the sirens in the middle of the night of the 19th- 20th of April after the first English planes dropped their bombs. Evidently, the first sightings of the bombardiers hadn't given rise to the sirens normally used to warn the population to flee into the air raid shelters to which each had been assigned. Quite possibly those on guard had thought the planes intended to drop their deadly loads further along the river. Alas, this delay caused many citizens to be out and about scurrying for their shelters during the thick of the bombing.

Over eight hundred civilians were thus killed in less than an hour's time. Others huddled close, calming crying children, sitting in cellars and sewer tunnels, with a suitcase or two of their most precious belongings. They cringed at every whistling noise as shells rained down around them, judging in a split second if the noise heralded their demise or not. Awful hours of waiting dragged, sometimes witnessing suffering nearby, the unlucky ones.

In general, the population clung to the hope that the Allied pilots would be accurate and that only the government buildings housing the Germans or their infrastructure would be targeted. Unfortunately, accuracy from a certain altitude is limited and the pilots couldn't know where the air raid shelters for the locals were located, couldn't hope to avoid them. It was a deadly game of chance.

Some inhabitants actually chose to sit tight in their homes, riding out the storms, lost in prayers. When it was over, the shelters would slowly empty, people tentatively creeping out from below ground, searching the sky for signs of any stray planes that could eventually dump their load on the unsuspecting. They would stagger toward their homes, surveying the damage to houses along the way, dreading what state their own would be in.

Neighbors and strangers took one another in when there was nothing left for a family to return to. Overwhelming outpourings of generosity sent survivors scurrying to pick up the pieces for one another, until the next time the sirens rang out. The dead were buried and the living were comforted. The wounded swarmed to Red Cross stations set up in clinics and hospitals. The firemen got to work, enlisting the aid of able-bodied men to assist in digging through the rubble for survivors.

The aftermath of one hour of bombing took days and weeks to clear up and even then the debris remained. Very little rebuilding was done. What was the good of it? Only more bombs would destroy what could be achieved.

In the meantime, children would skirt piles of brick and wood littering their paths to school. Some would scavenge through it looking for bits and pieces useful for blocking holes blown out of walls, missing windows and propping up wrecked doorways. Some buildings collapsed several days later, as if the building simply gave up trying to stay upright, surprising its occupants when an entire wall fell to the street exposing the apartments it sheltered to the view of passersby, like a child opening the front of a doll's house.

I was aghast, imagining what that would be like to have my insides torn open for public viewing.

Two weeks after the April raid, the Colonel rushed to Rouen to keep his appointment with the men who had come to visit in the night. His car navigated through the rubble of destruction. They slowly maneuvered around piles of what used to be homes, passing the ruined south side of the cathedral, whose organs had been silenced, blown to bits by Allied bombs. They drove up the *rue de la République*, through an area far enough away from the river to be as yet, relatively unscathed.

He noticed the *Tour Jeanne D'Arc* standing alone, coiffed with a peaked roof, keeping guard over the city, as it had since the Middle Ages. He wondered at its stamina, standing tall for so many years, witness to so many previous battles, as it once again, surveyed horrific damage further down the hill.

Dashing, two by two, up the steps to the *Hôtel De Ville*, he strode purposefully down the hall to an office and plunged inside, not knocking. He gave his information, asked a few questions and left as quickly as he had come, speeding off down the road back to me, his adopted home.

His conscience tormented him, seeing the destruction of this once lovely medieval city, county seat of the Norman kings of England. It was a terrible shame that so much ancient architecture having withstood the burden of time could be so quickly annihilated with modern weapons of destruction. He found himself to be bitterly confused about the significance of progress.

Now that he'd relieved himself of his burden of information, he dreaded the consequences of his actions. He questioned himself over and over about how much he could share, in order to protect those who deserved protecting. Yet he kept coming to the agonizing conclusion that he could say nothing, could help no one, and could only hope that he had made the right decision in handing over his map, in giving away Rolf's position as well as the locations of the other V1 sites he had stolen from Rolf's papers.

He prayed, as did the people in cities being shelled throughout France, that the Allies had a very good aim.

#

Rolf, unaware of the competence of the traitor just down the road from him, had in the meantime started his project. They took aim, carefully measuring the coordinates using the gyroscope to turn the rocket to the correct position. They released the chemicals to interact with each other. They stood watch in the ignition building. They waited, holding their breath.

It worked, exploding with a horrible roar to be heard for miles around. The rocket took off into the night sky, leaving a trail that looked rather like a comet. They cheered.

Several minutes later, on the other side of the channel the inhabitants of a tiny village stirred in their beds hearing a strange whistling rush toward them in the night. Some of them didn't wake soon enough to wonder what it was. They were extinguished before being alerted by the noise of its deadly approach.

The English papers spoke of accidents and fires that had broken out taking lives, but never exactly saying what the cause of death truly was. Inaccurate accounts of the bombs were given on purpose to the papers, hoping to foil the German attempts at refining their aim to reach London. Spies skimming the newspapers looking for clues to pass on to Rolf and his colleagues, were confused by the lack of accounts regarding the V1 bombs. No mention being made, they had very little accurate information to go on regarding a target being reached or not. So they continued, firing away blindly, making tiny adjustments, hoping to reach London, the goal which would ensure a maximum amount of destruction.

We were horrified when we learned what he was up to. I was unquestionably ashamed that my peaceful woods were harboring such engines of destruction. I was not alone. The birds, as if in rebellion, abandoned their nests in the immediate surroundings, the noise and electric smell being too disturbing for the raising of their young. The squirrels, voles and pine martens executed an eloquent exodus, leaving the woods to the Germans and their noisiness. The Germans fired rocket after rocket. We could hear them from home. It disturbed everyone, indeed, every living creature.

There was something intrinsically sacrilegious about the whole affair. The forest was usually a refuge for the soul, a sort of natural cathedral dedicated to life and all things spiritual. People found solace in its tranquility, answers in its silences, and hope in its everlasting depths.

This tranquility was wreaked, violated and insulted. The leaves on the trees shook in anger at every blast of nauseous fumes, whispering of lives lost in the minutes that followed, reverberating through the ground. Echoes of horror from across the channel ricocheted back to bounce off the trees and rocks, eventually drowning in the spring.

Rolf was ecstatic. He was firing away, as if at tin ducks in a shooting gallery, never measuring, or worse, possibly not caring, about the lives he took, too far away to see, too distanced to feel, a perfect killing machine.

On a bleak day in early June a miscalculation sent a missile directly into a neighboring village claiming the lives of fourteen locals who'd come to examine the missile lying in the center of town. Curiosity killed them. Rolf felt no remorse, except for the loss of the missile.

Crashing just three miles from us, the dead were our neighbors, people who attended our church, who married the cousins of our families and whose children played in the schoolyard with our own. Disaster was striking close by.

Events were accelerating and spinning out of control. The reckless were elated and the prudent were frightened. None were indifferent.

Echoes from lower Normandy where the Allies were stalking hedgerows, ferreting out isolated German strongholds, and driving them east and north toward us might have brought jubilation, but for us who lie in the path of the retreating army, their advance brought destruction.

#

"But there is absolutely nothing I can do to stop him! You've spent enough time with him to understand that nothing anyone could ever say to him will produce an ounce of strain on his conscience!"

Heinrich flopped onto his back, once again scanning the now familiar cracks winding across the ceiling above their bed. "Honestly, I wish I did have some influence over him, but he is after all, following his orders. Whether we agree with the logic behind those orders or not, he's doing his job, and failure to obey the Fuhrer's orders would only procure his court-martial or even the firing squad. I can hardly blame him for doing what is expected of him. Actually, my love, I can only be truly thankful that I'm not in his position! I hate to think of being made to carry out such orders."

He removed her hand from under her cheek, as it was propping her above him and pulled her head down into the crook of his arm, nestling her ear onto his chest. He found it much too difficult to hold up under her accusatory blue gaze.

She expected him to act, to convince his despot of a brother that he should place his life in danger and sabotage the V1 installation he had so painstakingly set up. As if Rolf would ever listen! They both knew that was unrealistic, yet she kept insisting he try. He wouldn't, indeed he couldn't. She didn't accept that, or even attempt to understand it. She was holding him to account, and unfairly so. He preferred that she gaze at the ceiling tracery and stop digging into his heart with her eyes.

Paulette expelled a disheartened sigh. "I keep thinking of us, as if we were there across the channel, sleeping in our bed with our babies in the next room. How it could be us. That we could die from his work. It's not soldiers fighting one another on a battlefield; it's unsuspecting, innocent people who die in their beds! Families like ours, parents like you and me, who lose their children in a second because of demons like your brother! It's unbearable!"

Tears of frustration leaked onto his shoulder and slithered into the cleft between her cheek and his arm pit. It was an unpleasant tickling sensation, but he dared not move, not wanting her to look him straight in the face again.

He didn't want to squirm under her insistent stare once again. He was ashamed of not being able to satisfy her demands, uncomfortable for refusing to try and a little miffed at her for pressing the issue. He pulled his right arm a bit tighter around her shoulder, pushing his fingers through her hair, trapping her in a safe position where she couldn't look at him. It was easier that way.

They stared at the ceiling, once again feeling their differences pull them apart, in spite of his holding on tight to her shoulder and hair. Their love-making had taken place before this prickly subject of conversation had been broached. He was glad of that. Eventually they would fall into an uneasy sleep, their physical needs guiltily satisfied, both of them thinking about those across the way, who might never wake from their slumber.

#

The information provided by the map was passed from one set of hands to another in a strange relay race against time. The Colonel would never know who had connections with the Allies: the 'who exactly told who' being irrelevant and extremely dangerous. He had done his part and should be at peace with himself.

Yet he lie awake at night listening for the next V1 to fire off its track, shrieking across the short space of land separating us from the coast, then across the hundred miles of water to southern England. It took under twenty minutes to travel the targeted distance of one hundred and fifty odd miles to reach London. Of course, the explosion that heralded its landing couldn't be heard by his ears, but he felt the horror just the same.

With a terrible sense of anticipation, the Colonel waited for another sound that would inevitably come, fearing it, even though he had helped to set it in motion. After a few sleepless nights, his body refused to worry any longer and fell into a deep, dreamless sleep.

#

The droning woke the household. In the seconds when the brain struggles to regain full consciousness, before its owner understands why he or she has awakened, bits of dreams or nightmares as the case may be, mix with reality to create an incomprehensible jumble of confusion. Some never passed through this phase, losing their lives while in a half-dream state. They were the lucky ones.

A second explosion ripped through my west wing, blowing bits of furniture through what was left of the walls and the bodies of those occupying the rooms located there. The noise was quite literally deafening. Only after a few minutes did sound slowly reappear like the roaring of waves in the ears of those survivors closest to the landing spot of the bombs.

The third explosive device landed in the woods nearby, behind the north pasture. The fourth found its target to the west of us. It caused a secondary chemical blast lighting the sky with orange and blue fire. The forest ignited and wood smoke added its tangy smell to the heavier chemical odors sweeping across the kilometer separating us from what had once been Rolf's V1 site.

Being an old building that had been adapted throughout the centuries to accommodate the desires of those I sheltered, my walls were not completely interdependent. In a shuddering, some of them collapsed, crushing the contents of the three floors under the roof through which the bomb plunged.

When the west wing toppled, my center and east wing remained upright. I could do nothing to protect those who had been sleeping in the west wing. I groaned under the wrenching strain of the roof struts, thick oak traverses which supported heavy tiles. Some gave way and others stayed put, twisting as only wood can do, absorbing the shock with some success. Other timbers split in a snap as loud as gunfire, a dry noise that comes from wood aged over the centuries.

Dust was everywhere, clogging the air that Paulette tried desperately to suck through her mouth. She had jerked awake in confusion, and had run in her nightgown to check the babies who, though wakened from the frightful noise, were fine. She picked one up, only then realizing that she hadn't felt Heinrich in bed next to her when she'd run into the adjoining nursery.

She left Marguerite in the crib, rushing back to find his spot in the bed empty, though traces of his body heat lingered. She called out Heinrich's name, but her voice was tiny, and she coughed with the dust. Gently, she lay Thomas on the bed, grabbed her chenille robe, a long shawl and two clean diapers from the neatly folded pile. She went back into the nursery to retrieve Marguerite, placing her alongside Thomas on the bed, before wrapping them both in the shawl and tying her bundle across her shoulder and around her waist as best she could. She tied one of the diapers across her nose and mouth before slipping into her clogs. She opened the door to the hallway with not a little dread.

As she stood on the threshold of their room, she looked down the hall toward the top of the main staircase. Across the landing she could see out to the fields in the west, the stairs standing alone, open to the night sky, the absent west wing no longer continuing on from the landing. The shock of it kept her immobile for an instant, while her brain assimilated this newly displaced view.

Her first coherent thought was the urgent need to leave the house, in case it fell, trapping them inside the ruins.

As she moved carefully along the hallway past closed doors, she opened them as she went, but found each one empty. She hugged the children to her chest with one arm as she did her best to stay close to the wall, fearing a sudden shift of the floors. I stayed true to her needs, not swaying. I had settled into a new spot, feeling smaller, yet stable enough for the time being. She felt my whispering plaster as it rained white clouds onto her hair on its way to the floor, settling from the initial shock.

Halfway down the hall between her rooms and the landing she noticed something on the carpet runner. She squatted to retrieve a bouquet of pink roses tied with a ribbon. The thorns had been carefully removed. She tucked them in her shawl, between her chest and Thomas.

As she reached the landing, looking down, she could almost see the next floor and thought it safer to be closer to the ground no matter what happened. She eased with caution down the inside of the steps, clutching the banister, testing each footstep before putting her weight on it. It was slow going, but she didn't dare hurry for fear of dropping the babies tied in a makeshift fashion about her torso.

The second floor looked much like the first as she tried to see down the darkened hallway leading east from the landing. She selfishly decided to evacuate with her precious bundle, and leave it to someone else to search out eventual survivors. She heard no voices, no shouting, none of the sounds one would expect after a disaster, only the crumbling, grumbling, sighing noises of debris settling to its final spot.

She felt terribly alone in a nightmare, the weight and warmth of the children alone proving to her that this was indeed, some wicked version of reality.

CHAPTER 31

May 1992:

"I would guess this dates from around the 15th century. It's a very rare find. It was buried in your yard, you say?" The *horloger* peered down his nose, frowning at Debra over the edges of wire rimmed spectacles. She had been leaning forward in anticipation while he inspected the box, but now stepped back, surprised to find her nose in proximity to his own. His eyes spoke of suspicion and his voice held a somewhat different message than the one conveyed by his words. There was an element of warning in it. Instinctively, she put up her guard as he elaborated on his question.

"Most often when an item of this historical value is found, it must be declared at your *Mairie* and is confiscated by the state to be evaluated before placement in a museum."

Debra's heart sunk.

"I see," she said carefully, "I assumed that since it was found on my property, that I had the right to open it. I hope I haven't done anything wrong. What makes you ascribe such an age to it? Wouldn't wood that was buried in the dirt for so long simply decompose?"

"Well, that would be true if it had been in the ground since the15ᵗʰ century. I suspect it was put there much more recently, only about fifty or so years ago." He stared at Debra, clearly waiting for her to cough up additional information. "I would guess you found it in the shelter of some trees, or a building perhaps? It looks as if it hasn't been exposed to rainfall."

"Along the wall of a shed," she nodded. "That's very strange. I know my house was occupied by the Germans during the war. The mayor told me so when we discovered bits of mortar shells imbedded in the wall of one of the outbuildings. Could it have been buried by them?"

"You understand that I am obliged to research the origins of this box. If it has been stolen by the Germans from a museum somewhere in France, then it must be returned to that museum. You would have no claim to it whatsoever. In the meantime, I will photograph it, measure and catalog it. You may keep it safe while we wait for the results, but if the government decides they want it, you'll have to turn it over."

She grinned in thanks. Evidently he'd judged her honesty and she'd come out on the good side. She chose to push her luck while she was on a roll.

"Can you open it before that? My curiosity has been driving me wild since yesterday." A small begging note lifted her eyebrows as she smiled, hoping to charm him into acquiescence.

A timid smile strayed across his face. "It is rather exciting isn't it? A few photos first, then we'll get it open. But, I'll be obliged to catalog the contents as well," he warned her.

"That's fine, I'm just dying to see inside, is all," she quipped, a hefty dose of enthusiasm lighting her eyes.

"This lock is much more sophisticated than I'd thought," he explained as he set out his tools. "Not an ordinary mechanism common to the times: this is a special piece, indeed." A good half hour later, the lock sprung under the careful manipulation of a set of tiny pins inserted in the keyhole.

They bumped heads as Debra moved in too close to take a look inside.

Nervous laughter lifted them both upright. The horloger rummaged in a drawer to produce a clean pair of white silk gloves, before reaching inside to pull out a small leather bound book tied shut with leather laces. He placed it gently on a white cloth spread on the table next to the box.

Anxious to see what else was inside, they bent over to peer inside. A metallic glimmer announced a gold locket fastened to a sort of brooch, itself nestled on a small sheaf of thick, skin-like paper tied with a length of what looked like braided yarn. The outer edge of the parchment was decorated with round flowers resembling primroses. Each of these items was carefully removed from the box and reverently placed on the cloth next to the book.

Under these was another notebook, folded in half. It looked to be of homemade manufacture, but from paper that was quite obviously much more recent in age. As the *horloger* pulled it out, the pages fell open, revealing a series of pen and ink drawings of people, nicely executed, dressed in clothing dating from the pre-war period of this century.

"Oh! Look! They seem so real, as if they could speak to us!" Debra exclaimed. "Who drew them? Is there a signature at the bottom?"

"Unfortunately, no. But these aren't that old, maybe if you take them to the Mayor's office in your village, someone there could direct you to one of the older inhabitants who just might recognize someone in these drawings. It would give us a clue as to who put them in this box, and maybe to who buried it in your yard, and when."

"How extraordinary! It's like the mystery novels I read when I was a girl! A sort of buried treasure!" Debra bubbled, close to bursting with exhilaration.

"Hang on though! Before you get too excited, remember what I said about the cataloging of the contents. As a licensed antiquarian, I have to do my job thoroughly and research these items. There's something else left inside."

He pulled out a velvet pouch with a drawstring. Carefully loosening the frayed ties he poured the contents onto the cloth. Five stones fell with a clink onto the cloth.

"Wow! What are those, do you think?"

"It looks as though they're rough semi-precious gem stones, although I'm not absolutely certain. A jeweler could tell us more precisely."

They examined the stones blinking dully on the white cloth. The *horloger* prodded them, flipping them over in turn. Had they been strewn in gravel, they would be barely noticeable.

"I thought gemstones were transparent and had prisms," she said. "These really look like a bunch of rocks." she added dubiously. She didn't touch them, tempting though it was, as they both bent down closer to the table.

"I doubt that they're just rocks."

Like a child who has too many presents to open on Christmas morning, Debra's attention hopped from item to item.

"What's in the book? Can you open it? I'm a bit afraid to touch it. It looks old enough to come apart in my hands."

The *horloger* carefully untied the bow in the leather lacing. The inside cover was inscribed in very fine, spidery handwriting: "*Marie Lucille Eloïse de Rochfort: 1er Avril de l'an 1740. Je suis née.*"

"It's someone's diary," Debra deduced.

"Not just someone, my dear. Marie de Rochfort. She was a bit of a celebrity in her day."

"Really? Who was she?"

"The daughter of a Duke, who was accused of dabbling in the occult. Greatly frowned upon by the church, at the time, I'm afraid. She ended badly."

"Oh! Do you think I could take it home and look at it? I'd be very careful. I'd love to try and decipher her handwriting. I'm just curious. I wonder how it came to be in the box?"

"Where did you say you live?" he asked Debra.

"Out in the countryside, about twelve kilometers from town, near Bacqueville," she answered.

"You don't mean the manor house that was bombed by the Allies, in Bout L'Abbé?"

"Well, I don't know about the bombing part, but yes, I live in Bout L'Abbé," she was intrigued. He obviously knew something about her home that she didn't.

"You have a very historic home. And yes, it was partially demolished in the Second World War. The Germans had taken over. Your house was part of a very large estate, of enough economic importance to the Germans to want to keep it running, for their own supplies, you see. But during an Allied bombing raid, aimed at a camouflaged V1 missile site nearby, the house was hit. This is very interesting, this box, since you found it there. Of course, some of these items are much older and quite possibly belonged to the previous residents of the house."

Debra sat back, amazed. She'd never given much thought to the past occupants of her home. Although sometimes she thought she could feel their presence, without ever thinking the house was haunted, she simply felt they'd been there before her. But now, to have them come to life, gaining a firm identity in front of her was fascinating.

"If you look at the box itself, it's decorated with roses carved in the wood. That's indicative of the owner's affiliation with the *Rose Croix* association. They were the successors to the knights of the Temple, *les Templiers*: the crusaders who fought to free Jerusalem from the infidels. You should do some research into who exactly lived in your house before you did. I think you'd find it interesting."

"But, I was told that the house dated from the 17th century. Surely the *Rose Croix* people came from an earlier time period?" she asked hoping he knew enough to fill in the blanks.

"My dear, the *Rose Croix* organization still exists today. It just goes by a different name. You've heard of the Free Masons, I'm sure."

"Yes, but I don't personally know any," she answered.

"Well, some say they hold the keys to a treasure unknown to the wider world, and that they guard a secret dating back from Christ's time on earth, something they'd discovered in Jerusalem." He turned the box over in his gloved hands looking through a monocle, inspecting the carvings as he spoke.

"And any artifacts which bear their symbols are of great interest to the association existing today. I think I'll need to do some research on the contents of this scroll." He picked up the tiny roll of parchment. "But I need to date it first, and humidify the skin enough to unroll it without damage. This could take me some time, so I'll just keep it in my possession for now. You may have the other contents tomorrow after I catalog them, but just for the time being. You do understand that I'll have to contact the national antiquities office, before I can let you have anything here for your own."

"Of course, but if I can take Marie's journal and the sketches home with me, I can contact the Mayor's office and find out if anyone knows who the drawings are of. And maybe I can find out a little more about Marie de Rochfort. I promise I'll bring them back as soon as you call me."

She left the *horloger*'s little shop with the notebook and the drawings wrapped carefully in a length of white cotton supplied by her new friend. She stopped at the library before going home, to see if she could find any references to Marie.

When she came home shortly before 4pm, she opened the door with a new awareness as she paused.

Standing still, she held her breath and concentrated very hard to send a palpable message to me, as if I wasn't always listening to her anyway. I forgave her ignorance, knowing that the idea was a novel one for her.

Debra asked for my help. She was intoxicated with the things she'd discovered about me and her predecessors. She wanted more details. She'd taken for granted all that had come before her and all that was left of the past: the traces hidden in my walls and in the furniture she'd hesitated about throwing out when she first moved in.

Of course I would help her, if only in confirming her findings when she was on target.

We would be starting something exciting together. I vibrated in pleasure.

She felt it and knew she held an answer.

CHAPTER 32

Mai 1944:

When Paulette reached the bottom of the staircase after an agonizingly slow descent, she found the front hall obstructed by piles of debris, fallen from the floors above her. Swirling dust was thick and the darkness so complete that she could only feel her way in front of her with one hand, clutching the bundle about her waist with the other. There was no way to call out, each gasp of breath drawn through the folded diaper covering her nose and mouth was barely enough. She forced herself to stay as calm as possible, to slow her breathing and to focus on getting outside.

Looking across the hall at the library, her numbed brain identified the acrid smell of smoke. Something was on fire. She didn't detect any movement, nor could she hear any sounds or cries, yet somehow she knew she should be able to. She hadn't been alone in the house when she went to bed, so why did she seem to be now?

It was evident that she couldn't try and escape through the ground floor of the west wing. It was completely demolished and some part of it was on fire. She tried to clear her head and envision the disposition of the rooms on the ground floor, guessing which way she should turn.

Reaching the door leading to the dining room she calculated the layout of the room in her head, determining that since it was located east of the stairway, it should therefore, be intact as it sat two floors beneath her attic bedroom. In principle, the door opened inward and though damaged, she thought she could still push it open a little. Before attempting that she needed to clear away one of the ceiling beams which had fallen across the frame. Doing this would require the use of both hands.

She placed the wriggling bundle on the floor a few feet away from her work after estimating which way the beam would be likely to fall if she could dislodge it. She covered the babies' faces with the other clean diaper unfolded to one thickness, allowing them to breathe air that was as dust free as possible, before turning back to the task at hand.

The beam was incredibly heavy, hewn of solid oak and measuring roughly ten inches on each side. It had been bigger yet when the workmen had hoisted it into place in 1673, the year my lower floor was built, being newly fashioned from a huge tree growing on the grounds for several hundred years before us. I remember how they struggled with its weight and cumbersome length. However, the master was adamant. He wanted a house with three stories, one that would be a visual testimony to his grand position in society. The support beams needed to be massive to bear the weight of the floors above, in addition to the orange clay tile roof which coiffed the ensemble.

Time had twisted and shrunk the wood rendering it denser than before. Oak dries to a hardness unequaled by the less noble essences of ash or the resinous woods used by the poor in their structures. Fruit woods: cherry or maple, can be wrought into beautiful, delicate furniture, but oak is the king of weight bearing wood.

All of which made it impossible for Paulette to budge the piece which had given way, lodging itself against the door frame. She pushed against it with all of her strength, barely moving it an inch. Frustrated, she groped about until she found a broken bit of railing from the staircase, also made of oak. This she wedged behind the lower edge of the beam, took as deep a breath as possible and pushed at it with a grunting effort reminiscent of giving birth.

The beam fell forward, toward her, a jagged edge catching her nightgown where her chenille robe had worked itself open during her efforts. A sharp pain in her calf told her it had also caught her skin. She sat down hard on the floor as the beam moved, the railing piece she had used as a lever clunking her on the head as it fell from behind the beam. However, the door to the dining room swung open and she let out a hoot of satisfaction at her success.

Crawling to where the babies were squirming under the diaper and shawl, she kneeled to rearrange her precious package once again around her waist and shoulder. She tucked the posy of roses inside her shawl once the babies were secure. Lifting them to her chest, she rose and passed through the doorway in a crouched position, climbing over the beam still partially blocking the entrance.

Fragments of moonlight shone blue across the dining room through the windows whose curtains hadn't been drawn shut. She stood upright and looked about her in surprise, the difference between the hall and this room being so very shocking. Here, everything was in place though covered with a thickness of plaster dust such as one would expect to find in a home that had been abandoned for decades.

Moving in slow motion about the room, she touched the surface of the cherry wood dining table, and stroked the mantle piece. She paused, looking up at the painting hanging slightly askew above it. In an automatic gesture, she reached out a hesitant hand, realigning the painting to its previously occupied, dust-free spot, with the tip of her finger. Strangely satisfied, she moved to the sideboard, her steps those of a sleepwalker perceiving an alternate reality.

There she saw the crystal brandy glasses and their decanter standing unbroken. Ruby liquid glimmered through the dust covered crystal. It swirled inside the decanter, rebelling at the disturbance. She lifted the stopper from the bottle and inhaled, looking for a sensation to jolt her back to reality from this strange nightmare in which she was a player.

The pungent smell and robust taste as she took a swig from the neck of the decanter crashed into her mouth, igniting nerve endings before settling in her brain, transporting her back to the awful truth and carrying with it the pain from her torn leg and the new lump on her skull. She shook her head as she replaced the stopper in the decanter before carefully returning it to its original resting place, to keep company with the matching dust covered stemware.

Thoughts a bit clearer, she moved to the window, opened it and looked outside. The fields were visible from this side of the house but not her parents' cottage. Looking down, she measured with a glance the drop down the half floor representing the lower kitchen level, through the bushes camouflaging the stone base of the house.

The hydrangeas were thick and heavy, already budded out with their bluish pom-pom flowers. Dropping into them from about eight feet above didn't look particularly inviting but since they ran all along the wall of this side of the house, it appeared unavoidable. She remembered how lovely the thick bank of bushes looked from the drive, as if the flowers were an exquisite skirt, ballooning out around the base of the house, dressing its foundations in a mass of blue blossoms.

Turning to the sideboard she rummaged through its drawers until she found a linen tablecloth. It was long enough, she hoped, to tie to the iron window latch and allow her to slide down slowly enough to break her fall, protecting the babies from the sharp branches of the hydrangea bushes.

Her initial adrenaline rush had subsided now and she hesitated about undertaking such a drastic escape, knowing it could put her children in danger. Yet, she was too afraid to stay inside, not certain I wouldn't collapse on top of them and not knowing if the bombing had stopped, or if the fire would spread in her direction. She listened outside for noise, still hearing none, not even the wind through the trees, although she could see leaves moving.

The need to escape won out and she tied the tablecloth to the window's ironwork knob, fashioning a series of knots in the cloth to help keep her from slipping if things went too fast. She re-adjusted the babies as tightly as she could before she tested the strength of the tablecloth by suspending her weight from it as it hung from the window latch.

Satisfied that her knot would hold, she swung her legs over the ledge, pushing aside a window box of geraniums. She shifted around so that her backside formed a chair and her bent legs were effectively sticking out against the wall, her arms holding tight to the taut tablecloth. That way if the babies came loose they would fall against her legs onto her lap as it were.

Her torn nightgown and the chenille robe hung beneath her rather like the drooping sails of a damaged ship. She took a step backward down toward the hydrangea bushes, easing out a little tablecloth as she went. Two more steps down and she felt the first of the prickly branches pushing against her bottom.

This was going to be the hard part. She had to push the bush away from the wall with one leg, while easing herself closer to the ground with the other. She chose the wrong leg, forgetting that she already had a cut on it which was immediately aggravated by scratchy branches and leaves. She cried out, but didn't let go, taking a few more steps before dropping to the ground through the bushes, her torso bent over her bundled children.

She stayed hidden in the bush for a minute collecting her wits, before checking the babies to see if they were alright. She opened her shawl and saw two blue eyes looking up at her and another set screwed tightly shut. The owner of those eyes also had his mouth open in a silent cry.

Suddenly realizing that it was indeed a silent cry, she frantically unwrapped the shawl and put her hand to Thomas' chest, feeling the vibration from his wailing. In spite of the rumbling feeling through her fingertips, she still didn't hear a sound. She took off the diaper covering her face and tried to shout, only to hear a strange growling noise resonating in her chest, and a tiny echo of voice coming from her lips. Although she was very disturbed by this lack of sound, she made the decision to put off thinking about it until later.

The fact that she seemed to be alone in harrowing circumstances was more and more shocking and the drive to find someone, to speak to someone and hopefully to hear a voice in return, was taking over. Swallowing her fear as much as possible, for a rising wave of panic would be completely inopportune; she recited a litany of priorities. The children's safety, finding Heinrich, checking on her parents, all of these things took precedence over her loss of hearing.

A few deep breaths later, she gathered her courage about her like a cloak, camouflaging her fear, and decided to embark once again on a search for her loved ones.

Crawling from under the hydrangea bushes on her hands and knees, she looked at her white nightgown, glowing in the moonlight where her chenille robe had opened. There were dark, wet spots around the hem where blood was oozing from her leg. She lifted the nightgown to get a better look at the wound and saw a large splinter of wood protruding from it. She jerked it out without ceremony. Reaching back under the bush, she grabbed the edges of the shawl, dragged it over the ground, carrying the children out on top of it.

When they were safe next to her, she turned back to her self inspection. Squeezing the skin around the wound brought more blood oozing out, hopefully washing away any extra dirt trapped under the skin. She ripped of length of cloth from the bottom edge of her nightgown and tied the wound shut with no intention of tending more to it at this time. Her primary obsession was to figure out what was going on, where everyone was and determine what to do next.

She had lost her shoes in the fall. She fumbled on her hands and knees, scrabbling through broken branches and a carpet of blue petals finally producing the footwear. Backing out, she stood up in the cool damp grass wriggling her toes while turning to the left and the right, deciding which direction would be the most likely to bring her to another human. She slipped her scuffed leathers on her feet then bent to gather the children to her chest, tying the shawl about her waist and across her back and shoulder. Paulette opted for the direction of her parents' cottage.

As she came around the side of the house in the direction of the front yard, she was confronted with the full view of the damage done to me. The sight paralyzed her.

My facade was crushed open on the entire west wing, which had once stretched off the main entrance to the right. It looked as if a giant child had toppled his building blocks in a fit of destruction, before setting the whole thing on fire. Flames reached to the sky, trying to lick the tops of the ash trees which provided welcome shade for the upper floors from the hot summer sun. One of them was already alight, sending sparks into the night sky like so many fireflies.

There was an awful smell of burning, not the comforting smell from wood smoke, associated with fireplaces lit against the cold, but another sort of smell that told of burning paint and cloth and wall papers, scorched shellac and varnishes: an acrid, bitter, destructive smell.

She couldn't believe her eyes, or her nose, her heart rebelling at the vision of all she knew, wounded and on fire. Incapable of motion as the damp seeped into her worn out shoes, she realized her world had turned into a representation of hell.

I was suffering horribly.

CHAPTER 33

As Paulette watched in silence, the fire ate away another of the oak beams separating the ground floor from its twin above. It fell to the wooden parquet of the library, sending up a cloud of smoke and a fresh volley of flying sparks and debris. The resounding crash was felt as a tremor through the ground vibrating the soles of Paulette's feet. She did not hear it with her ears.

Now certain of her hearing loss, she felt no grief. Instead, she was doing her best to assess the situation, to decide what must be done. Unruly thoughts flew about her like hungry bats, unable to settle on a single course of action. "Heinrich...her parents...keep the babies safe..."

She readjusted the diaper over her nose and mouth, hoisted the babies to a more secure position, holding them with both arms, before heading off in the direction off her parents' cottage. The heat from the fire forced her to step back several yards, away from my walls as she approached the burning wing. Walking along the breadth of the southern facade, she was mesmerized by the destruction. Her footsteps slowed as she crossed the gravel drive.

From there, she had a view of the cottages belonging to the farm employees. What she had seen up until this instant should have prepared her for the horrific panorama in front of her now. Unfortunately, it had not.

The inferno of smoke and flames had no beginning or end, no boundaries delimiting its perimeters. Flames leaped from one thatched roof cottage to the next in an endless line of billowing smoke, punctuated here and there by exploding flashes of red and orange fire.

In darkened silhouette against this hellish backdrop, creatures of all kinds rushed to and fro in crazed activity. Blackened shapes, resembling demons from her childhood nightmares ran about in frenzy. Figures raised their arms in the air, gesturing to the sky. Another pair chased each other, one beating at the other with some sort of limp weapon. Others were scurrying in and out of the burning buildings dragging inanimate objects from them.

To her left the horses stampeded around their pen in terrified circles. As she stood still, contemplating this incredible vista, a small grouping of a half dozen smoking chickens rushed around her feet. As they passed by her, the strong, bitter smell of burning feathers assailed her nostrils through the protective diaper.

Paulette turned her body full circle, searching for somewhere safe to place her bundle. She found no such place. Lost, she clutched her precious burden to her breast, realizing the only lives she could save were these two, tied about her chest. She couldn't bring herself to dump them on the ground where they could be trampled by frightened animals or people, nor could she put them in any of the buildings. They were unsafe. She was forced to be a spectator, protecting her most precious cargo, incapable of leaving them to take part in the macabre dance swirling about in front of her.

Backing into the shelter of the orchard, she sank to her knees, sobbing, ashamed of her inaction, yet incapable of abandoning her babies on the ground to an uncertain fate.

I knew her hearing loss was a blessing in disguise, for she couldn't hear the cries or the wailing coming from the people, nor the screaming of agonizing animals, nor yet, my own groaning punctuated with the gleeful cackle of the flames. Her eyes and nose tortured her enough.

She watched from afar for a long time, as one by one the figures dropped to the ground in exhaustion.

It was late spring in Normandy, and what usually happened, finally did. A light rain misted through the clouds of smoke and ash, transforming the yard to blackened muck. It hissed on hot timbers, dampening the whole sorry mess. The rain would ultimately extinguish the fire, whose enthusiasm for its devilish task waned.

In spite of disaster, dawn broke, inexorable. It lit a different view of a terrible new reality. Daylight was substantially less reassuring to those left behind. The light validated the visions of the preceding night, giving them substance, while annihilating vain hopes that it had been a nightmare.

In the gray of early morning, Paulette went into the undamaged barn and placed her children in a nest of straw, protected from the rain. Wrapping them tightly, for warmth, she checked for any sign of danger. Satisfied they were sleeping contentedly, she took her first wary steps toward the scene of disaster. She exited the barn, reticent, afraid of what the dawn light would show her.

The first figure she came upon was Lieutenant Bierdorf, lying prone near the entrance to what was left of her parents' cottage. His inert body glistened with rain, his face turned upward, mouth open, catching falling raindrops. He was partially trapped under a pile of debris, still Paulette made no move to free him. His unblinking eyes told her of his demise.

She entered the remains of the kitchen and found her sister, Roseline sitting on the floor clutching her doll, rocking forward and backward, crooning it to sleep.

Paulette said her name, yet Roseline didn't look up, simply continued rocking, lips moving in her lullaby. Touching her shoulder, Paulette asked Roseline where their parents were, using words she could not hear. The child raised glazed eyes to Paulette, mouthing things Paulette couldn't distinguish. Paulette lifted the child in her arms, carrying her across the yard to the barn where she asked her to watch over the children, before setting off again to the cottage.

This time she saw movement coming from the doorstep of the Quesnel cottage next to her own. Henri Quesnel was washing the ash and soot from the face of his wife Aimée, lying dead across his lap. Paulette felt the rumble of her voice in her chest, speaking questions, not understanding the answers he gave her. She patted him on the shoulder and moved away, driven by her eyes surveying the desolate scene before her, as she searched for others.

She saw Polka the Saint Bernard, lying on the ground next to Emile Levasseur. His eyes were open, blinking against the rain, his hand kneading the thick fur of his companion. She knelt at his side, "Where are you hurt? What can I do for you? Have you seen my parents?"

Looking at his lips, she saw them move feebly, but could not hear their whisper. His left hand fumbled at the buttons at the neck of his shirt. She helped him open his shirt front thinking he intended to show her a wound. Instead he pulled out a ragged piece of blue ribbon. On this was fastened a tiny key. He pulled as hard as he could, trying to remove it from his neck. She helped him take it off. He murmured something as he pressed it into her hand. She bent closer as he whispered again, trying to make her understand something. His breath was warm against her ear as he whispered his last sigh into her neck.

Polka rose and began comprehensively licking Emile's face, every parcel of skin around his eyes, nose and ears, as if to revive him. Paulette held his hands and cried aloud, sobbing her fears and anguish at his unheard message.

If only she could have told him that she had understood what he was asking of her. He died knowing she didn't understand. The dreadful thought overwhelmed her. The kindness he had shown her throughout her young years when she pestered him continually in the garden, asking an unending stream of questions, to which he patiently replied, occasionally presenting her with the plumpest strawberry, or the sweetest plum, had been rewarded with her silence. She could never do what he had asked of her. The unfairness of this was unbearable.

Eventually she rose and slipped the ribbon around her neck, pressing the key close to her heart. Although she was driven to continue her search, her feet were slower, dreading what else she must witness.

She turned into the walled garden, surprisingly intact, and headed in the direction of the door leading down to the kitchen. As she approached she saw her father, alive and dragging a large piece of timber up the stairs from the kitchen. He saw her, dropping his burden as he dashed up the stairs to fold her in his arms. He held her tight and she felt his torso shuddering with tears, mixing themselves with the raindrops in her already wet hair. They stood this way at the top of the steps for a long moment, wordless, each feeling the heart of the other beating strong through their sodden clothing.

He spoke. She felt the vibration through her chest and she stepped back to tell him she couldn't hear his words. He squinted at her in disbelief, then smoothed her hair from her face, brushing it away from her ears, inspecting them as if he might detect the reason they weren't working correctly. There was nothing to see. He was relieved.

She asked him about her mother, brother Yves and finally Heinrich. He looked straight into her eyes and spoke slowly.

"Your mother and Yves are in the kitchen. I haven't seen Heinrich. Where are the children? Are they safe?" The inventory of their loved ones was shaped clearly on his lips for her to read. She swallowed hard before speaking as clearly as she could, her voice a vibration in her chest as she told of the babies' hiding place and of their guardian.

"Can you help me unblock the stairs? I need help to get in there. I'm afraid they're trapped inside." He touched her elbow, encouraging her hesitant steps. They both took hold of the timber, successfully dragging it up the stairs. The rest of the debris was smaller pieces of wood, bricks and clumps of the mud used to fill in the spaces between the beams many years before. The stairway made things difficult, but after a half hour they reached the doorway itself, shut tight. Her father turned away, hurtled up the stairs one last time and dashed off across the garden, leaping over rows of peas and beans.

A few minutes later he returned in the same manner, bounding across the rows of carefully tended vegetables much like a horse in a steeplechase. He was carrying a mallet, a wedge and an ax. My old oak door had large strips of iron crossing its chest, proud to defend against unauthorized entry. I shuddered against the pounding of the hammer, forcing the wedge into the space where the inside bolt would be.

Paulette's father pressed his ear to the door, then shouted instructions to stand away. He raised the ax. The blow glanced off the old wood as if he had struck at a rock. Dropping the useless ax, he continued hammering the wedge along the perimeter of the door until it finally gave in. It opened just a crack. The bottom stuck tight against the flagstone floor. Something had gone off kilter, either the door frame had shifted with the caved in upper floors or the foundations on which the flagstones were lain had shifted with the blasts. In either case, the door would budge no further.

A dirty hand with scraped skin forced itself through the small opening, reaching for daylight. Paulette's father grabbed at it, clutching it in both of his hands as the volley of questions and answers slipped through the interstice. A vertical slice of face, with one eye, part of a nose and mouth under a shank of dark hair identified Yves. Paulette anxiously tapped on her father's shoulder, needing the news for herself. He turned his face in order to relay his words so she could see them.

Liliane, Marthe, a kitchen maid named Laurette and Franz were in the kitchen with Yves. He thought some of them might be dead. Certainly all were wounded and bleeding. He desperately wanted to escape. He was crying and panicked. They needed to find a way to break down the door and free them before the house fell down on them. Paulette understood as much as was necessary. There was a lot of work to be done and time had become a formidable enemy.

Papa attacked the other side of the door, relentlessly pounding against the frame. Small progress was made with each strike as fragments of the wood splintered away. Paulette cleared away the debris, keeping the stairwell free. The sweat of the work dripped down his face mingling with the drizzle, washing away the soot and grime and cooling his scorched skin.

After a seemingly endless effort, a small hole was made, enough for Yves to wriggle through. He fell into his father's arms, sobbing incomprehensible things, information to be picked from the jumble. Marcel stuck his head in the hole scanning the room. It was dark. No sign of movement came from inside.

Paulette sent Yves off to the barn to take care of Roseline, to reassure her things would be alright. He listened to her request, eyes wide, not believing they would be.

Marcel continued to hack away at the door removing chips of wood, enlarging the hole. Finally he was able to wedge himself inside, instructing Paulette to stay put. She waited, anguished.

After a long moment, she stuck her head in the now enlarged hole, toward the source of light encircling her father. He sat on the floor with his wife in his arms, but her hands were gripping him and Paulette could see their lips moving. Liliane was alive!

She saw the inert bodies of Marthe, and Laurette, the kitchen maid. She hoped they were resting, only wounded, yet knew it wasn't so. She did not see Franz. She called to her father, asking should she come in and help tend to her mother. He made a shooing motion to her, as if to send her off on an errand.

All the while she clung to a sense of calm regarding the fate of Heinrich. She'd not seen him, and no one else had either. She knew she must now begin her search.

Leaving the garden, she aimed in the direction of the west wing, or what was left of it. She knew the Colonel and Heinrich often sat discussing things in the library. It was a sort of refuge, perfect for secret telling. The books listened to their discussions, sometimes providing answers to questions with their knowledge, stored secure between leather bindings.

The library was burning. The words of the authors of the many volumes rose to escape from curling pages.

Voices flew off into the sky with the ashes, wisdom and fantasies scattering in the wind.

As she stood outside looking in at the burning furniture, bookshelves and their precious works, a hand reached out and touched her shoulder.

It was the Colonel, who turned her around, enfolding her in his arms.

She could feel his words escape into her hair, not hearing them, just perceiving the whisper of his breath. She struggled against his embrace, to pull away and tell him she knew nothing of what he'd said, to ask him the question she feared the most.

"Heinrich?"

He looked at the ground, clasping her hands while answering.

She wrenched one hand free of his grasp and jerked his chin up in anger, so that he must look at her, so that she could read his words. She made him understand her loss of hearing by slapping at her ears, and shaking her head, no.

He took a deep breath, and clearly mouthed the words, "Heinrich has gone to try and warn his brother. I don't know if he made it in time, or if he got away before the bomb hit its target."

She sank to her knees in the wet grass.

He knelt in front of her.

She slapped him, furious at the news, furious that his commanding officer could have let him leave her alone, with their children, to permit him to go and save that monster. She pummeled his shoulders and chest, again and again, none of her blows effective in either hurting him or relieving her pain.

She grew weak with it, dropping her useless hands to her lap, head hanging in the drizzle.

This was unfair, unjust, and unbearable.

He took her hands, and carefully spoke to her, saying the things that needed to be said, telling her what must happen now, telling her how to save her children and herself, revealing the secret to her escape.

#

Later, they left in the Mercedes: the Colonel, the babies, and Paulette, clutching a posy of roses. The car rolled down the length of the drive in a slow reluctance, then turned east at the end of the orchard.

I felt them go, another hole blown in my heart. Although saddened by another loss, I knew her leaving was necessary, knew that I couldn't protect them from the future, from another invading army, set out to do good, but causing damage in the doing of that good. Paulette and the children, had they stayed, would have paid a price too heavy for her sin of loving someone who wore the wrong uniform. Yes, I understood this, understood her decision, and agreed with it. Still, I regretted her absence, and struggled as her roots were brutally ripped from my foundations.

CHAPTER 34

1996:

Debra opened the front door and approached the rental car parked in the drive. She waited while the driver, a young woman of about twenty-five got out, waving hello, before helping a passenger to exit.

The passenger, a distinguished snowy-haired lady, stood up straight, her blue gaze sweeping over the facade of the house and inspecting the yard, as though searching for something. As she accepted Debra's warm handshake and greeting, the intense expression on her face was tempered by a hesitant smile. Debra noticed her take a deep breath and hold it in.

Debra was a bit surprised. The woman appeared to be steeling herself for an ordeal of some sort. She noticed Debra watching her and glanced up as if caught doing something wrong, before reaching for the young woman's arm to steady her steps.

They walked across the terrace to the front door. Debra ushered them inside, guests of the bed and breakfast she'd been operating for the past two years. It was the first time anyone from South Africa had come to stay and she was curious about this unusual pair. Still, she decided to let them settle in before asking any questions. She helped carry the bags upstairs, installing them in two of the rooms on the upstairs floor, down the hall from the master bedroom. Turning to leave, Debra invited the ladies to unpack, and then come down for a cup of tea or coffee in the sitting room when they were ready.

#

Theresa helped her grandmother unpack her belongings, carefully hanging the clothing in the armoire and arranging the toiletries on the cherry wood dresser.

"Gran? I'm going across the hall to my room to unpack. Do you want to come or would you rather stay here?"

"I'll be fine, dear, just come back and get me when you're done, and we'll go downstairs together."

The young woman planted a kiss on the white hair, and the grandmother patted her cheek in return, before watching her leave, with a smile. Teresa shut the door on her grandmother and silence descended on the room.

The lady removed her hearing aid, placing it on a tissue pulled from the pink box Debra had set out on the nightstand.

She stood still, closing her eyes. Breathing deeply, she touched the cherry wood of the dresser. A tear meandered along the wrinkles on her cheek. She listened as closely as she could.

I whispered a welcome to my old friend, purring with happiness at her return.

Across the hall, Theresa hesitated as she placed a pile of t-shirts in a dresser drawer, listening for something she wasn't certain she'd heard.

Downstairs in the kitchen as Debra was assembling a tea tray with cookies, cups and saucers, milk and sugar. Elsa lifted her head from her paws, cocking her head to listen.

Debra stopped, her hand in midair clutching teaspoons, listening.

A small sound escaped me in my happiness, and a soft breeze of anticipation blew into their hearts, old friends and new, assembled here under my roof. A deep satisfaction rumbled through the floors, climbing the legs of all, reaching up to warm lonely souls.

When the guests gathered around the teapot in the sitting room, easy conversation was struck up. The old woman commented on the carved wooden box, placed on the mantle.

Debra brought it over to show her, telling the story of where she found it and what she'd discovered about its contents over the past four years.

The old woman listened attentively, nodding from time to time, until Debra finished.

Reaching inside the neck of her prim blue blouse she pulled out a ribbon with a tiny key fastened to it, and held it out to Debra.

The End....for now!

Author's note

Some small amount of poetic license has been taken in the geographical details of the story, notably in placing Saint Catherine's spring in proximity to Bacqueville. It is located instead near Lyons La Fôret, in the department of L'Eure, and as such about 80 miles from Bacqueville. Still, it is such a magical place I felt it needed to be included in this tale. The legends surrounding it are vast and varied and more of them will be included in the sequel, because the spot is so very intriguing.

The persons depicted in this book are purely the product of the author's imagination, so if any of you feel targeted, please revise your opinion. This of course, does not refer to the obvious historical personages such as Adolph Hitler and his acolytes.

In attacking such a vast subject, much historical research was involved. I was lucky enough to have enjoyed some face to face conversations with very interesting people who supplied me with details galore.

Therefore, many thanks go out to long time friends of my family, Marcellin Gallais, who was a member of the FFI: "Forces Françaises de L'Intérieur" during WWII. His exploits as a young man intent on annoying the German occupying forces on the island of Noirmoutier in the Vendée region of France, were the meat of many a dinner conversation. His wife Alice, helped out with valuable insight into the daily life of the people of occupied France, as well as some interesting tidbits regarding ladies undergarments.

On June 6th 2009, the 65th anniversary of the Invasion of Normandy by the Allied troops, our president, Mr Barak Obama made an inspiring speech on site. During that exact moment, I was wandering through the woods near Pommereval, at the V1 site "Ardouval". Fortunately, I took it upon myself to stick my hand out in greeting to the only two other people in the woods that day. They were a German couple, and it seemed right at the time for an American and two Germans to shake hands in front of such a horrendous contraption as the V1 missile.

We spoke for some time, and I discovered that the very kind man was a professor of military history with the German army and that his wife's father had been one of the soldiers defending the beaches at Omaha, where our president was eloquently discoursing. She had felt uneasy being there when that happened, a dose of shame still evident in her admission of her father's part in the dreadful affair that was WWII. I felt sorry for her admission of that, wishing that enough had elapsed for her to put that aside.

I plied them both with many questions, which they very kindly answered in great detail, their French and English helping me overcome my complete ignorance of the German language.

Photos were taken, by them, as I, rather stupidly, had left my purse in the car park some distance away. However, to my great regret, I never took down their names, having nothing to write with, notes of their answers committed to memory only. I owe this anonymous couple a huge thank you, because as I walked away, secure in the knowledge that the tone of my story was on track, I felt as if I'd had a rendez-vous with destiny. It was one of those chance meetings that was meant to be, and I rushed home to embark on a frenzy of writing such as I had never experienced before.

I pour out my heartfelt thanks to you, dear sir and your lovely wife, hoping only that fate will once again intervene and that a copy of this book will land in your hands, and you can read my sincere thanks for yourselves.

And of course, my number one fan deserves a wink here, being of greater support than the most expensive sports bra, my mom: lover of books, supplier of details, purveyor of tidbits of welcome criticism, and endless encouragement. For you, Mom, with love.

My cover photo is by Laurent Charles: friend and photographer extraordinaire. Many, many thanks for his patience in the quest for the right door.

My friends and colleagues at Goodreads kept me encouraged and driven, having all "been there and done that". It's a wonderful thing to have a group of relative strangers become cyber-supporters, especially the exciting, witty, imaginative group in the "Ménage-à-Twenty" author list. I learned a great deal from these friends and fellow writers. Through them I found the courage to re-write, refine, re-work and reject, not an easy thing to learn. Most especially, (and he's going to hate me for using yet another adverb in the same sentence as his name) to Carlos Cortes, my favorite Spaniard, my patient hand holder, verbiage corrector and general hombre simpatico.

Positioned close to the end of this really long list, reigns supreme my excellent, oldest friend, Tanya Hodder, who single handedly convinced me to espouse a career change, suggested, set up and maintains my website www.france-vacations-made-easy.com. She also pushed me when I needed it most, encouraged me when I threw up my hands in despair and walked me, long distance, through all sorts of major and minor computer blips. Web mistress extraordinaire, and most excellent pal: Tanya, with whom I hope to always celebrate every little success because they are most assuredly owed to her perseverance.

Last but not least, my personal Emile was also a source of inspiration, his voice has echoed through my heart for the past 24 years. I regret only that it took me so long to truly listen.

And my heartfelt thanks also go out to you, who takes the time to read.

List of characters for "The Manoir at Bout L'Abbé"

Debra:

Debra Dubois: American married to Philippe 25 yrs old
in 1987, 30 years old when Philippe dies in April of 1992
Philippe Dubois: Debra's husband- 15 years older than
Debra: 45 when he dies
Susanna Dubois: first born daughter to Debra and
Philippe: born in 1987: age 5 when Philippe dies
Victoria Dubois: Second born daughter to Debra and
Philippe: born in 1989: age 3 when Philippe "
Sophie: Philippe's secretary and mistress, has a neurotic
older boyfriend
Patricia: Philippe's accountant/secretary and sometime
mistress is married and childless
Francoise: the Dubois family housekeeper/babysitter:
married and childless
Elsa: Dubois family dog-Charplaninatz: female
Minette: Dubois family cat: female
Psychologist lady: woman picked by Philippe, but in
aerobics class with Debra
Police officer: kind to Debra
Hubert: the Dubois family gardener
Mac and Cheese: Dubois family Scotty dogs

Paulette:

Paulette Fournier: 19 yrs old in April of 1943
Michel Fournier: Paulette's younger half-brother: 16 yrs old in 1943
Yves Fournier: Paulette's younger half-brother: 10 yrs old in 1943
Roseline Fournier: Paulette's younger half-sister: 6 years old in 1943
Maman: Madame Liliane Fournier Paulette's mother:
Papa: Monsieur Marcel Fournier: Paulette's step-father:
Colonel VonEpffs: 40 some years old, in 1943: Colonel in the German army
Heinrich Von Zeller: 18 yrs old in 1938: 23 years old in 1943: Lieutenant in the German Army
Rodolphe Maximilien Von Zeller VI (Rolf): Major in the Gestapo: 29 years old in 1943
Lieutenant Bierdorpf: friend and compatriot of Heinrich's, ex roommate: similar age to Heinrich
Père Lemarchand: village priest: Jean-Pierre
Marthe: the French cook: a woman
Franz: the German cook
Emile Levasseur: French gardener: older fellow
Henri Quesnel: Co-worker of M Fournier on the farm, father of Guillaume, Manon, Elisabeth
Aimée Quesnel: wife of Henri, coworker of Mad Fournier: mother of Guillaume, Manon and Elisabeth

Guillaume Quesnel: 18 years old in 1943, friend of Michel

Manon Quesnel: just turned 15 years old at the time of her death in 1943

Elisabeth Quesnel (Lizzie): 7 years old in 1943

Polka: the farm's Saint Bernard: female

Flo: female Percheron horse: Flynn's mom 6 years old in 1942

Maurice: male Percheron horse

Flynn: Percheron colt in 1942, yearling in 1943

Captain Steve Winthrop: 27 in 1943 escaped Canadian pilot

Pierre and Ginette Duchemin: pig farmers who help out Steve

Granny Leclerc: eldest generation of the pharmacisit's family in Yvetot

Capitaine Martin: leader of the resistance camp near Yvetot

Doctor Hervieux: doctor in Bacqueville

Lieutenant Schmidtz: Gestapo: understudy to Rolf

1830236R00305

Printed in Germany
by Amazon Distribution
GmbH, Leipzig